IF BY CHANCE

What Will Be - Book Three

Laura Ashley Gallagher

First published in 2022

ISBN: 978-1-3999-2197-8

Visit www.lauraashleygallagher.com to read more about Laura Ashley and her upcoming releases. You can sign up for her e-newsletters so that you're always first to hear about her new releases, updates and exclusives. You can also find her on Facebook, Instagram, and TikTok.

Please note: there are topics in this book that some readers may find distressing. You can find the list of content warnings on www.lauraashleygallagher.com

DEDICATION

For the women that left, and the ones that couldn't.
This one is for you.

PROLOGUE

Six years ago.

"Dead."

I stay still, not breathing as I slowly come around from a brief doze.

"Dead," the little voice repeats.

We're in a cemetery. Everyone is dead.

I risk peeking through one eye, but the sun is blinding. I put a hand over my eyes. Sight finally adjusting, I dig my palms into the grass and shoot upright, pressing my back against the stone.

Blue eyes greet me.

They look like mine, and it takes a moment to realize I'm not dreaming.

His dark hair falls over his forehead, and it's long over his ears. He giggles at my fright.

I shake my head. "No. I'm not dead."

He presses a chubby palm over his mouth, shoulders shaking.

What's so funny?

I fell asleep in a cemetery. My hair is in knots, and my face is blotchy from crying.

I look like a body they forgot to bury.

"Buddy, where did you go this time?" A man's voice floats through the air.

1

The little boy's eyes widen.

"Dada," he says, pointing in the voice's direction.

Heat floods my cheeks.

I look like a mess, I've fallen asleep at my best friend's grave, and I'm pretty sure I'm still drunk from my college graduation celebrations last night.

I hold my finger over my mouth.

"Go," I urge him. "Your dad is looking for you."

He giggles again.

Please go, kid.

Footsteps grow closer.

"Quick," I beg.

He needs to leave before his father thinks I'm trying to kidnap him.

I should have stayed dead.

He plucks a star-shaped sticker from his little t-shirt and sticks it to my forehead.

Shocked, I glance around. "Thanks."

He nods at me and pats my face. "Mama."

Holy shit.

He's going to get me in so much trouble.

He pokes the sticker again.

I wince.

That's not helping my hangover, kid.

"Star. Mama."

"No. I'm not your mama. I'm dead, remember?"

"Where are you, buddy?" The man's voice is growing more concerned and closer.

He can't come closer.

The sun is beating down on my shoulders, and I'm not sure if I'm sweating from the heat or if I'm panicking.

"You need to go. Your dad will be worried."

Giggling, he potters away, but before he can, I stop him.

I don't know why.

Like I said, I'm still drunk.

I pull a daisy from the grass and hand it to him.

He blows me a kiss.

How sweet.

Turning, he runs away onto the path and out of sight.

"Dada," he screams.

"Jesus, you can't keep running away like that," the man says, clearly relieved.

Kneeling, I peek over my best friend's gravestone, curious for a glimpse of the stranger with the deep voice.

"Sorry, Nick," I whisper to the ground. "I don't know why I'm apologizing to you. You're dead."

I'm so drunk.

The man is scooping the little boy in his arms when I peep over, careful to hide and not get caught.

His back is to me as he walks away.

The little boy giggles again, waving his flower while blowing me another kiss.

I wave back.

The man turns, and I quickly resume playing dead, falling on the grass again.

Please don't see me.

"Okay," the man says slowly. "That's not freaky at all. My kid is waving at dead people."

ONE

Now.

My fiancé makes a very distinctive noise when he's close to orgasm. It's a grunting of sorts, not uncommon to most men, but he wheezes like he's on the verge of an asthma attack.

I never paid much attention to it because I'm usually in on the act with him.

Until now.

Because I'm on the other side of the door and those female moans aren't mine.

I wish he cared enough to use those moves on me because she is screaming like she's being murdered.

My hand hovers over the door handle, my body hesitating because imaging what's going on in there is bad enough, but to see it with my own eyes may tip me over the edge.

My eye catches on the glint of my diamond engagement ring as it tips inside my fingers. It's always been a little big, and I never made the time to get it resized. I wonder if it was an omen—fitting to my current circumstances. One way or another, this ring isn't meant to stay on my finger.

I think about knocking, like it's rude to interrupt mid-orgasm.
How inconvenient.

Or I could simply walk away and pretend I didn't leave work early to cook him a meal for our anniversary and to celebrate my graduation tomorrow.

But it's not in my nature. I'll make both our lives miserable until I can't hold it in anymore, and just the thought of sharing the same bed with him now makes my skin crawl.

It's your goddamn house.

Well, not exactly. We haven't officially moved in together yet, but I spend most of my time here.

Maybe I always knew it would end. It took me six weeks to agree to marry him.

I love him, but being tied to one person scares the shit right out of me.

But he—the man currently on the verge of that asthma attack I was talking about—that man made me believe.

I open the door slowly, peeking through with one eye. They don't hear me. The two bodies thrashing around on the bed are too wrapped up in each other, and her screams are enough to pierce my eardrums.

The distinct smell of sex, the lavender detergent I washed the bed sheets in, and shame lingers in the air.

My stomach rolls.

His uniform is scattered across the floor, and a red lace thong is hanging from the bedpost.

I swear, I fell for the cop uniform before I ever fell for the man wearing it.

Sun-kissed blonde hair lies in waves over *my* pillow.

I tilt my head, staring like a creep.

Does he always clench his ass so tight?

The moment I'm more focused on how he looks from this side having sex, rather than the fact that he's having sex with someone that isn't me, I know it's over.

I won't lie. I'm a little disappointed, but I'll just add Caleb to the list of all the other men who let me down. He won't even come close to the top.

It's a long second before I decide to move my feet, and it's not to interrupt them because in that second, I realize, I'm merely a little hurt. The betrayal stings, but it's not the *current us* I'll mourn. I'll mourn the idea of us. Of everything I thought we would be when we first met. The knowledge of us ending isn't crippling like I think it should be when you're fully invested, and you love someone.

I'm sure it will become a little more unbearable in the morning, but it won't end me.

A part of me always knew our promises weren't made with our whole hearts, and just like my engagement ring, we never truly fit.

So instead of wasting my energy on an argument I don't want, I simply slip the ring off my finger, place it on the dresser, turn around and leave.

TWO

Sunsets and donuts—the ultimate guide to mending a broken heart.

But not just any donuts.

Oh, no.

These are Maggie May's donuts. These donuts can put back all the pieces of a freshly shattered heart and soothe old scars.

Well, they do, for a while.

The sound of the ocean and the feel of the sun on my skin also help.

I sip on my coffee to wash down the last of the sugary glaze before squeezing the box, dumping it in the bin, and taking my seat again on the bench.

Couples and families stroll on the beach while dogs rush in and out of the lapping waves. It's quieter than usual. Kids are back at school soon after spring break, and the tourists have gone home.

Just a few minutes for the sound of the waves to wash over my aching body—that's all I need.

I never knew heartbreak could hurt more than your heart. It's manifesting in this ball of fire and burning all the way to my fingertips. It makes my stomach churn, and the more I think about it, the more these donuts don't want to stay down. I swallow and curse myself under my breath.

Pull yourself together.

I've had more boyfriends than I care to remember, but none of them got under my skin like Caleb. None of them stuck around long enough to claw their way through my soul. The most sickening part is that he made me fall in love with him while doing it.

I never pictured a future with someone until Caleb. I never imagined myself getting married or having little rascals to love.

He forced me to see a future.

He forced me to dream and have hope.

Hope.

The worst of all emotions.

It's difficult to build, but is easily crushed in the second it takes for someone to decide they want to jump into bed with someone else.

Why didn't he let me go when we first started dating?

I pushed him away because I thought he was like all the others. But he always returned.

I pushed, and he pushed back.

He made me cave.

Me!

Granted, he always did it when he wore that damn uniform.

But he was sweet.

Too sweet.

Like my donuts, when I consume too much, they make me want to vomit.

Fuck him.

I didn't need him before, and I don't need him now. I survived this long.

Caleb didn't break me. I'm merely cracked, and cracks can be filled.

I take a steadying breath, hold it, and exhale.

"Breathe in the pain, allow yourself to feel it, and then let it go," I whisper the words my mother used to tell me. Although, she always said it while running around the house with sage to kill the negative energy after Papa got drunk and heavy-handed. "Breathe in the pain, allow yourself to feel it, and then let it go," I repeat, not wanting to focus on my father.

I throw my head back and instantly regret it.

When did that tree get there?

"Ouch." I groan, rubbing the back of my head.

"Are you okay?" a low, gravelly voice comes from the bench next to mine.

I've been caught.

I turn slowly, massaging my fingers over the growing bump on the back of my scalp. I'm too drained to be embarrassed.

His eyes narrow, pinned on me as I stare back. Brows furrowed, his hands clasp together to rest on muscular thighs as he leans over and scrutinizes me with a frown before pursing his lips.

"I'm good." I nod through another wave of pain.

He sits back. "You sure?"

"I'm sure. Thanks."

"It's just…" he trails off, his eyes narrowing again, but amusement dances on his lips.

Fuck you, stranger.

I've had enough of men.

"What?" I snap. "Why are looking at me like that?"

He runs a hand through his dark hair, and I glimpse at his muscular bicep.

Damn it, Claire.

I pull my eyes back to his, and that cocky smile tells me he noticed.

Whatever.

"Well?" I prompt, hoping he will stop staring so I can return to my wallowing.

"You've been looking at that ocean like it can solve world hunger, you're crying, you've got sugar all over your lips, and you just took a hard bang to the head."

I'm crying?

I wipe a hand across my cheek.

And what do you know?

I'm crying.

Licking my lips, the salty tears blend with the sweet crystals.

He's wrong.

I don't expect the ocean to solve world problems. I want it to solve *my* problems.

"How long have you been watching me?"

He looks away, thinking for a moment, and my hungry eyes follow his fingers as they run over the five o'clock shadow on his sharp jawline. "Since about halfway through that box of donuts."

Marvelous.

My embarrassment is surfacing, and I can't think of anything better when I say, "You know, you should never judge a woman and her donuts."

He shakes his head, and his shoulders lift with a light laugh. He tries to hide it, but I catch the subtle movement. "You won't find any judgment here." He throws his hands up in surrender.

"Good." I huff, pulling my long hair back from my sticky lips and crossing my arms over my chest like a child.

"Is your head okay?"

Oh, for God's sake.

Why does he insist on asking questions?

No, my head is a mess, and you don't want anywhere near it because this mood is contagious.

"It's fine," I clip and hate when I regret it. It's not this guy's fault I'm in a foul mood. That's all down to a six-foot, blond police officer with lips that can make me crumble. "I'm sorry," I mutter, turning to face the ocean again. The sun is setting, and it calms my erratic nerves. "Long day," I quickly explain.

"You can say that again."

"Long day," I repeat, a slow smile spreading across my face.

He chuckles. It's deep and sexy.

"Want some company? Misery loves company."

Who is this guy?

"Who said I was miserable?"

"Your face."

"Touché." I look at him from the corner of my eye. "Are you a serial killer?"

"No, but would I tell you if I was?"

True.

I shrug.

"Are you hitting on me?"

"See answer one," he quickly replies, and I can't help but laugh.

"Okay, but you should know, I'm stronger than I look if you try to kill me, and I won't have sex with you."

He simply smiles and doesn't look at me like I'm mad. All I see is understanding and something else familiar in his eyes, but I can't put my finger on it.

"That sounds fair." He moves down the bench, as do I, so we're sitting closer, our arms almost touching.

I reach into my handbag and pull out another box.

"Donut?" I offer.

"Sure," he agrees, and I appreciate it when he doesn't comment on how these will go straight to my hips. I must have the desperate look of needing to feed a broken soul.

"So," he starts before taking a donut from the box and biting down on it. His eyes widen. "Who made these? Angels?"

I nod.

He's not far from wrong.

"Maggie May is the closest thing you'll get to an angel. She has a bakery in town. She's tucked away down an alley on Main Street, but if you're lucky enough to find her, you'll never go to another bakery again."

"I can see why." He takes another bite while I take another glazed bun.

My ass says, 'Don't do it,' but my heart says, 'It will heal you.'

"I'll have to stop by with my son tomorrow before we head home."

"Ah, I knew you weren't from around here. City boy?"

"Guilty," he mumbles. "A friend has been trying to get me to come here for a while. It's our first time, but we'll be back. My son loves it."

How sweet. "What age is he?"

"Eight." His eyes gleam with pride.

He shakes the sugar from his hands and leans back, lifting his ankle across his thigh.

Focus on your donut, Claire.

I'm heartbroken, and a broken heart sometimes thinks anything with a pulse can fix it.

"So, why are you sitting here on a Friday evening eating donuts with a stranger?"

My eyes glance over at him once more, double-checking the serial killer vibes.

What the hell. I don't know him. He doesn't know me. And sometimes, it's good to offload on a stranger.

"I walked in on my fiancé having sex with another woman yesterday."

He flinches. "Ouch."

"Yep."

"Bastard," he adds.

"Yep." Silence. "Want to know what he said to me?"

"Why not?"

"He said I was married to my job, and I wasn't emotionally available."

My pulse races with the memories of Caleb arriving at my door last night, looking broken but sated, the engagement ring clutched in his hand.

"Ah, the coward's way out."

I turn in my seat to face him and swallow the last of my donut. "Right? Okay, I have a hectic job, and I'm hardly ever at home, and I was studying all the time, and he's a cop, so I know his job is stressful, and…"

His brows furrow, causing a deep line of what I think is frustration between his eyes, and he frowns.

"What?"

"You're making excuses for him."

"Am not," I fight back, horrified.

"Yes, you are."

"Am not."

"Why are you so defensive?" He smirks, and it annoys the hell out of me because it's a sexy smile. Smug. One side of his mouth lifts higher than the other, but it only enhances the fiery glint in his dark amber eyes.

It's infuriating.

"I didn't ask you to sit with me, you know."

"Now you're deflecting."

"Are you a shrink?" I bite back, his honesty scratching too close to a raw nerve.

He shrugs.

Fucking infuriating.

I swing back around and run my fingers through my long hair.

He's right.

Of course he is.

But I hate telling people they're right.

I blow out a long breath and cross my arms over my chest. "Old habits," I breathe, unsure if he even hears me. "Want to know something even crazier?" I don't give him a chance to answer before I continue. "I turned down my dream job in the city for him."

It's the first time I've said it out loud. I never even told Mandy or Garry, and they've been my best friends since we were four.

"I've never allowed a man to come between me and what I wanted to do, but somehow, I allowed him to change that. I said no to my future for the chance of a future with him. Truth is, looking back, I'm not sure if I even wanted a future with him. And now I'm angry at myself."

Have I learned anything from my mother?

"I'm also thinking there's truth serum in the donut glaze." Gulping, I fight the lump in my throat and close my eyes to ease the sting. I build the courage to look back at him, and he's staring straight at me.

"You want my opinion?" he asks.

No.

"Sure."

"He's an idiot. Want some advice from an old man?"

I scoff a laugh.

He can't be over thirty-five.

Although, his eyes say he has lived through another lifetime. Maybe that's what I recognize—the undeniable glint of a past, but I nod anyway.

"Don't waste any more sunsets on him. Don't sit here and look at something beautiful and make it ugly. When you look hard enough, you'll always find the good."

Wow!

"Oh, okay."

He scrubs a hand across his stubble and rolls his eyes. "Young people."

I slap the back of my hand against his arm. "I'm twenty-eight." His eyes go to the skin I've just slapped and back to me.

Too flirty?

Yep, rein it in, Claire.

He smiles, and I relax.

"Tell me something good." He turns to face me, and his deep brown eyes lock with mine. "Like I said, we have to find good in our days. Even the shitty ones." He runs a palm down his slacks.

I drum my fingers against my leg, thinking, and not going for the obvious answer right away. "I'm getting drunk tonight."

He raises a brow, uncertain and almost concerned.

"Don't look at me like that. It's not to drown my sorrows. Well, not all sorrows." A slow smile pulls at my lips. "I graduated today. I got my PhD."

He moves back, his eyes wandering over my face as the corner of his lips curl up. "You're a doctor?"

"Not the type that can prescribe medication, but a doctor all the same."

His eyes grow larger, and he grins so wide I think his face will crack. "You mean you've been sitting here crying over a scumbag who doesn't know your worth—and the night before your graduation, no less—when you should be celebrating? Congratulations"

I hate that Caleb's actions have tainted what should be an amazing day, and I hate myself even more because I can't shake the heaviness in my chest.

"Thank you. But we need to balance this out. Tell me something bad."

"You're a glutton for punishment."

"Maybe. But come on, misery loves company, remember?"

He takes a long breath, and his gaze darts away from my face to the beach and back again. He's contemplating.

"Come on," I urge. "I've just told you about my asshole boyfriend. Give me something."

He pinches the bridge of his nose. "It's my wedding anniversary today." I see the gold band on his ring finger.

"Aren't wedding anniversaries supposed to be joyous occasions? How long are you married?"

His eyes narrow to slits, and his nose scrunches.

Pain.

I'd recognize it anywhere because it sometimes creeps its way out of my shadows and says hello in the mirror. It doesn't scream as loud as his pain, though.

"Eight years," he answers, smiling but clearing his throat.

"Shouldn't you be at home with your wife?"

More pain.

I didn't think it was possible to see so much agony in the flecks of amber dancing torment in his eyes. I can almost see his pulse throbbing in his neck.

"I should be," he whispers, kneading a hand over his chest.

I shake my head, confused. "I don't get it. You're not telling me something bad, yet I think you are all at once."

He sighs and raises his head to look at me. "My wife died eight years ago." He laughs without humor and smacks his lips together. "Eight years tomorrow, to be exact."

My mouth parts and a knot forms in the lowest part of my stomach. His wife died the day after their wedding.

Ouch.

"Oh," I breathe, unsure of what to say, and chastise myself when my fingers twitch with the want to reach out and soothe him.

I was right.

There's another lifetime behind those eyes.

Another story.

Another love story.

He said his son is eight, too.

All my problems suddenly feel minuscule.

And was the air on this beach always this thick?

I throw my hands up. "You win. Your misery wouldn't have enough company in mine."

He laughs loud and throws his head back, his shoulders relaxing against the bench.

"Eight years and you still wear your wedding ring." It's more of an observation than a question. I eye the gold band, and my heart breaks a little more for him. He's a gorgeous man. I'm sure he has women throwing themselves at him all the time, yet he chooses the reminder of the woman he once loved to stay on his finger for everyone to see.

I remember how eager I was to get my engagement ring off. It was as heavy as a noose standing in that bedroom.

"Today is supposed to be the day I take it off. I worked myself up for it. Maybe tomorrow." He sighs, broad shoulders lifting and falling with every breath. "She was the good in my days. She reminds me not to look for the ugly when I watch the sunset. I only had her for a short time, but she somehow imprinted herself on everything I do. I get greedy and wish I had her for longer, but how lucky am I to say I had her at all?"

I swallow the lump in my throat and quickly wipe the tears streaming down my cheeks.

That's love.

Pure.

Unconditional.

Seeing the simple in the complicated.

Seeing the good in the bad.

We both turn away and without a word, watch as the sun sets far over the horizon.

"I'm sorry about your wife," I breathe as the sky begins to turn darker and the air cooler.

"I'm sorry about your fiancé." He runs both hands down his thighs, and I know he's about to leave. "I better get back. My son is with family."

"Thanks for sitting with me." And I mean it. My shoulders feel lighter than they have all day.

"Are you kidding? Those donuts made it all worth it." He smiles, and my tummy does a flip, but only because he can still smile after telling me his story.

We stand together, and I throw my thumb over my shoulder. "I better get going."

He points in the opposite direction. "Me too. It was good talking to you."

As we both turn away, I take a deep breath and let the sea air heal me.

"Hey?" he calls, and I spin around on my heels. "I never got your name."

How ridiculous.

We've been sitting there for almost an hour, spilling our guts out to each other, and we don't know each other's names.

"It's Claire," I shout back.

"Do a stranger a favor, Claire? Call whoever offered you the job you wanted in the city and ask for another chance. Everyone deserves a second chance."

I close my eyes and smile, a small ray of hope setting my chest on fire.

"And if by chance you ever find yourself in the city, I'll look out for you on a bench somewhere. Hopefully fewer tears next time." He winks and stuffs his hands in his pockets.

He turns to walk away again, but I stop him. "Wait. What's your name?"

He grins, and I think I'll always remember his smile.

"Jake," he answers. "My name is Jake." He turns, walks again, and bellows over his shoulder. "Oh, and Claire?"

"Uh, huh?"

"You've still got sugar on your lips."

Damn it.

THREE

"Hey," I breathe, forcing a smile. I hope my red and blotchy eyes have calmed as Mandy swings open the door to her and Alex's beach house. She smiles back, and I swear, Mandy's smile can calm even the wildest of heartbeats.

"Hey, you." She pulls me into her embrace, and I melt against her.

My friends know something is wrong. They've known since they turned up at my graduation earlier today, and I didn't even leave my gown on for a photo.

"Where's Caleb?" she asks. "Did you walk here?" Her brows draw tight as she looks over my shoulder and doesn't see my car or a cab pulling away. My shoulders round, and I hate it when my eyes water again. "Just come in. I have wine."

My savior.

She always knows the right things to say.

"So," I begin, walking with her through the house and toward the kitchen. I've always loved this house, and Mandy's at home here with her daughter and Alex. She deserves it. "I got a cab to drop me a few minutes away. I wanted a walk on the beach to clear my head."

Her apprehensive gaze burns a hole in the side of my face. "Why do you need to clear your head?"

"This is the answer to your first question. I don't know where Caleb is, and I don't care. He's probably buried in the screaming blonde I walked in on him with yesterday."

She stops walking and slaps her chest as she chokes on air.

I rub her back and laugh. "Jesus, he's not worth dying over."

She tries to speak, but it only makes me laugh harder as she fights with herself to form words. "I'm going to kill him."

I think that's what she says.

"What the hell is going on?" Alex appears at the doorway with Garry following close behind. "Are you trying to kill my fiancé before I even get a chance to marry her?" He chuckles and holds her by the shoulders so she's upright. "Breathe, baby," he instructs, looking at her like he always does—like she's the only woman to walk the planet.

"You don't understand, Alex. I'm going to kill him," she sputters, gasping, and breathing through her nose when Alex tells her to.

"Kill who?" Garry steps forward, eyeing me with suspicion.

"Hey." I kiss his cheek, ignoring his question. "Where's Sally?"

"At home, trying not to vomit her way through this pregnancy."

I grimace.

Poor Sally.

"You didn't have to come. You should be at home with your wife."

"Believe me, Claire. She wanted me out of the house."

I try to hide the smile when I squeeze his shoulder.

"Who are we killing?" His eyes roam from me to Mandy and back again. Mandy glances at me. Her eyes are sadder than I like. "That bastard," Garry curses, his hands balling into fists at his side.

"I'm lost. Can someone tell me what's going on? Are you okay, Claire?" Alex pleads.

Me, Mandy, and Garry have been friends for so long that sometimes we don't even need to speak. Our eyes say everything we want.

I pat Alex's chest. "How about you get me a glass of wine and I will tell you everything?"

Alex dips his chin, gives Mandy a once over to make sure she's still breathing, and we take our seats in the kitchen.

***

"That bastard," Alex echoes a half-hour later.

"See?" Mandy screeches, almost spilling her wine. Alex halts with his beer halfway to his mouth. "I want to kill him. I liked him in the beginning. I hate when my judgment about someone is wrong."

Same, Mandy. Same.

"And he hurt Claire. No one gets to do that."

My heart swells.

He winks at her, and I think my friend just melted. "If you want to kill him, I'll help. But maybe tomorrow, when you've had time to sleep on it."

"Thank you," she smiles, joking, before turning back to me, and all amusement leaves her face.

"You turned down the job."

This is why I love my friends so much. They know I'll get over Caleb. He won't be the end of me. Their biggest concern is that I put aside my life's dreams for him.

I shrug, defeated, while hoping all my answers are buried in the bottom of this wineglass. "I know."

"Why don't you try again? Ask for a second chance?" Garry suggests, and I groan inwardly.

That seems to be everyone's answer this evening.

"Where's the job?" Alex is scanning my face, and sometimes I think he can read me as well as my friends can.

"I'll still be working for The Hope Foundation, but the job is just outside the city," I mutter under my breath and say a prayer they don't hear me.

No such luck.

They gasp in unison.

Alex is the first to speak. He doesn't just volunteer for The Hope Foundation—he's a huge donor. The man built an entire housing complex, for Christ's sake. "Nora wants you to run the new shelter, doesn't she?"

"The women's shelter?" Mandy looks between me and Alex. She knows it well because her soon-to-be husband designed it and just finished overseeing the build.

"A women's shelter?" Garry echoes, and I wonder if they've turned into parrots. "That's been your dream since college. You would be amazing."

"I know," I moan before gulping my wine. "And I've been too embarrassed to speak to her since." I sigh, not meeting anyone's gaze until I see Mandy with her arm outstretched toward me. She's holding my phone.

"Call that woman right now, Claire Russell. You've known her for years. She loves you like a daughter. Ask for another chance."

I sit back in my chair, and I'm not the only one dying to laugh. "Did you just *full name* me, Mandy Parker?"

She puts a hand on her hip and blows a stray curl from her face. "Yes, I did. Now get your ass up and go call her." She nudges the phone into my chest. Her voice is softer when she says, "Don't let him win, Claire."

She's right.

Time to pump some steel into my backbone, but it's late and I don't want to have this conversation when I've had a glass of wine.

"I'll call her on Monday. I promise."

My mouth shakes as I try to smile. To hide it, I stare into my wine, swirling the liquid around like a whirlpool, wishing I could get pulled into it.

I don't need to look up to know it's Garry's arms around my shoulders. I glance at him from the corner of my eye, laughing under my breath when he pouts.

His bony chin digs into my shoulder as he mumbles, "Why so sad, friend?"

Biting the inside of my cheek to stop the tears threatening to fall— a tight, anxious lump makes it hard to speak.

"I've been with you guys since I can remember. It's three hours away, and it would mean being closer to home." A single tear leaks from my eye despite my efforts. I moved with them to get away from my childhood home. Going back might break me.

It's silly.

I probably won't even get the job, but the thought of leaving my friends makes me want to curl up in a ball.

They're all I have.

My family.

"Three hours is nothing." Mandy pulls me into a comforting hug until I'm smothered.

"I'll gladly drive three hours for a babysitter when this baby comes along," Garry jokes, his voice cocooned in our embrace.

When Mandy pulls back, she cups my face in her hands, her eyes heavy, brimming with tears. She sniffles and brushes my hair over my shoulder. "You came here with us. For us. You kept me afloat more times than I care to admit, all while never admitting you were drowning."

20

A sob tries to rip through my chest, but I swallow it until it's nothing more than a strangled breath.

"What would Nick tell you to do?"

Nick isn't here.

He can't tell me to do anything.

But imagining helps to soothe the burn.

I laugh, trying to lighten the mood. "He'd say, 'Claire, you're twenty-eight. Stop climbing through my window.'"

Our houses were next door, our bedroom windows facing each other. It only took ten steps to get to his room. I counted once. Ten steps, and I was out of hell.

He was Mandy's first love, Garry's best friend, and he was my...What was he? I always find it hard to put into words what Nick was to me.

A brother? Absolutely.

Partner in crime? Yes, again.

Someone who tried to shield me from all the ghosts I fought with, but only because he promised to fight them with me.

God, I miss him.

"You're going to change the world someday, Claire Russell." He told me that once when we snuck to the lake hidden beyond the trees at the back of our houses.

"You're going to be a famous footballer someday, Nick Sawyer."

Sitting on a slab of stone, we turned to look at each other—pupils dilated, the smell of weed wafting through the air, and we lost it. We doubled over, coughing and spluttering until our eyes were bloodshot, and we couldn't breathe.

"This isn't fun anymore," I moaned, feeling bile rise in my throat.

"I swear, if you ever tell Mandy we did this—"

"We need to survive it first."

He watched me, I watched him, and the blood drained from our faces in slow motion.

We spent our first time getting stoned, giggling until we were in pain, and then we rubbed each other's back when we vomited.

I still haven't uttered a word to Mandy.

Her touch brings me back. She's laughing, and I love how I've become so used to seeing her laugh now.

"That's exactly what he'd say, but only because he'd finish with, 'Claire, what are you still doing here?'"

My chest swells with emotion because I can almost hear him say it.

The hours pass by. My friends share the burden, taking some of the weight and carrying it as their own. Now and then, a voice echoes in my head:

You're going to change the world someday, Claire Russell.

FOUR

My list of things I need to do this morning is longer than my arm. The air is too thick, and a bead of sweat trails down the back of my shirt, making me shiver. Strands of hair stick to my face. I pull it up, twisting it into something resembling a messy bun before sticking a pen through it, hoping it will keep it in place until I get back to the office.

I've just finished my final follow-up of the morning. I always get a nervous knot in the pit of my stomach when I go to check in on our kids who are placed in the care of other families. Most of the time, they do great, and they're loved, but it's not always the case. Some people are good at hiding the warning signs from caseworkers like me, and I've gotten on the wrong side of families for my inability to trust. But I'm not there to make friends with foster parents. I'm there to make sure our kids are treated with care—as they should be—and if that includes rooting out the bad apples by sticking my nose in a little too far, then so be it.

This morning's meetings went well. School reports and inspections of the children in the home environment proved the kids were settling in.

I hope my judgment is right.

As I pull into the driveway of the children's home, I immediately hear the screams of kids. And not the good kind.

This children's home is owned by the Hope foundation. One of many homes around the country. It looks like any other house in the neighborhood. Two storeys, steps leading onto the front porch, a swing chair, and bicycles scattered around the garden. But the stories inside are enough to cause a chill in the very marrow of your bones.

I volunteered with them while I was a caseworker for the state, but the founder of the organization has been in my life since I was fourteen and was my college professor. Nora Johnson is a friend and a mother figure. When she asked me to come work for the Hope Foundation, I couldn't say no.

Getting out of the car, I'm immediately greeted by two screaming children running toward me.

"Claire. Claire," they shout in unison, flattening me against the door as they come crashing into my body.

Darren looks up at me with tears in his eyes, his bottom lip trembling. He's our newest child, but after four weeks, he's finally settling and getting to know his voice by the sounds of it.

He tugs at my t-shirt.

"Addie stole my cookie," he cries.

"Did not," Addie retorts, folding her arms over her chest and stomping her feet. As she speaks, crumbs of what I'm assuming is Darren's cookie fly from her mouth. It takes all my power not to snicker. At six, she's our biggest diva.

"Why did you take Darren's cookie, Addie? That was his snack."

"I didn't," she protests, flicking her blonde curls. Her words are muffled because it looks like she stuffed the entire thing in there.

"Addie, I've told you before that if you want something, all you have to do is ask. You can't go around stealing other people's treats."

"I did," she whines. "I asked Damien if I could have another cookie, but he said no because I would ruin my dinner."

With that, Damien appears at the front door, looking down from the porch, smiling but shaking his head.

"You should have listened, little lady. You can't have everything you want, and when you don't get something, you can't steal. That cookie was Darren's. Now apologize."

She huffs, leaning into her hip. I sometimes wonder if she's a teenager trapped in a six-year-old's body.

"Sorry," she whispers so low I hardly hear it.

"Like you mean it," I say, biting the inside of my cheek to stop the laughter from erupting. It's not funny. It's really not, but sometimes they're hard to take seriously.

She stands straight, meeting Darren's watery eyes. "Sorry. I won't do it again."

"Good girl. Darren, come on. I'll get you another cookie."

He shrugs. "I didn't want it, anyway."

Oh, for the love of all that is holy.

Turning to face Addie again, he says, "You want to play hopscotch?"

And just like that, the argument ends. All is forgiven, and they run away to play together.

I wish adults could take a leaf from their book.

Damien eyes me as I approach him, tilting his head toward the door, his eyes swirling.

Confusion contorts my face. "Do you need a massage? A knot in your neck?"

Jade eyes roll as he crosses his arms. "You have a visitor."

Blowing out a long breath, my chest deflates.

I was going to call her. I really was.

There are only a select few allowed inside the house, and Damien's eyes never swirl so much for anyone else.

"How long has she been here?"

"Only ten minutes. She's reading the kids a story."

Of course she is.

I love Nora like a mother, but I've been wallowing too much in my self-pity over the weekend to even think of calling her.

But she's here now, and there's no time like the present.

"Did she not tell you she was coming?"

I smack my lips together. "Nope."

"She's going to take you away from me, isn't she?" Damien shrugs, wrapping me in a one-arm hug as we walk inside.

Halting, I look up at him. "How do you know?"

"Oh, come on, Claire. That job has you written all over it. Your name has been attached to the place from the moment they announced they were branching out. You know they haven't hired anyone because they've been waiting for you. Nora's running the place herself." He lowers his voice, leaning closer like the walls have ears. "Apparently, there's some hotshot in the city super involved. Big money."

I don't know why I whisper back. Nobody's listening. "It's a charity, Damien. Donors are essential."

He rolls his eyes again. "I'm talking big deal. The Hope Foundation have always worked with children. It's the first women's shelter. All the funding came from him. The shelter…Him. The new education program…Him. The back to work program…Him. The—"

"Okay. Okay. I get it."

"All his idea too. He's got to have a lot of influence."

Pinching the bridge of my nose, I try to make sense of what he's saying, searching the white walls for answers.

Nothing.

"They've. Been. Waiting. For. You." He jabs a long finger into my chest with each word.

I rub the tender skin. "Ouch." Still whispering. "How do you know this stuff?"

"Sources," he simply says, beaming his perfect white teeth at me. "What I'm saying is, if you don't take the job, you're an idiot, and I will kick your ass."

Eyeballing him, I click my tongue against the roof of my mouth. "Who is he?"

"Who?"

"The hotshot."

"Anonymous. I heard rumors he was an old business partner of Nora's husband."

Ah, Tony Johnson—Nora's *late* husband. Widely inappropriate and loud, but his hugs were always the best.

I rack my brain for answers, but I was too young back then, too self-involved. Tony died six years ago, and I vaguely remember Nora selling his shares of the business.

It's strange.

These donors like having their names attached to The Hope Foundation. It props up their image.

Leaning back on my heels, I break the bubble of our conversation. "Can you let her know I'm back? You know how she gets when we interrupt reading time. I'll be in my office."

***

I haven't spoken to Nora since I called her to tell her I wasn't taking the job because I'm embarrassed, and I know I disappointed her. Not by refusing the job, but because I didn't trust myself and my gut instinct. I refused to listen to the one thing I always depended on.

She's called me, but I always let it go to voicemail.

Coward.

"You can do it," I mutter, trying to calm my erratic pulse. "Don't see the ugly. There's good in our days." I don't know why those are the words that stuck with me from my random encounter with another stranger in pain. I'm leaping and hoping I'll grow wings and fly. I'll suffocate if I don't.

I shake the tremble from my hands and take a calming breath as I hear her heels enter my office.

Just the sight of her eases the knot in my stomach.

She smiles, her arms already outstretched as she walks toward me. "Hello, love. It's lovely to see you."

I swallow the lump in my throat because I missed her more than I care to admit.

"Hi. I'm sorry I haven't stayed in touch. It's been a crazy few months," I ramble as she pulls me into her embrace. The familiar smell of her perfume makes my throat prickle with emotion.

She tucks a stray strand of grey hair behind her ear before repeating the gesture with me. "Nonsense. I understand." As she always does. "Congratulations on graduating. I'm so proud of you."

"Thanks." I choke on the word and wipe my sweaty palm against my trousers. "I received your flowers. They're beautiful."

"You deserve more than flowers. Against all the odds, you did it."

We both take a seat.

"I remember the day you told me you wanted to get your PhD," she continues. "I think it was your first month of attending college. You only started as an undergrad and when I called you for a chat after your lecture to ask you to focus more on your class rather than boys, you told me, 'Nora, I'm going to be a doctor one day. A girl can have fun and be smart, you know?'"

We both laugh.

I was right, but I was far too confident back then.

Sometimes, I miss that girl.

Besides, it was my first year of college, and college boys were a different breed to my eighteen-year-old mind.

"God, I was cocky, wasn't I?" I cringe.

"You always had that edge, Claire."

"I think my edge was sanded down and rounded out a little."

"No, dear. It's simply hiding. You only need to find it again."

I hope she's right.

There's still a spark in my belly. I know it. It just needs a little air to bring on the flame.

"How are you? How's everything going with the boy?" Nora's voice is apprehensive, and I grimace. I'm honest enough with myself to admit that I hate when I'm wrong, but not with Nora. She has a way of making me feel like all my wrongs are right and mistakes are just stops in our journey.

"You'll be surprised to hear that me and Caleb have broken up," I say, the sarcasm dripping off my tongue with each word.

She doesn't say anything for a moment. I feel her eyes on me as she sets her glasses further down the bridge of her nose and glares over them.

"I am surprised."

"I know you didn't like him."

Her voice is even and calm. She crosses her legs at the ankle when she replies, "I never expressed an opinion on the boy either way."

True, but I know her well enough.

"Well, it's finished. He wasn't worth the chance I took."

When Nora stays silent, I see my opportunity. If I don't ask, I'll lose all courage and never do it.

Sensing my unease, she speaks before I can. "I hear you may be having second thoughts about the women's shelter."

How does she know everything?

I gape at her, my jaw going lax before snapping shut again.

"Who told you?"

She purses her lips, shaking her head as the hint of a smile curls on her red-painted lips.

Then it hits me.

The only other person to know both me and Nora well enough. I'd kill him if I wasn't so grateful.

"Alex," I say, already knowing I'm right.

"He might have mentioned it."

Taking a deep breath, I grasp at confidence, pulling it from thin air. "I know I turned down the job. I don't have any right to ask for a second chance, but I'm asking. You were right. I can do it. I can do it well."

"Sweetheart, you don't need to explain yourself to me. It's yours. But you should know, it's not what you're used to."

Good.

I need to leap out of my comfort zone. I need to get my blood pumping again.

Sitting straight, I nervously run my fingers through my hair, sweeping it over my shoulder.

"I think it's perfect for you, Claire. It's a big undertaking, but I have full faith you can do it. You know I'd never offer unless I did. You'll be amazing for these families."

My heart is pounding, my mouth is dry, and my breathing is non-existent. "I hope so."

I know it's a big deal because Alex showed me photos during construction. It's not like the simple house I'm currently sitting in. It's a sprawling complex with twenty private apartments built inside. There are common areas, offices, playrooms, and everything any of those women and children could need. It's all there until they feel ready to enter the world again. The support continues when they leave to live independently. The foundation helps them to find housing, already having a head start on their education, should they choose to enter the education program.

This is a huge step in my career, and my fear is taking over.

"Claire," she says softly, "You were made for this. You don't just have the qualifications; you have real-life experiences. You know these women. You know these children.

"I know it's a big move. Take a month or two to get organized and make sure Damien is prepared here. If it works out—amazing. If it doesn't—you can come home. Don't spend your life wondering, *what if?*" She takes my hand, squeezing it firmly as she places it on her lap. "Do it for the young girl that wanted to make a difference. Do it for her."

I don't know why a single tear leaks from the corner of my eye.

Probably because I'm scared half to death.

Don't see the ugly.

I smile and ignore everything screaming at me on the inside. My fear is so loud I can't hear the chaos of children running riot.

But something else is trying to break through.

Excitement.

Hope.

A good nervous and a flame burning bigger than it has in a long time. It courses through my blood and makes my heart hammer in my chest.

To hell with fear.

I'm taking the leap and growing my own damn wings.

FIVE

When I was a teenager, I stopped crying for five years.

I can pinpoint when I stopped, and the second it started again.

I know many people live their lives not crying, but mine was a conscious choice.

After my father left, and I was released back into my mother's care, I broke down in school. We were in English class, reading Shakespeare, and through the silence, broke my guttural sob. I don't know what brought it on or if I tried to fight it. I only remember my cheeks heating when blurry faces turned to look at me.

I started and couldn't stop.

Embarrassment crept up my neck, my skin blotchy with shame. Garry ripped me from my seat, pressing my head to his shoulder before escorting me out of the class, through the halls, and home.

I didn't go back for a week.

And when I did, everyone looked at me differently. Whispers followed me in the halls, a snigger echoing against the walls and assaulting my ears.

There were so many rumors that I eventually stopped defending myself.

"Did you hear what her dad did?"

"She's a slut like her mother."

"I heard her vomiting in the bathroom. Bet she's puking up her food. Look how sick she looks."

All lies, but people believe what they want to.

I tossed my long hair around my face, kept my head down, and ignored it because my aching heart was doing little to protect itself against the daggers.

But that day, in English class, somewhere between staring aimlessly at the pages, and faintly hearing the teacher's voice drift in the air, I ruptured. My dams broke, and I flooded. I told myself my tears weren't worth it. They weren't worth the small payoff of temporary relief.

For a while, I rebelled. I ignored my real friends because I didn't think I deserved their care. I died my hair, smoked too much weed, and drank too much at parties. I even lost my virginity in the back of Oliver Whitlock's car, staring at the ceiling of the cabin, and praying for it to be over with so I could move on to my next wild adventure. My smiles dimmed, always a little forced, and my mind often wandered to places on its own, drifting off and dreaming, because at night, when I welcomed sleep, I only struggled with nightmares—always silent nightmares.

I didn't wake until my screams brought me back, or Nick could hear me from his house, and he climbed through my window, shaking me until I came around.

My mother, having crawled so far into her own despair, never came to me. She allowed my roars to waft through the house and swallow me whole.

When I allowed my friends back in, they brought me back from the brink, tending to a wound they didn't own without smothering me. But I didn't shed a tear, even when breathing became less of a struggle or I started processing through everything that happened.

I didn't cry when Nick had the accident, and I certainly didn't cry when he was in the hospital. Everyone had a role. Garry was on sports duty, updating him on their team.

Mandy cared and loved more than anyone I've ever seen, draining herself in the process. I'm sure if love could keep someone alive, Nick would have lived forever.

Me...Well, I gave him hell because on the days he got angry when his legs didn't work; he was too exhausted to stay awake, or he was getting sick of looking at four walls, he needed someone to argue with. I was his vent for anger. I took it, knowing every word was laced with affection.

On the inside, I felt like I was perishing with him, but I kept sympathy to a minimum.

Three times he told me he wouldn't make it.

Three times I told him he was being dramatic.

The week before he died, I strolled into the hospital room, not noticing the wires attached to him anymore. Mandy was exhausted, as were his parents, so I was there to torture him. They warned me he was having an off day.

"Why you?" he moaned, throwing his head back when I strolled in, popping chips in my mouth.

"Ready for our hike?" I slouched in the chair, kicked off my shoes before I propped my legs up on the end of his bed, and poked him with my toes. "Oh shit, I forgot you can't. The legs and all."

He didn't meet my eyes, staring straight at the doorway, but I could see the shadow of a grin threatening his lips. "I'm feeling lazy today. I think I'll stay in bed."

I shrugged, poking him again. "Walk it off."

"You're the fucking worst. Why have I been friends with you for this long?"

"Because you love me. Chip?"

Scowling, he plucked a handful from the bag.

We stayed silent for a long moment, engrossed in a *Friends* rerun.

I didn't look at him when I said, "You're worrying your parents and Mandy."

"And you?"

"Think you're being a drama queen."

"Fuck you," he cursed under his breath, his hands clenching into fists.

I'm sure if I was in his position, I would have felt the same—angry at the world for still spinning. But if roles were reversed, he wouldn't allow me to wallow either.

"Your panties riding up your ass today?"

"I'm sick of this place." The emotion made his voice thick. I was used to seeing Nick vulnerable, but physically, he was withering too. His well-defined muscles were fading, melting away into the white bedsheets.

"Pretty sure it's just as sick of you."

"I just..." he stuttered, swallowing the lump from his throat. "I just want to go home, Claire." Tears of frustration glistened in his eyes.

Wiping the crumbs from my hands, I grabbed his fingers, forcing them apart so I could place my palm on his.

"I know. I want you home too. It's strange not seeing you when I look out my bedroom window. Although, I don't miss catching you and Mandy in compromising positions." He laughed, but it caught in his throat. "We can't change how things are, so how about you focus on getting better for now?"

He sighed, defeated.

I searched my mind for ways to distract him. "I found a new hiking trail."

His eyes darted to mine, a line of worry between his brows. "I told you not to go on your own."

"I'm not. Garry comes with me."

"Mandy never said. Does she not go?"

"She loves you too much to leave your side. We practically had to drag her home this morning."

He winced but quickly replaced it with a smile, his eyes brighter than I'd seen them since I arrived.

There's a subject he never got tired of talking about—Mandy.

Their love always made my chest swell.

For long hours, we sat in silence, watched sitcoms, and stuffed our faces with too many calories. He often dozed in and out of sleep, muttering things that didn't make sense.

"Can you tell Mandy…"

Nothing.

He never finished the sentence.

We still have no idea what he wanted to say.

We only spoke when a nurse came to poke at him with something.

Before I left, I hugged him and squeezed his calf. "I'll show you that trail soon. Promise."

He was getting better.

He had to.

Smiling weakly, his heart knew something I refused to believe the three times he told me.

"I'll be on torture duty again in a few days. Love you."

He waved me off, rolling his eyes as he laughed under his breath.

"Yeah, yeah. Love you too."

Those words were the last we said to each other, which I'm grateful for. But the ache the image conjures hasn't lessened over the years because it was the last time I saw my best friend with air in his lungs. I still think about him when I hike, usually talking to myself out loud when no one is around, and I pretend he can hear me.

Sometimes I even shed the tears I didn't at his funeral.

My return to endless sobs didn't happen because of some life-altering event. When I look back, I realize it was an accumulation, a pain building, weighing me down and filling me until I exploded.

When the first tear spilled from my eyes, it was because of a faulty piano key.

My mother was deep into her second bottle of wine when I found my fingers dancing over the white and black keys. Some scales at first before I took a seat and played. It wasn't anything special, and I can't remember the notes now, but my fingers led the way, reverberating around the house and drowning out my mother's cries and the sound of pouring wine.

In another life—a life before that night—my mother was a musician, and I've played music since I was old enough to stack blocks.

I sat there for what felt like forever, playing the same tune until it was perfect.

At least it was until my finger hit F sharp, and only a muted note drifted in the air.

I played it again.

Nothing.

One note.

It was essential to my piece, and it was silent.

I pressed it over and over again, my finger becoming red as I pounded on the black key.

"Claire, can you stop?" Mama warned, appearing at the doorway, looking every bit a powerful beauty, still dressed in her silk blouse and black trousers. But her speech had become slurred in the hours since coming home from work. Her eyes brushed past me as she spoke, indignation dripping from every word.

She always looked past me.

Never at me.

"Mama, it's broken."

"You think?"

I tapped one more time, as if the fairies had come along and fixed it since I last tried.

She used to play every evening, but she hadn't touched it more than to dust in over four years. Papa bought it for her before I was born, and I can't help but wonder now if it was an apology. Like all the flowers that appeared days after he'd left her black and blue.

"Can we get someone to fix it?"

"It's an old piano," she explained, crossing her arms over her chest. "Things break and wither over time, baby girl. That piano is no exception. It's old. Not even music lasts forever."

Her eyes glossed over before she stumbled back down the hall to the kitchen and into the only company she desired—her wine.

That's when it happened. Frustration boiled over, spilling down my cheeks until I couldn't breathe. I slammed the piano shut, not caring if she heard, kicking it, and immediately cursing myself when pain shot through my foot. Storming to my room, I swung the door shut, threw myself on my bed, and screamed into my pillow.

I was angry.

More than angry.

I was furious, but no one heard my pleas or my roars. I tossed them out, scream after scream until my throat burned, and my body was exhausted.

I eventually fell asleep, only for my tears to wake me again.

I cried because of the loss, because of the what-ifs, and because I couldn't change any of it.

I missed my best friend.

I missed my sister.

I missed my mother even when she was standing next to me.

I hated myself for it, but a small part of me even missed my father.

I missed myself most of all.

So, this morning, when my car was packed with everything I needed, I turned to say goodbye to the people that have been with me every step of my life, and I cried harder than I've cried since the day the piano key gave up on me.

"I ch…change my mmm…mind. I don't want…want to go." I sobbed, stuttering over my words.

Garry cupped my face, pressing a chaste kiss to my forehead. "Yes, you do. You need to go. Besides, you have tenants moving into your house tomorrow."

I worked hard to buy that house. It's small, but it's mine, and I hate to think other people are going to make it their own.

"You're going to be amazing. I love you, and we'll see you soon," he said, squeezing my arm supportively.

I replied with more snot and tears.

Mandy and I said goodbye with a wordless hug, both too choked up to form sentences. We didn't need to. We already knew.

Mandy is like another sister, and sisters always know.

I left pieces of myself with them, the hole in my chest ripping wider. I'm stepping into the unknown, and it's a scary place to be without company.

The women's shelter is in the suburbs of the city, and only thirty minutes from my hometown of East Fort. I'm afraid being so close to where I grew up will ignite something in me, and not the type of flame I crave. It's a place where I left my dark shadows, and if they come back to haunt me, I might break just like the old piano.

"Well, if it isn't my long-lost sister." My sister rushes from the front step of my mother's house, jostling me out of memory lane. Arms already outstretched as I exit my car, I open the gate, and she pulls me to her.

"You're so dramatic, Amy. We spoke last night, and I was here two weeks ago."

Her embrace is tight, and she sways with me in her arms. "I can't believe my favorite baby sister is finally moving home."

I'll still be thirty minutes away, but it's closer than the three-hour drive to Penrith.

"Believe me, either can I. And I'm your only sister," I breathe as she pulls back and squeezes my arms. "Where's Mama?"

"She's pruning." Amy spins around and points at a rosebush. My mother's legs are poking out.

"She has her headphones in."

My mother enjoys getting lost in her own world. Walking to her side, I remove the headphones from her ears and kiss her cheek. "Hey, Mama."

She grabs my hand on her shoulder but doesn't look up.

She never does.

"Hey, Claire Bear."

The nickname makes me smile.

My curtain of hair falls over us as I lean into her. Removing her glove, she wraps the ends around her fingers. She always plays with my hair. "Still beautiful," she whispers, mostly to herself.

"Keep going," I tell her. "I can't stay long. The moving vans will be at my new place in an hour."

She nods, pops her headphones back in, and continues with her work.

Sitting on the step with my sister, I'm grateful she doesn't go inside. The house has ghosts in every corner, and I try to avoid them.

Leaning my elbows on my knees, I take a deep breath to rid myself of the knot that usually develops when I visit.

I glance over at Nick's house and smile because all my best memories are there. Two houses on one street, but the sun only shines on one. A dark cloud crept over my childhood home many years ago, and it never left.

My mother is humming a tune, lost in her gardening. This garden could win awards.

"How's she doing?"

Amy clears her throat and shrugs. "It's her first time outside all week."

My head twists back around so fast, my neck cracks. "Why didn't you tell me?"

Her brows rise because I already know the answer.

Guilt gnaws, and I lower my head. "I could have helped."

"I had it under control."

"You shouldn't have to do it on your own. I'm closer now. I can help."

She takes my hand and places it on her lap.

"I wasn't here when Papa left. I was too busy traveling the world, and I didn't look back. You stayed. You turned down amazing opportunities to stay here with her. I'm here now. My house is down the street. Me and Jen can do it. Besides, she's started coming into the shop with me."

"Really?"

She nods. "She still doesn't play, but she enjoys it when the kids come in. She loves to listen to them."

My sister owns a music shop in town and is the most talented musician I know. I've yet to find an instrument she can't play. She attended university abroad and traveled the world teaching. She came home once. It was supposed to be for a month, but she met Jen. Two years later, they got married. She opened a shop in town, never left again, and I've never seen her happier.

"She's getting better. You know how she is. There's nothing you can do, Claire."

She looks away from me, unspoken words lingering on her lips.

"I know," I whisper, fighting the sting behind my eyes.

She kisses the top of my head. "I'm sorry."

She has nothing to be sorry for. It's not her fault my mother hasn't looked at me since I was fourteen. She loves me. I feel it with every touch she grants. But my eyes remind her of another's.

I sometimes envy my sister with her red curls and emerald eyes. My mother always jokes that she's the postman's baby, but she looks like my grandma.

I'm exactly half and half, with my mother's dark hair and my father's blue eyes. I remind her of him. Truth be told, I sometimes look in the mirror and see him too. I hate it. I'm not sure what parts of me my mother finds it more difficult to look at—the parts of my father, or the parts of herself.

She won't get better when I'm here because after she's done with her garden or painting the house for the third time in a year, she drinks to forget.

My eyes don't let her forget.

Looking at her, you'd never guess the depths she climbs into when she's alone at night. My mother is beautiful. Time has taken an obvious toll on her, but her beauty shines through. High cheekbones, and despite years of hardship, there's hardly a wrinkle on her skin. She's slender, her curves always petite. My dips and curves are fuller. My grandma may have given my sister her red hair, but she gave me my ass.

Thanks, Grandma.

My mother's hair, the color of dark chocolate, is now flecked with silver, and her hazel eyes once shone brighter than any star. She's tall. Regal. I wish she'd hold her head higher because she has the cheekiest smile when I'm lucky enough to witness it.

After my father left, she wilted, like I fear I will. A flower in full bloom only to be sentenced to an endless winter.

She always hid the darkest parts of my father's personality. She sheltered his demons—probably nurtured them—so we wouldn't have to fall prey to his outbursts.

I'm afraid when he walked away, she didn't let his demons go with him, and they haunt her to this day.

We weren't always this way. Before that night, she was the mother everyone envied—beautiful, charismatic, funny. The type of mother who held my hand so tight crossing the road, it hurt. She was my best friend, and with one look, she knew when something was wrong. She used to tiptoe into my room and lie with me until I was ready to speak or simply run her fingers through my hair until I fell asleep.

She can't read me anymore because she would need to look at me to see it.

I didn't just lose my father that night. I lost my mother too.

He took the brightest parts of her with him. One last selfish act. She remains in the memories, always stuck, never moving forward. She's a shell of who she used to be.

Empty.

"Are you excited about the new job?" Amy nudges me, bringing me back.

I'm lost in a daze today.

"Nervous. It's different."

"You worked with women when you first left college, right?"

"I did, and I've been a part of studies for domestic abuse survivors." I swallow the lump in my throat. "Change is scary," I admit, looking back at my mother.

"Change is good. You've got this, sis."

I chew the inside of my cheek, studying each of my mother's movements. She holds a rose between her fingers, smells, and smiles.

I'm jealous of a rose.

"Does she know what my new job is?"

Amy hums. "I told her."

The irony isn't lost on me.

I'm spending my life trying to help women like my mother, when I can't help her.

Maybe someday.

Maybe someday, she'll look at me long enough to see she can get through it.

When I leave, I hug my sister and kiss the top of my mother's head.

"I'll call by next week," I promise.

"Claire," she calls as I open the gate. When I turn, her eyes connect with mine for a quick second, and in that second, I see all the pain it causes.

She dips her chin, her focus back on the roses.

My chest aches.

"I'm so proud of you, baby girl."

A single tear falls before I have the chance to catch it. "I know, Mama. I know."

SIX

What Nora said is a shelter isn't a shelter. At least, it's not like the ones I worked at, and it's nothing like the other shelters I've visited.

When I drove through the steel gates and pulled into a parking spot outside, my mouth almost hit the steering wheel.

"Nora, this is insane." I drag my eyes over the length of the building. When I look over my shoulder, her eyes are gleaming with pride, and she smacks her red-painted lips together.

"Uh, huh," she hums, swaying on her feet. It's a childish movement and yet she does it with so much grace. There's a toddler running riot in her soul—I've always been sure of it. "Welcome to Guiding Light Women's Shelter."

I swallow hard because although this place is beyond anything I imagined, it's more than a step up from what I'm used to.

It looks like one of those huge houses from a design show.

You've outdone yourself, Alex.

There's a large tunnel-like corridor with floor-to-ceiling windows connecting one side of the building to the other. The gardens are landscaped to perfection, with a paved pathway leading to large double doors. It's bright and welcoming, and I'm going to get lost. I know it.

Noticing my unease, Nora squeezes my arm as my eyes roam around the quiet gardens. It's beautiful here. Trees hide the shelter, granting the privacy some of these women so desperately crave. It's secluded, sprawling out over green grass, and it's strange, but if peace

42

had a smell, this would be it.

"Calm down, Claire. You were made for this. You'll be fine once you're settled."

"I don't know what I was expecting. It's different."

Why is my voice so high-pitched?

"That's the point."

I've just never seen anything like this.

I turn to face Nora, and she's still smiling like a child, but her eyes turn softer. I must radiate panic.

"Why did you choose here?" I ask.

The more questions I ask, the more answers I'll have, and once I have all those, I can make sense of this and try to wrap my head around how one person can manage this place. My fingers twitch, and I anxiously wrap my hair around itself in a bun, but I don't have anything to tie it up with so it falls around my shoulders again.

I'm sure it wasn't this hot when I left my house this morning. It's stuffy and a bead of sweat slips down my back, causing me to shiver.

Ignoring my obvious unease, Nora answers, "I didn't. The donor purchased the site. He approached me about building a shelter with the foundation, and he already knew Alex, so he contacted him."

Damien was right about everything.

And it makes sense. The Hope Foundation has an excellent reputation. Nora knows what she's doing, and if he wants to learn, he chose the best.

"Who's the donor?"

She tilts her head, her lips turning down like I should know better than to ask.

"Don't worry. You'll meet him"

Waves of nerves wash over me. "I will? When?"

She blows out a long breath, turning to face me fully. Nora is petite, but I always feel like she towers over me.

"Tomorrow. I'll introduce you at dinner. He has a family and usually doesn't work on the weekends, so please don't be late."

Oh, sweet Jesus.

"I thought he wanted to remain anonymous?"

She shrugs her narrow shoulders. "Plans change. You can save any questions for Mr. Williams."

Mr. Williams?

I gawk at her, swallowing the hard lump of unease lodged in my

43

throat, and fumble with the cuffs of my blouse. "You could have warned me."

"That's no fun."

Biting the inside of my cheek to stop more questions from spilling out, I stand straight and inhale a steadying breath. She won't give me more answers until I meet him.

"I told you about the new education program for the women," she continues, strolling toward the double doors. My heart races with every step.

I can do this.

"The shelter is close enough to the city for access to colleges. At the moment, we have two community colleges involved in the program and the city university. The city has what we need—transport, easy access, schools for the children. There's daycare inside for the children who are too young for school. Not all of the women choose to go back into education. It's an option, but one they don't have to accept. Some take internships, some are just trying to get back into the workforce, and some already had jobs coming here. Whatever they want to do to build a life for when they leave, we support them." She takes a deep breath and rests her hands on my upper arms.

"Look, I know this is a lot to take in, but I wouldn't have asked you if I didn't think you were capable. You won't be on your own in there. You have two caseworkers working with you. The support staff is here at night, should anyone need them. They're one big family. You'll add that extra edge. I just know it." She cups the side of my face with her small palm before brushing my hair off my shoulder. "You're a hard worker, Claire, but don't forget about yourself in there. Working with these women may be hard for you, and I know some of their stories will bring back painful memories. When things get too heavy, don't forget to take a moment for yourself."

I force a small smile before nodding.

"Now," Nora pats me on the back, "Pull yourself together, dear. Nerves don't suit you."

I huff and smooth imaginary wrinkles out of my shirt. But there's more. There's always more. I can tell by how her nose wrinkles, making the small lines on the corners of her mouth more noticeable.

"You need to cut your hair."

Not this again.

For almost fourteen years she's asked me to cut my hair, and for fourteen years, I've given her the same answer.

"No." I roll my eyes. "I'm waiting for my knight in shining armor to come and rescue me from my tower. Anyway, I got a trim last week. It's not that long."

She digs a finger into my lower back, forcing me to walk toward the door. "It's almost touching your bottom. Which…" She tilts her head, and I know exactly what she's looking at.

"My ass is fine. It's the same size as the last time you saw it," I cut her off.

She winks. "It gives the men a little something to hold on to, dear."

"Nora." I gasp, shocked that such words come out of a woman with so much elegance. Her narrow shoulders vibrate, and she tugs me forward while linking her arm inside my elbow.

"Don't *Nora* me. I've been around a lot longer than you."

I don't even know why she surprises me anymore.

"I missed you," I whisper, pressing my head against hers as we walk.

I see the hint of a blush on her cheeks, and she squeezes my arm as a security guard dips his chin in a greeting when we walk inside.

"Boys." She waves her hello to the two security guards standing around the lobby.

"Mrs. Johnson," they reply.

"Why is there so much security?" I lean toward her and ask under my breath. I eye the big machines. "And metal detectors?"

Nora leads us around them without any protest from security.

"This building houses women coming out of some of the most harrowing situations I've ever seen. We want them to feel safe. You'll meet Sam at some stage. He's our liaison police officer. We thought having a familiar face rather than different officers would settle any nerves with women who choose to come forward and press charges. Or if there's any threat to the shelter, we call him. Thankfully, we haven't had any."

"Okay," I breathe, trying to digest every crumb of information as my eyes roam around the large lobby.

I get acquainted with the security guards; two at reception, another two around the building. I'll meet the night shift staff in time, I'm sure.

Every door on the way in is coded. Hard to get in, easy to get out. It's safe enough without feeling like you're in a prison.

The large windows allow the natural daylight to illuminate every corner, and no matter where I look, I'm surrounded by trees.

I've already lost count of how many lefts and rights Nora takes when I ask, "Where are we going?"

We're interrupted by a woman walking toward us. She's strikingly beautiful—copper skin, enhanced by a yellow sundress, and her curls hang to her shoulders.

"You must be Claire," she smiles. "I'm Amelia. I'm a caseworker here."

"It's lovely to meet you." Her smile reminds me of Mandy, and my heart instantly slows.

She steps aside and gestures to the garden. "They're expecting you."

We take the last turn through open doors, and the sounds of laughter fills my ears. Benches line the garden, children play on the swing sets, music blasts from a group of teenagers to my right, and women chat in huddles.

I can't fill my lungs fast enough.

Smiles.

There are so many smiles.

I don't know why I expected a place so different from this.

I expected dark.

Hopeless.

It's called The Hope Foundation for a reason, Claire.

Chastising myself, I drink in the scene, my nerves soon replaced with excitement.

"Wow," I breathe, unsure if Nora hears me, but I'm sure she can see the tears swirling in my eyes. It makes sense now why she asked me to pop by on a Friday evening before officially starting on Monday—everyone is here.

"Nora," a lady calls, standing from her seat. A sea of grinning faces turns toward us, and I'm engulfed in greetings…and hugs.

I'm searching for words among the crowd as they guide me further into the garden, insisting I sit with them.

"It's so great to finally meet you, Claire. Nora told us so much about you. I'm Mia." Her blonde hair flows in waves, her green eyes sparkling in the sun. "This is Emma, this is Sofia, this is Isa, this is—" She stops when my mouth falls open, a blush spreading across her face. "Maybe we should give you a chance to settle in."

Squeezing Mia's hand, I drink in everyone around me. "I'm sure I will get to know you all pretty fast."

I smile as a little girl reaches over me for a chocolate biscuit.

46

"Hi," she chimes, with no second thoughts when she wraps a finger around my hair. "You have hair like Rapunzel."

My chest swells with emotion because I know that behind all these smiles, there are the darkest stories. "Thank you."

She potters away to her friends.

Another woman pours coffee into a cup for me. "Sugar?" she asks.

I usually don't unless I'm stressed so I think today calls for some. "Two please."

"We usually have group dinners on Friday in the main kitchen." Another woman informs me. I haven't learned her name yet. "You're more than welcome to join us next week."

"I'd love to." My cheeks hurt from smiling so widely.

Nora takes a seat to my left, and watching her trying to sit on the picnic bench is almost comical.

"We sure are going to miss you, Nora." Mia wraps an arm around Nora's shoulders before holding a hand toward me in apology. "No offense."

I shake my head. I get it. I missed her too. "None taken."

"Don't worry, ladies," Nora says confidently, scooping a spoon of sugar into her coffee. "You are in expert hands. Claire is young. She's better at this, and she will fight for you all. We all knew I was only filling in."

For me.

I'm not sure whether to be overwhelmed that she waited for me to agree or insulted because she knew things wouldn't work out with Caleb.

I'll take the compliment.

Tears well in my eyes, but I beat them away before they fall.

The hours pass and the sun begins to set behind the trees. They introduced me to the children, who insisted I play on the swings. I happily obliged.

Some teenagers even lifted their heads from their phones to say hello. Although, I think one or two grunted at me.

The fairy lights hanging from the trees switch on as the darkness creeps in, illuminating the garden like lightning bugs.

It's beautiful.

Effort and love were poured into this place. It's seeping from every corner.

Alex did an amazing job on the build, but whoever designed the interior did so with care.

"We better go." Nora presses her hand in mine as I stand in the doorway, still mesmerized. "We should let them settle in for the evening."

I nod, take a deep breath, and feel a real smile stretch on my cheeks. I feel...full.

And it has nothing to do with the copious amounts of food the women offered me all day.

We didn't speak of their pasts. I'm sure I will hear their stories.

I want to.

But today wasn't about that. I was privileged enough to see a glimpse of these women without the whispers of what happened to them.

Each one has strength beyond what most people can imagine, envious courage, and souls marked by a past.

A past not too dissimilar to my own.

"I can do this," I whisper mostly to myself.

She's sure when she grips my hand tighter, and says, "Well, of course you can, dear."

SEVEN

I'm late.

I'm exactly what Nora told me not to be.

I swore I'd be on time.

"Please, Claire, whatever you do, don't be late. He's a busy man and his time is precious."

She called me again last night when I got home from the shelter. Reeling from my time there, I opened a bottle of wine and swayed around my living room to music because why not, while burning sage…because why not?

I wasn't using Mama's solution to kill the bad energy from the shelter. There wasn't any. Swirling the burning stick, I was determined to cast my own doubts aside.

"I'm a busy woman. *My* time is precious," I retorted, putting my wine down.

It was a lie. I was drinking wine from a cup, in nothing but an oversized t-shirt.

Nora took a deep breath, and I knew she was biting her tongue. "Mr. Williams has worked with the foundation for a long time, and he has put a lot of money into the shelter. I mean, he funded the entire thing, Claire."

Okay, so he was important. I got it.

"You are both going to work closely together, so you need to be on time. And for the love of God, keep your mouth shut."

I clenched the phone a little tighter to my ear. "What's that supposed to mean? He wants a meeting with me. I'm assuming I'm allowed to speak."

"Yes, dear, I know. Look, he can come across as abrupt. Especially to those, he doesn't know. He's a complete sweetheart when you get to know him, but I know how you are. You like to speak your mind. Just don't take offense."

I stayed silent, unsure of what to say. She was right. I would never let some old, overweight, greyed haired man in a suit talk down to me.

But for Nora, and the women in the shelter, I could try to hold it back.

I would *really* try.

Nora spoke again before I could reply. "This is important. You two need to get along with each other."

"Ugh," I grunted. "Fine. I'll be on my best behavior."

She only made me more nervous to meet him.

But Mr. William's secretary called this morning, informing me he could not attend dinner, and he freed some time in his schedule for this afternoon. I could meet with him at his offices in JW Media.

How kind.

I don't know what happened. I woke at my usual time and went for a run. I even popped into the shelter again to get to know some more of the women. I wanted my face to be familiar to them before I start on Monday. When I arrived, a young woman was on her way from another local shelter. I wanted to stick around. It's a scary situation, and honestly, a part of me wanted to prepare myself for what was to come. Bruises marred her youthful face, purple swelling around her eyes. But I needed the wake-up call. My time there isn't going to be coffee and chats like yesterday. The reality I'm facing is much bleaker.

I left with plenty of time to spare, showered and dressed without panic. I even unpacked the last of my boxes.

But I underestimated city traffic, and now I'm sweaty, anxious, and slightly annoyed, because when I called the secretary to explain why I was late, she didn't even attempt to show understanding.

"Mr. Williams is a busy man. He won't wait for you all day."

They should put that on his headstone.

Mr. Williams.

He was a busy man.

"I understand. I'm not expecting him to wait all day. Can you simply explain I'll be ten minutes late?" I huffed, hoping she believed my lie. I'm going to be at least twenty minutes late, but she didn't need to know that.

I've done well—all things considered. After checking in at the lobby, an elevator took me to the thirty-third floor.

I try my best to fix my running mascara and wild hair, to no avail.

I arrive within fifteen minutes. Still later than I told the secretary I'd be, but five minutes earlier than I promised myself.

Small victories.

"Hi," I greet the young woman behind the desk. I don't even have to introduce myself because my heavy panting and disheveled appearance give me away.

"Ms. Russell." She nods curtly, her voice even. Her eyes go to the large office behind me, the person inside hidden by frosted glass. "Mr. Williams is waiting. You can go right in."

I take a deep breath and attempt to smooth out my blouse, but it's no use.

I look like shit.

"Thank you," I breathe, swallowing my nerves and ignoring various eyes on me as I walk to the office.

I tap my knuckles against the glass door, and my eyes immediately go to the tall figure with his back to me, staring out the window and onto the city streets.

Can he even see anything from up this high?

He's not old with grey hair.

And he is most definitely not overweight.

Great.

It would be easier to relax if I couldn't see his muscles strain against his tailored suit jacket when he crosses his arms over his chest.

I clear my throat. "Mr. Williams?"

Then my eyes go to the lady sitting on the chair.

Nora.

I offer an apologetic smile because I promised to be on time and I'm not. She winks at me, and my shoulders relax an inch.

"You're late." His voice is low, raspy, arrogant, and does little to ease my spiraling nerves.

Choosing honesty, I admit, "Sorry, I'm not used to city traffic."

"I hope you'll run the shelter with more diligence, Ms. Russell."

I swear, I think my mouth just hit the expensive carpet.

51

Nora's shoulders tense when she says, "Everything okay, Claire?"

Nodding, I hold my breath, my eyes still transfixed on the back of his head.

Then he turns, and I know I'm wrong. Now my mouth hits the carpet. It may have even broken through the floor and is resting in an office below.

His hair is so dark it's almost black, but the ray of light shining through the window shows it's darker brown. Brows pulled together; he stares through scrutinizing eyes. Every feature sits on a perfectly chiseled face, and full lips merely twitch at my shock.

Him.

I blink.

He blinks harder.

I inhale.

He sighs.

Only for his jaw tenses, I'd think he doesn't see me.

Because he should know me.

"Jake?" I croak, sounding like a frog.

His eyes narrow as he pulls out his chair and opens his suit jacket to show a trim waist beneath before he sits. "Please, call me Mr. Williams."

What?

Have I lost my mind?

No.

I'd never forget his face because he's gorgeous. I'm not blind. But he's also one reason I'm standing here.

"Ms. Russell, are you going to stand there all day, or are you going to take a seat? I need to be out of the building in thirty minutes, and you're already late."

I blink again, unsure if I've lost my voice as my legs begin to move. I take the seat on the other side of his desk.

Sweet Jesus, are these chairs made from marshmallows?

I don't look at Nora because I know she's already staring at me like I'm another species.

"I've asked you here today because the shelter is a special project, and the education program has recently received the green light. I want to make sure you can manage it properly."

I try to speak, but I can't. My mouth simply flaps open and shut like a fish.

He runs a finger over his jaw, and I'm convinced that if he pulls his eyes any tighter together, he will go blind.

Leaning back in his chair, he rests his arms on either side. It makes him larger, and I feel claustrophobic. "Ms. Russell, are you ill?"

I shake my head.

"Then can you stop gawking at me?"

I nod, but I'm unable to pull my eyes away because I'm trying to see something about him—something I don't recognize. Something that will tell me this is a case of mistaken identity, and he just looks really similar to the guy I shared donuts with two months ago. I'm trying to make sense of this.

"Ms. Russell, Nora warned me before this meeting that your mouth can sometimes get the better of you. You've had it open since you walked in here, but nothing audible has come out of it."

Nora sniggers but remains quiet. She's useless as backup, but I can't even react to the insult.

I blink again.

He blinks harder.

"Jake?" I repeat, leaning forward.

"That's my name, but I'd much prefer if you called me Mr. Williams."

What the fu—

"Ms. Russell," he repeats, agitation pouring out of him. His jaw twitches as he pinches the bridge of his nose. "Are you having a stroke?"

Maybe.

"*Are* you having a stroke, dear?" Nora adds, leaning forward in her chair.

"I don't know," I breathe, astonished

He shakes his head slowly and pins his eyes to me, searching my face for answers.

I'm glued to the chair.

"Jake?" I repeat, and I'm starting to think I don't know any other words.

"Oh, for the love of God. Yes, that's my name. If it gets you to talk, you can call me Jake."

I look away briefly to give myself a second to gather my thoughts. When my eyes land on his again, I think he's sure now I'm having a stroke.

"Do you remember me?"

Maybe I've lost all remaining sanity. It's the only explanation for why he's looking at me this way. He clasps his hands together and takes a deep breath.

Am I having a stroke?

"Remember you?"

"Yes. Remember me. We've met."

Haven't we?

I know we have.

What is wrong with him?

His lips set into a hard line before he speaks again. "Where?"

I search his face, but I'm seeing nothing in those deep, chocolate-colored eyes.

It's him.

I'd remember those eyes anywhere.

Now, if he could just smile. I'm pretty sure I've thought about his smile more times than I'd like to admit.

Maybe I've blown this completely out of proportion. I know I'm just a stranger, but we spoke for an hour.

Two strangers, sitting on a bench, eating donuts, and spilling our guts to each other. He was part of the reason I asked for a second chance with Nora. He's the reason I'm sitting in his office, staring at him too intensely while his jaw stiffens more and more by the second.

"In Penrith. On the benches by the beach. I hit my head, and I was crying. You asked if I was okay. We shared donuts and spoke for almost an hour."

He arches a brow, and there's a teeny tiny shadow of a smirk, but his stoic mask comes back down almost immediately.

"You were crying because you hit your head?"

I throw my hands out and roll my eyes.

"I was crying because my fiancé cheated on me. You told me about your wife," I say softly, but there's a moment of doubt when I look at his hand and don't see the ring I saw when I first met him.

His knuckles turn white, and I suddenly regret mentioning that part of our conversation.

"We won't be discussing my wife, Ms. Russell."

"Sorry," I murmur under my breath.

His eyes roam around his office before they land back on me, and for a second, I think he's going to say he remembers, but no words escape his mouth.

Nora's voice finally cracks through the air. "You bought the beach house close to Alex, didn't you, Jake?"

Thank you.

His eyes soften when he looks at her, and for a moment, I see his features warm with a hint of a smile. "I did. I was there. I'm not saying Ms. Russell is lying. I'm saying I don't remember her."

I sit back in the chair. "Nothing, huh?"

He shrugs. "I meet a lot of people."

He says it like it should make me feel better.

It doesn't.

Okay, so I've made a big deal out of something that meant zilch to this guy. I've thought about this man's words for months, and he doesn't even have a vague recollection of my face.

Ouch.

"Ms.—"

"I swear, if you call me Ms. Russell one more time, I'm going to cry. Call me Claire," I almost beg.

He shifts in his seat, and I blow a strand of hair from my face.

"Okay," he says slowly. "Claire, we should get on with the meeting."

I nod, shaking my hands of their tremble and nursing my bruised ego.

"I was hoping my donation toward the shelter and the funding for the education program could stay anonymous, but that doesn't seem to be the case."

"Why?" It's out of my mouth, and I want to suck it back in, but now is the time for answers. "Anonymous donations happen all the time. Why is this different? Why are *you* different?" I arch a brow. "Unless you're doing something illegal, Mr. Williams?" I meant it as a joke, but when his eyes harden and his jaw locks, I know he doesn't take it the way I intend.

I cross my arms over my chest and lean back. He's made it abundantly clear he doesn't know me, and yet, he insulted me more than once.

"I get it. A young, handsome CEO donates a large amount of money to a women's shelter. It's a story for the beautiful socialites who will throw themselves at you. It shows you in a softer light. It's good for your image. People love those stories."

"Claire," Nora scolds, her cheeks turning red.

She already told him my mouth gets me in trouble. He's expecting it.

I don't want to disappoint him, do I?

But the curl of his lips only serves as fuel to my fire. Then, for the first time, his smile reaches his eyes, and he chuckles. A full-on, loud, obnoxious laugh fills his large office.

And I hate it because now I know it's definitely the same man I shared donuts and my darkest day with because that same smile makes my tummy flutter.

Damn it, Claire.

"You think I'm handsome, Ms. Russell?"

Bastard.

He is going to be a pain in my ass.

I bite my lip before letting my frustration bubble. "Of course, that's what you'd take from what I just said." I roll my eyes and look away because his stare makes my cheeks heat.

"Enough, you two," Nora warns sternly, but the glint in her eyes betrays her efforts. She is finding far too much amusement in our petty argument.

"Apologies, Nora." Jake nods, and I grind my teeth so hard I think one cracks. "Ms. Russell appears to enjoy making assumptions. I wonder if she enjoys admitting when she's wrong?"

Hell will freeze over before I admit I am wrong.

Those fiery eyes come back to lock with mine. "Like I said, I was hoping to stay behind the scenes here, but that isn't going to happen, so certain things are expected. JW Media and The Hope Foundation will host a charity auction in the coming months. It's not specifically for Guiding Light, but it will mark the official opening."

I take a deep breath, swallow my nerves, and fight the urge to argue with him.

I shrug. "That's fine."

"There may be some interviews during the initial buzz."

"Uh, huh," I agree with a hum, already hating the idea.

Why couldn't he have stayed anonymous? Bet if he was old, they would have left him alone. But no, this guy has the bone structure of a Greek god with a body I can only imagine is carved from marble.

His gaze assesses me too closely, and I shift under the weight of his stare. "Why choose this line of work, Ms. Russell?"

I rear back. "Excuse me?"

"It's a simple question. You'll be asked it until you're blue in the face. I suggest you prepare a better answer. Is there a reason you wanted to help women and children?"

My mouth goes dry.

Oh, God.

"Jake," Nora pleads with a soothing voice.

"I'm good at my job. It's something I'm interested in."

Please don't ask again.

Can he see it?

Can he see the lies glistening in the tears wanting to fall?

"You'll be asked how you relate to these women. Can you? Can you relate? Personal experience?" he asks flatly, pinching at a raw nerve buried somewhere in the dark parts of my mind.

"Do I need it?" I shoot back. "Mr. Williams, I relate to these women and children because I will work with them. I will listen to their stories. I'll empathize." My spine turns to steel, and I sit so straight I think I slip a disc. "Maybe if you worried less about appearances and interviews and actually met the women you are so generously throwing money at, you might be able to relate as well."

I hear Nora mutter, "Oh no," but I choose to ignore her.

"With all due respect, I understand your job here differs from mine. But my concern isn't with my image, appearances, or how I will come across in interviews. My job is to make these women believe they deserve a second chance. My job is comforting children who curl up when they hear raised voices. My job is to make these women believe they're enough before they doubt themselves and walk back into the relationship that brought them to the shelter in the first place." I've no idea when I stand, but my palms are spread against his oak table. "That is my job, Mr. Williams, and I take it seriously. You can focus on your image. I will smile and answer questions. Then I will go home, peel off the fancy dresses and do *my job*.

"You may throw money at this project because you can, and it somehow feeds your ego, but I don't work for you. I work for those women and children." My chest is heaving, and there's the lingering pounding at my temples, but I don't stutter.

I do not stutter.

Because I believe in everything I said.

I also believe I'm about to be fired before I ever start.

57

This mouth *is* trouble.

But this isn't about me, and he had no right to ask. My past has nothing to do with him.

He sits back, linking his fingers over his broad chest. Then the smug bastard does something that makes my hand ball into a fist with the want to punch him.

He smiles.

"Mr. Williams, are *you* having a stroke?" My voice doesn't break—not once—but my chest is tight.

He tries to hide his smile as he looks over at Nora, but he doesn't try hard enough. His face looks like it will crack under the pressure of his grin, and it's the most beautiful thing I've ever seen.

"You were right about her."

Nora beams back. "I know."

"I'm right here," I add, confused by their exchange.

She glances between us. Her smile does little to calm my failing nerves. Clutching her handbag, she stands and kisses my cheek before winking at Jake. "My job here is done. I'm sure you can both sort the rest."

"You're leaving?" I screech.

Please don't.

But it's probably for the best. I don't need witnesses when I strangle this man.

Ignoring my panic, she simply walks away.

"I'll drop by the shelter next week to see how you're settling."

Head high, she turns on her heels and walks away, leaving me alone with him.

Heart pounding so hard I'm sure he can hear it, I slowly turn back to look at him. Eyes firm, I don't break eye contact, even when there's a quick twitch of his lips.

He scans my face, taking in every inch, and I'm not sure why my heart is hammering anymore.

"Sit down, Claire."

So now I'm Claire.

His mouth curls up on one side. "Please."

Taken aback by his sudden change of tone and the warmth in his voice, my knees hit the back of the chair, and I sit like an obedient dog.

"The shelter is lucky to have you. You're passionate, and you stand up for what you believe in. You just handed me my ass on a plate.

Interviews won't be an issue."

"I won't talk about my past. It's my past for a reason. It doesn't affect my job." I swallow again, a knot tightening in the lowest part of my stomach. His smile falters, and I regret saying anything because his smile somehow calmed my mood. Even if I wanted to rip his head off thirty seconds ago.

"You have my word. No one will ask about your past. I'll make sure of it."

I look down at my hands, hoping to hide the wobble in my voice when I say, "Thank you." Shifting in my seat, the leather squeaks beneath me. "I still don't understand. Why now? The shelter opened six months ago. Why announce yourself as the donor?"

A heated stare skims over me, but I don't move.

"Like you said, it's a past for a reason. This past isn't mine to share, but mine to protect." A pained expression dashes across his face, but it's hardly there long enough for me to notice. "When we announce the education fund, the official name will be *The Jessica Connors Education Program*. It's named after my wife."

The pain I briefly witnessed makes sense now.

I nod, understanding.

"I can't put her name to this and stay anonymous, and she deserves to be part of it."

His eyes glaze over, the sincerity in his tone leaving me lost for words.

I'm rarely lost for words.

"Two weeks," Jake finally says after a long silence. "I can visit the shelter in two weeks."

Oh.

"Great." I force a smile. "The group has dinner together on Fridays at six. You should come." My anger subsides, his confession leaving a sting in the back of my throat.

"Six o'clock is perfect, Ms. Russell."

EIGHT

Shortly after the meeting, I haul my ass out of those swanky offices. I get off at the wrong floor twice before I finally find myself outside JW Media and surrounded by the bustle of the city.

I'm so on edge I could combust. It's bubbling under my skin and making me itchy.

Maybe the specimen radiating potent masculinity and raw magnetism has something to do with it.

Why couldn't he have been old?

Instead, Jake Williams has proved to be one of the most beautiful men I've ever set eyes upon. I saw it when I first met him, but I was too busy wallowing to appreciate it.

I'm pretty sure I'm jealous of his tailored suit. I'd need to be blind not to notice the body it's hiding—trim waist beneath an open suit jacket and muscular thighs that strain against the material.

In the twenty minutes I sat in his office, he managed to erase the memories of kindness he showed just months ago.

Having him watch my every move in a job I'm already nervous about makes my stomach knot with anxiety and unwanted excitement.

To be fair, he's not the worst thing I've ever had to look at while working.

Watching him walk is entertaining.

"How did it go?" Mandy singsongs through my phone as I try to avoid getting trampled on.

I love my friend, but she's not who I want to vent my anger on right now. "Hey, sweetie. Is your husband with you?"

She remains silent before there's a hushed whisper.

"Put him on the phone, Mandy."

"I can tell by your tone that you're not happy. I would like to have noted that he is not yet my husband. Therefore, if he has done anything wrong, you cannot hold me responsible."

"Traitor," Alex hisses in the background.

"Duly noted," I agree.

He clears his throat. "Hey, Claire. What's up?"

Taking a deep breath, I grip the phone a little tighter. "Don't *Claire* me, Alex Hale."

"Oh, shit. She full named you," Mandy jeers.

"We're friends, Alex, right?" I ask, trying to concentrate on getting myself a cab without getting knocked down.

He hesitates for a moment before replying, "Yes."

"You could have told me who the donor was."

"Ah," Alex stalls, obviously unsure where this is going. "You've met Jake?"

"Jake?" I hear Mandy gasp. "You never told me he was the donor. Jesus, Alex, our kids play together."

That makes me feel a little better.

"I couldn't tell anyone." He fights back. He's such a sweetheart. I can hear the guilt in his voice. But he's still not off the hook.

"Oh yeah, we've met," I interrupt.

"And?"

"And you still could have told me."

"What difference would it make?"

Nibbling my lower lip, I deliberate whether to tell them I've met Jake before.

"Claire?" Mandy echoes, waiting for my reply.

"Hold on a sec."

My eyes wander to a neon light.

A bar.

I halt, glancing up, deciding if there's ever a day I need a drink, it's today.

It's cozy inside, and the heat stings my cold cheeks. I sit at the bar while a game plays on the screen.

The bartender swings a towel over his shoulder. "What can I get you?"

Holding my hand over the phone, I order a glass of wine.

61

"Are you in a bar?" Mandy wonders.

I fiddle with a beer mat between my fingers.

"Yep. Single woman, sitting at the bar, drinking on my own. I've hit rock bottom." I laugh, but something tightens in my chest. "Stressful couple of days."

As much as I want to believe it's the new job or how a man I hardly know makes my skin tingle—it's not.

Since visiting my mother, I've had a painful knot in my chest because a part of me knows that for her to get better, I need to stay away.

And it sucks.

I knew coming home would be hard, but there's no painkiller for the sting of rejection.

There's silence for a moment before she sighs. "I'm sorry." She doesn't scold me for being in a bar on my own because she knows. Probably better than most.

"Can we get back to why I'm in trouble?" Alex interrupts as I take a long drink of the chilled wine, grateful that I was too scared of city traffic to drive to the meeting.

"I've met him before," I finally say.

"Jake?"

"Satan, yes."

"Satan?" Alex barks a laugh. "I didn't know you knew each other."

"Okay, Satan might be a little dramatic. I let him get under my skin. We met in Penrith. It was months ago, but it was enough for me to remember him. He can't say the same for me. He didn't have a clue who I was."

"Liar. You can't forget a face like yours," Mandy bellows, offended on my behalf. She's a good friend. "I'd never forget your face."

Not the same, but I love her for it. "We've been best friends since we were four. I'm pretty sure if you got amnesia, you'd still remember me."

"True," she agrees.

"Sorry, Claire," Alex continues, interrupting our little love fest. "Jake didn't want to be known as a donor. It was confidential. I couldn't tell you, even if I wanted to."

"It's me, Alex," I remind him, gritting my teeth.

"It's business, Claire," he retorts.

Ugh.

Impenetrable.

"Alex, if you want to remain my friend, you need to brush up on your girl code." He chuckles, and I can almost see the roll of his eyes. "Take some lessons from your wife."

"Soon-to-be wife," he corrects. "I'm beginning to second-guess my decision."

Despite my irritation, I laugh. Blowing out some stress, I roll my shoulders to ease the tension.

"I can't believe he didn't remember you," Mandy sighs. There's silence for a moment before I hear a gasp. "Claire? Did you sleep with him?"

I choke on my wine.

How did she come to that conclusion?

"No," I sputter, trying to clear my airways. "I can assure you. I did not sleep with Jake Williams."

I feel a prickle along my spine, and I'm not convinced it's because of what I said.

"Don't sound so relieved." The deep rasp of his voice tickles my ear.

What the hell?

Am I hearing things now?

Spinning around on the stool, my lips part with a pop.

"Is he there?" Mandy whispers.

"Speak of the devil and all that," I murmur, staring up at him like he arrived by UFO.

I take another long drink, desperate to wet my dry mouth.

I've reached my limits on surprises for the day.

"Sweetie, I've got to go. I'll call you later."

I only hear her giggle as I end the call.

He removes his suit jacket, and despite my shock, my treacherous eyes rake in every muscle movement as he drapes his jacket over the back of the stool.

"By all means, you're welcome to join me."

He blinks in response, utterly unfazed as he takes a seat and orders a whiskey.

"Neat," he adds.

Of course.

"Are you following me?"

Another blink.

"So, who were you trying to convince you didn't sleep with me, Ms. Russell?" he asks, ignoring my previous question.

"We're in a bar, not a boardroom. I think it's okay to call me Claire. And I wasn't trying to convince anyone. It's the truth."

He shrugs his left shoulder before bringing the drink to his lips.

I become mesmerized just watching how his throat moves when he swallows.

Snap out of it, Claire.

Jesus, he's like a walking sex toy.

"If you say so. I guess I wouldn't remember."

Asshole.

Swallowing my anger, I lean an inch closer. It's hardly noticeable, but I certainly notice when his spine stiffens. "Believe me, Mr. Williams. If you had sex with me, you'd remember."

His fingers clench around his glass as he places it back on the bar.

He tilts his head. "Debatable."

I resist the urge to shake him.

"Why are you here?"

His eyes wander from me to my wine and back again. "I think it's the same reason you're here."

"To drown your sorrows?"

Shut up, Claire.

Shut the fuck up.

He frowns, a line forming between his brows. In the dim light of the bar, his eyes are almost black.

"Where's your son?" I ask before he can comment on all my many sorrows. His stare burns a hole in the side of my face.

More silence.

"You told me when we met," I explain.

I can't believe he doesn't remember.

"With his aunt and uncle. You'll meet them. Sam is the liaison police officer for the shelter."

Oh.

"It's a real family affair you've got going on over there, huh?"

"I need people I can trust."

"Is Sam your brother?"

He sighs and taps a finger against his glass.

I'm starting to think he doesn't like questions.

Well, tough shit. I love them.

And it was his choice to sit here.

"He's married to my sister-in-law."

I let the silence linger between us before I begin to fidget.

I hate silence.

"Are you always this moody?"

I expect no answer, but his shoulders shake, a chuckle coming from deep in his throat. He dips his chin before finally looking at me. I take a deep breath because with a simple look, I have an ache between my legs.

"No."

"No?"

That's it.

I chew my lip between my teeth. He watches just as intently as I watched him drink his whiskey.

Staring straight ahead, I swallow before saying, "Tell me something good."

When I turn to look at him, I swear there's a moment of recognition before it quickly disappears.

He smiles.

A real one this time, and it's beautiful. I can't help but smile with him.

Another drink.

As if attached to him by a piece of string, I lift my drink to my lips too.

"We finally found someone to run the shelter today. She thinks I'm a moody bastard, but I think she enjoys making assumptions. I also think she's going to be amazing for the women."

My smile fades.

This means a lot to him.

It's more than just a shelter.

There's a deeper meaning, and I may never find out what it is, but I understand it.

Suppressing the sudden prickle in my throat, I hope my voice doesn't break when I say, "I was there yesterday. It's beautiful." I nudge him playfully. "You'll see when you visit."

A hum vibrates from his lips before he smiles again. I don't think I can take another one. It holds a secret I'm not privy to—like even his smile is guarded.

When his hand comes toward my face, I freeze.

Slowly.

Closer.

And closer.

Is he going to touch me?

His thumb pulls at my chin, freeing my lip from the hold of my bite. *Holy shit, he's touching me.*

"Stop it," he warns and returns to staring into his dark liquid.

I can only blink.

Despite being on a busy street, it's early, and the bar is quiet. A game is playing on mute on the large screen, but nobody appears to be watching it.

I see a jukebox in the corner.

Perfect distraction.

Grabbing my purse, I feel his wandering eyes on me with every step. He's still staring at me when I sit on the stool again, smiling to myself.

With the same sexy smirk on his lips, he asks, "What did you choose?"

I wink. "You'll see."

When *You're So Vein* plays over the speakers, he throws his head back and laughs.

NINE

My eyelids feel glued together. My mouth has never been this dry—I'm pretty sure it's on the verge of cracking. And the banging at my temples is both punishing and unforgiving.

Cursing myself for forgetting to pull the curtains last night, I feel the sun on my face before I open my eyes.

What did I drink? The entire bar?

I open one eye, close it again as quickly and groan at my stupidity. I'm so hungover my bedroom doesn't even look like mine.

But then I feel a large hand sprawled over my stomach.

Who the hell is in my bed?

Slowly, I peel my eyes open, convinced even the slightest movement will wake my bed buddy.

And there he is—snoring lightly into his pillow, sun-kissed skin, every muscle contoured in the morning light, tousled dark chestnut hair with a five o'clock shadow across his jaw.

This isn't my bedroom.

Bad Claire.

So bad.

It's my partner in misery.

It looks like we both found comfort in our joint loathing.

Glancing around, I drink in the large room while trying to piece together what happened last night.

I remember playing a song on the jukebox.

He ordered more drinks.

We laughed.

Well, I laughed. Jake looked at me like he couldn't understand why someone made the sound so often.

I played more music.

He judged my taste.

But I wasn't drunk.

What did I do, and why can't I remember any of it?

My heart pounds deep in my chest, my skin clammy, and I swallow back the bile rising in my throat.

I glance over at him again, more eager than ever to get away.

I can't remember going to bed with him.

But I also can't remember getting home.

His fingers tighten on my skin, and even hungover, heat rushes between my legs.

I have a rule: never, ever, sleep with someone I work with.

With his touch, a moment from last night flashes.

I vaguely remember going to bed. He helped me after I dressed in one of his t-shirts.

I peek under the covers and release a breath.

I'm still wearing it.

But then he left.

How did I end up in the same bed as him?

Oh, sweet Jesus, did I pounce on him?

As much as I'd like to get the most from this situation, and a morning quickie might satisfy my salacious appetite, I feel like I was dragged through a bush while tied to the back of a horse, and I'm pretty sure I look no better.

"Shit," I curse under my breath, hitting the heel of my palm against my head and immediately regretting it.

How the hell am I supposed to get out of this bed without waking him?

Do I wake him and politely ask him to move but risk having the awkward morning-after small talk?

Or do I try the dive and crawl?

Neither, it would seem, because the man lying next to me leaves out a moan, and with a simple sound, he sums up exactly how I feel.

My chest deflates.

Awkward morning-after small talk it is.

"Morning, Trouble," he mumbles, turning away from me and onto his back.

68

Trouble?

Chewing the inside of my cheek, I force a smile while pulling the covers a little higher on my body.

"Morning. I'm going to freshen up, and I will be out of your hair."

His eyes narrow on me. His throat bobs while his eyes slide down my arms—the only part of my body exposed—and my stomach tightens.

I need to get out of here before I jump his bones again.

"Sorry, Claire. My son is due home soon."

Bonus points for not calling me Ms. Russell.

"It's fine, honestly. I need to go anyway, and we're both adults. Let's not drag it out. And please don't fire me."

His tired chuckle makes me squirm.

"I'm not your boss. I can't fire you."

Once I throw my legs over the edge of the bed, the room begins to spin.

I think I'm still drunk.

He grabs my elbow. "Wait. Fuck. I almost forgot. Let me help you."

I bark a laugh under my breath. "I'm pretty sure I can dress myself."

He walks around to the side of the bed, crouching in front of me. We stay still. He stares at my forehead. I stare at how those black boxers are hanging deliciously low on his hips. Line after line of abs, and I think I'm drooling.

Why is he still staring at my forehead?

He frowns, reaching his fingers up to brush them across my face, and everything in me goes to mush.

"How is it?"

"Nice." I smile, my breathing coming faster.

His eyes scrunch to slits as he laughs under his breath, and my face lights on fire.

What's so funny?

"I'm glad it's nice. But I'm talking about your head."

"My head? What's wrong with my head?" As I say it, I pat the back of my hand across my forehead, and like a tsunami, memories of last night come washing over me.

And oh. My. God.

World, open, and swallow me whole.

Last night, after we'd finished yet another random conversation, I plucked up the courage to ask, "What age are you, anyway?"

He gulped the last of his drink before nodding toward the barman for another two. Leaning back on his stool, he smirked, crossing his arms over his chest.

Smug bastard.

"Guess."

His knees brushed against mine, and I shifted on my stool. The brief contact made my skin tingle.

"Mmm," I hummed, eyeing him head to toe. "You're in great shape, so you like to take care of yourself. You were married. You have an eight-year-old son, but no grey hairs…Yet," I added, cackling.

Other people at the bar turned to look at me.

My laugh has always broken the sound barrier, and the alcohol made me merry.

"Maybe you dye it." I moved forward, getting a closer look at his hair. Long enough to run my fingers through.

I bit my lip to suppress a moan

"Do you dye it?" I whispered, curiosity getting the better of me. It looked natural, but who knows?

"No."

My heart stopped when he edged closer to me.

Too close.

I could feel his breath across my face. I almost buried my head in his neck and sniffed. Cedarwood, peppermint, and the hint of whiskey made my head spin.

"Thirty-four," I blurted, needing to distract myself.

"Thirty-eight," he corrected.

"No fair."

He looked good.

And I needed to stop.

In slow motion—at least it felt like slow motion—I watched as he raised his hand for the second time that night, curled two fingers under my chin, and pulled my lower lip from the hold of my bite with his thumb.

"I thought I told you to stop it," he rasped, the hint of a warning making my pulse erratic. I could feel my heart beating all over my body.

But because I'm a glutton for punishment—and I wanted to know what he would do if I didn't do as he asked—I chewed my lip between my teeth again.

He cocked a brow, his eyes fixated on my lips, and my mouth

watered with the want to taste him.

"You're trouble, aren't you?"

"I hope so."

"Fuck," he cursed, turning away, diverting his attention to his drink. "Go choose another awful song before—" He stopped.

Before what?

I wanted to ask him but thought better of it.

It was a bad idea.

Instead, I chose to take his advice.

And that's when it happened.

My world went black.

Everything after that is foggy—until right now.

"I hit my head," I say, suddenly realizing.

"Oh, yeah. Your leg got caught in the strap of your handbag, and you knocked yourself out."

This couldn't get any worse.

I bring my palms up to my cheeks to hide the furious blush. I'm practically radiating heat now.

"Oh," I let out, wanting to curl up in a ball and die. "Have you got a shovel around here?"

"For what?"

"I want to dig myself a grave. Promise you'll tell my family where I am so they can come to visit me."

He's laughing when he removes my hands from my face, and the more I look at him, the more embarrassment eats me alive.

I don't know why I'm hot anymore, but I think most of it's because he's half-naked.

"No stitches, but the doctor in the emergency room said you should stay with someone."

I'm a professional, grown-ass woman.

How?

How did I even survive to this age?

I don't have to worry for too long. I'm sure I'm about to perish from shame.

Falling back on the pillows, I murmur, "I am so sorry."

I was very wrong about this situation.

He didn't take advantage of me. *I* took advantage of him.

"Don't worry about it."

I want to vomit.

Maybe it's the concussion.

"Jake?" I finally ask, feeling my stomach sink. "How did I end up in your bed?"

Please don't say I came in here and propositioned myself.

"There was a thunderstorm," he says slowly, unsure if that's the answer, but I know immediately that it is.

I've feared thunder for over twenty years.

"When you found your way in here, you were shaking with a bloodied head. How could I say no?"

Great.

He's making fun of me.

"And?"

"And that's it. You slept. Nothing happened. I like my women coherent and not on the verge of vomiting."

Ugh.

"Everything makes sense now. Thanks for looking out for me, but I better go before I embarrass myself more." I say it to the ceiling because I'm still too mortified to meet his eyes.

He stands, looming over me while offering his hands to help me up.

The moment I begin to move, the door flies open. I drop my hands, throwing myself back down and pulling the covers over my head, praying to anyone that will listen that I didn't just flash whoever walked in here. I feel some of Jake's weight shift toward my side. He's trying to hide my existence, I presume.

"Dad, Sharon's cooking breakfast."

His son.

And Sharon?

Who the hell is Sharon?

But I bite my tongue. I'll be out of here in less than ten minutes. If I stay still and not breathe, I will make it out of here unnoticed by any humans, big or small.

But I really need to pee first.

"Morning, buddy. That's great. Why don't you wait downstairs with everyone? I'll be there soon."

Everyone?

I want to die.

"Okay," a young voice chirps. "See you in a minute."

When I hear the door shut, I sit up, leave out the breath I don't know I'm holding, and finally grab my clothes.

Jake holds up his hands before I have the chance to ask. "Sharon is his aunt."

"Another one?" I whisper-yell.

"His mother's best friend, but also her sister-in-law." He shrugs. "Like you said, it's a real family affair."

"How did he not see me?"

He stuffs his arms in a shirt. "He's like his father when he's hungry. The only thing that kid can see right now is food."

I'm panicking. The air is too thick.

"Do you not live alone with your son? How did they get in here?"

I swear, I think he's going to laugh at me, and I won't be the only one with a concussion if he does.

This isn't funny.

"I do. They have a key. We're a close family." *No shit.* "Breakfast was planned."

The more his words sink in, the more I think this concussion is an internal bleed. My head is throbbing, and sweat is crawling down my back.

One long stride and his hands are on my arms, steadying me.

"Claire, relax." It comes out of his mouth in a growl.

"How? Your wife's best friend is downstairs."

"Her brother and sister too," he adds. "But her parents are out of town."

"You have got to be fucking with me right now." I glance over at the window. "How far up are we because I can jump? If I fall on my ass, I'll bounce."

He laughs again, and I want to punch him. He didn't laugh this much last night when I *was* funny.

I feel like the worst person alive.

His wife may be dead, but she's still his wife.

I know nothing happened between us, but it doesn't look that way. Not to everyone else.

Needing to cool off, I turn on my heels with my clothes draped over my arms.

"There's a spare toothbrush in the cabinet," he calls after me.

I grunt at him.

I wash my face, careful of the bandage hiding a large bump and purple bruising, brush my fingers through my knotted hair, and dress.

I look like shit.

My heart is still pounding when I finish. Jake is dressed in grey slacks and a powder blue shirt.

Porn.

He's porn.

"I'm going to run now. Literally." I laugh nervously. "Thanks for everything. But you've got to smuggle me out of here." I know some of his family work closely with the shelter, and this is not how I want to meet them.

Damn it, Claire.

"You can join us for breakfast?"

I want to be sick again.

"Okay. Okay. I'll drive you home. But I left your handbag in the kitchen, so you'll have to wait."

I wave a finger around the cut on my head. "The one that caused all of this?"

"The exact one. Can I suggest pockets?"

"HA! You can suggest anything you like, but I'll trip over my own feet."

The windows downstairs are open, and the fresh air hits me the moment I step onto the ground floor. It does little to ease the banging in my head, but it clears the fog.

This house is beautiful.

"Alex built this?" I can tell.

"Two years ago."

Foot on the last step, I'm almost out of here, but that's when I hear it.

The sounds of people.

Oh, no.

I close my eyes, feeling my heart sink to the lowest part of my stomach.

He flinches. "I'll get your bag."

"Jay-Jay told us you had a friend stay over. Don't hide her away." A woman's voice echoes from where the kitchen is.

My mouth falls open, but Jake doesn't seem fazed.

Why doesn't he seem fazed?

Why isn't he sweating enough for both of us?

I am.

Is his family used to him bringing home random women?

I'm hyperventilating.

I jerk back as he rubs his palms up and down my arms, gathering heat in my body. "Calm down."

"That's easy for you to say. You're not the one walking downstairs in your boss's house, looking like you've been nicely fucked all night." My hand shoots over my mouth, physically preventing further word vomit. I shrug. "Sorry. It must be the concussion."

He steps closer, crowding me. My neck tips back to look at him. "I'm only going to repeat this once. I am *not* your boss, and if you were nicely fucked by me—as you put it—you wouldn't look like you do, and you certainly wouldn't be walking like this either. You wouldn't be walking at all."

My mouth hangs open, shuts, then opens again, but all that comes out is a whoosh of air.

"You're quite sure of your..." I swallow, searching for more words, "...abilities."

He tilts his head like he feels sorry for me. Like I'm missing out on something, and only he knows what it is. He lifts his shoulders in not-so-quiet confidence.

I run my tongue across my lower lip. I'm curious. "Had I not been clumsy and hit my head, would I not be able to walk this morning?"

"You managed the not walking all by yourself last night." I roll my eyes. "As for this morning, who knows?"

"You didn't think about it...last night?"

Because I did.

His jaw tenses, shoulders squared. "I never said I didn't think about it." He sighs, releasing the tight tension across his chest. His mouth quirks ever so slightly. "Come and have some breakfast. I'd feel better knowing you've eaten."

I don't need this today, but all I can do is shake my head in agreement because he stole my ability to speak.

A quick hello, so I don't seem rude, and I can leave.

With his hand on the small of my back, he guides me through the archway, and into the large kitchen.

I wish he wouldn't touch me. It's going to be hard enough explaining what happened last night without him touching me like we did more than sleep in the same bed. And it's not helping the spinning going on in my head.

A man is feeding a baby in a highchair while a woman with a sleek ebony bob is chopping fruit at the breakfast counter. The guy in the cop uniform must be Sam—the officer I was told about. And I'm assuming the woman on the floor is his wife. She's doing a jigsaw with a little boy. He removes his glasses and rubs his eyes before putting them back on.

He looks at me and smiles, big and bright, and simply waves. "Hi. I'm Jay-Jay."

Like a robot, my hand motions back and forth, and I think I say hi back. I can't be sure because my heart is ringing in my ears.

"His name is Jay. He added the second Jay recently because he thought it sounded cooler. It stuck," Jake explains.

"No. I added the second Jay because one sounded too much like your name, and you're not cool."

I like this kid.

Jake pokes my lower back when I laugh.

The woman cooking doesn't look up when she says, "Had yourself a little sleepover, did you, Jake?" I see her teasing smirk from here, and a burn claws its way up my neck. "I'm Sharon." She strolls toward me, wiping her hands on a towel before reaching out and shaking my hand.

I offer a wobbly smile.

She points around the room. "That's my husband, Pete. That's Sam." The men salute, casting Jake an amused smirk. Probably because I look exactly like I said I would.

Nicely fucked. In every way.

"Don't forget about me." The woman with long blonde hair looks up from the floor. When she moves, there are streaks of purple under her golden strands. "I'm April. Jake's baby sister. Well, sister-in-law."

"Hi." I look around, wanting nothing more than to curl up in a ball. "I'm Claire."

Everyone spins around to look at me. My cheeks burn, but I don't think they've stopped since I woke. Jake's eyes grow wide in a silent warning, and they don't utter another word.

What the hell?

"The baby is mine, and there are two others around here that are mine too," Sharon continues.

"Nice to meet you. I'm sorry about all this."

She pops a hand on her hip, her smile turning down when she averts her attention to Jake. "When I told you to make the most of a night to yourself, I didn't mean for you to pick up strays."

Ouch.

"Rein it in," Jake warns.

She leans closer, lowering her voice so only we can hear, and glances at my bandaged forehead. "What did you do? Ram her through the headboard?"

Okay, where's the nearest exit?

"It's not what it looks like," I start, but Jake rests his hand on my back again.

She blows out a long breath, and places her hand on my arm. "Sorry, I'm a bitch by nature, but now I have a toddler and eight-week-old twins. I could cry just standing here. My emotions are in a blender. My tits are killing me because I'm basically a dairy cow. I haven't gotten a period yet. My hair is falling out, and the babies sound like air raid sirens when they cry. But please join us for breakfast. There's more than enough."

Wow!

"Jesus Christ," Jake mutters, scrubbing a hand over his face.

"Thank you." It's all that comes out. It's impossible to produce any other words. It's not very often I'm rendered speechless, but here I am, with my mouth hanging open as she walks away.

Jake gestures for me to take a seat at the breakfast counter.

I look at him, pleading, saying, "Do I have to?" without actually saying it.

His breath is in my hair when he demands, "Sit."

I do.

I sit.

We eat.

We talk.

I don't hear a word of it.

I drink too much coffee.

Nobody mentions my bandaged head again, and I only hope Jake will explain.

It's normal.

They're a family.

They laugh, they tease each other, and I smile as I watch.

He's attentive to every word his son says.

Sharon eyeballs me a couple of times, and I can't help but feel like I'm sitting in what is usually an empty chair, or one she wished was filled by someone else, but she doesn't ignore me.

Every so often, I feel Jake's eyes on me. I nod, letting him know I'm only dying of shame and not my concussion.

TEN

"Ms. Russell." My name rolls off his tongue like forbidden fruit, amusement dancing around the letters, making my stomach clench, and my shoulders square in annoyance.

I should have known it was him. His power fills my office with raw masculinity, and I haven't even bothered to look up from the floor.

We're back to being formal. I woke in his bed and had breakfast with his family, yet he's still calling me Ms. Russell.

"Mr. Williams," I greet back, proud of how uninterested I sound, but my lips turn upwards despite myself.

Finally turning my head, he stands at my office door, arms folded over his chest, sans suit jacket with his shirt sleeves rolled up to the elbows.

Pure fucking arm porn.

Goddammit.

Look away, Claire.

Look. Away.

But my brain doesn't send the signal to my eyes fast enough, and they wander the length of his body—his suit pants and shirt tailored to fit every inch of him perfectly. With the top button undone, he looks perfectly fuckable.

Not that I would ever.

I would have.

But that was Claire from two weeks ago.

I've grown up since then.

He looks more relaxed this evening. His facial features don't appear as harsh, yet there's not a hair out of place. Just the appearance that the pole rammed up his ass has loosened an inch.

Maybe two.

But no one should have the right to look this good at seven in the evening.

I'm pretty sure my day's makeup has faded, and my hair is tossed from trying to pull it out with stress.

I feel him looming, peering over my shoulder.

"What are you doing?"

I sit back on my heels, grinning over the drawings.

"Putting these pages on a string so I can hang them up."

When I stand, he grabs one side, taking over when I struggle to reach high enough on the wall. He tacks both ends on either side.

Standing back, I cross my arms over my chest and smile.

He tilts his head, brows drawn tight.

"What are they?"

Tsking, I roll my eyes. "Self-portraits. The kids drew them."

He scowls.

My brain suddenly catches up, and I spin around. "What are you doing here?"

His eyes narrow, lips pulled into the ghost of a smirk, assessing me. It makes me uncomfortable, and I fight with myself not to shift on my feet. I'm not giving him the victory of knowing he makes me uneasy in all the right ways.

"Are you going to stand here all night? I have work to do."

"That is what you're paid for."

Holding back an exasperated growl, my fake smile never falters when I ask, "Can I help you with something?"

He crosses his leg at the ankles and leans against the door frame.

Far too comfortable for my tastes. I really have work to do.

"Dinner, remember? You were quite insistent."

Shit.

It's Friday.

And no, I didn't remember.

With the chaos of the week, I completely forgot. I haven't even warned the women.

"I remembered," I lie. "The dining room is down the hall and to

80

the left. You will meet the women there. You've probably already seen some of the kids running around here."

"You're not coming?" he asks.

"You seem like a confident man. I'm sure you're capable of introducing yourself."

He dips his chin. "I am. I meant you're not eating with us?"

Oh.

"It's been a long day, and I still have lots of work to do."

"I'm sure you can take a break."

I really can't.

He raises his wrist to look at his watch. "Aren't you supposed to finish at five?"

I almost laugh.

Yes, my contract says my job is the typical nine to five, Monday to Friday, but to hell with contracted hours. Especially in a job like this. I've no doubt I will be here many nights until I'm ready for bed and weekends, too. Some things are more important, and I'm still settling in.

"*Supposed* to be, isn't always *will* be. Problems don't appear when I arrive at nine in the morning and miraculously disappear at five when I go home. Perhaps it's different being a CEO."

I'm sure it's not.

He lifts his left shoulder, unaffected. "Perhaps. When's the last time you ate?"

Now that he mentions it, my stomach growls, angry at me for the breakfast bar I had this morning and for missing lunch.

My guilt must be written on my face because he takes one large stride toward me. "Walk," he demands like I'm a dog. "You're going to eat with us. I won't have you passing out on my watch."

Charming.

"Really, I can't."

The smell of garlic wafting from the kitchen isn't making my argument any easier, and my mouth waters.

"Fine," I finally give in when his glare becomes unyielding.

A mop of dark hair comes crashing into Jake's back. The boy's giggling is interrupted briefly.

Not even looking up, he mutters, "Sorry, Dad. We're playing chase." He waves at me. "Hey, Claire." His cheeks blush.

Adorable.

At least he doesn't call me Ms. Russell.

"Hey, Jay-Jay."

I walk to him, ignoring Jake standing so close I can feel his body heat and how his scent makes my knees lock.

"You met the kids already?"

His eyes narrow. That expression is all his father.

"Uh-huh," he says slowly, looking at Jake. "Can I play with my friends now?" He shuffles impatiently on his feet.

Friends?

This kid works fast.

When Jake dips his chin, he's off like lightning.

Stepping back, he gestures toward the door, the same self-assured tilt to his lips.

Why does he insist on looking at me like that—like he's always one step ahead?

"Ladies first." He stuffs his hands in his pockets before stepping aside. I'm not sure how a man built this big can move with fluidity, but he manages it.

He follows close behind. I sense him with every step I take, but I refuse to fidget. I don't want him to know he puts me on edge by just breathing the same air.

I spent many years teaching myself not to be intimidated by men, but Jake carries it in everything he does—his gait, the tilt of his chin, eyes that can pin me to one spot, the demanding tone of his voice.

By simply existing.

But sometimes a hint of mischief breaks through. I've seen it. I've heard his laugh. I've seen a genuine smile. He might not remember, but I do, and for some reason, I feel protective over those glimpses he once showed before he knew who I was. When I was just a stranger. I can't help but wonder what else he is hiding beneath the walls.

In my peripheral, he picks up some boxes from the table in the lobby.

I don't ask what they are.

It's hard for me not to break the tension by talking, but my tongue gets tangled in my mouth too often when I'm nervous, so I decide against it.

I let out a long breath when we get to the kitchen, grateful for a distraction. Steam rises from pots. Women are deep in conversations, some are singing along to the radio, and the kids are causing chaos as they run around their mother's legs. Two of the women are setting the large table. Another is breastfeeding her newborn in the corner.

That's going to make our uptight visitor uneasy.

Jake sees. He doesn't flinch.

Nothing.

Just a friendly nod of greeting to the nursing mother.

I don't know if it's because he's the only man in a room full of women, the magnetism he oozes, or that he fills the doorway, but heads turn.

"Ladies," I begin to say, about to introduce the very man who paid for the ground we're standing on, but the sea of greetings flying our way has my jaw snapping shut again.

This is familiar.

These aren't the welcomings of women meeting a stranger for the first time.

I was nervous because I didn't warn them, and I thought bringing a strange man in here was going to cause an upset.

"Oh, Jake, you made it."

"I knew I saw little Jay-Jay around here somewhere."

And a collective, "Hey, Jake," has my eyes darting around the room to make sure we didn't enter a parallel universe.

Standing still, my jaw goes slack, arms falling to my side while my brain tries to process, but there are so many thoughts I can't catch up.

A smiling Mia rushes to his side. Blinking, I follow the motion of her hands as she takes the boxes from him. "What did you bring for us this week?"

It's fucking dessert.

I swear hearts are flashing in her eyes.

"This isn't your first time here?" It's half a question, half a gob-smacked statement.

There's a chuckle from numerous women. Amelia takes garlic bread from the oven before popping a hand on her hip. "I've been here from the start, and Jake comes for dinner at least twice a month. Sorry, we should have told you he was coming," she informs me, like I'm not being swallowed whole by embarrassment.

They should have told me?

Instinctively, my fingers knot around the ends of my hair.

Hell is about to freeze over.

I was so wrong.

Checking my mouth is closed, I turn to look up at him.

My voice is a bare whisper because I'm too shocked to produce sounds. "You allowed me to believe—"

I suck in a breath as he leans closer, swallowing the rest of my sentence. I don't remember what I wanted to say. The smell of his cologne is dizzying, and his touch is warm as he tilts my chin back with a finger, snapping my mouth shut.

"Assumptions, Claire." The use of my name from his lips makes me gulp. "I warned you about them."

In the same breath, he turns on his heels. The smile on his face hits me right in the chest, the warmth in his eyes reminding me of the first day I met him.

"It smells delicious, ladies. What are we having?"

Someone points at a chair for him to sit. A little girl crawls onto his lap like it's the most natural thing in the world. She presses her palm flat against his cheek, and when he holds her hand and tickles her palm with his stubble, she giggles and squirms in his arms.

He pokes her nose.

I liquify.

Suddenly, this man is more of a mystery than he was two minutes ago.

I thought I had him figured out. I've met his type before—men who spend their life looking down at the world, smug and infuriating.

Oh, Claire, you don't know a damn thing.

ELEVEN

"You know you don't have to see them off every morning?" Amelia stands by my side at the front door as I wave at the kids on the school bus. She hands me a steaming cup of coffee.

"Thank you." I give one final salute as the bus pulls away. "It's a habit. I did it at the children's home."

When the bus disappears beyond the gate and out of sight, we retreat inside the house. Taking a deep breath, I drink in the lobby, searching for a sound.

There's none.

"It's quiet here during the day."

"Amazing, isn't it?"

I smile despite preferring the noise. At the children's home, even when the older kids were at school, there were always little ones pottering around in the morning.

"Don't worry, when they run in after school, you'll wish for the silence again."

In my office, we both take a seat. My cluttered desk is making me anxious, serving as a reminder of how much I need to do today.

I'm still getting settled, but after almost a month, I've finally learned everyone's name.

"I wanted to give you an update. Did you meet Emma when you started?"

I nod. She was here when I was introduced, but she left on my first day to go to independent housing.

"I called to see her yesterday evening. Her husband is back. He let me in but made me aware our services are no longer needed."

My stomach knots. "Her choice?"

"It looks that way. I couldn't get her on her own to know for sure, and I didn't want to press too much because she will be his target when he's pissed off about me calling. She said she was happy. He told her he's changed. He's going to anger management."

The usual then.

"What a hero. Is it a positive sign that he's trying, or is he a serial anger management attendee?" I've met too many of those.

"It's his third time. If he hasn't managed it by now, he never will."

"Oh."

"I'll keep an eye on them, but for now, there's nothing I can do. She's a grown woman. I've contacted the kid's school to let them know. I need them to be extra vigilant."

"Good decision. I'm sorry, though. It sucks."

I know the feeling when you've worked hard with someone to help them see their self-worth, only to have it unraveled by the charm of a monster. We may be warned about it, but it's impossible not to get attached to people in our jobs. We form bonds, and we don't give up. I know Amelia will be there if Emma needs her again. Which—the likelihood is—she will.

"She's not the first, and she won't be the last." Her shoulders slump, defeated.

Still, I can't help but wish it was different.

The greatest fear in life is the fear of the unknown. The fear of what will come next. Will it be better? Worse? More of the same? Should we take what we have in the case we don't get a fairer deal?

Risk.

It's like jumping off a ledge, not knowing what's at the bottom because the air is foggy.

But if we never jump, we never know.

My eyes catch sight of a face peeking inside my office. It's Leah. She arrived the same day I was late for my meeting with Jake.

She backs away. "I'm sorry. I didn't mean to interrupt. I can come back another time." She's skittish, child-like almost. Although, at eighteen, she's not far off.

I wave at her. "Come in."

"Honey, I was about to leave." Amelia winks before standing. "See you later."

I gesture for Leah to take a seat.

She takes a tentative step forward.

Then another.

"How are you doing?"

"I'm okay. I like it here," she replies, her eyes scanning my bookshelf.

"Do you like to read?"

She nods. "I couldn't bring my books with me." She pulls at the sleeves of her top, desperate to hide and make herself smaller. There's a healing bruise around her eye.

"You're welcome to take one anytime."

She turns to look at me, a watery smile threatens her mouth. I wonder when is the last time she properly smiled?

"Thank you," her voice is almost a whisper.

Smaller.

Anything to curl up and disappear.

"Would you like to take a seat?"

"Are you sure? I don't want to annoy you. I know you're busy."

God, that breaks my heart.

"You're not annoying me. Far from it."

Slowly, she takes another few steps, gently pulling the chair out to sit.

"Thank you," she repeats, her eyes drifting to her lap.

"Are you settling in?"

She hums. "Noah likes it. I know he's only one, but I think he's happier." She wipes her sleeve under her eyes. I'm not sure if she's crying, or if her eyes always look so full with constant tears threatening to fall.

"You're doing amazing. He's a beautiful little boy."

I smile.

She tries to smile back.

I bet her smile is beautiful when she uses it.

She chews her bottom lip, and I can almost feel the rattle in her chest.

"What kind of books do you like?"

Shrugging, she pulls on her sleeves again. "Fantasy. Sometimes romance." Her cheeks redden.

An escape.

That's the genre she's looking for.

Standing, I go to the bookshelf to pluck something I hope she will like.

I place the book on the table. "Have you read this one?" She shakes her head. "This one has fantasy and romance. See how you like it. When you're done, you can come and pick another."

Her smile broadens. It's a tiny hint, but enough for me to get a glimpse.

"That's kind of you. I'll be careful with it."

I lean forward, taking another sip of my coffee.

She takes the book in her hand, examining the cover and back. Still looking down, she says, "Can I ask you something?"

"Of course." If she chews her lip anymore, it's going to bleed. "Leah?" She looks up. "You can relax. And you can ask me anything. I don't know if I'll always know the answer, but I can guarantee I'll help you find it."

She takes a deep breath, and her thin frame relaxes. "The women here…they go to work, and some go to college. I think I'd like to do something. Maybe I could make something of myself."

Looking at her, I can't help the lump forming in my throat. I swallow it down.

I can't imagine what it must be like—living here, trying to trust new people when the first and most important relationship in her young life left her black and blue. But here is where her strength shines through. She may doubt everything. She may not know if she can make it through the day, but she's thinking ahead. She's standing tall so she can see over the bad days—the ones that have gone by and the ones to come—and she can see a glimpse of the days when she's stronger.

Little does she know, her strength is already rushing through her blood.

I see a warrior.

A survivor.

"What do you think you'd like to do?"

She scratches the back of her neck, then her face, and now her palms.

"I've always been fascinated with publishing." She looks up briefly before lowering her head again. "I don't know where to start, but I mean, I love reading."

More scratching at her skin. I reach out and stop her. She's going to hurt herself. Crouching, I meet her eyes.

"I might know someone who can help you out."

At least I hope he can.

He might tell me to get lost.

"Thank you," she whispers, an obvious wobble to her voice. "Can I ask one more thing?"

"Anything."

"I'd love to know how to do my makeup properly. I've tried online tutorials, but it never turns out the way it's supposed to. I wasn't allowed to wear it before. My boyfriend said if I wore it, I must be trying to impress someone. My mom died when I was a kid, so she never showed me."

"That doesn't mean you can't learn."

She lifts her left shoulder. "I love your makeup. It's pretty. Womanly." There's heat in her cheeks again. "Not that you need it. I bet you're beautiful without it. I just mean—"

"Leah," I cut her off. "It's okay. And thank you. I've always liked makeup too. Some people don't and that's fine and there are days when I can't be bothered. But on those days when I need a little boost, it's my go-to. And my mom didn't show me how to do my makeup either."

"I'm sorry. Is your mom dead?"

"No. She's..." She's what? "My mom suffers from her own demons."

"Who taught you?"

"My friend's mom."

The memory makes a grin stretch across my face. Nick's mother Kate sat me down when I was going through a phase of thinking blue was my color. Blue eyeshadow, blue mascara, blue eyeliner. The pictures still make me cringe.

I remember when she called me inside, sat me on the edge of the toilet, and handed me a wet wipe. I whinged because I didn't want to take it off.

"Were you in a fight with a Smurf? You look like a giant eyeball," Kate teased. "Your eyes are already so blue."

Then she grabbed her make-up bag and showed me how to apply foundation and what colors matched my eyes.

But most of all, I remember what it was like to have a mother figure. Someone to guide me. I don't think I paid attention to what she was doing because I was too busy staring at her, secretly hoping it could be my mother doing the teaching.

"I can teach you if you'd like?" I offer, hoping she will trust me enough with what I see as a big moment.

Her eyes grow wide. "You will?"

"It would be my pleasure."

I grab two fresh cups of coffee, spin her around toward the window, and grab my make-up from my bag. Her skin tone is similar to mine.

I take my time, telling her about each product, careful not to overdo it. She drinks in every sentence like a child learning about their favorite subject for the first time. She hangs on my every word. And that, I take seriously.

I hold up a small mirror. A single tear slides down her cheek.

"Beautiful."

"Thank you, Claire."

"I'll reach out to someone about getting you some work experience in publishing. It might be an unpaid internship, but it will be a start. If it doesn't work out, the local college runs courses."

She drops her head. "You think I can do it?"

Tucking a finger under her chin, I tilt her head back. "I think you can do anything you set your mind to."

When she leaves, I open my emails, shaking the tremble from my hands when I start typing.

To: jakewilliams@jwmedia.com
From: clairerussell@guidinglight.com
Subject: Internship

Jake,

I understand your company has a publishing department. One of our girls is interested in pursuing a career in publishing. She's only eighteen with no prior experience, and I'm at a loss where she should start.

Does your company offer internships? She's willing to accept it unpaid.

I think getting her into the workforce will improve her confidence and chances for a successful progression outside of the shelter.

If this isn't an option, I would like to put her name forward for the education program.

Kind Regards,
Claire Russell.

Xx

I press the send button before I realize what I've done.
Shooting up from the chair, I desperately press cancel.
"No. No. No. Do. Not. Send."
Your email has been sent.
"Fuck," I curse, sweat gathering at the nape of my neck.
I sent him kisses.
It's habit.
A terrible habit.
I send my friends kisses at the end of all my messages.
I want to cut off my fingers.
Sinking into my chair, I contemplate letting it go and playing dumb.
I can hope he doesn't notice.
No.
I need to do something.

To: jakewilliams@jwmedia.com
From: clairerussell@guidinglight.com
Subject: Internship

Jake,

Please ignore the kisses in the previous email. It's habit and now I want to die.

It won't happen again.

Although, like I said, it's a habit, so it may happen again.

Just always ignore it or block my email.

Kind Regards,
Claire Russell.

How do I successfully ramble through email?
"You're an idiot, Claire."
I need some sage.
No amount of deep breathing is going to get me out of this.
My computer dings and I think I'm going into cardiac arrest.

From: jakewilliams@jwmedia.com
To: clairerussell@guidinglight.com
Subject: Re: Internship

Dear Ms. Russell,

Please pass her details to the HR department. She can start when she's ready.
Her internship will be paid.
Kisses in an email are highly unprofessional.

Regards,

Jake Williams
CEO
JW Media

*heart emoji.

I laugh out loud.
He's human, after all.

TWELVE

Curling my toes into the carpet, I pace back and forth, staring at blank walls. It looks like a hospital in here. The walls are too clinical, and the carpet is doing little to absorb the echo.

"What to do. What to do," I mutter to myself, twirling my hair around in a bun before letting it fall over my shoulders again. "They already have a gaming room. A study room? No, that's a stupid idea. They'll hate me. A computer room? Now you know you're old, Claire."

They say talking to yourself is fine, but answering yourself is when you need to worry. I don't know who *they* are, but I'm too far gone now. I've been having conversations with myself in this room for over a week.

It's the only empty room in the shelter. I want to put it to use for the teenagers. I just don't know what to put in here. They have a games room of sorts. They call it the *hangout room*. But they're either too busy with their heads in their phones or talking to people on the gaming console, while completely ignoring each other.

They've been moaning because they can't leave the shelter, and I can't blame them. They don't get to go to school parties like other kids or meet friends after school. Their life is this shelter. They'll all leave someday, and new kids will take their place, but I want something to give them a start. Some motivation.

"There are only so many walks they can go on to burn their energy," I continue, searching the walls for answers. "Something creative.

Think, Claire. Think." I hit the heel of my palm against my head.

I halt mid-step, feeling eyes on me. I don't even have to look up to know who they belong to.

"She's talking to herself again," he murmurs, but it's not to me.

"Does she do it often?" It's Nora this time. She's joining us for dinner this evening.

They know I can hear them.

"I've found her mid-conversation with her shadow almost every Friday I've been here."

I scoff, looking up only briefly before continuing my pacing. They're disrupting my train of thought.

"I only do it on Fridays because it's hard to find intelligent conversation when you arrive, Williams."

A deep chuckle echoes against the bare walls, and no matter how hard I try to fight it, I smile. Over the two months I've been here, he's missed one dinner, and his damn laugh always pulls at my lips. He still reminds me how wrong I was about him, and I have yet to admit it.

Out loud, at least.

"What are you doing, dear?"

I wave my hand. "Nora, I love you, but just hush for a minute."

"She's bossy when she's talking to herself."

"She's a pain in the ass," Jake adds.

"Hey." I stop, crossing my arms over my chest, meeting his stare head-on.

Dipping his chin, he takes a step forward, and immediately the room feels smaller. "I knew I'd get your attention." He glances at my bare feet as I rock back and forth on my heels. "What are you doing?"

I throw my hands out, exasperated. There are too many thoughts swirling around in my head.

"It's an empty room." My shoulders slouch, defeated.

He blinks at me. "I see your observation skills are good."

"Shut up, Jake. We shouldn't have empty rooms. I want to do something for the older kids to get their creative juices flowing, and I can't think of a single thing."

"That's not very creative, is it?"

Smartass.

My only response is a blistering stare.

Two young girls pass the room, music blaring from their Bluetooth speaker as they sing along.

There's always music coming from somewhere here.

I wave after them. "They're on their own and too wrapped up in their phones, or together, but not together, and I'm not making any sense."

"You rarely do," he deadpans.

He's pacing with me now—brows furrowed in a scowl, hands tucked into his pockets, the sleeves of his white shirt rolled up as they always are on a Friday evening. I appreciate the effort, but he's distracting me. He looks ridiculously handsome when he's thinking.

We're civil with each other. We rip each other apart, but it's a joke...most of the time.

We're not friends. I don't know him. He doesn't know me. But we care about the shelter, and I appreciate how much it means to him.

I nipped his incessant emails in the bud quite early on, and he didn't like it when I pointed out he was a control freak.

I get it. He wants this to work. And he understands I don't hold back when I want to say something.

He's more involved than I originally thought, but I'm here to run this place. I told him when I met him that this is my job, and I take it seriously. He doesn't interfere. I sometimes feel like he's sitting on the sidelines to learn, and it makes me more nervous than it should.

At least he stopped calling me Ms. Russell.

"You're trying to get them to like you," he points out.

"Of course I am. Teenagers scare the shit out of me. They're the only ones I haven't gotten through to. I've worked with both women and young children. But teenagers are a different species."

"Oh, my dear child," Nora singsongs, tapping the toe of her shoe against the floor. "The answer is staring you straight in the face."

I stare up at Jake.

He shrugs.

"Jake?" I question, confused, as I turn to look at her.

Before I can say another word, Jay-Jay comes flying into the room, a sheet swinging from his hand.

"Claire, I got picked for a solo in our recital." His cheeks are roaring red, excitement pouring out of him. I have no idea what he's talking about, but it makes me giddy.

"A recital? I didn't know you played an instrument."

"Yep." He nods smugly, looking exactly like his father. "Piano."

"That's amazing. Well done."

Then all my thoughts settle, my eyes go wide, and everything clicks.

"Jay-Jay," I shout, jumping around with him. I kiss the top of his head. "You're a genius."

He stills, looking up at me while I continue jumping. "I'm not that good." He also gets his sarcasm from his father.

"Oh, but you are." Kneeling, I meet his eyes. Nora is right. The answer is obvious. I needed a little push, and Jay-Jay gave me the shove I needed. "I play piano too."

It's both comical and unnerving when he and Jake respond together. "You do?"

Nora's at my side, patting my shoulder. "Oh, yes. Our Claire was something of a prodigy."

"Don't be dramatic, Nora." Winking at Jay-Jay, I say, "She's a little deaf."

He giggles.

I stand, bouncing from one foot to another, pulse racing, and any tiredness I felt from the day is gone.

I spin on my heels and forget Jake is so close, I need to tip my head back to look at him.

Winking, I take a tiny step closer. I'm sure my grin is scary, but I need him if I want to do this.

He takes a tentative step back.

I continue toward him, fluttering my eyelashes.

"Hey, Mr. Deep Pockets," I try to say, but I can't hold it together long enough and burst into laughter.

Throwing his head back, he groans, and I'm almost ready to admit how wrong I was about him because he doesn't want to know what my plans are. He simply asks, "What do you need?"

THIRTEEN

"You're taking this very seriously. You look like a hippie." Jake eyes me when I open my front door. I pull at my dungarees overall, swaying on my feet.

What?

I use it for painting.

Instead, I smile and say, "Thanks."

Grabbing my bag, I close the door after me, choosing to ignore the heat in my cheeks when his eyes halt at my breasts. It's only a beat, but he doesn't hide it fast enough.

I take in his navy slacks and white button-down.

"I'm assuming you consider this casual?"

He shrugs. "These? These are my workout clothes."

Jake has one condition for my music room idea—I must decorate it myself.

First on my list is paint because those white walls give me a migraine. His sister-in-law, April, is an interior designer and decorated the shelter.

It's beautiful.

But she has other jobs, so it's just me and Mr. Sunshine.

He didn't offer to help. I guilted him into it.

"Where's Jay-Jay?"

"He stays with his grandparents on Friday nights. I'll pick him up this evening."

I pout, disappointed. "I was hoping he'd come. He's more fun than you."

A deep laugh vibrates in his chest. "I know."

I roll my eyes as he opens the car door for me. When I hesitate, he dips his chin, daring me to argue.

Who said chivalry is dead?

"It's a pretty mouth you have, but please do your best to keep it shut. I have a headache."

I press up on my tiptoes, finally seeing the glossiness in his eyes. "You're hungover."

"Just get in the car."

Sighing, I slide into the passenger seat before he slams the door a little too hard.

As he pulls out of my neighborhood, I turn in my seat and stare, loving how uneasy it's making him.

"Hot date?"

Shut up, Claire.

Why do I even care?

But I'm nosy, and he's impenetrable.

He curses under his breath.

"But you didn't have sex."

He's far too tense.

His eyes widen, the muscles in his jaw twitching.

"Nobody is this grumpy after getting laid," I explain.

He pinches the bridge of his nose, soothing what I'm assuming is a throbbing headache. "You're all rainbows and unicorns this morning. Can I assume you did?"

"Me and Henry had the best time last night."

His nostrils flare, his grip on the steering wheel so tight that his knuckles have turned white.

The hangover must be bad.

"Who the fuck is Henry?" he grits out, glancing at me from the corner of his eye.

"My vibrator."

He chokes, and I erupt into a cackle.

"Fucking hell, Claire."

"Don't be a prude. He's the best. He doesn't catch feelings, and he doesn't talk back. He's not a fan of cuddles, though."

Shifting in his seat, he taps his fingers against the steering wheel, silence engulfing us once more.

I hate silence, and he grabs my hand when I attempt to switch on the radio.

More questions it is.

"Was she nice?"

He shoots me a look before his gaze returns to the road.

"Who?"

"Your date."

"I don't date."

"Why?"

"Why do you insist on always talking?"

"Don't answer my question with a question."

He stretches his hand, and I follow his line of sight to his ring finger.

"When did you decide to stop wearing your wedding ring?"

Eyes blazing, nostrils flare, and I want to sew my mouth shut.

"I didn't. I lost it."

"Where?"

"Claire, if I knew that, don't you think I would be wearing it?"

Okay then.

Studying his profile, I choose silence for a moment, allowing him time with whatever memories he's lost in. His forearms are taut, and a heaviness settles in my stomach.

We haven't been on our own together since the night of my concussion. When he comes to the shelter, we're always with other people.

I think he reads my thoughts when he glances over at me, and my skin prickles under the heat of his stare. Eyes narrowed, confusion muddles his features before he blows out a breath and his focus returns to the road.

But the crackle of tension remains.

I open the window for air, feeling jittery as the leather under me squeaks from shifting so much.

"What was your wife like?" I keep my eyes on the passing trees because the words are out, and I immediately want to suck them back in.

There's a disconnect between my brain and my mouth this morning.

But there's something about him that makes me want to dig deeper, claw under his skin, and pull out his thoughts.

He doesn't react as I expect. I hear the tapping of his fingers against the steering wheel, and then he begins. "She was infuriating, stubborn, and selfish, but she was beautiful, strong, and selfless."

He's contradicting himself.

I think, to him, it makes sense.

My chest tightens, and the pain in his voice makes my throat tighten.

"Was she sick?" I ask quietly, afraid I'll burst the bubble he's in.

"Cancer. We thought she was getting better, but it was her time. That's what I tell myself. It's easier than being angry at her."

My head spins to look at him. "Why would you be angry at her?"

"Like I said," he sighs, "my wife was both the most stubborn and the most selfless person I've ever met. She hid her diagnosis when she got pregnant with Jay-Jay. I can't blame her for wanting to protect him because I know I'd easily give my life for him now, and I hate when I can't help but blame her either. Last night was one of those nights," he breathes.

That explains the hangover.

That's grief, I guess. There are five stages, but no one says those stages are in order. They jump out at you when you least expect it.

My tongue sticks to the roof of my mouth, words trapped in my throat.

After long seconds, I turn back to face him. "I don't think she meant to be either selfish or selfless. She sounds protective. She sounds like a mother."

She sounds an awful lot like *my* mother.

He swallows, his throat bobbing, and my fingers twitch with the want to reach out and touch the day-old stubble on his jaw. To knead out some of his tension.

But I can't do that.

I don't think it's my touch he craves.

He doesn't utter another word, and I don't ask.

I won't test my luck.

Distracting myself, I hum, drumming my fingers against my thighs. I keep my eyes on the road, refusing to squirm when I feel blistering eyes on me as he glances back and forth throughout our journey.

He doesn't moan about my singing. Instead, he taps a matching rhythm against the steering wheel with his ring finger.

"Fresh Air Blue? Claire, I'm pretty sure you're just fucking with me now."

I hold up my fingers. "Scouts honor. After my time with Henry last night, I did lots of research. Fresh Air Blue is the most calming color according to scientific research."

"Infuriating," he grits out so low, I'm unsure if he means for me to hear. Face tensed, he turns back to the shop assistant. "Have you got…" he hesitates before casting a doubtful glare my way, "Fresh Air Blue?"

The shop assistant nods, tapping the counter with his knuckles. "Sure. What size tin do you need?"

I clap my hands, eager to get going. "A big one."

***

Jake eyes the front of the music shop when we get out of the car. "Why here?"

To be fair, he didn't protest when I asked him to drive the forty minutes to East Fort instead of going to a music shop in the city.

It felt like the ultimate betrayal to go to another shop.

Besides, this one is my favorite.

I'm also not here for just instruments.

"The music teacher I promised. She's right in here with everything else we need."

My sister's head pops up from her hands when the bell rings on the door. "Hey, sis. What are you doing here?" She takes in my overalls. "Picasso called. He wants his clothes back."

I nudge Jake in the ribs when he snickers.

Her eyes dart from me and the rigid wall walking behind me.

"Hi," she says slowly, and I know she's wondering if I failed to tell her about a new boyfriend.

I wrap my arms around her neck and kiss her cheek. "Missed you." She smells like guitar strings. "Amy, this is Jake. Jake, this is my sister…Older sister," I tease.

She slaps my arm. "Bitch."

I'm unsure how to explain why he's here, so I go with the answer I know will piss him off. "He's my sugar daddy."

Her eyes widen.

As I walk away, he pulls at my elbow and drags me back to his side.

"Hello, Amy." His smile is so forced, he's going to sprain his facial muscles. "I am *not* her sugar daddy."

I stifle a laugh. "Today you are."

He shakes his head. "You're impossible."

I look back at my sister.

She's mystified.

"I'm kidding, but he's going to disagree with whatever title I give him. He owns the women's shelter."

Amy's lips part in an O shape as she nods slowly.

Still mystified.

I think Amy is always mystified.

Jake leans his elbow against the counter, crossing his legs at the ankle.

"Great to meet you, Amy, but please tell me your sister isn't always so giddy."

I feign insult.

Tough shit, big guy. I'm in my element here.

"Sorry. She's always this annoying." She's gifted with a real frown and the middle finger. "Seriously, what's going on? I didn't know you were coming by today."

Jake answers for me, his tone contradicting what he says. "Your sister had the fantastic idea of creating a music room at the shelter and roped me into helping."

Her smile broadens.

She's catching on.

Throwing my arms out, I spin around. "He's got the credit card. I need one of everything."

But she doesn't do cartwheels like I expect. Instead, her eyes twitch so fast between me and Jake, I think she's ill.

"Has she cast one of my mother's voodoo spells on you?"

Jake smirks, making me warm to my toes.

Amy notices.

Shit.

"Is that what the smell was this morning?"

I gasp, crossing my arms over my chest, and just shy of stomping my feet. "It was sage."

Amy slaps the counter. "You still burn sage?"

They share a knowing glance.

"You're ganging up on me." I pout.

With a long breath, Jake takes his wallet from his pocket and places his credit card on the counter. "Amy, I'm going to find painkillers. I trust you know your sister. Get her anything she wants."

She bites down on her lower lip before dipping her head and looking at me as if to say, 'Is he real?'

Yes, sis. He's real. I even touched him once to check.

He taps the counter twice and stands straight. "I'll bring back coffee. You're stressed or excited or whatever the hell that mood is, so I'm guessing you need two sugars?"

How does he know that?

I gape. "Uh, huh."

He turns to Amy. "How about you?"

"I'll have the same," she says, just as flabbergasted.

"Before you leave," I call after him. "Mandy's dad owns the restaurant across the street. They have the best coffee. Thanks, big guy." I wink.

His only response is an exasperated groan before he leaves, looking like something straight from a magazine as he crosses the street.

Amy skips to my side.

"He knows you take sugar in your coffee when you're stressed? Girl, you are so fucked."

I watch as she walks away, tapping his credit card against her palm while she eyes the acoustic guitars.

"He's observant." I shrug, eager to ease the pinch in my chest.

Damn it, heart. Don't start this shit with me.

Her lips pull upward. "Is there something going on between you two?"

"Sweet Jesus, no. He's just really involved with the shelter."

"He's hot."

"You're married to a woman."

"I don't want him to rail me. Penises are gross. But I'm also not blind. I can see, and I see how badly you want him to rail *you* because you don't think penises are gross."

She gags.

"Amy," I screech, face burning so much, I know I'll never hide it. "I do not."

Her laugh is loud and grates at my ears, but only because there's an echo in my head screaming, 'She's right.'

It may have crossed my mind once or twice.

"You need to practice your poker face because he'll eventually see the sex in your eyes and your panties falling off."

"My panties aren't going anywhere, and what does sex in your eyes look like?"

She spins my head around, forcing me to look in the mirror.

My cheeks are flushed, and I'm physically squirming.

She pokes my nose. "That."

I step out of her hold, averting my gaze to the floor to hide the blush. I don't want to see more of the truth.

"What's his story?"

"Widower. Single dad."

She grimaces. "Shit. That's rough. What age is he? He's hard to judge."

"Thirty-eight." I swing my foot along the carpet.

"A little old for you then?" It's more of a question.

I shrug.

I fucking shrug.

Like there's even a possibility.

"I knew it," she squeals.

"Shut up, Amy."

"It makes sense with your daddy issues."

"I don't have daddy issues."

She pops a hand on her hip, blinking at me. "You were engaged to a cop."

I see where she's going with this.

My father was also in the force.

I *do* have daddy issues.

"You also have the same issues," I remind her.

We always revert to arguing like children.

"Emotionally damaged are always the best in bed. With your combined emotional trauma, I bet you'd be fire together."

Jesus, she's relentless.

"Stop talking. You've got a credit card in your hand that I'm pretty sure doesn't have a spending limit. Have fun."

"Whatever, grumpy. I've got spare underwear in the back in case yours are wet."

"Shut. Up."

Needing to fidget, I run my fingers over the guitar strings before moving to the pianos lined against the wall.

"A music room?" she questions, eyeing me a little too closely. My chest deflates, grateful for the change of subject. "It's a great idea. Thanks for coming here. I'm about to make more profit today than I have all month."

Pressing the keys lightly, I notice the slight puffiness around her eyes. "Things aren't bad here, are they?"

"No, things are good."

"How's Mama?" I'm pretty sure she's the reason for my sister's exhaustion.

I wish we could share it.

She moves her hand back and forth, unsure. "I think she seems good. Well, as good as Mama gets."

A punch of guilt knocks the air from my lungs. I want to help, but I want my mother to get better, and she won't if I'm there. I've stopped visiting as often. Instead, I come to see Amy at the shop.

It's no coincidence she's getting better since I've stopped calling round. It hurts like hell, but the alternative is losing her completely.

"Doc prescribed new meds. They're agreeing with her a little better."

"Yeah, but I don't think she's supposed to wash them down with wine."

She frowns but agrees with a hum.

My heart aches. I love my mother, and when I don't want to wrap her up and protect her from the world, I want to grab her by the shoulders and shake her.

I want the mother I once knew.

I want to go back in time. Before that night. But going back would mean she'd suffer all over again.

"There's nothing you can do, Claire. We've tried everything. You've tried to help her in every way short of kidnapping her and forcing her to accept help. It is what it is."

But I hate what it is.

She takes a guitar from the wall. "What ages are the kids?"

Taking a deep breath, I beat away the shadows. I sit at the piano and start playing as Amy gathers instruments.

"Different ages. Not all of them will want to partake, but maybe ukuleles for the younger ones. Some music books too. Oh, and that karaoke machine over there. They can have fun in there when it's not being used for lessons."

"Are you teaching them yourself?"

"Nope." I keep playing as I look up at her. Closing one eye, she studies me. "You are."

She props her hands on her hips. "Excuse me?"

"You're the best music teacher I know, and you always loved it. Is there an instrument in this shop you can't play? I play the piano, and maybe some chords on the guitar, but I'm in no position to teach them. I need someone I can trust with the kids. We were those kids, remember?"

Her eyes pull together, but there's excitement bubbling in her smile. "What about the shop?"

"It's only two or three evenings a week when the shop is closed. Like I said, not all the kids will want lessons, and even then, the kids you teach will leave, and new ones will take their place. I just want to give them a start and pique their interest in music. Who knows? Maybe if it works out, we can start making plans for them to continue their lessons when they leave."

Walking to my side, she kisses the top of my head. "Your heart is beautiful. And thank you."

I spin around.

"You'll do it?"

She rolls her eyes. "I suppose. It's not like I have anything better to do."

I pull her into a hug.

"I'll get everything ready, and have the guys deliver it on Monday." She tugs at a strand of my hair and tucks it back into the knot on top of my head. "Play for me? I might be better at everything else, but you still play more beautiful than anyone I know."

My fingers get to work as she prepares what we need.

The bell rings, and I know it's Jake. I don't need to look.

In my peripheral, Amy takes a coffee cup from him as she whispers, "She's in her happy place."

I smile.

"At least she's quiet there," he adds.

I scowl.

She potters away, laughing under her breath and refusing Jake's offer of help.

He doesn't interrupt, but his eyes remain on me for what feels like endless minutes, until finally, I catch sight of movement. He places my coffee on the floor next to the chair.

His breath sweeps across my neck, inducing a violent shiver as he whispers, "Coffee. Two sugars. Keep playing." My head almost snaps back, but he's so close, I can't move. "You're beautiful when you play."

I swoon.

***

The music room is painted in Fresh Air Blue.

So is Jake.

I made sure of it.

He looked too pristine.

Maybe he'll invest in overalls now.

I key the room, making sure the kids can't spy and ruin the surprise.

After we say goodbye to everyone, I wipe a paint-coated hand across my forehead. I tried to clean up, but I'll need a long shower to get the rest.

Chest heaving, Jake pulls me by the wrist as we step outside.

He's dragging me around a lot today, and I can't say I'm completely opposed to the idea.

"You are not getting into my car like that."

Meeting his stare, I crane my neck to look at him. "Want me to strip?"

His grip tightens as his brows shoot up to his hairline.

I hold out my hand. "I took two towels. Your leather seats will remain paint-free. If you're not happy with that, we'll simply have to drive commando."

I bite down on my lower lip to smother a laugh bubbling in my throat. His eyes drop and my threatening laugh dissolves. I swear his fingers are scorching my skin.

His white button-down is covered in light blue blotches, but he's kept his hair and face free of my markings.

I want to change that.

Dropping the towels, I move too quickly, and he can't step out of the way fast enough when I press my finger to his forehead and spread the paint down his nose.

I pop my bottom lip over my top and rest my hand on his chest.

"Jake, why so blue?"

In the next breath, his hand goes to my lower back, pulling me toward him until my chest is flush against his.

I gulp.

He's crowding me and stealing my air in the process.

The vein in his temple is throbbing and I'm so close I can see the blood pulse in his neck. Slowly, he lifts his hand and simply tucks my hair behind my ear.

Breathe, Claire. You're going to die if you don't breathe.

Not saying a word, he leans over, grabs the towels from the concrete, and wraps an arm around my knees.

It takes me a moment to realize the world is upside down.

"Jake," I scream. "Put. Me. Down."

"You're the bane of my existence," he growls, but I can hear the obvious amusement in his tone. "And you're fired."

My scream has gained us some spectators. They're gawking at us from the front door as Jake strides to the parking lot. I can't make out which women are currently giggling at our show because the world is bobbing up and down.

"You can't fire me," I bite back, flailing on his shoulder as his muscles dig into my stomach.

"Then I'll have Nora fire you."

"Nora loves me. Now put me down."

"No."

My eyes fall to his perfectly sculpted ass.

Payback.

I slap both hands against his slacks, pressing hard, and making sure I leave my painted handprints on either ass cheek.

He stills.

I try to look up to see his reaction, but I don't have the energy.

"I do love finger painting," I fume.

"Fucking infuriating." And there are some more choice words as he walks again.

I strain my neck to look back at the shelter. "Bye, ladies," I shout. "See you on Monday. Enjoy the rest of your weekend."

Their laughing is still echoing in the air as I hear a car door open, and I'm thrown onto the towel-covered seat with a thud. He lays the towel on his side and gets in.

Turning to me when I open my mouth, he pinches my lips together.

"So much prettier when this is shut."

"Asshole," I mumble against his fingers.

I want to open my mouth and fill the silence on our drive back to my house, but my skin is still stinging from his touch, and the heaviness between my legs is distracting. Instead, I keep my arms crossed, and say a silent thank you when he turns on the radio.

Pulling into my driveway, I get out without uttering a word. I lean in before leaving. He's hysterical. Perfectly put together, yet destroyed in paint.

And somehow, he's more handsome than he was when he picked me up.

It's not fair.

My laugh finally wins. I can't allow him to have the last word. "Blue really is your color." I shut the door, and don't look back.

He doesn't leave until I'm inside and he sees the lights come on.

An hour later, when my doorbell rings, I'm freshly showered, back to looking like myself, and not a cartoon character.

Opening the door, my stomach immediately grumbles as the smell of food wafts in the air.

I was too busy today and forgot to eat.

The young woman holds out a bag. "Claire Russell?"

I tilt my head, staring at the bag like it contains a grenade.

"I didn't order food."

She checks the receipt. "You're Claire?"

I nod, confused.

"Enjoy."

"Thanks," I say slowly, grabbing my purse to give her a tip.

She holds up her hand to stop me. "Believe me. They've already tipped enough. Have a good evening."

She walks away and leaves me with the mystery, steaming bag.

My phone dings and my heart slowly crawls into my mouth.

Jake: You didn't eat today. I won't have you passing out on my watch.

FOURTEEN

Jake storms into the shelter on Tuesday evening like he's announcing the end of the world. Shoulders rounded forward, raindrops cling to his black trench coat. His usually perfect hair hangs over his forehead—it's almost inky black when wet.

The panic in his eyes has the blood in my legs turning to lead, and I shoot up from the kitchen chair.

It's not Friday.

"I didn't know you were coming this evening."

I watch as his throat bobs, swallowing hard to contain whatever emotions are threatening to overwhelm him.

Aware of his surroundings, he forces a weary smile to everyone around.

He inhales. I take a breath with him as he leans in. "I need your help. Can you come with me?"

"Go," Amelia urges. "I've got things covered here."

I don't question him. I simply grab my coat and phone.

Struggling to match his pace, he escorts me to the front seat of his car, shielding me from the rain with his umbrella with every step.

The sun is set deep in the sky, and the grey clouds rumble with thunder in the distance.

I shudder.

"Scared of thunder?" he asks, not looking at me as he shakes off his coat and throws it in the backseat.

Swallowing hard, I try to hide the tremble in my hands. "Something like that."

He doesn't taunt me about how childish it is. He doesn't take the opportunity and my spine stiffens. The air in the car is too thick, his leather seat too noisy under me. I want him to joke. I want him to insult me if that's what it takes to lighten the mood.

I want normal.

"What's going on, Jake?" I finally ask as he speeds past the steel gates and onto the road.

He's gripping the steering wheel like it'll evaporate if he lets go.

Only silence ensues.

Trying a more comfortable tactic, I ask, "Where's Jay-Jay?"

"With his grandparents."

That's it.

It's the only thing he offers me.

I don't handle walking into the unknown very well.

I need answers.

"Where are we going?"

He glances at me before concentrating on the road. Then he does it again.

I don't know what possesses me, but I reach out and knead my fingers into his forearm. He tenses under my touch.

"Jake?" I plead, a lump so big in my throat, I fear I'll choke on it. "Stop the car."

"No," he clips.

"Stop the fucking car." My voice is louder than I intended, but it has the desired effect as he swerves to a halt on the side of the road. His breathing is so harsh, I'm sure he's consuming all the oxygen.

"I left with you. No questions asked. But I need to know what's going on."

The only sound in the car is our panting, the rain pelting against the windows, and the wipers.

He steeples his fingers over the steering wheel, leaning his mouth against them.

"I know someone. She's in trouble. She called me tonight needing help." Slowly, he turns to look at me. The anguish marring his face makes me want to reach out and soothe it. "I need you to make room at the shelter."

Oh, shit.

I run my tongue over my dry lips. Again, I don't ask questions. It's not what's important.

"Drive," I order.

Twenty minutes later, it's city lights I see in the distance. My stomach rolls, bile rising in my throat.

Shaking off any remaining emotion from our silent car journey, I pull out my phone. He needs to start answering me so I can make arrangements at other shelters if she doesn't have children.

But as I open my mouth to speak, he pulls into a bus shelter. City bustle engulfs me. Traffic passes by as normal, not knowing the dark sides of what life holds.

The car lights reflect in the rain, and then I see her—huddled together with a little girl, hoods covering both their heads, shivering in the evening chill. The little girl has long hair like mine. It peeks out from the side of her coat and flows to her waist. My chest tightens.

Memories assault me, and I fight to bury them. The woman sitting inside the bus shelter with a swollen eye and bloodied lip isn't my mother. The little girl glued to her hip with her neck buried in the crook of her mother's neck isn't me.

No, these people aren't me and my mother, but they are mirror images of my past. I remember standing out in the cold with my mother while she looked for somewhere for us to stay while my father cooled off.

"Papa just needs a little space, Claire Bear," my mother would say, stroking my hair and trying her best to keep me warm while ignoring her own pain. I just wanted my mother's tears to stop and once I was with her, nothing else mattered. I didn't understand what I did wrong. Why would Papa need space from us? He loved us, didn't he?

"Claire?" A warm hand rests on my shoulder and squeezes some life back into my motionless body. I swallow and shake my head. "Are you okay?"

No, but I will be.

I'm not important here. The woman standing on the edge of the path, reflecting particles of a broken soul, and the little girl trying to fall asleep in her arms—they matter. I gather my memories and stuff them into the farthest part of my mind.

The woman stands, and her belly juts out from her unbuttoned jacket.

I cover my mouth to stifle the sob.

"She's pregnant," I say, mostly to myself. Gasping, I pray she can't see my reaction. "Jake. Her face."

He follows my line of sight.

I said face, but whoever did that made sure she was unrecognizable. Favoring her right leg, she's swollen, bloodied, cut, and bruised, and yet the strongest emotion in what I imagine are beautiful features is shame.

In the middle of a busy street, she stands, dripping blood, and no one stops.

Sometimes I'm ashamed to be human.

"Fuck," Jake roars, hitting his fist on the steering wheel over and over again.

I grip his arm in an iron hold, smothering the sob bubbling in my chest. "Stop," I shout. "Get it together. She's scared out of her mind. She doesn't need another man with a raging temper."

My words sober him, and he nods. Shaking the remaining raindrops from his trench coat, he opens his door. When he notices I'm not following, he looks over his shoulder.

"She doesn't know me. I'm a stranger," I explain. "What's her name?"

"Beth."

"Tell her I'm here. Wave at me when she's ready."

He takes a moment to scan my face before dipping his chin and exiting the car. He rushes under the bus shelter. The coat he's wearing isn't for him. He shrugs it off and places it over the little girl's shoulders.

After long minutes of watching their lips move and calming my breathing, a quick tilt of Jake's head tells me it's okay to leave the car.

I pull the collar of my coat tight around my neck, sheltering myself from the bitter breeze. Rain seeps into my shoes, but I hardly notice.

This is your job, Claire. I remind myself, straightening my spine and gathering my emotions.

"Hi," I breathe, smiling the way I've perfected.

Her lips merely twitch.

I don't reach out my hand. I stay a foot away, granting her space. The little girl still clings to her hip.

"Beth, I'm Claire." I think she tries to smile, but her lips are so badly cut, I'm not sure. I crouch, looking into eyes that mirror very much my own. "What's your name?" I ask the shivering little girl.

"Hannah," she answers, curling her face away into her mother's arm.

"You're going to be all right, Hannah."

Beth's body is shaking. "It's my fault. I'm so sorry. I told him I was leaving, and he snapped. He was drinking. He passed out, and I just ran."

I open my mouth to reassure her, but Jake's voice stops me. "Hey," he says softly, leaning closer but never touching her. "This isn't your fault. It's not your fault," he chants it and Beth's dams burst until she's fighting for air. I don't think she means to, but her body crashes against Jake's and it's like second nature to him when he wraps her up, supporting her unsteady legs. "It's not your fault, Beth," he mutters against her hair, and something in my chest cracks wide open.

Standing, I roll my shoulders back and get to work. My emotions can come into play later, and I appreciate it when Jake doesn't interrupt.

"Beth," I urge. "I need you to look at me." Her blotchy eyes meet mine. "I promise you're safe, but I need to ask you some questions."

She nods.

"Move your mouth for me."

She does as I ask, and I have the haunting feeling she's been asked these questions before.

Her jaw isn't broken.

"How's your leg?"

"It's an older injury."

Jake throws his head back.

"How're the baby's movements?"

"Good." Her voice is wobbly. "She's moving right now."

"That's good." A wave of relief washes over me. She glances to the ground, and I catch her attention by snapping my fingers. I don't want to be rude, but she's in shock, and she'll begin to wonder, diving into the darkest places of her mind. "Eyes on me," I remind her. I lower my voice, mindful of little ears. "Did he kick?"

She shakes her head. "He was drinking."

So, his words were nasty, but the power behind his punch wasn't the same.

If this is what he does to her when he's drunk, I don't want to imagine his temper when he's sober.

"We should get you to a hospital," Jake interjects.

She shakes her head frantically, tightening her grip on her little girl's hand while the other protects her bump. "No. I can't, Jake. He'll find me. You know he will. He knows too many people."

Every word and tear is desperate.

"No hospital," I agree, ignoring how Jake is shooting daggers through the side of my head. "We're going to get you settled at the shelter. I'll call our nurse and she will check you out. But Beth, if she feels like you need a hospital, then I will have to insist."

Her hallow eyes connect with me, and for a moment, I swear, she sees it. She sees history repeating itself.

"Okay."

Her stare averts, but I quickly snap it back. Her chin quivers as I twirl my fingers in the little girl's hair. Beth doesn't break eye contact.

I dig the tip of my finger into her arm. "You feel that?"

She nods again.

"You're not back there. You're here. You're safe." She chews her raw lip, and the tears falling from her chin are as heavy as the rain. "Did he hurt her?"

I don't need to look at the little girl. She knows what I'm talking about because a mother always knows.

"Not physically."

Ice cold air fills my lungs, escaping in a cloud because I know.

I get it.

He hasn't touched her, yet, he has all at once.

I try not to react when she reaches out and takes my hand in a grip so tight, I almost flinch.

Jake rushes to grab the umbrella and ushers us back to the car.

Her hand remains in mine as I guide both her and her daughter into the back seat, but even then, she doesn't let go, so I don't force it. I slip into the back seat with them, aware of Jake's careful watch in the rear-view mirror. They both fall asleep, and I call our nurse.

I also call security and let them know we'll be arriving through the back door. I don't want the children to see. I ask if Mia can be there when we arrive.

She'll know what to do.

I may relate to Beth, but I haven't been there. Not in the same way.

We're like dominos by the time Jake pulls into the shelter. Beth is asleep on my arm, Hannah on hers.

I wake her with a gentle nudge. Hannah doesn't stir when Jake takes her out and holds her securely in his arms.

No words are spoken until we step inside.

Mia holds out the apartment key, and I'm not sure how she expresses so much emotion in a simple smile, but Beth immediately relaxes into her hold, loosening her grip on me but never letting go.

"Oh, honey, he did a number on you."

With the commotion, Hannah stirs in Jake's arms. He puts her down, and she immediately goes to her mother's side.

Beth doesn't release her grip around my fingers, and I'm reluctant to.

"Why don't we let Claire say goodbye to Jake? She'll be right with us." Mia nods at me and Beth lets go, finger by finger.

I turn away to hide it, but a tear sneaks past my defenses, lingering on my chin as I inhale a shaky breath.

The apartment door closes, and silence smothers me. I press my palms on my thighs as I lean over to fill my lungs.

"Fuck, Claire, I'm sorry," Jake whispers, like he's the one to blame.

Shooting up, I shake my head. "Don't ever believe this is your fault. I'm still adjusting, is all," I explain through a watery smile. "She's lucky to have you."

I mean it, but he stiffens, and I know there's not an ounce of him that believes my words.

I use old tactics and dig my finger into his bicep. Truth be told, it probably hurts me more than him.

"You feel that?" I ask.

He scowls but nods.

"This is real. You opened this shelter to help these women. One just happened before your eyes. She's lucky to have you."

His neck jerks like he's having trouble registering the message.

I hold his face in the palms of my hands, struggling on my tiptoes to reach him. "Thank you. Where would Beth have gone if a place like this didn't exist? Don't shit on yourself. You're a good man."

I fall back on my heels as he wipes the stray tear from my eye.

"And you?" he asks, struggling with the emotion in his tone.

"Trying to change history," I answer honestly. I let my arms fall to my side. "I should probably check on her"

He stretches his neck but is quick to respond. "I'll wait in the car."

"I'm going to be awhile."

"It doesn't matter."

He isn't going to leave until he knows she's settled.

"You can wait in my office."

***

Jake doesn't hear me when I enter the office an hour later. Elbows pressed to his knees, his head is in his hands. I can't see his face, but his shoulders are hunched forward, every muscle in his back straining through his shirt from tension.

Gently closing the door, I walk to him and rest my palm on his shoulder.

I offer a tight smile, but my lips struggle to turn upward.

He swallows. "How is she?"

"Tired. The nurse would like her to get the baby checked out in the morning, but the heartbeat is good, and she's moving. Hannah has a bunny at home and is struggling to sleep without it. Beth wants to go back and get it."

Horror fills his eyes. "It's okay. I've called Sam to let him know. He'll have a car check her house in the morning, and if it's clear, Sam will bring her to get her things. Hannah is six. She's too young to understand everything, and if a bunny brings her some comfort, she should have it."

The information doesn't make him relax. Sitting, I reach out and squeeze his knee.

"She's safe here, Jake."

He turns to look at my hand, and I almost snap it back, but he links our fingers, keeping my hand in place. A shock rushes across my skin.

"I wish you were right."

There's so much suffering in his eyes, I feel it. It's in the clench of his fist, the strain across his forehead, and the heart, I'm sure, is breaking.

"While that bastard is breathing air, she's never safe."

In a place full of hope, he sounds hopeless.

I dip my head to meet his eyes. "I need you to promise me something."

As if reading me, he sighs. His breath tingles across our interlocked fingers.

"It's not a promise I can keep."

"You need to. You can't seek him out. I don't know your story, or Beth's but I know this is personal. I know you're angry, but please don't go back. It will only make things worse."

Frustrated, he stands, and my hand drops to my side. I immediately feel his absence.

"You know what happened the last time someone protected him?"

"I'm not protecting—"

"Fucking Beth happened, Claire. He's been getting away with this for years." I jump as his palm comes down on my desk. "It was almost Jess. It was almost Beth. There are too many almosts. Someday, he won't stop. He won't stop until it's too late."

My blood runs cold. Swallowing the bile rising in my throat, I try to stand, but my legs are shaking.

My voice breaks as I whisper, "Jess? Your wife?"

He turns his head over his shoulder, hardly glancing at me before his lids shut tight over his eyes.

This *is* personal.

It's more personal than I ever imagined.

"I got to her in time," he rasps, his voice a whisper in the silence. "I got to her in time."

Oh, no.

My throat is dry, and no matter how hard I swallow, I can't rid myself of the lump. A tear slides down my cheek and falls to my lap.

"Jess wanted to forget about it, but he beat her so badly, the police tried to press charges anyway." There's silence, and for once, I have no desire to fill it. "They weren't even together anymore. She was pregnant with Jay-Jay, and when he found out, he showed up at her apartment."

I close my eyes, struggling to absorb any of this.

He laughs without any humor. "You know what Rob does for a living? He's a family law lawyer. Beth was too. But he wanted her to stay at home, so she gave it up." He laughs again, but it only causes a chill to run down my spine. "His father is a judge, and yet, there's no justice for people like him. They do what they want when they want."

Finally finding power in my legs, I stand but don't approach him. I simply stay quiet, hoping he will say more.

"He disappeared. For years, I didn't hear his name. Until Beth showed up at my office one day wanting to know about Jess. This shelter was only at the design stage. So, I did the only thing I could. I got her the hell away from him. Soon after, he fell off the face of the planet again. Beth wanted to press charges. Sam was trying to build a case against him, but he was met with resistance from fucking everyone. No one wants to prosecute a judge's son. When he got word of what Beth was doing, he showed up, claiming he had changed. They have a family. She wanted to believe him."

No hint of bitterness. He gets it.

Turning to finally meet my eyes, he runs a frustrated hand through his hair while blowing out a long breath. He glances around. "This place. Everything I've done is to understand."

It all makes sense.

His wife.

This shelter is for her.

Everything he does is for her.

Something claws at my chest, ripping at old wounds until they bleed out.

We're both spending our lives helping women because we couldn't help the ones we loved the most.

"Jake," I try to say, but my voice breaks. Shaking the shiver from my bones, I stand straight and take a small step toward him. I might not be able to make him understand everything, but maybe I can help. And if it soothes only a fraction of his pain, I want to.

"I didn't know your wife, but I know these women. They fall in love like everyone else. They give their trust and expect the person they love to protect it. It starts slowly. They hear simple things like, 'You don't need so much makeup,' 'I don't think your friends like me,' 'You said no last night'. They're experts at isolating.

"Eventually, these women question their own choices because every decision is made for them. I talk to them every day. Do you know what they want? They want to go to a hair salon but they're too afraid to go on their own. They want to walk down the street and not look over their shoulder."

My voice shakes, remembering Leah in my office.

"I had an eighteen-year-old girl in this room asking if I could show her how to do her makeup because she wasn't allowed before coming here. Just like that. She wasn't allowed.

"The kids want to be kids. They want to feel normal. Coming out of a relationship like that is the scariest thing because you doubt your

119

every move."

With a deep breath, I pump enough courage to say, "You told me about your wife when she was sick. I think she made those decisions because she finally had the freedom to do it." I bat the tears away, refusing to set them free. "*No* is such a small word, but it's our most powerful. It's a choice. But when someone ignores it, it becomes our weakest."

His head falls between his shoulders, but it's only a split second before my words hit, and it snaps back. He's trying to hide the rage in his eyes, the signs of a knot twisting in his stomach, the fear.

I see it because I know it.

Those shadows mock us. They taunt us until we build the courage to swallow them whole again.

The moment his eyes connect with mine, he sees it too.

And I hate myself for it.

I hate that I've let it show.

He takes a step forward, but I hold out my hand to stop him. "Stop," I breathe. "This isn't about me. I know because I've seen it with the people I work with."

I wish I was a better liar.

He ignores my pleas. Instead, he simply takes another step in my direction, so close now I feel the heat from his body. Desperate to divert his attention, I drop my gaze and open my mouth to say something.

Anything.

But he stops me, gripping my chin between his fingers and forcing me to look at him.

No words are spoken.

Not out loud.

I shake my head because I can't say it.

I can't give it air because it will ignite, and I'll be the one to burn in the flames.

"I need you to promise me," I repeat, skin burning from his touch, but he doesn't let go. "I'm here to help her, but I can't do that if I'm worried about what you're doing. It won't help her case if you go after him."

His chest is heaving, and I can't tell which emotion will win the war he's waging. Pressing my palm to his chest, his heart races against my fingers. "Trust me, Jake. Eliminating the monster doesn't banish the demons. Promise me you won't go after him. Not now."

His thumb traces over my lower lip, and I allow myself a moment to fall into his touch. Fingers curling into his shirt, I'm urging him to speak.

Say it, Jake.

Please say it.

Hand cupping the side of my face, his words bring me little comfort, but I have to accept it. "For now. I promise."

FIFTEEN

My ringing phone pulls me from my sleep. Trying to see with one eye still closed, I fumble to catch it before it vibrates off my bedside table.

Staying up most of the night, I called the night staff every hour to check on Beth. It was at least five before I got to sleep, too busy tossing and turning to close my eyes. When I did, vivid dreams haunted me until I woke in a cold sweat. But even now, as I catch sight of Sam's name on my screen, a pair of troubled eyes still occupy my thoughts.

After leaving my office, I resisted the urge to call or text Jake, knowing that if I wanted him to trust me to help Beth, I needed to trust him to keep his word. There was already enough blood spilled without adding his blood to the mix. The thought alone makes me nauseous.

He's right. Rob is getting away with this for far too long, and with it, he's grown confident. Too cocky. In his eyes, he's untouchable. He has people in his corner. People—I think—are just as responsible as him for every vicious word and shattering punch.

Jake's anger isn't impulsive. He's harbored this for years and allowed it to fester. It's too deep. Too embedded in him to step away. But it's dangerous—for everyone.

And yet, I can't blame him.

I was there.

Trying to rid the world of a monster.

But there's always more.

Always.

Swallowing the bile in my throat, I throw my covers back before sitting up and answering the call.

"Hey, Sam." My voice is hardly a whisper, tiredness creeping in and making it break.

"Sorry, Claire. I didn't mean to wake you."

"You didn't," I lie. I'll need to skip my run this morning. Although, I'm pretty sure my body is too exhausted to even attempt it. "I'm leaving soon." Putting the phone on speaker, I run the shower and brush my teeth. "Are you at the shelter?"

"On my way. We have two officers at his house, but nobody's home. Given the information I have on this asshole, I'm going to guess he knew we were coming."

"I'll be there soon. I'll come with Beth."

"Great. See you soon."

"Sam," I stop him before he ends the call. "How's April?"

This can't be easy on her either, knowing the man that abused her sister is back.

"Planning a murder."

"Well, I guess she's lucky she married a cop."

He laughs, but he sounds equally exhausted as me.

Thirty minutes later, I'm showered and dressed and on the verge of really cutting my hair. My arms are too tired from holding the hairdryer, and it's still partially wet when I give up.

"We're going to need a lot of sage today," I mutter, grabbing my keys while trying desperately to loosen the knot in my neck.

I feel like I've been run over by a truck.

Stepping outside, my eyes fall to a box at my feet.

I can't remember ordering anything.

Another one of my wine-fuelled shopping sprees, no doubt.

I grab the box and get in the car. I'm about to rip the tape with my key, but it's already open.

No name or address either.

Pulling back the cardboard, I glance inside.

A cuddly toy?

My heart stops. The blood in my veins turns to ice, and it takes all my strength to move my trembling hands.

A note inside reads:

Claire,

We haven't met yet, but I understand you're helping my wife through this terrible misunderstanding.

I'm sure you'll agree, a child's place is with both parents.

I only hope to be reunited with my family, and I'm sure you're working hard to achieve this.

Please pass this on to my little girl. She must miss it.

I'll be in touch.

One more thing. She's always loved music. While she's in your care, you might find time to teach her.

Under the letter is a white bunny with the name Hannah stitched to the ear.

***

"Fuck," Sam curses, staring at the box like it holds an atomic bomb.

I swear it weighs the same.

"It was on your doorstep?"

I only nod.

"I've been threatened at my job before. He's not the first egomaniac I've had to deal with."

"It's your home. He's sending a message."

A chill runs down my spine.

"It's bully tactics," I fight back, refusing to acknowledge the churning in my stomach.

"Have you seen his wife's face?"

"I know," I blow out, running my fingers through my hair as I begin to pace. Or maybe I was always pacing. I don't remember.

I hardly remember driving here.

"I need to bring these to the station. Don't go home."

My heart sinks.

"We need the bunny."

Crossing his arms over his chest, his eyes scan my face like I've lost my damn mind.

"You have a stalker, and you're worried about the bunny."

"Stalker is a little dramatic, Sam."

"Explain the music comment."

I can't, and nausea rocks in my stomach.

"Beth only arrived last night. Do you think he's been following me before now?"

A torturous second passes before he shakes his head slowly and shrugs.

I'm going to be sick.

"He's a fucking psychopath. He knows Jake helped her before. Maybe he was expecting it, or maybe he's trying to get under Jake's skin."

It will work.

He's going to lose his mind.

"The bunny," I plead, feeling a headache coming on. "She doesn't sleep without it."

I reach out to grab it, but he dodges me.

"I'm trying to build a case here. You're not getting the bunny, and I'm going to repeat this once more. Do. Not. Go. Home. He's dangerous."

Sighing, I grab my phone, snap a picture of the cuddly toy in the box, and slip my hands through my coat.

"Where the hell are you going?"

"Don't worry. I'm not going home."

"You should stay here. I need to bring this to the station. I'll be back this evening, and we can discuss."

I can't stay here. My mind will run riot.

"I won't be long. I'll be back before you are." I try to reassure him, but he'll need to handcuff me to make me stay.

"He won't like this, Claire," he shouts after me.

No doubt who *he* is.

I spin on my heels, taking backward steps. "Then don't tell him."

"I have to tell him."

"Just give me a few hours."

"At least tell me where you're going?" His eyes are bulging out of his head.

"To find another goddamn bunny."

SIXTEEN

"The karaoke machine is going down a treat." Amy appears at my side. I'm not sure how long I've been standing at the door of the music room, just watching the kids have fun, but it's long enough that my feet are almost numb.

I nod. "They love it."

"They've all signed up for music lessons, you know?"

My heart swells.

I thought some might be interested, but everyone is giving it a go. I've even seen some of the mother's come in for lessons with Amy.

"It's amazing."

She presses her shoulder against mine. "You okay, sis? You look exhausted."

I used the kids as a distraction, but the nausea is back. At least I got the same bunny for Hannah. It took an extra flutter of my eyelashes to get it stitched on such short notice, but if she was aware it wasn't the same one, she didn't say. Her smile was enough to ease the anxious weight I've carried around since this morning.

"Long day," I murmur, not wanting to cause her to worry. Not yet.

Her eyes tighten, and I know she doesn't believe a word of it, but she doesn't question me.

Kissing her cheek, I pat her back. "You can clear them out. I'm going to finish some paperwork."

"Knock, knock." The light tap on my office door takes me out of my work-induced trance. Looking up, I'm greeted by Sam's frown.

I hold out my hands. "See. I'm still alive." I smile, sitting back in my chair and stretching my stiff neck.

He doesn't smile back.

Party pooper.

But my chest is tight, and my eyes have been stinging with unshed tears all day.

He leans against the door frame and crosses his legs at the ankle, his thumb hooked in his belt loop like always.

"Any update?"

I feel his frustration when he shakes his head. He offers one of his lopsided grins, but it does little to relieve the tension in this office. "Believe me. I'm trying."

Nothing makes Sam nervous, so why is he suddenly shuffling on his feet?

"Do you want to tell me why you're standing in my office looking like you've kicked a puppy?"

He taps his knuckles against the door again.

Once. Twice. Three times.

"I'm going to give it to you straight." He blows out a long breath, and I have a sneaking suspicion I'm not going to like where he's going with this. "He's the scum of the earth. He'll do anything to get his family back. Anything to take back what he sees as his. It will eat him up knowing Jake is involved. Their history is too volatile. Too emotional."

Shifting in my seat, the leather becomes sticky and uncomfortable beneath me, and a violent chill runs down my spine.

"What are you not saying, Sam?" I finally ask, clearing my throat of nerves.

"I'm not comfortable that he came by your house. In his eyes, you're getting in the way of him being with his family again."

I swallow the bile rising in my throat.

Yep.

I definitely don't like where this is going, and I feel like I'm narrating the start of a true-crime podcast.

"Is there someone you can stay with?"

And there it is.

My heart drops to the pit of my stomach, and I wipe my clammy hands against my thighs. But my spine turns to steal, and I curl my mouth into a shaky smile. I've had threats made against me before—maybe not as severe or as personal as this one—but it's part of the job. It comes with the territory. After years in this line of work, I've come to expect it. I shouldn't have to. No one should, but I can't control it either. There are crazy people everywhere.

I wave my hand in dismissal before filing my paperwork back into their folders. I haven't finished, but I need to focus on something other than what Sam is saying.

"I'm sure I'll be fine. But thank you."

He takes a pleading step forward, but I refuse to look up and meet his gaze because I already know what I'll see.

I'll see he is right, and I don't want him to be.

I'll get security cameras.

Fuck.

Part two of the true-crime podcast has begun.

I don't have another option.

Staying with Amy means putting her in danger. As for my mother, just me being there puts her in danger of alcohol poisoning.

I could suggest a hotel, but I know what Sam is saying. It's not about where I stay. He wants me to be with someone. Strength in numbers and all that.

Sounding a little more desperate than before, Sam says, "Claire, he came to your house. What next? We need to be sure this asshole doesn't go a step further."

A step further?

My mouth goes dry, and I shudder. "What's a step further?" I ask, my voice breaking under the pressure that someone could be out there doing God knows what.

"I don't know. I just want to make sure you're safe. I wouldn't ask otherwise."

I'm about to argue, but when I open my mouth, it snaps shut again because over Sam's shoulder I catch sight of Jake storming into my office, eyes wild with rage.

"Why the fuck wouldn't she be safe?" The rasp of his voice coats over me, but not with the familiar warmth I'm used to.

Fuck again.

Closing my eyes briefly, I give myself a second to gather my thoughts and steady my breathing.

"Jake," I start, getting to my feet.

"Why aren't you safe, Claire?" When his eyes land on me, I feel my blood pulse everywhere. His jaw twitches and molten eyes turn to nothing but steel.

He's angry.

Not just a little inconvenienced, either. I can practically see the steam rising from his ears, and that vein in his temple is going to explode.

"Claire?" he repeats through gritted teeth, seeking a more educated reply than my gaping mouth.

He's about to go Hulk in my office, isn't he?

I lick my dry tongue over my lips, desperate for an out or time to explain this. I don't need two men berating me this evening.

"I was going to tell you when I left here. Rob called by her house this morning." Sam interrupts our staring contest, and my mouth falls open again, sucking in all the oxygen in the office.

Why did he have to go and do that?

Jake is silent, but there's a storm brewing. His murderous glare snaps back to me, and his anger vibrates, bouncing against the walls until it consumes the air around us.

"Did he hurt you?"

Frantically shaking my head, I hold out my arms like I have physical evidence. "No. He didn't hurt me. I didn't even see him."

"He left Hannah's bear in a box, and a not-so-subtle letter," Sam explains.

I'm going to kill him.

And it's a bunny.

Jake straightens his tie, pulls at his sleeves, then balls his hand into tight fists.

I don't know what to do. The weight of his stare is making me uncomfortable and oddly heated all at once.

To distract us both, I pick up my handbag from the floor and stuff my belongings inside. I need to get out of the way of his warpath. Sam landed us in this when he opened his big mouth. He can deal with Jake's tantrum.

I try to smile, but it falters before I say, "It's fine. Really."

"Fine?" he booms, and I think that vein is definitely going to rupture. He scrubs a frustrated hand over his face, stepping forward and taking what looks like a calming breath. It doesn't work. His shoulders square, and his knuckles turn white at his sides.

"Why didn't you tell me?"

Because I knew you'd act like this.

I don't say that and gesture toward Sam. "I told him. That's the policy. Besides, I'm sure it's nothing."

He grinds his teeth but averts his deathly stare to Sam.

Thank the heavens.

He was making me anxious.

"Sam." I've never heard someone's name spoken as such an icy warning.

Poor Sam.

"Calm down. I'm looking into it, but I think it's best if Claire stays somewhere else. A few weeks at most."

The blood drains from my body and pools at my feet.

"Weeks?" I screech. "Jake said it himself. Nobody wants to prosecute him. What if it takes longer?"

"It won't. They should grant a warrant for his arrest." That means nothing. "The captain appears to be taking it more seriously now that you're involved."

"Fuck him. He should have taken it seriously the first time, and the time after that. I'm not the one with bruises."

They don't disagree.

I don't know when I begin to pace, but focusing on the carpet under my bare feet is keeping me from spiraling. They ignore my distressed state and how I'm on the brink of a cardiac arrest, instead choosing to continue their conversation.

About me.

About my safety.

How did everything turn to shit so fast?

I'm sweating.

I don't like this.

I don't like this one bit.

My control is slowly slipping away. It makes my hands tremble and an ache claws at my chest.

When Jake turns his attention back to me, the crease between his brow deepens. He scrubs his fingers over his stubbled jaw. I don't know why I think it's okay to follow the movement, and I get stuck watching him. If he notices, he doesn't say because when our eyes lock again, they're narrowed, and he's assessing me like a piece of furniture he needs to move.

What the hell is he thinking in that gorgeous head of his?

He nods toward my shoes on the floor.

"Grab your things. We're leaving."

My head rears back, but I stay firm on my feet. "I can drive myself home, but thank you."

A very low yet powerful groan rumbles in his chest. "You're not going home. I'll have someone pick up your car."

I huff a laugh, crossing my arms over my chest. He's not making any sense. "That's stupid. Nothing is going to happen on the drive back to my house."

He curses under his breath and that blazing fire returns, flecks of amber burning in brown pools. "You're not going to your house. You're coming home with me."

What?

He says it with so much conviction, I almost believe him.

"No, I'm not."

But he doesn't reply. Instead, he exhales sharply, and I become desperate for air.

I blink.

He blinks harder.

I take a step back.

He takes a confident step forward.

I don't know what kind of dance this is, but I don't want any part of it.

"No, I'm not," I repeat, wishing my voice sounded stronger, but it breaks.

"Yes, you are, Claire." His voice certainly doesn't break because this deluded man is serious.

Mother of pearl.

He's not backing down, but I'll be damned if I do.

Hell will freeze over before I agree to stay with him.

He's being ridiculous. I won't get slaughtered in my own house.

Right?

Right.

My eyes grow so wide, I'm sure they'll pop right out of my head and roll to his feet. I glance toward Sam for help, but he's useless to me. All he offers is a shrug and, "It's not a bad idea, honey."

Because it's a terrible idea.

It's the worst idea I've ever heard.

Jake takes another menacing step toward me, and I take another one back.

We've resumed the dance.

"What about Jay-Jay? It's not good for him to see you take a random woman home."

I swear, there's a shadow of a smirk playing on his lips.

Asshole.

"I'm not taking you home to have you screaming my name every night."

For the love of all that is right in the world, why did I just clench my thighs?

"And you're not some random woman. Jay-Jay is crazy about you, and you know it."

Goddammit.

He just managed to turn me on and melt my heart all at once.

Not fair.

I open my mouth to respond, but I stutter, my tongue tangling around the words I want to say.

He takes another step forward and I shuffle back, but he's getting closer, like a wild animal hunting his prey.

"Get your things, Claire. Now," he demands, all hint of amusement leaving his tone. "Don't fucking test me on this."

It's in this moment, a condition I don't have a name for, but has plagued me since childhood, wins out in my inner turmoil. And when my mouth opens next, it isn't to argue with him, but a wave of uncontrollable laughter erupts from my throat, causing my shoulders to shake and my stomach to ache.

I know both men are probably looking at me like I've grown extra limbs, but it's a nervous reaction. I can't help it.

Scrubbing the flesh of my palms across my cheeks to wipe the tears, I try to say, "I'm so sorry." But I only giggle more.

"Are you laughing?" Jake asks slowly, unsure how to deal with me and my poorly timed outburst. "Seriously?"

"I'm sorry. I'll stop," I trail off, only to burst into another fit of uncontrollable giggles.

"Is she okay?" I hear Sam's voice, but I can't see him because of the tears blurring my vision, and my cackling is drowning out all other sounds.

"Who made my sister nervous?" It's Amy, but I can't see a thing because I'm hunched over, and my stomach is cramping. "What's going on?"

With a calming breath, I try to stifle it long enough to explain. "I'm sorry. I have terrible fight-or-flight instincts, and I freeze. Especially when someone is prowling after me like you are. I get nervous and laugh."

Jake stands so straight I think I hear his spine snap.

He's not any fun.

He doesn't see the funny side at all.

Honestly, either do I, but right now, if I don't laugh, I'll cry.

"Are you fucking with me?" he snaps, proving his lack of amusement to my current predicament. "He was at your house, and you laugh when I step too close. What would you ever do if you came face to face with him? Roll over and chuckle?"

I bite my lip and swallow another wave of laughter. "Probably," I choke out.

Wrong answer.

His body stiffens, and he pinches the bridge of his nose before pinning his eyes back to me.

"Claire?" Amy snaps my attention to her. Her face blanches. "What's going on?"

Sam explains under his breath, and with every word, her eyes widen. Tears brim, and it breaks my heart. It also brings me back to reality.

"Amy," I plead. "I'm fine."

"Stay with me," she offers.

"No," Jake explodes, making me jump. He turns to Amy, and there are a million unspoken words between them. "I need her safe. I need her with me."

She nods in agreement.

"Amy," I scold. She's my last resort for backup. "I don't need a babysitter."

"Listen to yourself, Claire. Don't make her mistakes." A single tear slips from her chin.

"What about Jay-Jay? I won't put him at risk."

"He's leaving with his grandparents in a few days. They're going to the beach house."

"Since when?"

"Since now."

Talking to Sam, he doesn't break our eye contact when he speaks. "Sam?"

"Uh, huh?"

"Do me a favor?" Jake asks flatly, shooting me a wicked smirk.

"Sure thing, buddy."

"Cover your ears and close your eyes or get the hell out of here because I'm pretty sure I'm about to do something illegal and kidnap this frustratingly stubborn woman. If I have to carry her out of here myself, she's coming with me."

I freeze, but it's not so funny this time.

He would never.

Would he?

Sam chuckles, and I hear his footsteps leaving.

"I need to get home to April, anyway. I'm sure you two can sort this out."

Jake grins that shit-eating grin that makes me want to punch him. "Thanks."

"Yeah, thanks for nothing, Sam."

Amy's body comes crashing into mine, almost knocking me off my feet. She wraps her arms around my neck. "Please, Claire. If anything happens to you—"

"Nothing is going to happen to me."

"Sure, because you're going to stay with Jake for a while, right?"

Hanging my head, I close my eyes, desperate for this day to be over. I can't deal with the worry in her eyes.

She's squeezing Jake's shoulder when I look up, whispering to him. He nods in response to whatever she says.

"Call me right away. I'll be back tomorrow evening. I love you, sis."

My backup is slowly dwindling. Not that she was much use to me. She's leaving us to argue this out, knowing I have no other choice.

When Sam and Amy leave my office and close the door, I think they may have taken all the air with them. The oxygen is heavy and my chest heaves, anticipation coursing through my veins. I back up, desperate to say something before he makes good on his threat. My *could-be* stalker is not what I'm afraid of tonight, but the man with dark-honey eyes and shoulders plenty big to throw me over.

As much as I'd suddenly like to experience it again, I think it's best to try to calm this situation with reasonable conversation.

"I appreciate the thought and you wanting to open your home to me, but I'm a big girl. I can take care of myself."

"Claire, I'm serious. I *will* carry you out of here."

"I snore," I argue, raising my brows and crossing my arms over my chest.

I don't think I snore, but he doesn't need to know.

"My walls are soundproof."

Of course, they are.

This ruins the argument about playing my music too loud.

"I'm a terrible cook."

I'm amazing, but again, what he doesn't know won't hurt him.

He tilts his head and for the first time tonight, I see a genuine smile split his lips. I don't know if it's because he knows he's winning or because of my pathetic excuses.

"I'm not asking you to stay with me so you can feed me and my son."

"I'm messy and annoying and—"

"Jesus Christ, Claire, I don't care about any of that. I don't care what you are once you're safe."

When he leans forward against my desk with his palms flat against the wood, his head falls between his shoulders, and my frustration melts away. Instead, I want to reach out and ease the tension across his chest. My heart swells and twists until I'm counting with each heavy breath.

"Please," he murmurs in a desperate whisper. "I need you to be safe, sweetheart." His voice is so low that I'm unsure if he meant for me to hear it.

But I do, and a single, heavy tear falls from the corner of my eye because when he looks up again, every feature on his face is awash with pain.

He doesn't need to say another word. It's written all over him.

My brain loses the battle with my heart. I'm at his side, gently squeezing his shoulder, hoping it soothes him.

No more fighting.

No more silly bickering.

He's right, and I need to be sensible.

And Jesus, I'd do anything to take that look from his face.

His eyes land on my resting hand, the crease on his brow deepening again, and I've lost my mind because I reach out, feathering the line with my thumb to ease it. He doesn't react, and my heart stops. Then it pounds so loud it's likely he can hear it. And when we both exhale together, he leans into the comfort my touch is offering. I feel his breath across my palm, and every inch of me tingles.

"Please, Claire. I can't—" He stops, taking another deep breath, his broad shoulders straining against his suit jacket. "I just need you to be safe. I made you a promise last night, but if you get hurt, I won't be able to keep it."

Well, what do you know?

Hell has frozen over again.

"Okay," I whisper, urging him to look at me. "I'll stay with you." My shoulders sag, but most of it is relief from knowing I don't have to stay alone.

He leans back. "Okay?"

I shake my head and offer a small smile. At least he doesn't look like he's in pain anymore. "Okay."

Strong arms come around my back and pull me tight to his chest. My heart all but stops.

"Woman, you drive me crazy. Why do you always have to argue with me?"

I laugh under my breath and hug him back because his touch makes my legs shaky, and I need something to steady myself.

"Because it's so much fun."

He continues to speak to me but never loosens his grip, and I feel his lips press against the top of my head. "You're the person who laughs at funerals, aren't you?"

My shoulders shake again. "Oh yeah. My best friend died when I was nineteen. It was one of the saddest days of my life, and none of my other friends had the time to cry because they were too busy waiting for me to break into laughter. I was doing so well until the priest slipped on a step."

He pulls away, holding me by my upper arms. "I take it back. I'm bringing you to your house."

"Hey," I scold, nudging him.

Cupping his fingers under my chin, he tilts my head to meet his gaze. "Come on. Get your things. We're going home."

I forgot how big his kitchen is.

It's bigger than my entire house.

Who needs a kitchen this big?

Nothing is out of place.

Yet, it feels homely.

Warm.

And I'm beginning to think he has an obsession with trees. The surroundings are similar to the shelter. A sprawling house lost in its own forest.

An escape.

Hidden.

I'm just getting used to finding my way around the shelter, and he's set on making sure I get lost here, too.

His anger subsided enough by the time we got here to get some information out of him. He moved into this house two years ago.

That's it.

That's all the information I got.

I asked why he moved, but I only received silence as an answer.

It's my own fault for being nosy.

Jay-Jay's paintings hang on the fridge, an unfinished Lego set is on the table, and the long hallway from the kitchen is littered with photo frames.

Curiosity getting the better of me, I examine each one carefully. All in black and white. I study the newborn draped over a woman's shoulder. Her profile is beautiful, the black and white casting shadows on her face, and her loose curls hang over her shoulder as she stares at the sleeping baby.

There's more of Jay-Jay—crawling, laughing on a swing set, holding the first tooth he lost. A gummy smile beams back at me. Every milestone is right here on this wall.

His very own memory lane.

The last one is a wedding photo. She's thinner than in the other pictures but no less beautiful. Her veil blows in the wind and she's smiling up at Jake. His hair is shorter, fewer ghosts behind his eyes, and those familiar broad shoulders fill out his tuxedo. He's bigger now, every muscle more defined, if it's even possible.

A tear falls before I have time to catch it because he's so full of hope in the photo, it makes my chest ache. He doesn't know what's coming.

Was it the last time she smiled at him like that?

Was it the last time he smiled without pain?

I suddenly feel like I'm intruding on an intimate moment and quickly return to the kitchen.

We stopped by my house on the way, and Jake scoped it better than the FBI. I half expected him to shout 'clear' after every room.

He's bringing my bags to the guest bedroom.

The kitchen door flies open like a hurricane has whipped through the house.

"Claire!" Jay-Jay shouts, running toward me, stopping short of hugging me. His eyes are bright, excitement making him shift on his feet.

I ruffle his hair, and his arms come around my waist, making my chest warm. After the evening I've had, I need a hug, and this kid gives the best.

"Dad told Grandma your house is leaking, and you get to stay with us."

Good thinking, Jake.

"I'm sure they will fix it in no time. You and your dad will have your man cave back."

God, I hope it is.

I hate the unknown.

He shrugs, adjusting his blue-rimmed glasses. His glasses are different colors every time I see him.

I think this eight-year-old is cooler than I'll ever be.

"We never have people stay with us."

Jake was telling the truth. He doesn't date. Or at least they're not around long enough to meet his son.

"You can play my piano if you'd like? It's down the hall."

This move just got a little easier.

"Thanks, handsome."

Jake enters the kitchen with a smaller lady, and I immediately feel like I'm looking at an older version of the beautiful woman in her wedding dress.

"This is Rose. Jay-Jay's grandma. Rose, this is Claire." Jake introduces.

She's pale—the rosy cheeks I imagine she has drained of all color.

She knows I'm here because of more than a leak.

Fiddling with the strap of her handbag, she offers a sad smile.

I try to smile back.

She pinches Jay-Jay's cheek. He backs away, his face reddening. "Grandma," he moans.

He's adorable.

"Me and your dad were talking, and now that you're on summer break from Friday, how about me, you, and grandpa leave early for the beach house?"

I can't see his face, but I know he's bursting with excitement.

He nods. "Awesome. Are you coming, Dad?"

"Your dad will be busy." Rose answers. "We'll leave on Saturday. He'll join us at the usual time, and maybe he and Claire could join us for a night or two before then."

I can feel the twitch in my lips.

Back with Mandy and Garry.

I'd give anything to be there right now.

"I'd like that," I say, glancing at Jake. His eyes pull together. Whatever he's thinking now is causing him pain.

I know him well enough to know that being without his son for weeks isn't the norm.

He's sending him away because he's scared for his safety.

"We'll be there, buddy." He hugs Jay-Jay, his eyes closing as he grips his son's sweater. "Say goodbye to Grandma. We'll go upstairs and get you ready for bed."

When we're alone, my throat feels tight, and I scratch at the skin, needing to open my airways.

To her, I'm a strange woman in her grandson's home.

Tears well in her eyes before she tilts her head and offers a watery smile.

"Can I hug you?" she murmurs, her voice wobbly.

Relief instantly washes over me, and the breath I don't know I'm holding escapes in a whoosh.

"Of course." I think she needs one as much as I do.

Her hugs are as good as Jay-Jay's, but they have a maternal squeeze.

When her chin wobbles, I take both her hands before I have time to think about it.

"I'm so sorry this is happening to you," she cries, taking a tissue from her pocket and patting her eyes. "We thought that man was out of our lives for good."

A sorrowful lump lodges in my throat. "Please don't be sorry. Don't apologize for him. And I'm sure Jake is just being cautious."

Her palm cups my cheek, and I swallow the prickle of emotion. "I know you don't know me, but please take my advice. I've known that man upstairs since he was a boy in diapers. Me and his mom were best friends long before then. Life has changed him, but his heart is the same." Her tears stream freely now. "Trust him. He's cautious for a reason."

She laughs through her sniffles. "You might want to kill him because he'll watch your every move. But that man bears crosses that weren't made for him." She glances at her feet, lost for a moment before she looks back at me. "Some people are born with darkness in their soul, and I believe Rob is one of those people. His darkness was allowed to flourish. Don't underestimate him, sweetie. He almost stole my child from me in the cruelest of ways. I can't bear to think of him stealing another mother's child. Listen to Jake. He's a good man."

She wipes a tear from the corner of my eye, and all I can do is nod in agreement.

"I know."

Because I do.

I know Jake is a good man.

He's amazing.

But I also know darkness flourished in my home.

Darkness grew and blocked out all light.

It left a chill, and it starved us of the sun.

Even on beautiful days, when the sky heated our skin, three steps inside my childhood home, and it was cold.

I squeeze her hand.

"I know," I whisper, putting trust I don't have in a man she's begging me to give a chance.

SEVENTEEN

The evening sky is threatening rain as I pull into Jake's driveway. My body feels stiff, my eyes heavy from lack of sleep, and I've ruined a new shirt because the kids were doing finger paintings at the shelter today. I couldn't stand back and watch like a normal adult. My inner child crept out, too giddy not to join in.

Jay-Jay has his head in a book when I go inside, sprawled out on the rug, the television on mute.

"Hey, handsome. How was your day?"

He glances up, pushing his glasses back onto the bridge of his nose before offering a small shrug. His face is sullen with no wide smile that I'm used to.

"Grandma is in the kitchen. Dad isn't home yet." It's then I notice the blotchy patches under his eyes, heavy with tears.

There's a little tug in my chest. "You okay?"

"I'm fine," he simply says before sighing and going back to his book.

He's lying.

"You're sure?"

"Uh, huh."

I don't press further. If he doesn't want to talk about it, I won't force him. Maybe he'll talk to Jake. I hate to think of him being upset.

"Hi, sweetie." Rose grins as she cleans the countertops. "How are you settling in?"

It's been two days.

It feels like a hotel.

And I don't want to settle in anywhere.

I won't be here long enough.

I better not be here long enough.

Instead, I say, "Fine."

She laughs under her breath, like she knows exactly what I'm thinking. "There's a casserole in the fridge. I can heat it in the oven if you'd like? Jake isn't exactly a domestic god."

I laugh as I hang my coat on the hook. "That's kind of you. Thank you. But I ate at work."

She smiles again, not fazed, before putting the cleaning products back in the cupboard.

"Do you take care of Jay-Jay every day?"

A proud smile graces her lips. "It's the best job in the world. Jake wanted to hire a nanny when he was little, and I wasn't having any of it. Now I just mind him after school. To be honest, there are so many of us looking for his attention. I'm surprised Jake gets any time with him. He's a good father. He made a lot of sacrifices to be at home as much as possible. But he's a businessman, and on nights like tonight, when he can't help it and needs to work late, I prefer to come here so I can cook. At least I know Jake is eating a home-cooked meal."

How sweet.

"He's lucky to have you."

Her eyes glaze over for a moment. "We're lucky to have them."

Sniffing the fresh flowers she places in a vase, I ask, "Any idea what's up with Jay-Jay today?"

She shrugs before putting her hands on her hips. "He's been like that since I picked him up from school. He wouldn't tell me."

I chew my lower lip between my teeth.

"Don't worry, honey. I'm sure it's nothing."

I force a small smile, knowing his tears weren't nothing.

"It looks like there's a storm coming. You should go home before it hits. I can watch Jay-Jay."

She thinks about it for a moment before peering through the window and into the angry sky. "You don't mind? Jake may be a while longer."

"Honestly, it's fine. It will make me feel useful."

The wrinkles around her eyes set deep as she grins. After grabbing her coat, she squeezes my shoulder. "You're a good girl."

I instantly feel like a child.

"Maybe he'll open up to you," she adds.

"Hopefully."

When Rose leaves, I ponder back into the living room. He's still holding the book but not reading it. So much contemplating for someone so young.

I sit on the sofa, careful of the dry paint on my clothes. I really need a shower.

"What are you reading?"

He jerks back. He didn't even notice me come in here.

A small smile curls on the corner of his mouth. From the pictures I've seen, he looks exactly like his mom. Just as beautiful as her, too. But that smile is all Jake, and I find myself smiling in return.

"Harry Potter. It's just the first one. Dad won't allow me to read the others until I get a little older." Another sad sigh.

I roll my eyes. "Muggles."

His face lights up. That smile I missed this evening flashes at me, and I feel some tension roll off my shoulders. But as soon as it crosses his face, it falters again. Chin quivering, he coughs to hide his sniffles.

I don't comment on his tears because I don't want to embarrass him, so instead, I ask, "Everything's good at school, right? Is someone bothering you?"

He scrubs a hand across his cheek. "It's not that," he says as he pushes himself to his feet, taking a seat next to me.

Please open up, little man.

"The other kids were making cards for their moms today."

Oh, my damn heart just cracked and broke into a thousand pieces.

With a deep breath, I lean into the sofa, the weight of his confession knocking me back. He follows, pushing his body close to mine. I wrap a comforting arm around him, hugging him because what else can I do? I can't bring his mother back. I can't prevent him from getting sad when his teacher has the stupid idea to make cards for mothers when there's a kid in the class without one.

It's not even Mother's Day.

Fuck you, teacher.

"You know, you can still make the card and bring it to the cemetery. I think your mom would like that. And you could give one to your grandma. I bet that would make her day. I know your mom isn't here buddy, and it sucks, and nothing will ever replace her, but you've got so many women in your life that love you like a mom loves a son. Sharon and April too." I can only see the top of his head when he nods. Tossing his mop of hair, I lightly squeeze his arm. "You know, I had a woman in my life growing up. She's my best friend's mother. And every year, when it's Mother's Day, I buy her a card because even though she's not my mom, she looked out for me and loved me like a mother does." A tight lump forms in my throat because, truth is, without Kate, I don't know where I would be now.

"Does your friend still give her cards, too?"

I close my eyes, fighting tears and the tightness in my chest. "He can't right now."

He looks at me, his blue orbs glistening. "Why not?"

It's an innocent question, it is, but I don't want to load more on him. His grief is already heavy enough.

"He's far away right now. But I'm sure he would love to."

We stay silent for a long moment. The light from cartoons on the television is the only light illuminating the room.

He looks up again. "Don't worry, Claire. Just because your friend is far away doesn't mean he doesn't love her. My mom is far away too, and I love her."

He smiles, and I swear, he knows. But when the grin finally reaches his eyes for the first time tonight, I feel better. He squeezes my hand, and the tiny cracks this sad conversation caused begin to heal. The shadows retreat until all that's left is his smile.

It's dark in here, but he lights it up.

"Want to watch a movie? I can make some popcorn." I'm not sure who needs it more.

His head bobs enthusiastically. "Sure." When he stands, his eyes narrow on me, and his nose wrinkles. He looks like his father again. "Claire, you've got paint all over you."

I don't know why, but I blush, and he rolls his eyes.

Who's the kid here?

"I better wash up first. Read some of your book, and when I get back, we can watch the movie."

***

Music is playing through the speakers and popcorn is popping in the microwave when Jay-Jay saunters into the kitchen, his feet dragging against the tiles.

It took me ages to get the paint out of my hair, and now the rain is pelting against the window. It's so dark, I only see my reflection when I look at the glass. He pulls himself onto a high stool at the breakfast counter, dropping his face in his hands as he watches me with a pout.

I wish I could wash all that sadness away from his face. I can almost see his heavy heart weighing him down when I notice his fingers tapping to the beat of the music.

Interesting.

What's better than dancing like a crazy person to lift your spirits?

Absolutely nothing.

I should know. I started bopping around my bedroom as a child, and I never stopped.

I'm not sure who's listening to my prayers, but I send a silent thank you when *Happy* by *Pharrell William's* starts playing.

Moving my head from side to side, I sway towards the speaker, slowly turning up the volume until I have to shout over the music. Jay-Jay's head pops up, his eyes wide.

"What are you doing?" he screams, covering his ears with his hands.

I laugh, shaking my hips like a crazy person. There's no rhythm, just jerking movements, limbs with no control, and every worry drifting to the back of my mind.

"Dancing." I shimmy to his side, patting my thighs. "Pop your legs up here." He's laughing, but he does as I ask. A few seconds later, he's giggling until his face is red when I pull his trainers off and toss them across the room.

I grab his hands, dragging him off the chair. He collapses into me, the sound of his laugh the most beautiful thing I've ever heard.

"Come on. Dance. It makes everything better."

Wiggling his eyebrows, his shoulders begin to move up and down, then his legs, matching my flailing body around the kitchen. We jump until our muscles burn, both our faces coated in a sheen of sweat, but so deliriously happy.

The microwave pings in the background. I ignore it.

One song blends into another, and I'm not sure whose idea it was to race each other by running and sliding in our socks.

There's a long hallway from the kitchen to Jake's office, and it's the perfect racing spot.

Memory lane.

"You're really bad at this," Jay-Jay says, breathless.

"I'm wearing the wrong socks."

I'm losing by two when we set off again, determination furrowing my brows. We both take off on a run. I begin to slide when the kitchen door flies open, and I crash into a brick wall of wet flesh. Instinctively, I put my palms up to steady myself, but my tired legs betray me, and I stumble backward. He's fast when his arm snakes around my waist, setting me back on my feet.

Looking up, I try to hide the blush across my cheeks, but I'm pretty sure I'm so out of breath he can't see it, anyway. And my stupid stomach does a weird flutter. His hair is soaked, drops of rainwater falling onto his face. One lingers on his lower lip, and I find myself licking mine. His eyes drop, as does my heart.

I clutch at the shoulders of his suit jacket. The material is soaked through.

"Sorry," I mutter, but the only thing my body is aware of is his touch.

His eyes roam from me to Jay-Jay and around the kitchen before a raging glare sets on me again. It's so different from the heat in his eyes just a moment ago, I rear back.

"What the hell is going on? Why is the music so loud? Are you trying to make my child deaf?"

Flinching, I step back and out of his hold.

You're welcome, asshole.

I swallow the sting in the back of my throat before opening my mouth to speak, but Jay-Jay cuts through the music. "We were dancing and racing in our socks."

Every muscle in Jake's face is tight, the vein in his temple throbbing. I'm in trouble.

"Are you trying to break his legs, too?"

I'm a little lost for words. I was only trying to help. I open my mouth to speak, but the only thing to leave my parted lips is air.

Jake shakes his head with a frustrated sigh before walking away, kissing Jay-Jay on the head and saying, "Get dressed for bed. I've got some work to do, and I'll be up then to say goodnight."

Then he walks away. Just like that, he disappears down the hall, the set of his shoulders stiffening with every step he takes. One final disapproving look back, and he disappears into his office.

I was just scolded, put back in my box, and taught my place in the time it took for the last thirty seconds of the song to play.

My hands ball into fists at my side, so much rage rushing through my blood, I feel hot to the touch.

When I look at Jay-Jay, my heart breaks all over again. His frown is set in place, his shoulders rounding forward.

He didn't even ask how his day was.

Jay-Jay shrugs, defeated.

Oh, no.

We didn't dance our way to exhaustion for that same look to come back.

"Wait here for a sec. I need to speak to your dad."

Shoulders squared, I storm toward the hallway, determined to get answers and an apology.

I deserve a damn apology.

Jay-Jay deserves a bigger one.

But as I round the corner, I quickly jump back before getting knocked out. The same brick wall I crashed into a moment ago slides toward me. He skids to a stop in the middle of the kitchen—that damn smile that makes my heart stop a permanent fixture on his face.

He points at me and Jay-Jay, winking when he roars over the music. "Gotcha. I can't believe you had sock races without me."

I'm going to cry.

Wet suit jacket discarded, his shirt's top buttons are open, and oh, sweet baby Jesus, the sleeves are up.

My heart swells in my chest. Any anger I felt leaves my body on my next exhale.

Jake's laughter booms over the music as Jay-Jay runs into his arms, laughing with him.

I'm pretty sure my mouth is still on the floor when he puts Jay-Jay down, spins around, and starts shaking that perfectly sculpted backside of his like nobody's watching.

Not fair.

He shouldn't be able to put me through such a rollercoaster of emotions in such a brief space of time.

I think I've got whiplash.

Leaning into my hip, I cross my arms over my chest, failing at looking unimpressed.

He can move.

He throws a smirk at me. Like he doesn't know it makes my stomach flutter.

He needs to be careful with those.

Those smiles are dangerous to such a fragile heart.

He shuffles over to me, my anger dissipating with every step closer, and when the rage finally retreats and leaves my body, I smile so wide my face hurts.

"Not funny." He swings his hips. Jay-Jay's knees buckle from laughter. "Careful. You'll do yourself an injury at your age." He turns around and wiggles his ass at me again. I hold out my hands, pushing him away. "Oh, God. Stop. My eyes. They're burning."

But I'm laughing so much now that my stomach is tightening.

He turns serious when he spins back around, taking my hands and dragging me into the center of the kitchen. "Come on. You started this."

God damn it, heart, get back in my chest.

Jay-Jay joins us as Jake spins me around. Then we go back to jumping around like it's the cure for every problem in the world.

"It's not raining anymore. We should show her the place," Jay-Jay roars over the music.

Out of breath, I lower the volume.

"What place?"

Jake looks astonished.

"You want to show her, buddy? You never bring anyone out there."

I shrug and hold my hands out.

I promise I didn't use any of my voodoo spells.

Jay-Jay jumps again. "Yeah."

"Okay then. Ms. Russell, grab your coat and shoes."

"Where are we going?"

He winks. "You'll see."

I'm apprehensive, but I've always been curious by nature, so I race them to get ready.

Jay-Jay wins.

Stepping out back, the yard lights switch on, but the closer we get to the trees at the end of the garden, the darker it becomes. I can't see a thing.

Like they can read each other's minds, I feel the warmth of two hands take mine on either side.

"You need to be careful in here, Claire," Jay-Jay warns, sounding like a wise old man.

"Yeah, watch your step," Jake agrees, but I couldn't fall if I tried. They're both holding onto me like I'm learning to walk.

Another couple steps in, and they stop. Looking up, there's a clearing in the trees, and in the darkness shine thousands of stars.

My mouth falls open.

He wanted to show me this.

Well, so long, heart.

Jay-Jay tugs at my sleeve and points at the sky. "See the really bright star up there?"

I nod, too astounded to form words. "That's my mom."

A sob chokes me, but when I look over at Jake, he simply nods and smiles.

"We couldn't see the stars at our old house. Dad said it was because of the lights from the city."

That's why he moved.

He built a damn house because his son couldn't see the stars.

"Look, Claire, there's another bright one right next to mom. I think that's your friend."

There goes my flimsy composure.

Holding a hand over my mouth, I hug Jay-Jay to my side, my heart so swollen I'm sure it's going to combust.

"Thank you for showing me this. It's beautiful here."

This time the tightening around my hand comes from my other side, and over Jay-Jay's head, Jake reaches and wipes away a stray tear with his thumb.

My heart stops.

The only thing I'm aware of is us three in this clearing, watching the stars in the sky.

Tonight, it's the cure.

It soothes pains, dresses old wounds, and eases the sting of scars.

When an hour later we're sprawled across the couch watching a movie, Jay-Jay's legs across my lap, his sleeping head on his father's, and we're all stuffed from cold, stale popcorn, Jake squeezes my shoulder, mouthing, "Thank you."

I should be the one thanking him and the beautiful boy he has in his arms because I know all the hearts in this house are a little lighter tonight.

Including mine.

EIGHTEEN

Jake was shirtless this morning.

Shirtless and talking to me.

I have no idea what he was saying because he was shirtless.

Half-naked.

Bare flesh.

Coated in a sheen of sweat.

Sweatpants hanging too low on his hips after a workout.

I almost had an orgasm while drooling into my breakfast.

It's his house. He's allowed to walk around how he likes, but he needs to warn me, so I know not to change my underwear until after breakfast.

I've never seen him so casual, so disheveled, and I found myself wondering if that's how he looks after sex.

Another orgasm.

I need to go home and get Henry.

"Does your bodyguard know you're here?" Amy glances at me from the corner of her eye as she finishes ringing up a customer.

I've been in such a daze. I'm standing here looking for a handle to a door that's already open.

God damn Jake and his orgasm-inducing body.

Imagine what his hands can do.

Imagine what his *Henry* can do.

Stop it, Claire.

Amy ignores my glare and my obvious confusion.

I push myself onto the counter when the customers leave. "Jay-Jay is leaving this evening. I wanted to give them time on their own. Although he seems excited to see Ava."

"Mandy's Ava?"

"Yep. Their beach house is next to Mandy's. She tells me Ava is a little smitten by him."

"Oh, shit. How long before Alex threatens the kid's life?"

I laugh. "Not long now. Poor Jay-Jay. He's a sweetheart."

"Claire," she warns.

I hold out my hands. "What? I get attached to everyone. Don't start."

"I'm surprised you're allowed out without the special service."

"I'm under strict orders to only come here and text him when I arrive. As if your skinny ass can fight off an attacker."

"Text him then," she orders.

"Ah, let him sweat."

"Jesus, Claire," she groans, taking her phone from her bag. "I'll do it."

I grab her phone. "Okay. Okay. I'll text him. Since when do you have his number, anyway?"

She joins me on the counter. We swing our legs like children.

"Since my sister has a stalker, and he's the only one protecting you right now."

I roll my eyes.

I hate when they call him a stalker. He made a threat. Once. And yes, it's scary he knows where I live, but I still think they're blowing this out of proportion.

She sways with me. "It's killing you, isn't it?"

"What?"

"Giving up control."

My grunt is enough of a reply.

I'm not giving up control. It's much worse. I'm losing it. I don't have a choice.

"You know it's only for your own safety."

There's a glisten in her eyes, and it kills me.

Chewing my bottom lip, I finally tell her. "His father is a judge."

Fear freezes her features. I know the sinking feeling settling in her gut. I had it the first time Jake told me.

"Then hopefully he'll do what Papa did and disappear."

Squeezing her hand, I hug her with one arm. "It'll work out."

Brushing a curl away from her face, she looks up. "Mama never did anything about Papa because he was a cop in town. The one time she tried, his buddies in the force backed him up. Then he took his rage out on her face."

I flinch, swallowing the bile in my throat.

"They're not all like that. Sam is working hard to build a case."

"For what?" she scoffs, sitting straight again. "To be refused at every turn. Who wants to prosecute a judge's son? We were pariahs after he left. Rumors did the rest. None of them wanted to listen to the truth." She stands, pacing back and forth as tears stream freely from her eyes. I should have kept my mouth shut. "The things they said about Mama having an affair. They spoke about her like she was the one to blame."

I look away, afraid she'll see the truth in my eyes.

"I know. I was there, Amy."

She stops pacing, her face turning a shade of red I haven't seen before. "And what? I wasn't?"

Already exhausted from this conversation, I stand and tuck her hair behind her ear. "You know that's not what I meant."

"It's the truth. I was too busy being selfish."

"Amy, you weren't selfish. You were nineteen. You were living."

"Yeah, but I left you behind, and look how that turned out. Our father almost—"

"He didn't almost anything," I snap, hating when memories assault me. "I'm here. I'm still here. And so are you. You're here now. Let's not go down memory lane," I beg, staring at our interlocked hands.

"I hate that this is happening again," she chokes out, finally calming.

"It happens every day. Unfortunately, Mama isn't the first, and she's far from the last. Papa did us all a favor when he left. Other women aren't so lucky."

She kisses the top of my head. I instantly relax. This is an argument we have too often. She feels guilty because she left. I feel guilty I couldn't change things when she did.

"I don't know how you do it. Work with those women every day. Listen to their stories. You're amazing. I wish Mama would let you help her."

I smile, but it falters. "I wish I didn't remind her of him." Her eyes water again, but she doesn't deny it because we both already know.

Shaking my shoulders, I try to lighten the mood. "We don't have a genie, so that's enough wishes. I'm going to make the same deal with you as I did with Jake. No more stalker talk. I want to pretend it doesn't exist unless we get another update. I live these stories every day at work. I don't want to carry it home with me, and I didn't come here to relive the past. I'm half-expecting the violins to play on their own."

Through a sob, she throws her head back and laughs.

"It's a deal," she agrees, wiping her eyes with her sleeve. "Play for me?"

"Of course."

The music erases the weight on our chests and extinguishes the burning memories. I continue to play even as more customers come and go from the shop, and people are pulled in by the sounds floating out onto the sunny street.

"Can you come back tomorrow?" Amy laughs, kissing the top of my head when I stop playing.

"I should have put out a hat. I could have made a profit."

She sits on the other side of the chair and plays on her end. It's a song from our childhood. Mama got sick of us fighting over the piano, so she taught us music we could play together.

Over the years, we became more attuned to each other, and we just go with it.

As I join in, she asks, "Now that his son is leaving, you're both going to be on your own in that big house, huh?" She wiggles her eyebrows suggestively.

"Stop it. That's freaky."

"So, you weren't thinking about him when you walked in here all flushed?"

How does she see everything?

"Okay, he's attractive, and he knows it. I may have had a mini fantasy."

"Did something happen?"

"No. He was shirtless this morning."

"That's it? As in, you saw his chest? You can go to any beach in the country and see a man's chest."

I smack my lips together. "Not this one."

She grimaces. "If it doesn't have a vagina, I don't want it."

And he definitely doesn't have one of those.

Grey sweatpants leave little to the imagination.

I flush again.

"Claire," she gasps, laughing at my reaction. I stop playing, only to hold my hands over my face, trying to hide my embarrassment, but it's no use.

"It's fine. I'm fine. Now that Jay-Jay is leaving, he'll work all the time. We'll be passing ships."

"In the night," she finishes.

I blow out a breath, frustrated with my lack of control and lack of orgasms today.

"I can't go there. That would be a shit show waiting to happen. Besides, he's married."

She blinks slowly.

Then again.

"I'm pretty sure the *till death do us part* applies here."

"I don't think it applies to him."

His life's purpose is Jess.

I wish it didn't make my heart melt for him, but it does.

I almost get lost in another daydream when she waves her phone at me. "You forgot to text him."

Reluctantly, I pluck my phone from my pocket.

Three unread messages.

He's over the top.

Jake: Did you arrive?

Jake: You'll be the death of me.

Jake: I'm getting in my car.

Shit.

Me: Stay at home. I got seduced by a piano. I arrived at my destination at 14:00. Over and out.

Jake: I don't appreciate your tone.

154

Me: You can't determine a tone over a text message.

Jake: With you, I can. Text me when you leave.

Me: Yes, Sir.

Jake: Careful, Claire. I might make it a requirement for you to call me Sir from here on out.

Me: Careful, Jake. I might enjoy it.

Are we flirting?
I'm on the brink of too many orgasms today.
I text again, putting an end to whatever the hell we just jumped into.

Me: Tell Jay-Jay to have lots of fun. Give him a hug from me.

Jake: Give the kid a break. He's still blushing because you kissed his cheek.

Me: He's adorable. Okay, got to go. Amy is staring at me because I'm ignoring her and texting you.

Jake: Don't forget to text me when you leave.

Me: Yes, Sir.

The bubbles on my screen bounce around for a long minute before he replies.

Jake: I'm changing your name on my phone to Trouble.

Me: I didn't think you'd know how to do that at your age.

Jake: Trouble and infuriating.

Me: What's my middle name?

Jake: You don't want to know.

NINETEEN

"Jake?" I call from my room.

My phone has disappeared.

Or I've left it somewhere, and I don't know where.

I walk to the other end of the landing. His bedroom door is partially open, so I knock.

I've been in this room before, but somehow, I still giggle under my breath when I step inside.

I'm a teenage girl.

Everything in this room is dark—his bedding, the walls, the oak wood furniture, and the grey padded headboard.

It's Jake.

Floor-to-ceiling windows make the trees swaying outside look like a moving picture.

"Jake?" There's a wobble in my voice, and I cough to clear it.

The shower shuts off, and I think about leaving, but I need my phone.

"I'm out here, so don't walk out naked."

I'll never take it.

I'll combust on his carpet.

A plume of steam escapes the bathroom as he steps out.

In nothing but a towel.

Wiping the side of my mouth to check if I'm drooling, my eyes follow each droplet of water as it glides over each muscle.

Lower.

And lower.

Over the deep V in his pelvis before it absorbs into the white cotton towel.

I lick my lips.

I'm jealous of a droplet of water.

"Claire?"

My eyes snap back. My cheeks aren't the only part of me burning anymore.

"Am..." What the hell did I come in here for? "Oh, I lost my phone."

Silence and an amused snigger are his only response.

"Can I use your phone to call mine?"

"Get on the bed."

My mouth falls open.

"Excuse me?"

His eyes narrow. I'm shifting on my feet to ease the throb between my legs.

"It. Is. On. The. Bed," he repeats slowly.

Oh.

I'm fantasizing and hearing things again.

And I'm wet now.

I could suggest he wear a onesie when he's indoors, but I know he'd still look like sex-on-legs.

"Are you feeling okay?"

No. I keep thinking about how, with one movement, I could whip the towel from your waist.

"Great. Thanks."

I turn and grab his phone from the bed.

"You should put a password on this."

"Why?"

"Don't you have sensitive information on here?"

He runs his finger over his jawline and shrugs. "Like what? Anything related to work is already password protected. What else would I have on my phone?"

Shaking my head, I cast my eyes back to his screen. "I don't know. Pictures you don't want people to see." His brows almost reach his hairline. "Never mind."

He steps forward, putting his hand over mine and blocking my view

158

on the screen. "Claire?"

Sighing, I find enough strength to look up at him. His wet hair is falling onto his forehead. I'm reaching out and pushing it back before I can register what I'm doing.

He stiffens under my touch, and I drop my hand like it burns.

In the same breath, his thumb parts my lips.

I'm all too aware of how naked he is under the towel, and my clothes are suddenly itchy. He grazes his finger along the sensitive skin, but I feel it everywhere.

"What have you got on your phone?"

I drop my head. "Nothing."

As he steps back, I almost groan when cool air takes his place. He presses his palms against the bedside table, leans back, and crosses his legs at the ankle.

The corrupted part of my brain is begging for the towel to drop, just for a second. I want proof his grey sweatpants weren't being generous to him this morning.

But I already know the answer.

Everything about this man is intimidating.

I'm sure whatever is hiding under the towel is no different.

He chuckles. It's deep and dark and sends goosebumps across my skin. "You're full of surprises."

"I don't have naked pictures of myself. I'm not stupid. But men are and they love dick pics."

He nods toward his phone. "Check."

It takes all my power to keep it in my hand.

Biting down on my lip, I shoot him a crooked smile. "No need. Your towel has slipped."

He. Doesn't. Flinch.

Cocky bastard.

The towel hasn't moved. I only wanted to make him squirm like I am.

"Put your clothes on, Williams. You're distracting me." I'm not embarrassed to admit it because he already knows. Nobody gets this flustered for nothing.

When I dial my number, the name that pops up isn't mine. "You really changed my name to Trouble?"

"And infuriating," he reminds me.

"What about the middle name?"

"Guess."

"Hmm," I hum, rocking back and forth on my heels. "Sweet?"

He barks a laugh.

Not that then.

"Brilliant?"

It's going to be something less savory, but I enjoy annoying him.

"Amazing? Pretty?" I laugh, but he stops. The twitch of his lips stills me and my smile fades. "You think I'm pretty," I sing-song.

Rolling his eyes, he secures the towel at his waist and walks to the bathroom. "Go find your phone. And Claire, it's not pretty." He glances at me from over his shoulder. "Pretty isn't enough."

He closes the door, leaving me with my hammering heart.

***

I find my flashing phone under my bed five minutes later.

My heart drops into my stomach.

Ten missed calls in the time I've been in Jake's room. All from Amy and Jen.

What the hell?

Hands fumbling, I call Amy, but it goes to voicemail. When I finally get through to Jen, her voice is shaky.

"Oh, thank God, Claire," she lets out.

"What is it? Is Amy okay?"

"It's your mother. She's having a meltdown, and no matter what Amy tries, she won't calm down. She's calling for—"

"Me," I cut her off. I already know. "I'm leaving now. I'll be there as soon as I can."

I'm fumbling with the shoelaces on my boots when Jake strolls into my room.

"I need to go see my mother. I'll be back later."

"You're shaking."

I ignore him.

Why can't I tie my laces?

He crouches, pulls my hands away, and begins tying my laces because I forgot how to perform a basic skill.

"Take a breath. I'll drive you."

"I'm fine, Jake. Nothing is going to happen."

"I know. I'll drive because you're shaking."

160

Deciding not to argue, I simply thank him and grab my coat.

It's been a long time since Mama had a break like this. I should have seen it coming. I felt it the last time I was there. I could sense the distance in her, the disconnect from the rest of the world.

On the way, Jake rests his palm on my knee to stop it from bouncing. I try to concentrate on his touch, but I'm too distracted thinking about what I'm about to walk into.

I don't know what version of my mother will greet me tonight.

When we pull up to my childhood home, my stomach knots. I hate this house. I should have burned it to the ground years ago.

The familiar lump chokes me. Nothing about this place brings memories I welcome. There used to be good times here. Early on, we were happy together as a family. But I store those memories in a box labeled *before*. Everything *after* overshadows all the good. Its strength pushes it back until I can't find the good anymore.

"Claire?" Jake intertwines his fingers with mine, bringing me out of my reverie. "You good?"

I swallow back my fear and nod.

I wonder what he's thinking, pulling up to what looks like a beautiful home.

To me, it's derelict.

The person inside is only a shell, living in a shell of a home.

"It used to be beautiful," I whisper. He doesn't correct me. To everyone on the outside, it is beautiful. I don't know why I feel the need to tell him. Maybe it's embarrassment bubbling in my chest. "She's really house proud. We always had the most beautiful garden in the neighborhood."

That's always a good memory that peaks out of its box. During the summer, if we didn't go to the lake, she spent all day in the garden planting flowers and, in the evening, she played the piano while dinner was cooking. The sound of her playing beautiful music drifting through the neighborhood was always the sound of coming home. I can't remember the last time she played. Or maybe she plays all the time, and I don't come around often enough to hear it. I'd do anything for just an echo of those sounds.

I shake the thoughts away, knowing entering this house always brings ghosts out of the shadows. I can't let it consume me tonight.

I take a deep breath, fill my lungs, and pump my backbone with some well-needed courage.

Time to face it.

"I won't be long."

"Take all the time you need. I'll be right here." He tries to smile, but it falters, and his fingers slip through mine again before I turn around. His eyes land on our hands and then on me, his grip tightening until my trembling subsides. "You're good." The simple tilt of his lips is enough for my heart to stop hammering and my shoulders to relax.

Nodding, I squeeze him back. "I'm good."

I twist my hair in a bun a couple of times before letting it fall to my waist, then scratch at my neck like I can free the blockage.

Amy stands on the front step when I open the gate.

"She's lost it. For real this time."

My sister is exhausted and frustrated.

I get it.

"She only wants you." The bitterness in her tone stings, but I ignore it. "Even Kate came by to help, but she wouldn't talk to her."

"What did she drink?" I finally ask, not meeting my sister's gaze. My eyes roam over the house of horrors.

"What didn't she drink?"

Nodding, I squeeze Amy's shoulder.

The house smells clean, like lemons, bleach, and sage. Which can only mean one thing—she had a sober day and scrubbed until her fingers bled, then rewarded herself with a bottle of whatever she could get her hands on.

"Someone get my baby," she screams from the living room.

She's screaming to herself. Or maybe it's the demons in the wall. I can't be sure.

Oh, Mama.

Dropping my bag, I rush to her side.

"Mama!" I shout, grabbing her face in my hands. "I'm here. Look at me."

Please look at me, Mama.

She does.

She looks at me for one, two, three seconds.

Then frantically, she pats her hands over my body.

"You didn't visit. I thought he'd hurt you."

With my blood struggling through my veins, I look over at Amy standing in the doorway.

Did she tell her about Rob?

Amy shakes her head, answering my unasked question.

I almost burst into tears when I see Jake standing behind her back. "I asked him to come in. We might need him," she explains.

She's right. My mother is close to passing out.

Swallowing my pride, I look back at the stumbling woman in my arms. "Mama," I say quietly. "Come back from the past. Look. I'm here. I'm okay."

Delicately, she presses each finger to my throat. I know what she's doing, and it's going to break me.

"My baby couldn't breathe."

I suck in a shaky breath, feeling my throat burn. Grabbing her wrist, I yank her hand away. "Stop it, Mama. You're not back there."

"If you just stopped screaming. You should have stopped screaming."

"Mama!" Amy shouts from the corner.

She turns away from me and reaches for the wine bottle on the broken piano, but I get there first.

Even angry and desperate for alcohol, she can't find it in herself to look at me.

"Look at me, Mama."

She looks at the floor.

My heart shatters.

But she needs to face this.

"I was trying to save your life."

Bloodshot eyes glaze over, and I can almost see the break. "And I lost my damn mind saving yours."

Each word is like a knife, slicing at me slowly. It's not enough to kill me, but it's enough to make me suffer every cut.

Gasping for breath, she collapses onto the couch, and rocks back and forth. "And I'd do it again. I'd do it again every day."

Kneeling, I sit back on my legs, peel her hands away from her face and start braiding the ends of her hair. She relaxes into my touch.

"Remember when we were little, and you brought us to the lake in the middle of winter? I was too scared to get in because the water was cold. I sat there for so long, just watching you and Amy have fun without me. You let me be. You never pressured me. And when you felt I was ready, you said—"

"Claire Bear, if you never jump in, you'll never know the adventures you're missing," she finishes.

A good memory.

Her laugh is hoarse as she mirrors my fingers in my hair. "You broke your leg that day, baby girl."

Even Amy laughs now.

"That's because she got brave, Mama," she adds.

"But it was an adventure, wasn't it?"

She's still swaying, but she nods.

She's going to crash soon.

"I only have his eyes. My spirit is yours."

Eyes closed, heavy tears fall to her lap. "That's what I fear."

She won't remember in the morning, so fighting the moisture threatening to fall, I finally ask, "Do you hate me because he left?"

A guttural sob rips through her chest before she cups my face and presses her forehead against mine. "I hate myself because *you* left. I lost a piece of my Claire that night. He took it with him like he had a right to it."

I'd give anything to say she is wrong.

She tangles her long fingers in my hair. "You always had the most beautiful hair."

I return the gesture, twirling her dark chocolate strands in my palm. It's shorter than mine.

Her eyes flutter closed, and her weight shifts to my shoulder.

"You made sure of it," I whisper, but she's out. "Okay, Mama. Let's get you up."

I try to lift her, but for such a slight thing, she's heavy.

A firm hand squeezes my shoulder.

"I've got her, sweetheart."

With ease, he wraps his arms around her back and legs. She doesn't stir.

My embarrassment can eat me alive later, but for now, I need to get her into the shower.

"Can you bring her upstairs?"

He dips his chin, walking as if it's the most precious cargo he's carrying.

To me, she is.

My heart twists, looking at him as he watches her, trying to make her comfortable in his arms even when she's unconscious and probably can't feel a thing.

You're in good hands, Mama. I bet his arms are the most comfortable place in the world.

"What can I do?" Amy asks as we go upstairs.

"Can you get me a change of clothes? And maybe some coffee for Mama."

She doesn't ask questions. She simply nods and leaves for her house down the street.

I switch on the shower and check that the water isn't too cold before shaking off my jacket.

Unwavering, Jake stands with her snoring on his shoulder.

"Bet you didn't expect this tonight?"

The smile he offers in return is too sad.

Choosing to ignore the ache in my chest for another time, I pull off my boots and socks and step inside the shower.

I don't look at him, but I know he thinks I'm crazy—standing there, fully clothed and soaking wet, with my alcoholic mother in his arms.

I reach out. "You can put her down. I've got her."

He hesitates, so I nod, eager to get this over with.

A small part of me understands why my mother won't look at me. I can't look at Jake for the same reason. I'm afraid of what I'll see.

He places her in my arms, steadying me when I stumble against the wall with my hands under her arms to support her weight.

It's been a while since I've needed to do this.

"I'll be down soon."

"Claire," he pleads.

"Please, Jake. She'll be embarrassed if she wakes and sees you here."

I'm sliding down the shower wall when he leaves and closes the door.

My mother sputters when the cold water rushes over her face.

It may be uncomfortable, but she's alive.

We both are.

***

My mother is mumbling on the edge of the bed once I finish drying her hair.

I change into the dry clothes Amy brought.

I look like a teenage pop star.

Bubble-gum pink t-shirt and flared jeans.

Did she also go back in time?

She did this on purpose.

Jake appears at the door like he teleported. I still don't understand how he moves around so quietly. Someone so huge should make noise.

In the craziness of what is tonight, he manages to smirk at me. I know he's trying hard not to laugh.

"I know, okay? I look ridiculous. She's not steady enough to walk. Can you carry her?"

"Of course," he says, like it's not the slightest inconvenience. I pulled him away for the night and not once has he made me feel guilty. "Amy will stay with her tonight. It's easier if she sleeps downstairs."

"You can stay. I can come back for you in the morning."

"Thanks, but it's best if I don't. Hopefully, she won't remember I was here."

His eyes pull together, feeling my pain for me.

"It's fine. It is what it is."

Downstairs, I stand in the doorway with Amy as he places my mother on the couch. She stirs, her eyes fluttering open from her drunken slumber.

"You're handsome," she slurs.

Me and Amy share a look before bursting into laughter.

Poor Jake.

She pats his chest. He doesn't move away. Instead, he crouches at her side and allows her the moment.

"I have two daughters, you know?" She looks at him with one eye still closed. "Although you're gorgeous, you're not Amy's type." We're both shaking with silent cackles now. "But Claire, I think she would like you."

Really, Mama?

"You should know—she's a big deal."

Jake takes her hand when she reaches for him. "I've heard."

"Don't break her heart, Mr. Handsome. It's too big. You'll look after my baby girl, won't you?"

She's dozing again.

"Always," he murmurs as her eyes close.

***

"Claire?"

His voice brings me back. I'm too lost watching the trees in the darkness as we drive.

"Hmm?" I turn to him and smile.

"You're lost. Talk to me. Tell me something good."

Filling my lungs, my eyes divert to the trees again. "I got to see you in just a towel today."

His laugh fills the car.

"But I'm exhausted, so you can't remind me I said that in the morning."

He takes my hand and places it on his lap as he drives. I think he's trying to keep me from diving back into my head. "Deal."

The silence consumes me, and the words bubble from my chest and linger on my lips. I don't know why I start talking, but I think he deserves an explanation.

"She wasn't always that way. My father drank all the time, but I never saw my mother touch a drink until my father left," I start, still staring into the darkness.

"I was a daddy's girl. He brought us everywhere on his shoulders. Amy got jealous when she got bigger. If we weren't fighting over who got time on the piano, we fought over who my father's favorite was." His grip tightens, but his thumb massages my fingers.

"I don't remember the shouting. Not as much as Amy. She protected me from a lot. The first time I saw my father hit my mother was the same day I became too big to sit on his shoulders. He said her dress was too short.

"Amy snuck out to a party with her school friends one night, and when I heard my parents fighting, I cried, and I couldn't stop. My father's punishment was to put me out on the front porch in the middle of the night during a thunderstorm. I don't remember seeing my mother, but I'm guessing she was unconscious somewhere. My best friend, Nick, lived next door. His father found me and brought me inside.

"The arguments became a weekly occurrence, but I don't remember it because I wasn't there. The moment I heard them shouting, I climbed through my window and into Nick's bedroom. His window was always open, just waiting for me." I don't wipe the tears. There's no point. "They never asked why I was there. Nick just woke me up for school, and I would eat breakfast with them. His parents did everything to help, but my mother wasn't ready to leave. She couldn't. He made sure of it." Unease rocks in my stomach. "Amy was older.

She was starting to see through him. But he put me in the car one night and told me we were going on an adventure. I don't remember how long we were gone. Two days maybe. But when we got back, my mother was frantic. He wanted to teach her a lesson. He wanted her to know he could take me away.

"When I was fourteen, Amy got a scholarship abroad, so she wasn't around anymore. I don't blame her for it. I would have left too." I laugh to suppress the sob wanting to escape, but nothing about this is funny. "My father was a cop. He received an award for his service. That same night, he almost beat my mother to death. I stood at the stairs and watched as his rage overpowered him. He lost control. I can still hear her jaw shattering." I bite my lips together, the images replaying so vividly, I can almost smell the blood and sweat that lingered in the air that night. "I just screamed. It's all I could do." I grip his hand like it's the only thing keeping me planted to reality.

Going back in time, I run my finger over the raised scar at the back of my head before scratching at my throat. His pained eyes meet mine before focusing on the road. He brings my hand to his lips, kissing each finger. I don't know how his touch holds so much power, but I find the courage to keep going and repeat the words he said to me in my office. "My mother is the way she is because I was the almost that went too far."

I don't realize I'm gasping for air until Jake skids to a stop at the side of the motorway.

"Jake, I'm fine," I protest through a sob, scrubbing my hand over my face.

Jesus, get it together.

"Yeah, fuck this. I'm not."

He's out of the car and unbuckling my belt in the next breath. In one scoop, I'm out and wrapped around his body. His arms don't let my feet hit the ground, and my ankles lock around his waist.

"You're safe, baby. I've got you." I hear his hushed words in my ear as cars fly by us on the road. "God, Claire, I've got you."

TWENTY

I drift out of my light slumber when a cool breeze sweeps across my body. Fighting to open my eyes, they flutter when a warm hand cups my face, a thumb caressing my cheek.

"We're home," Jake whispers, crouching at the passenger side.

I yawn and stretch my stiff limbs, offering a small smile. "I'm sorry. I was awful company on this road trip."

"Absolutely," he agrees, chuckling under his breath as he stands and takes my hand, helping me out of the car. "And you snore," he adds, mischief dancing in his smile. "And drool."

He unlocks the front door, ignoring my panic as I stop dead in my tracks. I pat my mouth frantically, my cheeks already burning.

"Do not," I retort, horrified, but finding no evidence of his accusation. His booming laugh fills the empty house. I elbow his ribs. "Not funny." But his laugh always warms me, and I smile.

Leave it to Jake to help me forget the day—even if it's only briefly.

Because when the silence engulfs me once again, my stomach churns with a ball of anxious nerves, and my chest burns so badly, I touch my skin to check if it's hot.

It isn't.

Just simple pain hammering away in there.

I don't know why I'm surprised. It's always this way after visiting my mother.

Years of rejection doesn't get easier.

Before I allow the threatening tears to fall, I swallow the defeated lump lodged in my throat since we left her house, and I do what makes me the world's worst daughter: I shove it in a box and stick it in a dark corner of my mind.

"I was thinking," he starts as we enter the kitchen.

"Did it hurt?" I joke, biting my lip to stop the laugh.

He doesn't reply to my teasing. He simply glares at me from the corner of his eye, but there's a shadow of a smirk curling on his mouth.

"I was thinking," he repeats. "I know you're tired and probably want to go to bed, but you haven't eaten. I'll order takeout. You can sleep then. Or if you don't want to do that, we can watch a movie, and you can get shit-faced drunk."

My heart swells, and I can't help but smile. I lean my hands on the counter and prop myself to sit on it, my legs dangling against the cupboards.

He doesn't need to do this for me. He's already letting me stay here. Albeit, I didn't have much of a choice. But he's doing it for my safety. And as much as I kicked and screamed about coming here, I'm glad I did. I'm grateful I don't have to be alone tonight.

"Thanks, Jake," I breathe, hoping he knows I mean for everything.

For looking out for me.

For having my back.

For being the friend I so desperately need.

But when his eyes meet mine, I lower my head to my lap from the sheer embarrassment of all he had to see tonight.

Then I forget how to breathe when he curls two fingers under my chin, tilting my head back up.

"Up high. You have nothing to hang your head for."

My heart stops when his eyes land on my lips. It's hardly long enough to notice, but I notice everything he does. I notice every glance. I notice every movement toward me.

"Besides, you're far too beautiful to spend your life looking down. Don't deprive the world."

I gulp, feeling the ball of nerves in my throat settle in my stomach, fluttering around like I've never had a man look at me like this.

Because I haven't.

Most importantly, Jake has never looked at me like this, and I'm surprised by how my body reacts to the wildness in his eyes. Instinctively, we both lean forward, and the next breath I take is the only control I have, hoping it will somehow pull him closer. Hoping it will make me forget because I'm suddenly not thinking about anything else other than how his mouth would taste and what it would be like if he pressed his lips against mine.

Would it be rough or gentle?

My thighs clench, and I run my tongue over my bottom lip.

But what the fuck am I doing?

We can't do this.

Whatever *this* is.

We can't even think about it.

Bad idea.

Terrible idea.

I don't know if his mind goes to the same place as mine, but we both seem to realize what a mistake this would be, and we lean back at the same time. His embarrassment isn't as evident as he clears his throat and dips his chin.

I jump off the counter like the moment never happened. "I don't think I'll sleep. How about you order food? I'll go have a shower and change, and we can watch some chick-flick."

He pulls his brows together, not liking my suggestion. But hey, I'm the one with the mommy issues tonight.

"And we can *both* get shit-faced drunk," I say, ignoring how unimpressed he is by my choice of movie. "Then I'll sleep."

He doesn't argue.

***

I shower quickly, not wanting to give myself too much time alone. Too much time to think. For my thoughts to consume me like they always do. They hurt, and they burn, and they rip me apart from the inside out because even when I'm as clean as I can be, sleep shorts and a t-shirt on, I still look in the mirror and see all the things my mother sees.

Eyes that don't belong to me.

Eyes that hurt her.

Eyes that hurt me.

They haunt every waking memory and terror-filled nightmare. If I could gouge them from my head, I would. I'd do anything to look in the mirror and see something different. To not see the shadows dancing like a ghost behind my tears. But no matter what I do, the pain builds. It boils and bubbles in the pit of my stomach until it's agony, and my body folds, my knees buckling. I open my mouth to scream, but nothing comes out.

Silence.

It's always silence.

Empty sounds.

Nothing to fill the void in my chest.

My throat is on fire, and the memories surround me.

His heavy frame hovered over her fragile body while her eyes struggled to stay open.

"You were perfect once, but now you're a whore." He continued to mumble, most of his words incoherent, his own body exhausted, heaving from the punishment he'd served.

Mama moaned as she tried to pull herself up, the air leaving her lungs sounded painful. He held her carefully, like those same hands didn't just leave her bloody and bruised.

It's over now. He's had his fill. He'll calm down. They'll be better tomorrow.

Mama propped herself up on her elbows, her head bobbing back and forth. A loud inhale echoed around the room, wheezing in her chest, and her golden orbs set into a hard, determined gaze.

"Don't say it, Mama," I whispered, but they didn't hear me from where I was standing at the end of the stairs, my body almost curling into the wallpaper.

Her lips came close to his, so close I'm sure he could taste the copper from the blood running freely from her lips.

"If I'm anyone's whore, I'm his. Amy already despises you. I'm taking Claire with me. Away from you. You're a pathetic excuse for a man."

My heart dropped into the lowest part of my stomach; a lump so thick in my throat I thought I'd choke on it.

I couldn't see his face because his back was to me, but I could imagine his raging glare, his shaking hands, his inability to swallow his anger.

I wished Amy was there.

She'd know what to do.

He raised his fist in the air, the tension along his arm making the veins protrude.

He's going to kill you, Mama.

I couldn't lose her. Not more of her.

So, I did the only thing I could think of. I swallowed the lump away, resolve settling in my blood. I closed my eyes, I opened my mouth, and I screamed.

I screamed until my throat burned. Until my eyes stung. Until the air in my lungs ran out.

I screamed until an iron hold wrapped around my neck, squeezing the scream out of my mouth until it was nothing more than a whimper.

My head crashed against the wall. Something thick and warm flowing down the back of my neck.

My eyes shot open, bloodshot and heavy from tears that wouldn't fall.

"Papa," I tried to say, but I only made a silent motion with my lips.

"You need to stop screaming, baby girl. I don't want to hurt you. I love you. Me and Mama are going to sort it out."

But Mama was sleeping on the floor.

"Papa," I tried to beg, my weak hands beating and scraping his arms, desperate for him to let go. "Please, Papa."

I couldn't feel the floor.

I needed air.

I couldn't breathe.

But Mama was safe.

He wasn't hurting her anymore.

My arms went limp, jerking against my sides.

"I love you. I love you. I love you," he said over and over again, his tears soaking his t-shirt, my tears soaking the hands squeezing the last of the air from my tired body.

My vision blurred, and my body was enveloped by a comforting warmth.

It's over now.

He won't hurt her anymore.

My last attempt to call his name failed. I closed my eyes, my mind and body ready to fall into a deep and peaceful sleep.

My fingers clutch at the rug under my feet, desperate for something to come and take the pain away.

Anything to feel numb again.

People think feeling numb is a bad thing.

Not to me. Not when the alternative is this.

I try to stop it—the tsunami rushing over me, pushing me down, further and further until there's no chance of air.

No light.

Darkness everywhere.

I fight against it, unmoving, but inside I'm kicking to the surface until every cell in my body burns.

And it all comes crashing down. The memories I always fight to bury—the sounds of screams, clashes, dishes smashing, the sound of flesh breaking.

And after…Silence.

Silence always followed. I promised myself that someday I'd open my mouth, but I swallowed the silence until it ate at my words, and my voice drifted away because the day I opened my mouth and fought the silence, I lost myself to my screams. I fought to win, but in the end, I lost. I lost more than my voice that night.

All the tiny memories repeat in my head. Everything that has gotten me here and my mother there.

All the times she looked at me but saw somebody else.

"Claire!"

I don't hear the door opening or what must be the rush of feet, but another silent roar escapes my tired lungs when his arms wrap around my waist, scooping me up from the ground with ease, and out of whatever depths I was climbing into.

"Christ, Claire." Frantically, he brushes my hair off my shoulders. "Sweetheart, look at me."

Everything feels heavy.

My shoulders.

My tears.

My thoughts.

Everything is so dark and weighted.

It's not always like this.

But facing my reality with an outsider there to witness it may have made it too real. It burst the bubble around where I'd tucked the memory of that night.

My body curls in on itself, relaxing into his arms as he sits on the edge of the bed.

Like a security blanket, his hands wash over my body, fingers in my hair, rubbing my back until my breathing evens and my blurry eyes come into focus. I'm not sure how long we sit here—with him soothing my aching muscles from what seems like the inside out. And me, trying to focus on anything other than the war happening in my head.

"Look at me." His voice is soft but demanding, a hint of worry buried under his words.

It's too late to be embarrassed now, so I lift my head, scrubbing the flesh of my palms across my cheeks.

Both hands cupping either side of my face, he erases the last of my tears with the pads of his thumbs, and I lean into his touch because it's bringing comfort I desperately need.

"I'm sorry," I mumble, my voice sounding small.

He shakes his head firmly, the indent of a concerned line between his brows. "Don't. Never. Not to me. Do you hear me?" I just stare at him like he's grown another head. He's walked in on me having the mother of all meltdowns. "Do you hear me?" he repeats, curling his fingers under my chin, forcing me to meet his eyes again.

I only nod before another sob ruptures. The emotions of the day are taking too much of a toll.

"Tell me what to do. It's killing me seeing you like this. What can I do?"

I swallow hard, desperate for my voice to come out in more than a whisper, but it betrays me, and my words become strangled around my tongue, saying things I don't think I realize have repercussions.

"I want to feel. Something. Anything other than this."

His hands stop still on my upper arms when my eyes find his mouth.

I don't know what I'm asking.

I don't even know what I'm doing.

But I don't care.

I shift on his lap, feeling the effects of my words.

He knows what I want.

"Claire?" He searches my face, my name a mere growl from his throat. But his hand slips around my waist, holding me closer.

"Do I look like a monster to you, Jake?"

He rears back with a whoosh, my question knocking what little air is in this room from his lungs.

I bite down on my lip so hard, I'm sure it will bleed.

"Why can't she look at me?" I whisper, knowing he will never have the answers. "I spent my entire life protecting her. I was a child and the parent, and she can't bear to look at me in the eye because I remind her of a monster."

Am I?

His jaw ticks, and with two hands on either side of my head, he holds me firm. I try to look away, but he won't let me. "Look at me," he demands.

I do.

"I'll only say this once because if I hear those words coming out of

175

your mouth again, I'll go crazy. You are not a monster. You're bruised and cracked and hurting. You're fighting. But you're surviving. And for all of that, you're perfect."

My heart cracks wide open. Those little crevices he has chiseled away at for weeks explode into a thousand pieces.

"Then help me feel anything but this pain."

I knead my fingers into the hard muscles in his shoulders, his body tensing beneath me, my thighs clenching in response. Because if I'm finding comfort in his arms, I bet I'll find even more in his bed.

It's hungry. It's desperate. It's raw.

And then I recognize what I saw in his eyes the first day I met him by the beach.

Pain.

The whisper of a ghost.

Our ghosts are different, but they haunt us the same.

"Don't you want that too? I see the pain in your eyes every day. Don't you want a night—just one night—where you're not consumed by the gaping hole in your chest?"

The fire in his eyes is tamed. It's still blazing but controlled.

His touch becomes softer as he strokes his thumb across my cheek, following the path he's outlining on my face, and I stop breathing when he slowly runs it over my lower lip. "It will change things."

"Only if you let it."

"You deserve more than what I can offer you, Claire. I can't give you more. This is all I have. It's not sweet. It's not gentle. That man is long gone."

"Good," I breathe, my lungs screaming for more air. I don't want sweet and gentle. I want to forget. "I'm not a doll. You won't break me." I worry my lip between my teeth. "I'm not looking for a happily ever after. I won't cling to you. You won't have to run from me. Nobody ever does. I always run first."

He flinches, but it's true. You can't get hurt if you don't stick around long enough.

His fingers dig into my spine, as if he's afraid I'll fall apart if he lets go.

Maybe I will.

"Help me feel, and I'll help you forget."

Or remember.

"Claire," he rasps against my ear, pressing me flush against him.

176

"Don't worry, Jake. I've spent my entire life with people looking at me and seeing someone else. One more can't hurt."

Another flinch.

This time he drops his hands, and the absence of his touch causes me to shudder.

"Jesus Christ, Claire."

Well done. You've horrified him.

But I'm giving him what he wants. It's a simple transaction.

For one night, we can help each other.

But when he doesn't move or say a word, my body tenses, embarrassment creeping in until my cheeks burn, and I want nothing more than the world to open and swallow me whole.

Silence.

And more silence.

More silence than my injured ego can take.

What the fuck am I doing?

Panic takes hold, and the glossiness in his eyes is screaming something at me.

Pity maybe.

Anger?

Hunger?

Thinking I'm fucking delusional?

My best guess is all the above.

But he has no right to look at me this way.

"Don't fucking judge me. You have no idea," I snap, fighting the burn behind my eyes, willing the tears not to fall again because this time, they're not for my mother. They're for how crazy I sound, and how I allowed the anger to control me until I could hardly breathe.

Attempting to stand, I make it halfway before he jerks me back to him. He pulls my legs to either side of his waist, goading me as I straddle him. He sucks in a breath, hooded lids daring me to keep his gaze. But like the coward I am, I look away, his intensity making my heart pound so hard against my chest, I'm sure he can hear it.

I want to fight him, to scream at him to let me go. But when he holds my face with both palms—enough to almost hurt—I know he won't let me move. I try to look away again, to move, to escape the boring hole he's staring through me, but he won't budge. His scent invades me. Cedarwood and peppermint and roaring masculinity. All fucking Jake and my head spins.

"I have no idea?" he snarls. "Listen here, princess. Don't fucking tell me what I know. This pain. I've lived with it for long enough to recognize it when it's staring back at me."

He sees it too.

He closes his eyes, swallowing hard, his frustrated breaths making his chest heave, and every time it brushes against my breasts, I try not to squirm.

"If you want something. Ask for it."

I hold his stare, trying to read between the lines.

He doesn't want me to beat around the bush, and I'm diving too much inside my embarrassment to even utter the words, so I do the only thing I know how at this moment.

I deny.

Because denial may keep my heart intact.

My breathing is too shallow, and I can't seem to fill my lungs. My voice sounds weak, and even I'm unconvinced when I say, "I don't know what you mean."

A slow, uneven, and devilish grin curls at the corner of his mouth. "Don't go coy on me now, sweetheart." His thumb strokes the base of my throat, applying enough pressure for my eyes to roll, and my thighs clench on his lap.

He couldn't have not felt that.

Jesus, Claire.

But when I shift my position, I feel exactly how hard he is between my legs, straining against his slacks. He tilts his hips, and my head falls back, foggy with need. The rough pad of his thumb pulls my lower lip from the hold of my bite.

"Say it," he demands, edging so close that my breath catches in my throat. "Tell me what you want."

Why is he doing this?

What does he want me to do?

Beg?

No, thank you. I'd like to keep my pride intact, even if my dignity has fallen to shreds.

Feeling a burning flush across my body, I press my palms to his chest, pushing against him, and straightening my legs until I'm upright.

I'm embarrassed and angry. And yes, the man turns me on to no end, and right now, I hate him for it.

"Fuck you, Jake. If you don't want me, you only have to say." I rush out of the room as fast as my legs will take me. He doesn't get to see me bare my soul until I'm raw and then pick at the wounds.

"Claire," he calls after me as I round the hallway. I'm almost to the stairs when his voice booms against the walls. "Goddammit, Claire. Stop!"

I stand still, stuck to one spot, unable to put a foot in front of the other. I already hear his footsteps stalking toward me. I turn around as he reaches me. Goosebumps prickle my skin, and I blink away the tears threatening to fall.

He leans closer, our lips almost touching, his eyes never leaving mine. "Don't fucking tell me what I want. Especially when it's something I've thought about since the day I set eyes on you."

I gasp, filling my lungs and unable to let it go again.

He's thought about me.

In that way.

About us doing...

Holy shit.

"You have?" My voice is breathy. I don't have to say it, my words are drenched in lust, and my panties are no better.

"I've thought about fucking you on every surface in this house since the moment you walked through my door."

Oh.

Heat swarms in my belly, my breasts aching for his touch.

Anywhere.

I need to feel him.

My back meets the wall. I didn't even notice him leading me here. I straighten my spine. There's no going back now. Not that I know he wants me too.

I press up on my tiptoes. He's impossibly close.

"Even here?"

His eyes shut, and he groans. Then I feel the firm grip of both hands on the back of my thighs as he lifts me high around his waist.

"Even here," he agrees, his voice husky.

He swallows.

I swallow harder.

"I need you to tell me what you want, Claire."

Be bold.

Be brazen.

Just say it.

179

"I want…" My insecurities get the better of me. I'm not known for my lack of confidence, but I've never been this forward, and Jake is prying it out of me like he'll die if he doesn't hear the words.

Or he'll put me back down, say goodnight, and we'll start all over tomorrow.

And that option doesn't involve him being inside me tonight, and I honestly think I'll go crazy if that were to happen.

"Claire, you want me to what?"

Three deep breaths.

Count to five and…

"You. I want you, Jake. I want you to fuck me."

He sucks in a breath. More silence for a moment. The only sounds filling the hallway are our heartbeats pounding in our chests.

Feeling his muscles tense beneath my fingers, I dig my nails into his shirt, but I'm unable to find purchase, even as I slide further down his toned torso.

His lips brush mine as he whispers, "I knew you were going to be trouble."

I know I'm wrong.

This will change things.

But my foolish, aching heart won't listen.

And I need to protect it.

As if sensing my hesitation, he slips back but only an inch, our chests still pressed against each other, my breasts heavy from the friction.

"We need rules," I say, my voice barely a whisper, hushed in the atmosphere of this landing. "If we're going to do this, we need rules."

Whiskey eyes coat over me, and those alone make me dizzy.

I'm drunk on him.

An addict.

And I know the further we dive into this, I'll become intoxicated, and I won't be able to stop.

He cocks a brow. My heart slams against the walls of my chest when I notice a brief moment of amusement.

"I know where this is going. For me and for you, we need rules."

His throat bobs as he swallows hard. Another animalistic flick of his hips, and my head falls back against the wall.

"Rules," he agrees with a dip of his chin.

My nerves creep in until they're clawing at my insides. But I know

I can't back away from this.

"Don't kiss me."

There's a flash of realization.

This isn't just for me.

This is for us both.

I know if he kisses me, I will fall so deep and so hard into him, I will lose myself. Maybe not all of myself, but I will most definitely lose pieces, and truth is, I've already lost too many. I don't have enough to make me whole.

The wall beneath me feels cool against my skin, and I concentrate on that.

I know this look.

It's recognition.

He knows.

He knows what kissing involves, and there's an intimacy to that neither of us can deny.

This isn't about intimacy.

It's not about love.

It's raw, it's primal, it's bared back. It's clawing at flesh and taking what's underneath.

We both want the same thing.

We want to pretend.

It's sick, but so am I.

This heart has been withering for a long time.

"No kissing," he replies hoarsely, his breath mingling with mine.

"One night," I say, determined, knowing that I need this, and I allow myself to do it.

I need one night.

He needs one night to pretend. To fall into oblivion. To nip this attraction in the bud and release it from our system.

We'll feed our hungry curiosity and move on.

"One night," he agrees against my mouth.

Even after setting our rules, the same want is in our eyes.

I need him.

I need his body on mine.

I need to feel.

I just need.

I probably need more than I'm asking for, but I don't have time to dwell on it as his hand fists in my hair, tugging as his mouth finds the hollow of my neck. I shiver, so wound up I almost come undone. Still flat against the wall, his body is hot, burning, and I'm engulfed by blue flames licking my skin. My moan is loud, becoming strangled in my throat as my voice betrays my body.

There's an unspoken rule.

One neither of us dare to speak because when we do, it will give weight to our confession. To our promise.

No falling in love.

His tongue lashes against my skin. I know in my heart it's not strong enough to mark, not strong enough to bruise, but it does.

An electricity fires throughout my body until I can't take it.

"Jake," I cry.

He peels me from the wall. I wrap my unsteady arms around his neck, climbing, wanting support, anything his body can offer.

He walks in the opposite direction from where we came.

We're not going back to my room.

We're going to his bedroom.

His bed.

His territory.

Inside, he sets me on my feet, only to step away from me.

He wants to look.

"Strip," he orders, his voice full of primal lust.

Running my tongue along my lower lip, I don't argue. There's nothing in his demanding tone left to argue with.

He's a man that knows what he wants, and he's used to getting it.

I'm what he wants.

The thought alone sets goosebumps racing across my skin.

His eyes dance over me, undressing me whether or not I do it.

Clawing at my sweater, I pull it over my breasts. I didn't put on a bra after my shower, and he instantly notices, his spine becoming ramrod straight.

My nipples draw painfully tight, watching as his gaze slicks over me, desire making my knees lock. With fumbling hands, I discard my sleep shorts.

I'm naked.

I'm naked in front of Jake.

It's more than just in the flesh because his eyes show me something I never expected to see when I asked for this.

He sees…me?

Or is he looking at me in search of somebody else?

Inhaling a shaky breath, I decide to return to pretending.

I don't know who he sees when he looks at me, and I don't want to think about it.

I don't want to think at all.

Isn't this the point?

Our gazes lock for a long beat, the sight of him consuming, branding me with scorching eyes. Our staring snaps, but the air around us only grows thicker, and no matter how hard I try, I can't get enough oxygen to satisfy my greedy lungs.

Dragging his eyes across my body, he slows as he takes me in. My breasts, my abdomen, my sex, all the way to my toes, and back to my face. Like a lasso, I'm hooked to every slow pull.

Why haven't I felt this before?

With anyone?

I loved Caleb, didn't I?

And yet, I never felt the pure electricity as I do when Jake looks at me. It's thunder and lightning striking across my body until I'm no more than flesh and bone.

Bare.

For him.

"You're fucking beautiful."

With his confession, my mouth goes dry because I've never heard anyone speak to me with such conviction.

He doesn't avert his gaze again, not once as I walk closer to unbutton his shirt, holding back on ripping it apart so I can finally uncover what's beneath.

Taking my time, I skim my nails across his shoulders, whimpering when his muscles go rigid across his chest. Knowing I cause such an effect on him pumps me with confidence. Palm flat, I guide my hand over his abdomen, my fingers treasuring every inch of silky olive flesh.

My hands tremble with nervous anticipation.

He stops my movement, placing his hand over mine as it hovers above the waistband of his slacks. Holding my jaw in a gentle grip, he tips my head back to look at him, and what I see knocks the air from my lungs. Desire burns deep, but he spares me a moment to show a soft smile, giving me another chance to back out.

He's in this.

He's not going anywhere, but he wants confirmation.

I nod, not expecting the gentle stroke of his thumb across my jaw. His other thumb dances the same motion on the back of my wrist.

His voice is gruff when he says, "Baby, you're safe with me."

My body goes lax, leaning into him for the support I so desperately need, and my blood boils, rushing through my veins, ready to explode.

And I do.

I lose it.

Unable to wait another second, I break our gaze, only to unbuckle his belt. His reassurance has calmed my trembling hands, and I manage to pull the leather through the loops in seconds, the sound making my core flood.

The belt drops to the ground with a thud, but I hardly hear it as my heart whooshes in my ears. Releasing the buttons on his trousers, I push them around his ankles, hyperaware of every second I can feel his breath in my hair. He toes the material until they're off, and then all that's left between us is the thin material of his boxers.

My eyes widen at the bulge straining against the cotton, and I shudder, feeling every hard inch of him against my stomach.

A skilled hand wraps around my waist until my body is flush against his.

Suppressing a moan as I wet my dry lips with my tongue, I cling to his shoulder with one hand while lowering the other into the waistband of his boxers, freeing him, and discarding the material with the rest of our clothes.

Excitement builds, making my head spin.

Lowering my starved eyes, I wrap my fingers around the sleek length, my thighs clenching in response. I devour him, taking in everything.

This man isn't just big in stature, and I'm suddenly glad he showed me the softness in his eyes just moments ago because if he were to take me with any hint of anger, I'm sure he'd rip me in two.

His head falls back as I wrap my hand around the base of his cock, appreciating the feel of him as I give one tug and soothe my thumb over the tip.

"Fuck, Claire," he rasps.

He guides me backward until my legs are against the bed. My thighs meet the mattress, and I fall back.

Totally at his mercy, I glance up at him, finding no evidence of the intimidating man I'm used to.

Another slow smile.

More reassurance.

You're safe with me.

It works. I've never felt so untouchable in my life.

His muscles, the set of his jaw, maybe even a part of his heart may be hard, but when he looks at me with those molten eyes, they're burning but yielding, forgiving, and easy.

He doesn't look at me with indifference.

He looks at me, and I don't see the reflection of somebody else.

Carefully pushing my shoulder, he guides me until I'm flat against my back. He takes that moment to engulf me. It's almost like he's taking every inch as part of an inventory. He scans over my features, restraint causing a line between his brows.

He's focusing.

And it's all on me.

I should be self-conscious or cower away, but I don't. The time for shyness has long since passed. And I don't know what he's doing, but he makes me feel like I'm the only woman that's ever been looked at this way, and it heals my wounded confidence. I place my hands at my side, my hair like a halo around my head.

But I'm nobody's angel tonight.

The devil won this battle.

He can look.

Mouth setting into a hard line, there's a hint of a familiar agony, and I don't expect him to repeat the same words: "You're beautiful, Claire."

I feel the weight of him press me further into the mattress and his skin is so hot against mine, I melt into him. Digging his hands into the matress on either side of my head, he cages me in with strong arms, and his mouth is above my ear as he whispers, "I'm going to make this feel good for you, baby."

I shudder violently, already willing to beg for more.

Sliding my thighs against his narrow waist, locking my ankles at his back, I force him closer.

His breathing is heavy, and I'm glad for it because I don't think I can breathe at all. He's doing it for us both.

"Please, Jake," I plea, and I'm surprised when the embarrassment doesn't surface.

A long second.

Another.

A painful breath escapes him, and he's everywhere.

Bruising fingers dig into my hips, his mouth finding my nipples, taking each one and sucking, teasing, and nipping until I cry out beneath him. He tastes every inch of me, a skilled mouth over my stomach, my thighs, my calves, leisurely working his way back before flicking his tongue over the sensitive skin of my inner thigh.

I buck against him, my body unable to take more teasing.

Drinking me in, his tongue takes a single caress of my core, the sensitive bundle of nerves contracting to the feel of him, and I instantly leap, my back arching off the bed.

"Fuck yes," he groans. The vibration against my already sensitive clit has me fisting the bedsheets. He slips a single digit between my folds before it's his mouth again. The power of his tongue has me jerking away, and liquifying against him all at once.

He glances up.

Another soft smile.

More reassurance.

You're safe with me.

Then he grips my hips, yanking me closer until he's buried within me. His mouth is punishing, unforgiving, and relentless. He continues until the burn begins to build. I feel the slip of a single long finger entering me, punishing me from the inside out. My body is desperate for release, and as if reading me, he adds another finger, and I lose it. Too much heat swirls in my stomach and my thighs quake.

I cry out his name louder and harder than I've ever cried a man's name before.

But as I chase the orgasm, he releases me, and I almost cry for a different reason.

He stands on muscular thighs before leaning over, coming so close my heart stops when I think he might kiss me.

He doesn't.

Instead, the words from his mouth almost make me unravel.

"I want to watch you come while I'm inside you." A growl rumbles from deep within his chest.

He hasn't even been inside me, and I know I've gone too far.

It's in the way he looks, never taking his eyes off me, even when he fishes a condom from his drawer, ripping the foil and slipping it over his engorged cock. There's a glint of something. The same flimsy thread I'm holding onto is daring me to snap it.

And even though his mouth hasn't touched mine, it doesn't mean I don't feel it.

I feel it everywhere.

It's dark in this room, but the moon cast enough light through windows for me to appreciate him as he stands. Our only audience is the trees howling in the wind.

Before I take my next breath, I'm on his lap, my back still flat against the sheets as he pulls my legs up around his shoulders. My body vibrates.

Anticipation courses through my veins because I know he's big, and he's probably going to break me, but I know I'm going to enjoy every second. I dig the heels of my feet into his shoulders, slowing him.

His chest heaves as he inches a hair closer, enough to watch my face.

I can only imagine what he sees—lust-filled eyes, no shame in how my mouth parts, or the unspoken pleas from my tongue.

That familiar smirk etches on his lips. The same lips that were wrapped around my sex only moments ago, licking me with expertise until I almost exploded on his tongue.

"Jake," I warn, suddenly nervous.

"You can take it, baby." He winks, and I know I'm done for.

He doesn't thrust into me the way I expect. His knees dip into the mattress, my legs stretching higher on his shoulders. His cock slips up and down the wetness of my core, teasing my entrance, and immediately, I feel the stretch.

I whimper, shutting my eyes.

He stills, unmoving, the tip of his erection inside me. The pad of this thumb brushes my lower lip, down my throat, his hand squeezing briefly until it dips into the valley of my breasts, stopping only once to pluck at my nipple. He continues his journey, his eyes still on mine as he travels lower.

Lower.

And lower.

Pressuring his thumb against my clit, I shudder against him once more.

"Jake," I swear.

If I cry his name one more time, it will become imprinted on my body.

It probably always will anyway.

He doesn't give in to my begging.

And is he…grinning?

This bastard is smiling at me.

He dips his thumb into my mouth, running it along my teeth, and I bite.

Wincing, he hisses my name.

He pulls my lower lip from my teeth. "You know that drives me crazy."

"I hope so."

He takes his time, slowly pushing further. It takes everything in me not to scream. I dig my teeth into the knuckles of my fingers to suppress it.

The moment he sees me do it, he rips my hand away.

"Don't," he warns, every second filling me more. "I want to hear you. Tonight, those sounds are mine."

I claw at his arms, fighting the sting. But it only lasts a moment until pleasure takes its place, my knees quivering, thighs trembling.

"Christ, Claire," he groans, throwing my legs to either side of his waist.

Arms caging me in, he looms above me.

Face to face.

Chest to chest.

We don't kiss, and somehow, I regret ever making the damn rule because with a kiss we can close our eyes, feel each other's mouth, and swallow each other's moans.

But with this…We stare. We watch. We look at each other. Through each other.

At first, it's one slow thrust of his hips after another. He's hardly moving, yet it's just as intoxicating.

Then he begins the torturous onslaught of his cock inside me.

He cups the side of my face, his thumb finding my lips again.

"God, this fucking mouth," he grumbles, every dirty word causing me to clench around him.

He pulls out completely, filling me again in the same breath.

Over and over.

My body shakes, my breathing erratic.

"Harder, Jake."

I need it harder because I can't look at him anymore.

It turns out—his eyes are more deadly than his lips will ever be.

He stills, and before I know it, he draws back, pulls out, and I'm left empty.

Cold.

My heart drops with the sting of rejection prickling in my throat.

What the fuck?

"You don't need harder." The words are hardly out of his mouth, and he flips me over so fast my stomach somersaults. I squeal, pursing my lips to stifle the nervous giggle. "You need deeper." His tone leaves me with little to laugh about and suddenly there's a nervous knot forming in my stomach.

Deeper?

He can't possibly go any deeper.

I fumble, my body already too spent to support my own weight. He takes over, grabbing me at my waist until I'm pressed against him once more, my face flat against the pillow, nails scratching at the material so hard, I'm going to rip it.

Jake is used to getting his way.

In everything.

In his boardroom, his bedroom, and now with me.

I usually like control. I hate losing it. With Jake, I don't know what it is, but I easily submit to him. His words replay in my head every time doubt sneaks up and eats at me.

You're safe with me.

I'm a psychologist's wet dream.

I lost control once. Then I fought to win it back, yet here I am, willing to give it over to Jake.

But here's the thing: this time it is *willingly*.

I have control over my control.

I hold all the cards here.

I don't even realize my smug smile when I glance over my shoulder, watching him position himself. As if sensing me, he catches me watching him, the look on my face drawing a hushed chuckle from his chest.

Slap.

Right on the ass cheek.

I moan and back into him.

A devilish smirk curls in his mouth, the dark fire in his eyes knocking the breath from my lungs. "You really are something else."

He doesn't give me time to think about anything before he pushes into me. No going slow or warning this time.

I struggle to adjust to his size, but my treacherous body is already growing familiar.

Fucking deserter.

Calling out, I hear my voice echo around every dark corner of the room. His response is a satisfied groan.

For every scream, he thrusts harder, knowing exactly what he's doing to me.

And I only feel him.

The unbearable pain in my chest is nothing but numbness now.

Memories don't invade my mind.

I don't think about why I'm in this house with Jake in the first place.

I can breathe.

I'm on the brink, my eyes blurring as I fall closer toward complete oblivion. Then those skilled fingers dip between my thighs, rubbing my core until I'm nothing more than molten. The licks of his fingers become more demanding, drawing the orgasm with so much skill, I see stars.

The sensation of his soft lips pressed against my spine tips me over the edge, the tenderness of his kiss a complete contrast to the way he's working my body.

I detonate.

Every inch of me shaking, I come with his name lingering on my lips.

Steadying me with both hands on either of my hips, he pushes in and out of me with abandon. He never loses rhythm as he closes in on his own release.

Shocked by my body's response to him, another orgasm rattles my bones.

My name is the last word floating in the air as we both come undone, lost in each other.

His panting slows before he collapses beside me.

Chests heaving, and both coated in a sheen of sweat, we turn to look at each other, the effects of what we just did slowly creeping in.

He cups my cheek.

Another soft smile.

"Don't." He presses a kiss to my forehead, resting there for a long moment. "We can process tomorrow."

I take his advice and bury the emotions threatening to destroy me.
He doesn't turn away.
We don't put our clothes back on.
I don't leave.
I clean up in his shower.
He joins me, and we start all over again.
We can process tomorrow.
The night is close to demented.
It's fucked up to the highest degree, begging for a whole carved so deep by our pasts to be filled, we drain each other.
We're selfish.
We give everything and steal more.
I don't give myself time to regret it.
Not when I'm with him.

TWENTY-ONE

I wake before the sun rises, feeling stiff and unrested. I tie my hair back, dressing quickly into my joggers and crop top. I slip my arms into a black hoody before grabbing my headphones and creeping out of my room. Jake's bedroom door is closed, and I don't want to wake him. Only because I don't want to look at the face that invaded my dreams all night.

I've had one-night stands before. I've never lost sleep because of them.

And considering we did very little sleep together, I'm exhausted.

I climbed into my bed before he woke yesterday morning, and I didn't see him all day. With Jay-Jay gone, I assume he went into the office. Probably to avoid facing what we did.

I'm not ready yet. I don't want to look at him and see his regret.

I shake my tired limbs, hoping to erase the obsessive thoughts about him too. I feel like a teenager with her first crush.

Fighting yet another yawn, I tiptoe downstairs and into the kitchen. Head in my phone as I start my running playlist, I grab a glass from the cupboard for water.

"Good morning, Trouble."

"Sweet SpaghettiOs," I screech.

The glass tumbles from my hands, bouncing off the counter but not breaking. I scramble to catch it before it rolls to the floor.

Gasping, I spin around, my hand on my chest, trying to calm my erratic heartbeat, but it does little to help. How is this man just as gorgeous in sweats and a t-shirt?

Fucking walking orgasm.

"Don't scare me like that. I almost died."

He chuckles, taking the last gulp of whatever disgusting green shake he's drinking.

"Sweet SpaghettiOs?" he questions, far too bright-eyed and bushy-tailed for six in the morning.

"I wanted to say sweet fuck, but one kid at the shelter has a habit of cursing when he gets a fright. The only way I can get him to stop is to tell him to say the silliest thing he can think of. It works for both of us, it would seem."

"Well damn," he says, leaning his hip against the counter. His mouth curls up into the warmest smile, and it thaws my icy nerves. "That story is so sweet. I think I'm getting a toothache."

I want to roll my eyes, but there's no sarcasm in his tone.

"Call me Mary Poppins."

"Have you always worked with kids?"

He's in a chatty mood.

I blow out a breath, my brain still laying cozy in bed. It's not good to talk to me before I have my morning coffee.

But I said our night wouldn't change things.

This is normal.

I think.

"My first job out of college was in a women's shelter, but the jobs led me toward children. I wanted to move when my friends did. Too young and too scared to stay in the city on my own, I packed up and moved to Penrith. I was lucky. I got a job right away as a caseworker with foster children, and I got stuck. Comfortable."

He runs his fingers through his hair as he hums, shifting his weight from one foot to another, thinking.

His expression softens. That sleepy bed head gives him a rugged appeal. "Do you want kids of your own?"

The question is so out of the blue, I almost choke. I swallow, gawking at him.

"Would you judge me if I said no?"

"I'm not a sexist prick. I don't think a woman's worth is defined by her ability to reproduce."

I wasn't expecting that answer.

"I don't know," I reply honestly. "I love kids. Do I want any of my own? I'm not sure. I've seen women happy with and without children." I finally fill my glass with water, having no idea why I'm nervous.

Maybe talking about reproducing with Jake has me jittery. I don't want babies with him, but it's what people do to make those babies that have me flustered.

"I've also spent most of my life parenting my mother." I try a light-hearted tone, but he frowns, and my chest tightens.

He turns serious, casting his eyes over my face. "Any kid would be lucky to have you in their life. Whether they're yours or not."

I stare into my glass, my throat suddenly stinging. It's too early for so much emotion.

"How about you?" I ask, directing his attention away from me.

"Kids?"

"No, aliens. Yes, kids. Do you want more?"

He cocks an eyebrow. "Aliens would be easier." I laugh, feeling the weight of our previous topic lift. "I think I'm missing something for more kids."

"What's that?"

"A wife," he deadpans.

Now I really roll my eyes. "How about you step out of the dark ages, old man? People don't have to be married to have babies."

He tsks. "Young people." I swallow the water before I spit it out. "I know that. Me and Jess weren't married when Jay-Jay was born, but I always thought if I did it again, I'd like to have what I had the first time, and marriage isn't on the cards. Not for me. Nobody gets that lucky twice."

His gaze turns somber, and it takes all my power not to reach out and touch him.

"Don't rule it out. Nobody knows what tomorrow brings. Or today. You might leave this house today and meet the next love of your life." Thinking of him spending the rest of his life alone makes me oddly uneasy.

He runs his fingers over his lips. "You're a romantic."

I shrug my left shoulder. "What's life without some romance?"

Something dark and hungry flickers in his eyes, dancing over my skin. I take a deep breath because my lungs are suddenly burning.

"I didn't see you yesterday?" It's a dangerous question because I probably won't like the answer.

He flinches, closing his eyes to hide the guilt.

"Processing," he admits so low I hardly hear it.

Yeah, me too.

I get it.

Casting my eyes to the ground, I grab my headphones. "I better go, or I'll never be back in time to get ready for work." I don't look at him because my chest is heaving.

One look from him and everything tingles.

But as I try to walk away, the block that is Jake Williams stands in my way. I try to step around him, but he mirrors my feet.

Craning my neck back to look at him, I blow out a dramatic sigh. "I don't enjoy dancing, big man."

"Where do you think you're going?"

"For a run," I say slowly, in case he's hard of hearing.

His expression remains impassive. He's unreadable, but he's so close that his scent invades my senses, making my head spin.

"There's a gym down the hall."

"Well observed," I reply, trying to keep my voice from breaking.

"Use it."

"I like running in the fresh air."

Still staring.

Still making my stomach tie in knots.

But I refuse to look away before he does.

"It's dark outside. I don't think a run is the best idea given your current predicament."

This is why I tried to be quiet coming down here. I wanted to get out for my run and back before he woke. But the look he's giving me is pure steel, unwavering as he flashes a shadow of a smirk.

He knows he's right.

I know he's right, but I don't want to admit it.

"You're not leaving for a run, Claire. We can work out together."

I swear there's a glint of heat in his stare, and I know we're both thinking of our last workout. Heat rushes up my neck, and his smile widens.

Asshole.

I sigh, my shoulders drooping forward.

He's won, and he knows it.

Raising his hand, he feathers his thumb across my cheek. "You're blushing."

Well done, Captain Obvious. I can't breathe either. Can you see that?

"Am not," I lie, casting my eyes to the ground.

He laughs, low and gravelly. The sound assaults my ears and does unwanted things between my legs.

I feel him inch closer, and my breath hitches. "Afraid to get a little sweaty with me, Claire?"

Oh, mother divine.

Why?

Why does he do this?

My next inhale is shaky, my knees locking, but I fight through. He may have a valid point about going for a run, but I refuse to allow him to win this, too. I'm not going to be the only one fuelled by being horny on the treadmill.

Biting down, I stretch up on my tiptoes, my mouth skimming his chin, his stubble tickling. Wetting my lips, we're so close my tongue touches his skin. He doesn't move, but his every pant is matching mine. My nipples pebble against his chest, and the stiffness in his jaw tells me he notices.

Good.

Fluttering my eyelashes, I take one last sweep of his face, trying not to get sucked in by his hooded lids and the heat radiating from his body, before I whisper, "But I'm so good at getting sweaty on my own."

I purse my lips to stifle the giggle ready to erupt as his eyes widen.

Falling back on my heels, I take a step back, not sure what he's going to do now. His hands ball into fists, the veins in his arms protruding like he's fighting to hold back—and oh, there it is—he's pitching a tent in his pants.

Success.

Patting his chest one last time, I step around him with a bounce.

"Come on, big man," I summon as I leave the kitchen and toward the gym. "I'll even let you watch."

While throwing his head back, he digs his teeth into the skin of his knuckles, biting down, and a groan comes from deep in his throat.

He spins around, the golden specks in his eyes turning dark, pinning me to my spot. He drags his eyes from the floor, dancing over every inch of my body, pulling me in like a magnet. But I still can't move.

One step forward, and my heart leaps into my throat.

Not this again.

"No, Jake," I warn, holding out my hand like I'll be able to stop him with my imaginary powers. I'm pretty sure my full force wouldn't make a difference. "Don't you dare."

Another step.

My throat tightens, and I cough to clear it.

Great. I'm choking on air now.

"Please," I beg, the familiar feeling bubbling in my stomach, and I know it won't be long before I erupt into nervous giggles.

One last confident step forward before he growls, "Run."

Holy shit.

Spinning around, I try to quicken my pace, but it's no use. His strides are too big, and I'm scooped up and wrapped around his waist before I can blink again.

"Stop, Jake. Please." My eyes blur over with tears of laughter, my body bouncing with every easy step he takes down the hall.

I feign a struggle, but when a man like Jake picks you up and runs away with you, you don't fight—you strap yourself in and enjoy the ride.

I try to quench my disappointment when he doesn't take the stairs. I don't know why. We agreed to one night, but the idea of having his body on mine one more time is too much. I know I won't be able to say no because I want it more than I want air in my lungs.

Halting outside the gym, he pins me against the wall, his eyes stripping me bare.

"You're a little more trouble than I expected."

"I hope so," I whisper, breathless and too turned on to form proper sentences.

Hovering over me, he leans forward. His breath across my face causes me to whimper, and the stiffness in his pants is hard against my core. My eyes roll, the friction and having him this close doing little for my resolve. My defenses fall apart, crumbling between us until all that's left is body against body.

His hands leave my legs, one cupping my ass, the other pressed against the curve of my back. Hot mouth against my throat, my head falls back, giving him more access.

Giving him everything.

Across my jaw, he doesn't stop kissing me until his eyes meet mine again, entirely at his mercy when his hand delicately flattens against the base of my throat.

"Have you any idea how hard it is for me to let you go right now?"

Then don't.

Oh, God, please don't.

"I thought having you would stop me from wanting you. But now I know the sounds you make when you come undone, and you've made me an addict."

His head falls against mine.

"Jake…"

Grinding his teeth, he shuts his eyes, and I can almost see his restraint in the momentary dent between his brows.

My eyes feel heavy with tears that won't fall, and my chest is too weighted to even think of breathing.

Painfully, he lowers me back on unsteady feet, his eyes never leaving mine. He keeps me upright with his grip on my upper arms, moving only to place a soft kiss on my forehead.

I close my eyes, relishing in the feel of him.

A quick pulse of his fingers against my skin, and he disappears into the gym, leaving his curse lingering in the air after him.

Flattening my palms, I fall against the wall, hoping to relieve the heat rushing under my skin.

It went too far.

It went too far the moment I stepped inside this house.

Now I'm panting against the wall, wondering why a single tear is leaking from the corner of my eye and why my body is already mourning his absence.

TWENTY-TWO

"Claire," Jake answers because hello must not be the cool thing to say anymore when answering the phone.

"Jake," I deadpan.

"I'm in the middle of a meeting, so anytime you're ready."

"Oh shit. Sorry. I can call you back."

A door clicks in the background. "I stepped out. Is everything okay?"

"I'm just calling to let you know I'll be late this evening."

There's silence for a moment before he responds. "Why?"

"I have a date."

His breathing picks up, and I purse my lips to stop myself from laughing.

"I'm kidding," I say before he has an aneurysm. "I'm going shopping with Amy. I don't have a dress for the auction next week."

Because I've been too distracted by you.

I'm half expecting him to argue with me about it, so I'm shocked when his only reply is, "Just keep in contact."

As if I'm going to be kidnapped.

"Some of the guys are coming over for poker night, but I'm going to cancel."

"Don't cancel. Don't change your plans just because of me. It's your house." And I already feel guilty enough.

Silence.

"Jake, please."

"If you're sure?"

"I am. Guys need playtime too."

"Claire, I need to go."

Charming.

"See you later."

"Don't forget to check in," he reminds me.

"Yes, Sir."

He groans.

***

Smiling like an idiot, I push the kitchen door open with my ass—my hands too weighed down with bags to use my motor skills. The rustle of my bags makes my appearance more of an announcement as I spin around and see Jake and the boys playing poker at the table on the far side of the kitchen.

"Hey, Claire," Pete and Sam holler, hardly looking up from their cards.

Offering an apologetic smile, I hold out a heavy hand and gesture for them to continue.

"I'm only getting a bottle of water. I'll be out of your hair, and it will be a woman-free zone once again."

Jake doesn't say a word, leaning an elbow on the back of his chair as he takes a gulp from his beer bottle, but it's me he's drinking in. Hot amber eyes rake over my body, and it sizzles all the way to my toes.

He cocks a brow and then tilts his head toward the clock, like I'm on a curfew.

Whatever, Dad.

I roll my eyes.

He smirks.

My gaze averts to another man sitting at the table.

New man.

He's brand spanking new to me, at least.

"Hey." He salutes. "It looks like none of these assholes are going to introduce me. I'm Logan."

Walking to the table, I reach out and shake his hand. Strong hand. Muscles flex on his tattooed arms as he stretches, his dark beard giving a masculine feel to his boyish jade eyes. "Claire. Nice to meet you. Nice

200

tattoos," I compliment.

"Thanks."

Logan is cheeky. The peek at my cleavage as I lean over almost went unnoticed.

Not by Jake, though.

A quick look in his direction has me almost grunting. If his jaw doesn't snap from tension, the hole he's boring through the side of Logan's head will surely give him away.

He takes another long drink.

"Logan has a tattoo shop in the city," Pete explains.

"I've always wanted a tattoo," I voice my thoughts under my breath, trying to distract myself from Jake's molten glare.

I don't have to look at him to know his eyes are on me.

I feel it.

I don't know why, but I always feel it.

Pursing my lips, I fight the pull, concentrating on Logan as he takes his seat again. He tugs at his black t-shirt, hanging loose over his stomach, but his biceps are struggling with the material.

Is he flexing?

"Nice to meet you, Claire." His smile is warm, but it's no match for the icy man sitting next to him. "You settling in okay? Jake tells me you moved back here recently."

"It's great."

Apart from having a stalker.

But I don't say that, choosing not to dull the atmosphere. I think stalker-talk would be an instant mood killer.

"And my roomie here is all sunshine and rainbows, as you can tell."

The guys unsuccessfully try to stifle their laughter.

Pete plucks crisps from a bowl before looking up at me as I rest my palm on the back of his chair. "He's been watching the clock like a madman. Now I know why."

They're teasing him, but knowing he was worried makes me shift on my feet, surprised by the rush of heat in my stomach.

I wait for him to deny it, to tell them to fuck off for telling me or play it off like it's nothing, but he doesn't say a thing.

I risk a glance at him, only to be pulled into dark honey eyes. There's the tension in his shoulders only I would notice, and the indent of a frown between his eyes.

He was worried, and if I know Jake, it probably killed him not to

201

pick up the phone, or better still, get in his car and look for me.

I told him I was going shopping. What more can I do?

And now, I'm not sure if the look in his eyes is anger or if he wants to punish me in the most delicious way. Chewing on my lip, I fail to concentrate on suffocating the fire burning in my chest or the tingles unfurling between my legs.

"You're good?" His voice is thick and coats over me, confirming my suspicions. He's both relieved and turned on that I'm back, and the notion makes me want to jump into his arms…or his bed.

I nod, still transfixed. "I'm good."

"It was getting late." It's all he says, and it's the only explanation I need.

"Shops were open late. We had fun."

He tips his chin, understanding. "Good."

The tension rolls off us, and I feel the shift, the weighted air becoming lighter. He leans back again, more relaxed.

Better.

Those full lips edge up into a slow grin, reaching his eyes, and washing over me like a soothing balm. With another drink of his beer, he winks, and the breath I don't know I'm holding escapes in a whoosh.

"Grab a beer and join us, Claire." A voice knocks us out of our oblivion.

It's Logan again. Pulling over a chair, he slots it beside his and taps on the back of it.

"Oh." Why am I nervous? And it has nothing at all to do with Logan. I throw my thumb over my shoulder. "I just want to have a shower." I swear there's a groan from my left. "It's been a busy day. I'm just going to grab my water and relax in my room. You men can do…" My eyes scan the table. I've never played poker, and I have no desire to learn. "Whatever it is you do."

Saying goodnight, I grab my bags and water, feeling eyes on me with every step I take.

Before the kitchen door clicks closed, I hear Pete's voice. "She's home. Are you going to stop watching the fucking clock now and play?"

I can't help but smile.

***

202

An hour later, I'm downstairs again after spending most of my time showering and lathering my body in my new honey body butter. It smells like heaven, and I keep sniffing my arm.

The rain started while I was in the shower, and by the time I finished, thunder was rumbling in the distance. I'm playing off my being here as nothing more than grabbing some popcorn for a movie and not admitting I just wanted company for five minutes because I'm afraid of the weather like a child.

The guys don't seem to mind, and they involve me in conversation, but I'm still trying my best to be invisible when Logan sneaks to my side, startling me. I was too preoccupied with the popcorn bag expanding in the microwave.

I need better hobbies.

Smiling at him, I try to hide my blush as he grabs four beers from the fridge and sets them on the counter.

"What's that smell? It smells like frickin' heaven."

My thoughts exactly.

I laugh, removing the popcorn bag and shaking it before putting it back in. "It's me. I smell like heaven," I joke, holding up my arm to him.

He arches a brow, holding back his chuckle.

"Have a whiff. I smell great."

Cautiously, he leans forward and sniffs.

"Fuck." He backs away. "That is good."

"Body butter," I explain, but he looks confused.

"You rubbed butter on yourself?"

I shift on my feet, his eyes too heavy as they make no apology for sweeping over me. "No. It's like a lotion."

He nods. "It smells amazing." He runs a hand through his messy dark hair, the bulges of his biceps hard to miss.

"Your tattoos are impressive. Did you design them yourself?"

"All but one." He points to a small unicorn inside his elbow, looking completely out of place on his sleeve of black ink. "My niece drew it."

Well, my damn heart.

"I think I just melted. What age is she?"

"My princess is five."

I can't help but grin, my heart swelling in my chest. His hard

203

exterior is deceiving.

"It's beautiful. Maybe she can draw one for me when I finally get balls big enough to get one." I immediately want to suck back the words. They sound too presumptuous and deceiving because I meant it differently than his eyes are suggesting.

"You got any plans next weekend?"

Oh, no. Please don't ask me out. I'm not good at this stuff.

"Am… yeah," I stutter, trying to hide my face behind my curtain of hair. "I've got the charity auction."

"So you do."

I jerk as an all too familiar voice rasps from behind, jumping again when the microwave beeps and a clap of thunder booms through the window.

Give me a break. Please.

"Jittery?" Jake questions, sauntering to the sink, his skin briefly touching mine as he walks by. The contact causes me to jolt, and I wrap my arm around myself.

"Nope," I pop, smiling, and demanding my greedy eyes to stay on Logan as he speaks.

He glances over my shoulder to Jake, eyeing him for a moment before stuffing his hands in his pockets.

I can't help but feel he's testing something.

"I'd love for you to come down to the shop sometime, Claire."

"Like fuck she will," Jake grits low enough for only me to hear.

My gulp is audible.

"You might take the leap and get the tattoo you wanted. You free Sunday?"

My heart pounds, my body flushing.

Why does Jake have to be so close for this conversation? But honestly, I'm searching for a way to let Logan down without sounding like a bitch. He's hot. On par with Jake kind of hot, but he doesn't make my skin tingle with anticipation, and my stomach doesn't tighten at the sight of him.

Opening my mouth to respond, it quickly snaps shut again when Jake cuts in, his body so close to my back, it makes me shiver.

"She can't. She's going to be tied up on Sunday."

I choke on air, swallowing to clear my throat.

I didn't miss the insinuation in his voice, and by the glint in Logan's eyes, either did he.

What is he doing?

Sensing the tension and my cheeks flaming, Logan flashes me a warm smile, his eyes darting from me to Jake.

He's making this too obvious.

"I thought as much." What does that mean? "Maybe another time."

With a stern shake of his head, Jake says, "Not likely, buddy."

Grinding my teeth, I point a finger at Jake while keeping my eyes on Logan. "I'm sorry about him. He's obviously hormonal."

Logan chuckles, dipping his chin before casting a knowing look in Jake's direction.

They're both smug bastards.

I wait until Logan is back in his seat before I spin on my heels. I slam straight into flames, his fiery stare licking my skin. For a second, I forget what I want to say.

"What are you doing?" I whisper, grinding my teeth, and finally finding words.

His expression is impassive, giving nothing away about what's going on in his head. "You don't want to go on a date with Lullaby Logan."

"Why the hell not?"

"I've been friends with him since college. You'll be another notch on his bedpost. Nothing more."

Ouch.

I ignore the sting in my chest, lowering my head in an attempt to cool my boiling blood.

He infuriates me sometimes.

Curiosity getting the better of me, I ask, "Since when do you call him Lullaby Logan?"

"Since right now."

"Why?"

"Because he'll bore you to sleep."

"You don't know that," I retort.

"I do because I know you," he replies with the same even tone to his voice.

"You don't know shit."

He has the gall to snicker.

"First, I'm just a notch on his bedpost, and now he will put me to sleep. Decide. Besides, maybe I'll enjoy *sleeping* with him."

Jesus, Claire, you can do better than this.

My argument is running dry, unlike my panties, because I can't think straight when he stands this close.

Not backing down, I tip my head back.

"Maybe I don't mind being a notch."

He leans an inch closer, crowding me enough for my already thumping heart to leap into my throat.

"I do." He stands straight again, the amusement coiling around his lips. "And I don't share."

What the fuck?

"I'm not yours to share. And maybe the grass is greener on Logan's bedpost."

With a menacing step forward, I'm forced into the corner, my palms flat against the granite, trying to provide some support to my shaky knees.

I'm suddenly grateful for the size of this kitchen, and how the guys are too occupied with their conversation to notice us.

"Jealousy doesn't look good on you, Jake."

It looks fucking amazing on him.

I squash the corrupted and damaged thought to the back of my mind.

"But you look incredible on me."

"Do you always have an answer for everything?"

"Do you always get this wet when you argue with me?" The words roll off his tongue like ecstasy, knocking what little air I have from my lungs as my treacherous body trembles.

I scoff, my eyes leaving his to compose myself.

"Don't answer my question with a question." I press forward on my tiptoes. "I'm not a possession. Put your penis away and stop pissing a circle around me."

He ignores me, running the pad of his thumb across my cheek. When his breath hits my ear, my eyes roll.

Bastard.

"It turns you on to argue with me. You enjoy it."

I do.

"No. I don't."

Leaning back, I press my hand to his chest. "It's a pity there are other people here. You could check for yourself."

"Then don't make a sound."

My eyes go wide, a sharp inhale setting my lungs on fire as his hand slips inside my sleep shorts.

I bite down on my lip to stop the moan and try not to squirm too much to avoid catching the attention of everyone behind me.

Dipping his fingers inside the thin material, a smug grin captures his features. The rest of the kitchen and everyone in it melt away.

"Liar," he breathes, slipping a finger across my core.

I curse my body for giving him evidence that he's right.

"I'm going to assume it's not Lullaby Logan making you so wet right now."

My eyes fall closed as he motions in circles around my sensitive heat, my knees buckling as I cling to his shirt.

I whimper as he backs away. He continues to stare at me as he lifts the same finger and sucks on it like it's the sweetest candy.

Jesus.

My mouth gapes open with a pop before he curls two fingers below my chin, pressing my lips together again.

"Closed, sweetheart. It's far too tempting hanging open like that."

I blink, coming back to my surroundings.

Did I just dream that?

Embarrassment floods my face, but there's no sign from the guys that they noticed anything. I hear a stupid joke floating in the air, followed by hysterical laughter.

But nothing is funny, and I'm suddenly dealing with a heaviness in my pelvis.

Adjusting himself in his slacks, Jake grabs his beer, pokes my nose, and walks away, quickly re-joining the group.

Catching my breath, my teeth grind together so hard I'm surprised they don't crack before grabbing my water and forgetting the popcorn.

I'm not hungry anymore.

I'm about to storm out when Sam pipes up. "You going to bed, Claire?"

My eyes zone in on the troublemaker, sitting back in his chair and scanning me like we share a secret.

Because we do.

Never dropping my gaze from Jake, I answer, "Not yet. I'm doing some D.I.Y."

I shut the door as he sputters on his beer.

***

I hate thunder.

It's a stupid childhood fear I can't shake. But being left out in a storm all night as an eight-year-old stayed with me.

Everything is trembling, and deep breathing or music isn't helping.

I'm tempted to go downstairs again and distract myself by playing the piano. It always helps, but I don't want to interrupt the guys.

My head snaps back as my door opens. I can only see his silhouette in the darkness.

I smile, though he probably can't see it.

It's embarrassing. He shouldn't see me on the brink of a panic attack.

"What are you doing here?"

He steps into the room, and it suddenly feels smaller.

I need more space, not less.

My breath is shaky when he pushes my hair back from my shoulders.

"You're scared of thunder."

I stay still, afraid that if I move, the sob bubbling in my throat will escape.

He remembers.

"Where are the guys?" I whisper.

"I told them to go home."

"Why?"

"Because you're scared of thunder," he repeats.

My throat prickles with emotion, and I cling to his shirt like it's the only thing keeping me from crumbling.

The same warm smile I remember from our first night together washes over me.

You're safe with me.

I flinch as lightning flashes.

"Breathe," he instructs, running his finger over my collarbone, along my shoulders, and down my arms, repeating the motion until my breathing evens.

Our eyes lock, and the familiar pull snaps between us.

"Did you touch yourself?" he asks, leaning closer and pressing his lips to my neck.

He's distracting me, and I grab onto it.

My heart stops listening to my head as I grip his hair at the back of his scalp, trembling with the feel of it through my fingers and his lips below my ear.

I throw my head back and whimper, too focused on him to notice anything else.

"No," I say, my voice husky as I dig my fingers deeper.

He hisses and repays me by nipping my skin with his teeth. "Why?"

"Because I wanted you to touch me. But we made rules. We agreed to one night." My voice is so low, I can't even convince myself.

"I broke it already. I've thought about being inside you every night since you were in my bed. It's driving me crazy knowing you are sleeping right down the hall." His thumb laces over my lower lip. "Fuck the rules."

The thread snaps.

We're pulling each other's clothes off in the next breath.

I'm in his arms, and he's carrying me to the bed in the breath after that.

On my knees, he keeps me upright with his arm around my waist. He pulls my hair back, peppering kisses along my skin from behind. But he never touches my lips.

My addiction to him is too much.

I need a fix, and he's the only thing to satisfy it.

His gruff voice vibrates against my ear when he orders, "Hands on the headboard."

I look at him over my shoulder, cheeks blushing. "Why?"

"Because I intend on fucking you, so I suggest you hold on to something." His fingers spread over my stomach, sliding between my legs. "Now, hands on the headboard, or I'll tie you to it."

As much as I think I'd enjoy it, my body is demanding we don't waste more time.

Biting down on my lip, I do as he asks.

His finger circles my clit. I shudder with my back pressed against his chest.

I'm already close when I feel him sheath himself inside me. I cry out, adjusting to the familiar stretch.

There's another boom of thunder, but I hardly hear it as he does exactly as he promised.

He fucks me.

Hard.

Deep.

In every delicious way I remember.

Keeping me anchored with his arm, he grips my hair, forcing me to look at him, but my body is too wound up, and I'm so close, my eyes flutter closed.

This pool of energy will eventually leave us raw, wounded, and crumbling. I might not know how to salvage what's left of the wreckage, but I know what I need now.

"Open your eyes and look at me, baby."

Our eyes connect, and I explode, shivering when heat unfurls between my legs.

"Good girl. Now scream for me."

I do.

I come with his name on my lips, clawing my nails so hard into the back of his neck, I'm sure it will leave a mark.

Lightning dances across the room, but I only see him.

He doesn't let me go.

Not once.

You're safe with me.

It's a lie.

My body is safe.

I feel it with every gentle touch.

But my heart might be starting to betray me.

TWENTY-THREE

I set the roasting dish on the counter and busy myself getting plates, still wiggling my body around and singing like I have a note.

I don't.

I'm brutal.

"Ah-hem."

My body stiffens, and I slowly straighten, turning to see Jake standing at the kitchen door. His eyebrows rise, and his amused grin is so wide, I'm sure it's hurting his face.

It's not Friday, but tonight is a special group dinner at the shelter. Even Amy is here.

"Please, don't stop on my account. I'm enjoying the show."

I roll my eyes, walking to the table to set the plates down.

"Perv," I tease, but he chuckles.

"Your dancing is great, but keep the singing to a minimum. You'll summon the wolves."

Jay-Jay comes strolling into the kitchen, head buried in his book. "I think she sounded good."

I jump up and down, too excited to contain myself. "Jay-Jay," I scream, running to pull him into a hug and ignoring how his cheeks redden. "I missed you, dude." I poke my tongue out at Jake. "See. I've got a fan."

Now it's Jake's turn to roll his eyes.

Jay-Jay hugs me back before pulling away and straightening his glasses. "I've been gone two weeks, Claire."

He's so much like his father.

"I know." I lean closer and whisper, "But you're more fun than your dad."

"I know," he agrees with a nod.

He's going back to the beach house tomorrow, but I'm glad Jake listened to me when I told him it's safe for him to be here for one night.

I slip my hands into oven gloves and carry the dish to the table. I feel Jake glancing over my shoulder.

"This smells amazing. You said you couldn't cook."

"I lied."

"Why?"

I glance at him from the corner of my eye. "Because you were threatening to put me over your shoulder."

"I'm still tempted."

I smile up at him. "All empty threats, Williams."

He tilts his head like he feels sorry for me. Or maybe he's accepting the challenge.

My stomach flips.

"Sit. Eat. Enjoy."

The women and children come pouring into the kitchen when I call them.

"You didn't have to do this on your own, Clare. We don't mind helping." Mia hugs me.

"I know, but you're leaving us tomorrow. I wanted to see you off properly."

Her eyes water. "Thank you. I'm going to miss everyone so much."

"It's not goodbye. I'll be around to see you in your new home, and you're welcome to come visit anytime. Now, let's eat. I haven't cooked this much since I was in college and living off pasta."

She wipes a tear from her eye but laughs.

When I sit, Hannah climbs onto my lap to braid my hair. It has become a habit of ours over the weeks. She braids my hair. I braid hers.

We call it the Long Hair Club.

Very original.

The minute I gave her the bunny, she took an instant liking to me.

She still doesn't know it's not her original bunny.

Beth's cuts are healing, and her face is taking its natural shape again. She's settling here. The women have welcomed her with open arms, as they do with everyone.

Hannah looks up at me as I take a mouthful of lasagne. "Mom says you're going to a princess ball. You should wear your hair like Elsa."

"You think?"

"Uh, huh. Or put curls in it."

I much prefer the curls idea.

"Will you put curls in your hair too?"

She frowns. "I'm not going to a ball."

Either am I. It's a charity auction, but I don't correct her.

"Hannah," Beth scolds. "Leave Claire alone to eat her dinner."

I wave my hand. "She's fine."

Hannah rolls her eyes, and we get back to our hair conversation as the rest chatter.

Amy pokes her head in. "When we were young, our mama called her Rapunzel."

Hannah's eyes light up. "I'm cutting all my hair off, you know?"

I clear my throat, my head suddenly aching like she threatened to cut mine. Hannah's hair is long too, and I remember how protective I was over it as a child.

Okay, I still am.

"Why?"

Beth explains. "She wants to donate it to a charity that makes wigs for children with cancer. A girl in her class did it. When everything settles again, I'll bring her to the hair salon."

Wow!

This little girl is braver than I'll ever be.

"That's amazing."

"We'll see. She loves her hair too much. I'll be surprised if she goes through with it."

"Will too, Mom," Hannah whines, offended.

You go, girl.

Beth looks down at my fingers and laughs. Instinctively, I've started twirling the ends around my hand. "Don't worry, Claire. You can keep yours."

Thanks.

Hannah turns to eat her dinner while still sitting on my lap. Amy leans into me as I finish the braid.

"Does he always look at you like that?"

Confused, I whisper, "Who? Like what?"

"Jake. Like he wants to eat you and not the lasagne you just cooked."

I try to turn, but she stops me. "Don't look. It will make it obvious."

I think she's making it pretty obvious already.

Eyes wide, she rears back. "You had—" She stops, glancing around at the children sitting at the table before choosing her words. "You played on his swing set, didn't you?"

I hate that she reads every situation so well.

"I did no such thing," I answer honestly.

I've never played on a swing set with Jake.

Has he fucked me within an inch of my life?

Absolutely.

But I've never played with him.

"Then why are you flushed like you've just been on a swing set?"

"No idea what you're talking about."

"You're a swing set whore."

I gasp, trying not to attract other attention. "It was more like a merry-go-round."

She chokes on her pasta. "I can't believe you didn't tell me. How many times did you ride the merry-go-round?"

We've hardly slept.

"Too many," I answer honestly, feeling his eyes on me as I speak.

I say a silent prayer of thanks when Mia stands and interrupts us. "I'm not one for speeches, so bear with me. I'm leaving tomorrow, and it doesn't seem real. This place has been my life for nine months and you've become my family." She takes a deep breath to stop her emotions from bubbling over. "I was here the day this shelter opened. I've seen women come and go to better and worse places. But I never thought I would be one of them. If you asked me a year ago where I would be, I never would have said I was going to be a woman working toward a degree, and about to move into my own home." She squeezes her teenage son's shoulder. "That my son would be safe every night." She points her glass toward me, and tears fill my eyes. "Claire, you arrived only four months ago, but you've made the world of difference to our children. We come here for their protection. And then we meet someone like you. You want to protect them, but I see how hard you work every day to make sure they succeed. Last year, I lost sleep

214

because I wondered what road my son would take. Do you know what his ambitions are now?" She looks around the table and nods to Amy. "He wants to teach guitar." Amy squeezes my hand, and our tears are shed at the same time. "To you, Claire, it might have been a music room. Something to fill their time. But right here, in this shelter, you've provided a world of opportunity."

I scrub the tears from my face as she turns to Jake. I immediately see his discomfort.

She laughs through a sob. "Thank you," she whispers. He nods, offering her a warm smile. "Jake, you were the first man I encountered when I came here. Thank you for teaching me you're not all the same. Thank you for bringing your son up with your morals. I can stand here all night, and I'm sure I speak for all these women here when I say, we all hold a torch for you because when the day finally comes—when we can move past this—we know where the bar is set."

He stands, still uncomfortable with the compliment, but he holds Mia in an embrace, whispering in her ear.

"Ah, shit," Amy says quietly, wiping tears from her eyes. "I think *I* just fell in love with your merry-go-round. You're so fucked."

Yeah.

I'm so fucked.

TWENTY-FOUR

As I finish the afternoon emails, a light tap sounds at my office door.

With the sight of Amelia's face, my legs go to lead, and I shoot up from my chair.

She holds out a hand and smiles. "Nothing's wrong."

I blow out a long breath.

"Sorry to interrupt, but there's a lot of people waiting out here. They said they're here for the party?"

I shake my head, searching my mind for plans I can't remember.

Nope.

I'm not losing my mind.

"What party?" I glance over her shoulder to where people are setting up different stations.

What is going on?

I have an auction to get ready for. I don't need craziness today.

"I thought you would know. They've all been cleared to come through by Nora."

I rush to the door, and I think I may be in the wrong building. Everyone is pouring into the commons area to see what the commotion is about. There are people I don't recognize.

Everywhere.

Is that a DJ?

And a clown outside?

I hate clowns.

A lady approaches me, dressed head to toe in black, her blonde hair curled around her shoulders. "You must be Claire. I'm Natalie." She reaches out her hand for me to shake.

I take it, feeling no less confused than I was a minute ago. "And you must be the lady with answers?" I hope she takes it as a question because it is one.

"I'm the hairstylist. I brought two of my girls with me, and two makeup artists. It's okay for the DJ to set up by the window, right?"

I think I've swallowed my tongue, so I nod and try to clear my throat.

"Okay, ladies," Natalie bellows as she walks back to the center of the room before I can ask her anything else. "I've heard some of you would like to have your hair done and learn some makeup tips. We are getting some virgin cocktails ready for you, and the kids will be entertained."

Everyone cheers and the room lights up with excitement.

Seriously, I've entered a parallel universe.

"Claire, we're having a party."

At the sight of Jay-Jay running toward me, everything suddenly settles in place. As he hugs me around the waist, my gaze levels to the man staring at me. Standing in the corner, he's leaning against the wall, arms across his chest, and legs crossed at the ankle, with a smile that coats over every inch of my skin.

It was him.

He did this.

He remembered what I said.

Does he remember everything?

"Hey, handsome boy," I choke as I embrace Jay-Jay with one arm while pressing my other palm over my mouth to stop the sobs from escaping. "It looks like we're having a party."

He stomps with excitement before running away to find his friends.

"Thanks, Claire."

"You're the best."

"This is amazing."

All these compliments are coming in my direction from the women, but they're telling the wrong person. Yet, I can't take my eyes away from Jake and how his smile is making my skin tingle.

"Ladies, this wasn't—" I'm about to correct them, but Jake shakes his head and places a finger over his lips.

I stand there for what I think is minutes, unable to move, unable to comprehend all of this.

Does he realize what this means to these women?

To the children?

To me?

And suddenly, I don't care how hard my brain fights with my heart because my feet are moving. He straightens, and his smile falters because I'm pretty sure I can't control the emotions on my face.

"I'm going to hug you now," I warn, but I don't give him a chance to answer before I throw my arms around his neck. He doesn't hesitate, and with a deep breath, I feel warm hands against my lower back.

"For a minute there, I thought you were going to hit me." He chuckles into my hair, and I hiccup because I try to laugh with him, but a sob cracks in my throat. "Hey, don't cry." His laugh is gentle, and I try to hold back a moan when his hand motion circles on my back.

I pull away, lowering my head as I dry my wet cheeks with the back of my hand. But when I look around the room, more tears fall. This time, they fall over the massive smile on my face.

When his hand comes up to tuck a strand of hair behind my ear, he steals my next breath with his touch. "Keep smiling, sweetheart."

I gulp, and he can probably see me trying to swallow my nerves. "Thank you, Jake. This is amazing."

He leans closer. It's only an inch, but everything in me melts. My lips tingle, and if I just push up on my tiptoes, I can press my lips to his. I can get lost in him again and find myself.

Find us.

It will break another rule, but I can't find it in myself to care.

"Let's get dancing, kids."

Damn it.

The sounds of screams and booming music over the speaker break our connection. He offers me a small smile and takes a step back.

"Non-alcoholic cocktail?" Jake tilts his head toward the tables in the corner.

I lean into him, patting my hand against his chest, only to drop it again when a tingle rushes through my fingertips.

Not here.

Not now.

"Oh, Mr. Williams, you know how to treat a girl."

He shakes his head before placing his hand on my lower back and pushing me forward.

Once Jake has handed me something sweet and fruity, we stand side by side and watch the scene unfold. This took a lot of organizing. I know Jake cares about this place. I know his heart is bigger than he lets anyone see. But this…This comes from the most caring of hearts. It's a heart that's breaking through my own, breaking down cement walls I didn't know I built. All without knowing and ever being able to tell him.

Witnessing it…Being here with him like this and him allowing me a glimpse into the warmer side of his soul is enough. I can't ask for more.

He won't give it, and I probably don't deserve it.

This is enough.

I risk a glance at him, afraid he'll see how my heart is playing my emotions on my face, but when I do, he's already looking at me. I smile, suddenly nervous, as I tap my fingers against my cup. He takes a sip of his drink while stuffing a hand in his suit pants pocket. He grimaces.

"Not to your taste?" I ask, stifling another giggle when he shudders.

"Did they dump a bag of sugar in there?"

I roll my eyes. "It's a cocktail. They're supposed to be sweet. Live a little."

"I'd prefer to live without a toothache."

I grab his cup and put our drinks back on the table. Gripping his tie, I pull it until it loosens, unbutton the top of his shirt, and run my fingers through his hair.

He's not impressed.

"Lighten up." I shimmy away from him as the music plays. "Dance." I kick off my shoes, choosing to slide along the floor with the rest of the children.

"Sock races," Jay-Jay demands, screaming as he charges toward me.

"I think your dad felt left out last time." I wink at him. "Come on, Jake. Bet I'll win."

I laugh into his arms as he wraps a hand around my waist and carries me to the end of the corridor.

He chuckles against my ear. "Let the games begin."

***

I've never been prouder of these children as I am right now, watching as they cheer for Hannah when it's her turn to get her hair cut.

"You're up, Hannah."

But something isn't right. The excitement has faded from her blushed cheeks, and she's clinging to Beth so tight, her knuckles have turned white. My chest cracks open when her chin wobbles and endless tears stream from her eyes.

Beth holds her close and shakes her head. "She doesn't want to do it. She's nervous," she mouths to me as her little girl tries to control her hiccups.

I hold my drink out to Jake. "Can you hold this for a minute?"

"Sure," he agrees, taking the drink and arching a brow.

I ignore his unasked question and go to Hannah's side, crouching down until my eyes meet hers. "Hey, sweetie, how are you doing?"

She sniffs and hides behind her curtain of light brown hair.

"You nervous?"

She nods and twists the strands around her finger.

I get it. To anyone else, it might seem silly—being so attached to hair. After all, it will grow back. But I see this little girl. I see the vibration in her shoulders and how she is fighting to keep control of what she can. I see her because I see parts of myself in her fear.

I lost control over a lot of things when I was growing up. My hair was mine. I let it grow because I could. Nobody forced me to cut it, so I didn't. Ever. Apart from trimming the length, it has always remained long. It became my crowning glory and something I hid behind. Honestly, I still do. It allowed me to stand out and blend in all at once. I didn't want my circumstances or the rumors to be what defined me. I took control where I could. So, instead of being the girl with an alcoholic mother and a father who couldn't be bothered to stick around, I became the girl with the beautiful hair. Some part of me carried that reasoning to adulthood.

All the way to this moment, right now, when I look at Hannah and want her to define her life in other ways.

But I won't force her into another circumstance she has no control over. She needs to know that when she says no, people take it seriously.

Her words mean something.

I hear her sniffles at my side. "I want to keep my long hair, so it will be like yours when I grow up. I want to be beautiful like you."

Oh, Hannah.

I wipe her tears with the palm of my hand. "Sweetie, you are beautiful and not just because of your hair, but because you're kind and caring. You've got so much more that makes you beautiful in here." I place my hand over her heart, and she exhales. "But if you don't want to cut your hair, you don't have to. You don't have to do anything you don't want to do."

"But...B-but, Claire," she stutters, scrubbing the flesh of her palm across her cheeks. "I said I was going to do it. Nobody else's hair is long enough."

I offer a comforting smile, and rub my hand down her arm, feeling settled in my decision.

"Mine is."

She gasps, as do the others crowding around us.

Am I that obvious about my hair?

"I'm going to cut mine. You only need to enjoy the party, okay?"

I give her a quick hug before standing and walking to the salon chair to sit. I refuse to look at anyone because they'll see my nerves making me tremble. My eyes are wide, and my chest is burning.

It's ridiculous, I know, but I can't help it.

I wipe my clammy hands against my thighs, sit back, and force a smile as I glance at the hairstylist through the mirror.

"Let's do this."

Her brows turn down, and her hesitation is making me nauseous.

"Honey, this is a lot of hair you've got. Are you sure about this? Most girls with hair this long have it this way for a reason.

I guess women really treat their hairstylists like therapists.

I press my lips together before reaching my hand back to Jake. "Drink, please." My voice is too quiet because my throat feels like sandpaper, and I lick my dry tongue over my lips.

Without meeting his gaze, he hands me the plastic cup and squeezes my shoulder. I roll my eyes because I don't have to look at him to know he has that ridiculous smug smirk plastered on his lips. The women going to mush around me tell me as much.

"She won't do it," Nora speaks up, tapping her pointed heel against the floor.

"I almost forgot you were here," I fight back.

"Doesn't matter. You still won't do it."

She's goading me.

I know it.

She's not smiling, but her eyes are. I shouldn't fall for it. I should keep my mouth shut, but my nerves have gotten the better of me.

"Will too," I retort childishly before gulping on the fruity liquid and wishing there was something stronger in there.

"You can do it, Claire," the children chant.

Great.

No pressure.

"Hey, Hannah," I call, noticing her tears have dried. "I need someone to hold my hand."

Her face lights up, and she skips to my side.

There are far too many eyes on me, and my cheeks are burning. Even when Natalie wraps a black cape around my neck, she is constantly eyeing me like I'm about to run for the hills.

I swear my leg twitches a few times because my body is screaming at me not to do it.

After Natalie measures the amount of hair she needs, she glances back at me and smiles. "It won't be that short."

I'm going to be sick.

"How short?" I ask, immediately regretting it when she slices her hand to just below my shoulders.

It's not short.

Not to other people, at least.

But to me, she may as well shave it.

Jesus, get a grip on yourself.

I nod, hoping my voice sounds stronger than I feel when I say, "Okay, just do it."

I squeeze my eyes shut and focus on the hushed chatter around me.

"Wait," Hannah's little voice speaks up. "I want to do it with you."

Tears of sheer pride wet my cheeks. "You don't have to."

"I want to." She hops up on the chair next to mine, looks at me to say, 'we've got this', and we both take a deep breath. "But I can't reach your hand from over here."

"I've got you, baby girl." Beth is wiping her face as she holds Hannah's hand.

"And I've got this baby girl." Jake's firm grip takes my hand and squeezes. I don't need the sound of his voice to know it's him because

I think I'd know his touch anywhere. It's the only time my skin tingles, and I can't help but torture myself when I wonder if he feels it too.

Why does he have to do things like this?

But I take his comfort because I need it.

"Ah, I see now." Nora pipes up from the corner with the most annoying grin. "Rescued from your tower, were you?"

I glare at her.

She's putting two and two together and getting five.

"Nora, haven't you got other people to torture or the souls of young people to drink?"

Jake almost chokes.

"HA!" she cackles like the witch she is. Sometimes, I don't know why I love her so much. "I only drink the souls on Sundays, dear. You should know that."

I roll my eyes and blow out a long breath, choosing to ignore the amusement she's getting from my panic.

I press my eyes shut so hard it hurts, but I don't want to see this.

"I'm going to be sick," I mutter to myself, swallowing back the lump in my throat.

"You're going to break my hand," Jake says, laughing his ass off. I open my right eye and shoot him a warning glance, but it doesn't have the desired effect because his shoulders roll with more laughter. I squeeze him tighter. "Squeeze all you like," he teases.

"Shut up, Jake."

"Okay." His agreement shocks me enough to open my eyes.

"Why aren't you arguing with me?"

"Because you're freaking out enough." He motions his thumb in circles over my knuckles. "You've got this."

Then it happens.

I hear the snip of the scissors, and my eyes go wide.

He was distracting me.

In a second, the years I've clung to my hair like a safety net evaporate. I feel the weight slip from the back of my head, and oddly, I don't think the heaviness lifted from my shoulders is from the hair.

Natalie holds up the mane of hair, still swinging from an elastic. "All done. I'm going to style what you've got left, and you can be on your way."

I don't let go of Jake's hand, even as Natalie finishes, and Hannah runs to hug me when hers is done.

"You look so pretty, Hannah."

She blushes and sways. "I like it."

I'm glad.

Natalie pats my shoulders. "You're done. I ran the curling iron through the ends. Want to see it?"

Nope.

"Sure."

I risk looking at Jake for his reaction. If it's hideous, I'll see it in his eyes. But he's staring at me like I've grown another face.

"What? Is it horrible?"

I almost don't want to know the answer.

"You really are beautiful under there, huh?"

My heart stops and swells in my chest all at once.

"So beautiful, Claire."

"Thanks." It's all I can say because, with a simple look, he has stolen my vocabulary.

"Now do me a favor?"

"What?" I ask skeptically.

"Smile for me. You look like you're trying to figure out the most complicated maths equation."

I don't want to just because he teased me about it, but I do.

"Ah, there she is. Always smile. Your smile makes everything better."

TWENTY-FIVE

"Jay-Jay, Grandma is here," Jake bellows from down the hall.

"He'll be right there," I answer.

"Can we play for grandma?" Dark lashes flutter over those big blue eyes, and I melt. His cheeks are still red from the party, and when the adrenaline wears off, this kid is going to crash.

Honestly, I may fall asleep at the auction tonight.

"Sure."

He runs from the chair and returns seconds later, pulling Rose by the hand. Jake is close behind.

I taught him the duet I used to play on the piano when me and Amy were kids. We practiced for hours last night, and he demanded we do it again before he leaves.

"This is exciting." Rose smiles, waving at me. "I love the hair."

Heat crawls up my neck, and it's probably more visible now because I have nothing to hide behind.

I cringe. "Thank you. It will take getting used to." I try to tangle my finger at my waist, but there's no hair there anymore.

That's one way to break the habit.

"I'm sorry you and your husband won't make the auction tonight."

"Don't be, honey. I hate those events. I much prefer to look at the ocean with a glass of wine."

I almost swoon.

Me too.

Jay-Jay takes his seat. I nod at him and tap my feet. "Ready?"

He dips his chin confidently.

"One, two, three, four."

He begins, and after a couple of beats, I join in on my end, but I know the notes so well, I spend my time watching him getting lost as he plays, remembering how it felt when I was his age. How amazing it was when all the practice finally came together.

Concentration pulls his brows down, like he's commanding his little fingers not to slip.

My mother and father would stand at the doorway just like Rose and Jake, and they'd watch me play, sometimes for hours, because I would demand they stay until I got it right.

Eyes watering, I swallow the emotion clogging my throat when the piece comes to a close.

"Giochi come un angelo," I whisper.

My body freezes, too trapped in a memory to realize what I'm saying.

Why the hell are those the words that came out of my mouth?

Eyes narrowed, Jay-Jay looks up at me as Jake and Rose clap.

"What does that mean?"

"Oh." I smile, but it falters. "It means 'you play like an angel.'"

"Do you speak Italian, Claire?" Rose asks, the same curiosity on Jake's features.

Choosing honesty, I shake my head. "Not a word. My father's side of the family is Italian. He always said that after I played. It slipped out," I explain, ignoring the tremble in my hands as I fumble with a thread on my shirt dress.

I'm blaming the haircut.

The memories trapped in my hair must have escaped.

"Italian? With a name like Russell?"

It's an honest question. She doesn't mean anything by it, but it doesn't stop my throat from closing.

"Russell is my mother's name."

I don't tell her why I changed it. Maybe it's the color draining from my face or the obvious tension in my shoulders, but she doesn't ask anything else. She simply smiles. It's warm, and I immediately relax.

I don't look at Jake.

I don't want to see it.

"Can you teach me another song when I come back?"

226

Uneasy with the number of emotions I'm going through today, I ruffle his hair and choose to stay on the honesty train. "I'll be going home soon. But we can play at the shelter when you visit."

"You can always visit us here," he suggests, eyes bright. He leans in, lowering his voice. "Dad isn't as good at sock races as you."

Looking at Jake for help, a small part of me crushes. He's stoic with nothing readable in his expression.

Soon, I'll pack my time here away with all my other memories because outside of this house, we don't exist.

We've created our own black hole, pulled toward each other, and sucked in.

I fear that when I finally claw my way out, I'll leave part of myself behind.

With him.

"Maybe," I breathe, kissing the top of his head.

Hugging Jay-Jay, I leave, ignoring the eyes following me as I walk away.

***

"You can stop crying now. You'll see him again next week."

I sniff, wiping my nose.

I'll be back at my house soon.

I think.

It should give me hope. It should make me feel better.

I hate it when it doesn't.

"I know. I just hate goodbyes."

"He'll be back next week," he repeats slowly, like I didn't hear him the first time.

He's making fun of me.

He hated saying goodbye to Jay-Jay, too. I see how much he misses him in how he hangs his head after their phone calls every night.

If I have this ache in my chest, Jake must be crumbling on the inside.

Jay-Jay didn't care.

He laughed when I cried.

Just like his father.

"You know, he spent more time with you when he was here than me." That makes my heart hurt again. "We had an amazing day, and you're fogging up the room with tears."

My glare is blistering, but he merely scowls at me.

We did have an amazing day, and everyone was still having fun when we left the shelter because we have to get ready for a stupid auction.

I'm sulking.

I wanted to stay.

I'm on the verge of stomping my feet when I say, "I don't want to wear a dress."

Leaning over me, he scrubs his palms over my face to dry my cheeks.

"Go naked. That'll raise money."

"Go away, Jake."

Laughing under his breath, he scratches the back of his neck before pulling me up from the bed.

I feel like bursting into tears again.

I knot my fingers in my hair, but there's no hair.

I never thought cutting it would put me through such emotional turmoil.

Arm around my waist, he backs me into the wall—the air whooshing from my lungs is hot.

"I need to leave for a while."

Shocked, my mouth parts. "You mean you're leaving me alone? You won't be watching my every move?"

"There's security on the gate."

I groan under my breath. "There always is."

He ignores my frustration.

"I won't be long. Make sure you're smiling when I get back."

I force my lips upwards.

"A real smile."

I roll my eyes.

He tucks a strand of hair behind my ear. It's still weird when I don't feel it around my waist. Instead, it falls in waves to just below my shoulders.

My shoulders!

I'm bald.

He winks at me, and my cheeks twitch. "At least I can still do this." His fingers sprawl over the back of my neck, sliding into my hair. He tugs and presses hot lips to the base of my exposed throat.

Panting, I whisper, "We need to stop this, Jake."

"I know."

"It was a terrible idea."

"The worst." But he doesn't stop the tour of my neck with his mouth, and I crumble.

My heart wins again.

My brain needs to up its game. It hasn't won yet.

Relishing in the feel of him, I close my eyes.

"Do you have to go?" I moan, a throb aching between my legs.

"I don't want to." He backs away with a sigh, eyes still heavy. "But I have to meet someone."

I wiggle my brows and run a finger down his shirt buttons, like that will entice him to stay. "Who?"

Let him go.

Everything inside is screaming at me to run.

It's familiar.

It's the same sense I always get when my heart is on the verge of falling.

And I always listen.

I always run.

But his eyes keep my feet and my heart pinned to one spot.

"Your questions are going to get you in trouble someday."

I shrug, swaying back and forth. "You don't call me trouble for nothing."

He kisses my nose, and it comes awfully close to my lips.

It's too tender. Too intimate.

My heart stops, but he doesn't notice.

Lips tingling with the want to touch him, disappointment floods when he steps away, keys swinging from his fingers. "Your questions aren't why I call you trouble."

"I know."

It's because I can't stop having sex with you, and my heart is in trouble.

I laugh to hide the wobble in my voice, biting down on my lip as he walks away. "I hate to see you leave, but I love to watch you go."

He turns, feigning shock. "Ms. Russell, are you staring at my—"

"Your ass," I finish. "Oh, yeah."

Shaking his head, he taps the door frame with his knuckles.

"Trouble?"

"Yup?"

"I think I have a surprise that will cheer you up."

"I don't think I can take much more," I admit, already searching for hair at my waist that's no longer there.

"Just come downstairs."

Eyes narrowed; I take his outstretched hand.

"It's in the kitchen. I'll see you in a couple of hours."

He leaves me standing in the hallway, wondering what the hell is going on. But when I open the kitchen door, the scream is real, as is the person sitting on the stool.

"Mandy," I squeal, running to her side.

Her tears fall with mine.

"I can't believe you're here. You said you couldn't make the auction."

She did.

I remember her saying as much just yesterday when I called her.

She winks at me. "I lied. I wanted to surprise you." She runs her fingers through my hair, and her eyes almost bulge when they stop at my shoulders.

"I know." I almost cry again.

She spins me around, not believing it's gone. "I love it."

"Really?"

"It suits you."

Standing back, she plucks her phone from her pocket and takes a picture. "For Garry," she explains. "He's been worried about you."

I know. He texts me twice a day.

"I feel like I'm missing my right arm without the two of you."

My heart twists.

I hug her again, needing her more than ever.

"Where's Alex?"

"He's gone with Jake somewhere. He'll pick me up in a few hours so I can get dressed back at the hotel, but I couldn't wait until the auction to see you."

That answers my question.

Emotion clogs my throat, so instead of letting the tears flow, I grab her hand. "Come on. Let's go steal some of Jake's fancy wine."

***

Wine glass swinging from her hand, she strolls down the hallway leading to Jake's office.

Memory lane.

"This house is amazing."

Topping up my glass, I nod. "Of course it is. Your fiancé designed it." Blushing, she smiles proudly. "I'll feel claustrophobic when I go home."

It's not just because this house is a castle compared to my townhouse.

He won't be there.

Either will the piano playing little boy I've become attached to.

I try to laugh, but it breaks.

"How long more do they think this will last? It can't go on forever."

She's right.

And if I'm smart, I should leave.

He can't keep me here.

What is Jake going to do? Tie me to the bed?

I almost laugh at myself.

The sick fucker would enjoy it.

But I could leave. I could stand right now and march out the door.

Why don't I?

Because I can't.

Jake is right. I'm a romantic, and I've become really good at pretending.

I love staring risk in the face and laughing.

This time, I'm risking everything.

"Rob seems to be one of those slippery bastards. He gets through the cracks. But he's been silent since the day with the bunny. Not a word. I've tried convincing Jake that he's probably gone. If he knows she won't go back, then maybe he's given up. He won't hear a word of it."

"He knows this guy better, though, right?"

I hum, biting the inside of my cheek to distract myself.

"You're safe here. That's all that matters."

Gulping the wine, I try to hide the heat rushing up my neck.

My heart is in more danger inside this house than it ever was outside.

She studies the photographs, smiling like I did when I first saw them. "He's such a sweet kid."

"How's our girl's crush?"

Rolling her eyes, she shrugs. "Growing every day. She thinks she's sixteen. Alex is convinced her only purpose in life is to give him high blood pressure."

I laugh into my glass. "That's what daughters are for."

Her eyes cast down, lost in her thoughts for a moment. "She's asking about Nick a little more lately, so I'm glad she has a friend she can relate to in that way. It might not make sense to them now, but when they're older—hopefully, they'll understand each other, and the loss they share."

It's cruel that they have to understand it at all.

"Have you been to see him lately?" she asks.

"Nick?"

She nods, still staring at the photos.

"Yeah." I roll my eyes. "He's still not talking to me."

She almost spits out her wine.

Sobering, there's silence between us for a moment. "His wife was beautiful, wasn't she?"

I purse my lips because Mandy makes me feel like I'm in a confession booth. I never keep anything from my friends, but I've kept this.

I locked this dirty secret away for myself.

But Mandy being here is making the secret so big, I can't contain it. I'm afraid she'll see the truth in everything I don't tell her.

"She really was," I say honestly.

Eyes watering, I drop my gaze to my glass. When I look back at her, she's staring at me, mouth turned down.

"Oh, Claire," she breathes.

I knew it.

I knew I wouldn't have to say a thing.

Taking a seat on the stool next to mine, she wraps her arm around my shoulders. Our heads press together, sighing.

"We agreed to one night," I confess, voice cracking.

"It wasn't one night, was it?"

"No," I blow out.

It's every night.

Except for last night because Jay-Jay was here, and I was exhausted anyway after I spent hours teaching him new songs on the piano. Even then, I couldn't sleep because my body has become accustomed to Jake's heat at my back.

Run, Claire. Fucking run.

I shake my head, trying to rid my bones of the shiver. "It's silly. It's only because we're in this house together, and with everything that's going on. I'm sure it will go back to normal when I leave." I don't sound convinced.

I run my tongue over my teeth, desperate for the lump in my throat to ease.

"He still loves his wife."

With a soft smile, she's quick to reply, "I still love Nick. It doesn't mean I love Alex any less."

"I know," I choke, batting the treacherous tears away.

This is different.

Mandy's love story wasn't complete.

I have the sinking feeling Jake's is.

TWENTY-SIX

"Claire," Jake bellows for the third time.

I swing open the bedroom door. "Jesus, keep your knickers on. I'm coming."

"We're going to be late."

Unless there's the world's worst traffic jam, we're not going to be late.

Trying not to sweat my makeup off, I grab my phone and red lipstick, and hurry downstairs.

I hate being put under pressure, but Jake is an expert at it.

And there he is. Standing at the end of the stairs, looking every bit like the wet dream, he is. Jake in a tuxedo is next level, and it's going straight to the box of memories labeled, *dirty and corrupted.*

To be used at a later time…obviously.

I wolf whistle and slap his ass as I rush past him. "You look hot for an old man. I just need to grab my clutch in the kitchen."

Fingers inside my elbow, I'm yanked back, crashing into him. I wobble in my heels, but he steadies me.

Flushed, I blow hair from my face. "Stop dragging me around."

"You didn't even give me a chance to look at you. Stand still."

Too shocked to form words, I roll my shoulders as he steps back.

Whatever he's doing, it's not looking.

I feel naked under the heat of his stare. Like a magnet, I take a step toward him, heart hammering.

He swirls a finger, demanding I spin around.

I do.

Because this man controls me with his own gravitational pull.

"Christ, red is your color, Claire."

I moan when I feel his breath on my neck.

I can't remember the satin feeling this heavy on my skin when I first put it on.

My head falls back, shivering against him when he moves my hair over my shoulder and presses his lips below my ear.

His knuckles feather my spine, and goosebumps dance over the bare skin. "Where's the back of it?"

Blowing out a laugh, I spin slowly in his arms. The heels make it a little easier to look at him.

It's not completely backless. The red satin dips midway down my back.

With a devilish smirk, he cocks a brow. "Red lips too?"

His thumb reaches out to touch them. I rear back.

"Don't you dare. You'll smudge it."

There are only two places I want to smudge this lipstick.

One would break a rule and the other—well—we don't have time for.

"Let me guess, your underwear is red too?"

Straightening his bow tie, I run my teeth over my lip.

He stiffens like he always does when I do it.

You're a tease, Claire, and you're getting yourself in so much trouble.

"They would be if I were wearing any."

We're going to be so late for this auction.

***

To my disappointment, we arrive early.

He cursed profanities I didn't even know were words before we left, threatened me in the most enticing way I've ever been threatened, and almost broke the steering wheel when I crossed my legs, and the slit in my dress slipped, shouting, "Stay fucking still."

He's very over the top and grumpy when he's turned on.

The auction is taking place on the rooftop of JW Media.

As we enter the lobby, I take a step away from him. We might not be able to hide that we arrived together, but I don't want people to know I constantly have a heaviness in my pelvis because of him.

People are streaming in, heading toward the elevators and onto the rooftop.

Tonight is a big deal, and it's unusual to see him so nervous.

"You good?" I whisper as we wait for the elevator.

He dips his chin, not looking at me. "I'm fine."

Grumpy Jake is back.

When the doors open, he guides me inside with a hand on my elbow. There are other people in here, but I'm only aware of him as he greets familiar faces.

Every set of eyes is on us.

On him.

He doesn't say a word, doesn't move, yet draws all the attention in this metal box.

My heart is going to combust in my chest. He doesn't look at me, but the tension rolls off him. All I can do is fidget with my purse and wipe imaginary wrinkles from my dress.

Halfway, he leans over me and presses the button for the thirty-third floor.

"I need to get something from my office," he explains.

"I can meet you up there."

"You're coming with me."

I don't argue. I'm afraid if I do, the elevator will collapse from the pressure.

The doors open, and again, he guides me out, like I'll fall through an imaginary hole in the ground.

The floor is dark with only dull desk lights guiding the way.

"Jake?" I whisper. I don't know why. There's nobody here.

He glances at me from the corner of his eye as we walk.

Trying to fill the silence, I ask, "When did you rebrand from the Lynwood Agency to JW Media?"

"Six years ago."

I wait for him to continue, but he doesn't.

Impenetrable.

"Why?"

He blows out a breath, frustrated with my questions as he opens his office door.

"You knew Nora's husband?" he asks, practically pushing me forward.

Stepping inside, I nod.

"When Tony died, Nora gave me first refusal on his half of the company. She didn't want it, and her life has always been the foundation. I borrowed enough money to make me sick and went for it."

"I'm going to take a wild guess here and say those loans no longer exist."

There's a shadow of a smile on his lips.

He's proud.

He should be.

"What did you need in here?"

In the next breath, he spins, shutting the door over my head and pinning me to it.

My purse slips from my hand, my body going lax.

"You," he growls.

There's a harsh rise and fall of his chest. The office is dark, but his eyes are the darkest thing in here.

Swallowing, my voice is breathy when I say, "You're mad?"

Possessively, he grabs my hip. "One night. One night I spent in my bed without you, and it drove me crazy."

I guess neither of us slept last night then.

We've gone too far.

There's a pinch in my chest, burning and burning until I'm desperate for air in my lungs.

"And I've been hard since I watched you walk down the stairs in this dress."

He crowds me, the familiar pull too much, and I know the thread is going to snap again.

My mouth waters because I'm hungry for him.

I want to taste him.

"Did you bring your lipstick with you?"

I can't help but smile.

"A girl always brings lipstick."

"Good, because you're about to ruin it." He cups the side of my face, fingers massaging my scalp. "On your knees."

Thank the heavens.

Raising two fingers to my head in a fake salute, I wink. "Yes, Sir."

TWENTY-SEVEN

While everyone is distracted by the auction, I try to break away and find Mandy and Alex. I'm exhausted from talking, and my cheeks hurt from smiling.

Nora finishes the auction with a painting from a well-known artist, and it sells for a jaw-dropping amount of money.

Mandy reaches out her hand as I take my seat by her side. Alex's arm drapes over the back of her chair.

"You're still smiling." She points to my sore face.

"I can't stop," I say through clenched teeth, trying to relax my facial muscles.

Turning, I feel a familiar heat at my back. I fight the shiver. He leans in, his breath across my neck.

"There you are."

Fluttering my eyelashes dramatically, I pout. "Miss me?"

His voice is low, gruff, and every inch of my body reacts when his thumb sweeps over the exposed skin where my dress dips. "Always."

For a moment, I forget we're in a room full of people.

People that don't know we've seen each other naked.

"Claire." Mandy tugs at my arm. "Nora is calling for you."

"What?"

Spinning around, my eyes find Nora's mischievous smile.

The auction should be finished.

Why is she calling me from the stage?

"Ladies and gentlemen, we have one last item tonight."

Frantically, I grab an auction sheet from the table, my blood suddenly burning.

I'm already shaking my head when she ignores me and announces, "It's a last-minute entry. It won't be on your auction sheet."

"Shit, shit, shit," I mutter under my breath.

I'm going to kill her.

I know what she's doing.

"Our final auction tonight is for a dance with our beautiful Doctor Claire Russell."

The rooftop erupts into applause.

I'm going to die.

Mandy bursts into a fit of nervous giggles while Jake tenses at my back.

"What the fuck?" he curses.

Eyes wide, I silently plead with him to help me. "Did you know about this?"

"No idea," he answers honestly, running his fingers across his jawline.

"Who is going to pay for a dance with me? This is ridiculous. I thought this was an auction to make money." I don't even know who I'm talking to anymore. I'm just hoping someone will carry me out of here.

A bomb scare could work.

Jake is looking at me like I've grown an extra head. "Every goddamn man with eyes is going to want to dance with you."

I don't have the brain capacity to process the compliment.

"Claire, if you could make your way onto the stage," Nora continues, my heart pounding so hard it's hurting.

The spotlight swings around, blinding me, and every head in the room spins toward me.

"Oh, shit." I sigh, standing on shaky legs, and contorting my face into another unnatural smile.

Swallowing my nerves, I press my palm against the back of my chair, eyes darting from Alex and Jake.

"I swear, I will castrate both of you if your arms aren't sore from holding them up by the time this is over."

Mandy winks. "Are you sure, though? That man over there is

239

already holding up his hand."

A chill runs down my spine as I follow the direction she's nodding. I spoke with him earlier, and he followed me to two other conversations, sweating through his tight tuxedo, and laughing at everything I said, like I was the most entertaining human to ever exist.

I'm mildly amusing at best.

He was a nice guy, but I don't want to dance with him.

"I'm kidding." Mandy laughs, rubbing my arm supportively. "We've got you."

It's for charity.

It's fine.

It's really fine.

I'm not sure how much a measly dance can raise, but every little helps, right?

Jake presses his palm against my lower back, guides me over the white sparkling dance floor, and toward the stage. I've never been more grateful for his hand because I'm sure I'm as unsteady as a newborn giraffe.

Through a fake smile, I mutter, "You're pissing another circle around me, aren't you?"

I meant it playfully, but when his fingers grip my waist possessively, spinning me around to face him, there's nothing playful about how his jaw tenses. The spotlight is still on us, but I suddenly don't care when he looks at me with so much heat, he could set the building on fire.

He leans an inch closer. Not enough for everyone to notice but enough for my stomach to churn with a ball of nerves. "You're beautiful, sexy as hell, and one of the smartest people I've ever met. Go up there and own it. I've told you before that you're too goddamn beautiful to hang your head. You're doing the world an injustice by hiding yourself."

I've never wanted his mouth on me as badly as I do right now. I'm more than willing to let him claim me.

"Jake," I whisper, knowing there's eyes on us everywhere, and not all are strangers. His family is here.

But his eyes are only on me.

And I feel them everywhere.

My heart is hammering in my chest for a different reason now, and it has nothing to do with the possibility of dancing with the sweaty man, but everything to do with the amber eyes and delicate brush of knuckles down my arm.

"But don't be mistaken, Claire," he continues. "I'll sit back and watch these men practically drool over you, but I'm taking you home. Then I'm finally going to strip you of this dress, and I'm going to fuck you until it's my name you're screaming from that beautiful mouth."

My eyes flutter before I blink the fog away, shifting to ease the throb between my legs.

I've never wanted to leave a party so fast.

"Mr. Williams, you'll have to let her go if we intend on finishing this auction," Nora pipes through the speaker.

Ignoring the furious blush spreading across my cheeks, he leans back and winks.

"Go," he orders as one corner of his mouth curls into a soft smile. "And for fuck's sake, don't start laughing."

He knows me too well.

Dazed and taking extra care not to trip over my dress, I take the steps onto the stage, unable to see the crowd anymore. The lights are blinding. Nora kisses me on each cheek, and I pinch her arm for good measure.

"You're evil," I say, never breaking my smile.

"All for a good cause, dear."

A good cause, my ass. She's taking pleasure in this.

She rattles off a spiel like I'm at a cattle mart. The lights dim and I wish they'd stayed on because I'm being ogled like a heifer, too. With the city skyline as our backdrop, it's the most beautiful cattle mart I've ever seen.

"Ladies and gentlemen, our finest item of the night, and we'll start the bid at one thousand dollars."

I can't help it when my mouth falls open.

"Nora," I whisper-yell. "No one—"

"One thousand to the gentleman in the back."

What?

Rearing back, I scan the crowd, but another hand rises before I can see who made the first offer.

She really should have warned people that my dancing skills aren't worth this much. I've got two left feet.

"Two thousand."

Another hand goes up to the left of the room.

Interesting.

He's attractive.

But I don't want to dance with anybody because the only man I want to dance with is standing with his hands in his pockets, enjoying the show while I hyperventilate.

The further the numbers go, and more hands rise in the air, the more I'm beginning to sweat, but my stupid smile never falters. And I'm about to do exactly what Jake told me not to do.

I hold my hand over my mouth, acting shocked at the amount of money someone will pay for me to step on their toes.

I am shocked, but I'm also biting the flesh of my palm, so I don't break into hysterical laughter.

"Ten thousand. Going once."

It's the sweaty man, and I can't even look to Alex or Jake for help because who in their right mind pays that much money for a dance?

"Going twice."

I'm going to be sick.

My eyes land on Jake. I don't expect him to help, but I know just looking at him will calm my trembling hands.

Our stare locks, and with a slow wink, I melt all the way to my feet.

"Thirty thousand."

There's a collective gasp, but mine is the loudest. Hushed whispers follow, and I'm pretty sure I've become the envy of every woman here.

I couldn't care less.

I would have danced with him for free.

But, oh, my poor heart goes and swells so much I can hardly breathe.

Nora stutters before gathering herself and rattling out the words faster than I've ever heard her speak. "Sold. Congratulations Mr. Williams."

There are cheers and hollers from all directions, but I hardly hear them as Nora takes my arm and practically pulls me down the steps and back onto the floor of the rooftop.

The music starts again, and people are already making their way back onto the dance floor.

"Nora," I call, forcing her to face me. "Why didn't you tell me you were doing that?"

"All to prove a point."

My eyes almost jump right out of my head. "What point? How to induce a panic attack?"

Blowing a long breath, she leans in close, her eyes glancing over my shoulder. I know it's Jake on his way to claim his prize.

Her speech is hurried, her expression turning serious. "We're in a room full of stunning people, yet his eyes have followed every step you made tonight. I've been around for a long time. It's not just a spark between you two. And you're only kidding yourselves by thinking you're hiding whatever it is you two have going on." A slow grin edges on her lips, but it's forced, and I know he's close. "This is my point. You two. Together. I knew what the outcome would be. He may have just spent thirty thousand dollars for a dance, but there's no limit to what he would have paid to make sure someone else doesn't touch you. You're a smart girl. Open. Your. Eyes."

With a dip of her chin, she turns and walks away, leaving me reeling and stuck to one spot.

She's right.

We've been doing a very poor job of pretending.

There's no room left for argument in the circus we performed in tonight.

"That was a big circle you pissed around me," I whisper, feeling him tower over me at my back.

His breath is on my neck when he rasps, "I'm not in the habit of sharing what's mine."

His.

The tingles when he calls me that knock me back, my knees almost lock.

"You're an idiot. That's a ridiculous amount of money for a stupid dance," I say, hating when I hear the wobble in my voice. But I can't look at him.

I've been denying the truth of it.

But this truth doesn't set me free.

It's breaking my already fragile heart.

"Another man isn't getting his hands on you, Claire."

Grabbing my waist, he spins me around and presses his hand on the small of my back.

"Where are we going?" I ask as we shuffle forward.

"I'm getting you the hell out of here."

I was hoping he'd say that.

TWENTY-EIGHT

Something's changed.

In me.

In him.

In us.

I don't know what it is yet, but I feel the weighted shift.

We drove home in silence. We didn't touch, yet my body is singing like he was everywhere.

Music floats in the air when I walk into the living room. I throw my purse on the couch and switch on the fire.

I don't think it's cold, but I've got a chill in my bones, and I think turning on the fire with remote control is the coolest thing I've ever done.

His heat is at my back before I can turn, wine glass ready.

I dip my head in a curtsy. "Thank you, Sir."

He rolls his eyes.

He holds the glass to my lips for me to drink but doesn't let me hold it. His eyes remain on me as I swallow the liquid before he takes it again and places it on a side table with his tumbler before reaching his hand toward me.

"I think you owe me a dance?"

I gawk at it like it's on fire.

He really is an idiot.

Loosening his bow tie, I slide it from his collar and throw it on the chair. I press my lips to his cheek, but he moves, and it comes awfully close to his mouth.

"Let me change," I say, needing a distraction from the way he's looking at me.

When I try to walk away, his hand tightens around my wrist, pulling me back.

"I thought I told you I was going to remove this dress."

"So you did."

"Dance with me." His voice is thick, betraying the playful smile on his lips.

"Nora should have warned people before she put me on the market. I can't dance." I look away, suddenly nervous, my stomach tying in knots.

He steps closer, crowding me, making every inch of me tingle with awareness. He tucks my hair behind my ear.

Tentatively, his hand slips to my waist, his other hand spreading out to interlock with mine. "I've seen you dance."

"You've seen me flail. I can't dance."

When I don't move, he says, "I didn't get the privilege to feel you in my arms tonight, and it's always a privilege to hold you."

I think my heart stops. A shaky breath escapes and I tighten my hold on his arm to support my unsteady legs.

Oh no.

This isn't good.

My chest feels heavy in all the beautiful ways I don't want it to.

But there's a short circuit somewhere because I think my heart stopped listening to my head a long time ago.

"Dance with me, baby," he repeats, but our feet have already started to move to the soft sway of the music. We hardly do more than a shuffle, but the world feels like it's spinning at lightning speed around me.

He tucks me closer, my front flush with his chest, and if he notices how my body trembles, he doesn't say. He leads with confidence—like always. I try to inhale deeply to calm my pulse, but breathing around him is hard.

I can't take my eyes off him. I'm afraid if I do, my mind will catch up and realize what's happening here, and I'm not ready to admit it yet.

As if reading my thoughts, his body shifts closer. I open my mouth to speak, but my words get trapped somewhere deep in my throat. I lick my lips because his eyes have wandered there.

"Jake?" I whisper, everything in me screaming for him not to come closer, but thinking I'll die if he doesn't.

"Claire?"

Another inch closer.

"What are you doing?"

I don't think he blinks, and he doesn't hesitate when he says, "Not kissing you is torture, but I'm afraid if I start, I'll never be able to stop."

There goes my heart.

Fully and wholly.

Because there's no going back after this.

When my heart shatters, I'll never be able to put it back together. The pieces won't fit the same.

It's almost like he's waiting for me to stop him, but I can't.

I couldn't if I wanted to.

And I don't want to.

I want to taste him.

Another inch closer, and his lips are hovering over mine.

"God, you're perfect," he breathes before his mouth presses to mine.

I stay still, not knowing if I should move because I don't want to. I'm afraid if I open my eyes, this won't be real.

The small vibration at the back of his throat when he begins to move makes me whimper, desperate for more.

His kiss is soft. Like he'll break me if he deepens it. He pulls away slowly, but I don't open my eyes.

"Christ," he rasps.

His mouth comes crashing against mine.

It isn't gentle this time.

It's rough.

It's demanding.

It's annihilating.

I gasp. My mouth parts, and when his tongue brushes against mine, I moan.

I claw at his shirt as if I can somehow open him up and melt into him. I'm sure he's breathing for both of us, swallowing my every pant and whimper. I feel his fingers in my hair. He tugs, tilting my head back, opening me up for a bruising kiss.

I was right.

With his lips on mine, he kisses away questions, answers, and all the words in between.

His kiss has wrecked me. All the guarded parts of my heart explode, and fragmented pieces pour out. He might not know it, but he's taking every one of them, and no matter what I do, I know I'll never get them back.

I don't want them.

They're his.

Go easy with them, Jake.

I'll never run far enough from this. It's with me. It's nested its way into the deepest parts of my soul, and I'll carry it forever.

This flame burns so deep, I ignite.

I'm not a phoenix. I won't rise from the ashes. I'll simply suffocate in the aftermath.

I don't come back from this.

I don't come back from *him*.

Ripping at the buttons of his shirt, my nails claw at the skin, but he hardly notices, guiding me with expertise to the couch. It hits the back of his knees.

"Sit," I order, panting as I break away from him.

My turn, big man.

He sits.

With his knees wide, I stand between his legs. He leans back, hungry eyes looking over me.

I slide the straps of my dress off my shoulders until it pools at my feet.

He doesn't move.

Not a twitch.

But I see how his body stiffens. He swallows, but I'm sure it's me he's drinking in.

His gaze drops to the red lace between my legs.

Pressing forward, I squirm when his breath hits my stomach. He thumbs the material and snaps it against my skin before running a soothing tongue over the burn.

"You lied," he murmurs against my flesh.

"I know."

I try to reach for my heels, but he grabs my wrist.

"Leave them on."

It's almost painful when he slips my panties down my legs, leaving them to rest with my dress. I pull at his shirt, desperate to feel his skin on mine.

When he's shirtless, I press my palms to his shoulders, pushing him back as I climb on his lap.

I take my time, reaching between my legs, unbuckling his belt, and freeing him. The friction of him against my core is so intense, I shiver. He takes my nipple in his mouth, swirling his hot tongue around, and in the same breath, I guide him inside me.

The air enters my lungs in a gasp as he fills me.

It's too much.

It's always too much.

I slow, adjusting to the feel of him.

He watches as I lower myself, dark eyes branding every inch of me.

Blistering hands press against the flesh of my waist as he leans forward, our pants a whisper against each other's lips.

Skin to skin, he holds the side of my head, stilling me before I sink impossibly deeper, but he doesn't stop watching me.

"What are you doing to me, Claire?"

I'm not sure if there's pain or surprise in his eyes, but it leaves a fear-soaked lump in my throat.

What are you doing to me, Jake?

We're ruining each other.

One broken soul seeking to be mended by another when we know it's impossible.

But we're diving in anyway.

Consequences be damned.

Arm around my waist, he cages me against his body as I move.

A tender touch of his thumb along my lips, and he parts them only to replace the touch with his mouth. This time my moans don't echo around the room because he devours each one.

Tongues fighting for dominance, we fall into a familiar wildness. His groan vibrates in my mouth as my core clenches around him.

I hold tighter to his shoulders.

One sure thrust after another renders me senseless, and my thighs quiver.

"Jake, I'm going—"

He doesn't let me finish. Our kisses are too greedy.

I can't breathe.

I don't think he can either.

But we don't care.

We're breathing for each other.

We're each other's life support.

My scream is muffled against his mouth as the heat between my legs builds and builds. A shudder crawls up my back. My nails mark his skin, and my lips are swollen from his kiss, but I only feel him.

His body remains stone as I liquify. With the aftershocks of the orgasm, I shudder against his mouth.

Hardly catching my breath, he presses up on his feet while still inside me, hissing as my high heels dig into his back.

"What are you doing?"

"Bringing you to my bed."

We don't make it.

Five steps in—he fucks me against the wall of the stairs.

Fourteen steps in—he fucks me again.

When we finally make it to his bed, I'm close to passing out.

We give and take in equal measure.

We don't fight for control.

We give it.

We take it.

And I savor it.

His taste.

His touch.

Then I lock it away because this will end, and if by some miracle I make it out alive, I will pull the memories out to help me breathe.

TWENTY-NINE

"You know we're eventually going to have to leave this bed?"

He groans against my throat, nuzzling his head in the crook of my neck.

We woke so tangled in each other, I wasn't sure where I ended and he began. Sleepy eyes met, and like all the times before, we were all over each other.

It's not healthy. We've created our own vacuum inside this house.

He grabs my hip, pulling me closer. He's hard again.

How?

"You know, for an old man, you're insatiable."

With just the vibration of his laugh against my skin, I'm wet. He has that effect on me.

But I'm sore.

Everywhere.

And my body needs a break, even if I don't want one.

I yelp as he slaps my ass.

He leans on his elbow, cupping the side of my face before he runs the ends of my hair through his fingers.

He's silent for a moment, deliberating.

"What?" I prompt.

"Does Amy get her red hair from your father?"

"Oh." I wasn't expecting that question. "Am...No. She gets it from my grandma on my mother's side. My father's hair is the same color as mine."

He nods, still lost in his thoughts.

"You can ask whatever you want to ask, Jake."

He scans my face before reaching for my hand and lacing my fingers in his.

"Did he ever reach out to you again after that night?"

I shake my head, still mad at myself for feeling the sting. "No. I don't remember a lot. Mama kept most of it hidden. I know he filed for divorce shortly after he left. It was quick. He didn't fight her on anything. Amy was past the legal age, so it was only me. He relinquished his rights to me, and I never saw him again.

"He was a well-liked cop and climbing the career ladder. He knew a lot of influential people. I'm sure the advice was to leave and not look back.

"I kind of wished he had. Not for me, but so we knew where he was. At least my mother wouldn't live her life with the fear of him returning."

Embarrassment bubbles as emotions make my eyes water, but when I attempt to drop my gaze, he holds my chin. He's wordless, but I know what he's saying.

Head high.

"Everyone on the outside said he was such a sweetheart. Nobody could understand why he would just leave his family. It was the first time my mother allowed people to see the bruises. Not everyone was supportive. Some said she must have done something. Anything to justify why the town's favorite cop up and left his family. Rumors started about my mother having an affair."

He flinches, like he's in pain for me, and takes my hand again.

I need it.

Choosing the moment to finally hand over some trust and utter the words I've never spoken has my heart hammering in my chest. "She was having an affair. Amy doesn't know. I've never told her because, to me, it doesn't matter. And I've never brought it up to my mother. I don't want to give him an excuse for what he did. But that's what their argument was about that night, and I know it's why my mother carries so much guilt. It doesn't matter what my mother did, he would have snapped anyway. He would have found an excuse."

I take his hand and guide his fingers to the scar on my head.

His body tenses.

"I don't remember much of the aftermath, but there was so much blood in my hair, they wanted to cut it." I laugh, remembering the tantrum I threw. I was more concerned about my hair than the bleeding. "I created chaos." He smiles, and it eases my erratic pulse. "They shaved a small patch so they could stitch it."

He wipes a lone tear before it falls. I inhale a shaky breath and continue. "The most devastating part is: they tried to say my mother hurt me, and that's why my father left. Despite her bruises, they put me into foster care, and I got a place in a Hope Foundation children's home."

"That's how you know Nora," he says.

I nod, smiling. "She was good to me. She's probably the reason I am where I am."

"If that night didn't happen, where would you be?"

That's a loaded question, and I'm not fond of what-ifs, but I enlighten him and answer. "I was offered a scholarship when I was seventeen."

He squeezes my hand, his eyes never leaving mine, attentive to every word. My heart melts a little right here in this bed.

"For social care?"

"No. It was the same scholarship as Amy's. Music."

His eyes widen. "Why didn't you take it?"

I shrug, content in my decision. "It meant going abroad. I wasn't just a car journey away. Besides, I wanted to help people like my mother. People like me. I love music, but I play for myself. I play because I think it's the only thing keeping me connected to my mother. She doesn't play anymore, and I think a part of me plays for her. The university was close enough to home, which meant I could stay with her while studying. Amy came back during my final year. My mother wasn't getting better with me there. If anything, she was crawling deeper into herself. So, I moved with my friends to Penrith."

He runs a soothing finger over my collarbone. "You're still young, Claire. You can still see the world."

I bite my lips together, afraid of what will come out if I open them.

"I traveled after college," he continues.

I slap his arm playfully. "It must have taken a long time back then— traveling by boat."

I'm rewarded with another slap on the ass.

"I can't say it benefitted me much, but I think it would suit you—

being a jet setter."

I smile despite the knot churning in my stomach and pull at an imaginary thread on the sheets. "I know you've always worked in some form of media. Is that what your parents did?"

He barks a laugh. "No. My father is a veteran, and my mother was a librarian before she died." So, he worked his way up to get where he is now. As if he isn't impressive enough. "My father still runs five miles a day, but he had a heart attack four years ago. He was too proud to move in here with me and Jay-Jay when I built this house." He blows out a frustrated breath. "He's stubborn."

"No." I feign shock. "And yet, you're so patient."

He simply glares at me, his lips twitching. "So now he lives in an over-priced retirement village and demands I bring him Starbucks every Sunday when I visit."

"Starbucks?"

"Iced venti London fog tea latte with soy, cinnamon powder, and cinnamon dolce syrup." He rambles off the order like it's second nature.

My mouth falls open. "Wow! I think I'm in love with your father." His lips curl into a crooked smile. "Let me guess. Your order is tea. Black. No milk. No sugar. Boring with a sprinkle of no adventure." He hates coffee.

Winking, he grips my chin. "You're paying attention, Ms. Russell."

We stay silent for a long minute as he gets lost in his thoughts again. The air grows thick before he finally asks, "Do you regret it?"

"What?"

"Not taking the scholarship?"

Back to this again. "Not really. I don't have time for regrets. I'll never know where it would have led me, and I love what I do."

Teasing and in my best attempts to distract us both, I throw my leg over his waist. "Now here I am, in your bed with you. All caught up?"

I laugh.

He doesn't.

When he leans closer and presses his lips to mine, I forget everything.

My heart still stops because since we woke this morning, I forgot we're doing this now.

We're kissing.

We broke another rule.

But we've kissed so much, I think we're trying to make up for all the kisses we didn't allow. My lips are swollen, but he's branded them. He's marked on the skin.

It's long, hard, deep.

Everything pours out of him, and I drink it back.

Words are useless when his mouth is on mine like this.

He doesn't have to say it.

I already know.

He's angry at the world for me, but he doesn't have to be.

I survived.

I'm here.

So is he.

He pulls away. We're quiet for a moment, and I concentrate on his breath across my skin.

My inner danger radar is screaming at me again. I need to say it.

"Jake?"

His thumb traces circles around my cheek. I want to swallow the words on the tip of my tongue. I want to pretend a while longer.

He backs away, leaving me breathless and dizzy.

"What is it, Trouble?"

Suddenly nervous, I divert my gaze over his shoulder.

"I need to go home soon."

His brows pull down, and the fear swirling in his eyes is something I've seen more often than I'd like. We've avoided talking about it because I asked him not to.

"He hasn't made threats. He's been quiet and—"

"That's what worries me. He's too quiet."

"Jake," I plead. "I can't stay in this house forever. I have my own. It feels wrong. I'm here, but your son isn't."

I'm avoiding the obvious. We don't exist outside our vacuum.

"Believe me, if I could send you both to the beach house, I would. Jay-Jay isn't here because Rob almost took him from me once before. I wasn't going to put him in the firing line of his retaliation." His voice rises with each word, harsh breaths making his chest heave. "You're in danger because of someone from my past. I won't allow him to hurt somebody else. I can't."

"I'm in danger because of my job, Jake. Not because of you. He's not the first, and he won't be the last one to threaten me. I can't pack my bags and move in here every time it happens."

And we can't keep having sex.

"Beth is about to have a baby, but she wants her life back. She wants to go back to work. We can't keep hiding."

I reach out, pressing my palm to his arm.

Relaxing, he closes his eyes and lets out a long breath. "Give me a week," he relents.

My heart won't survive a week.

"Just let me get eyes on him. He's fallen into the unknown now, and I don't like it. I'm sure he knows the police are looking for him, but I want to make sure the bastard doesn't make another move."

"How are you going to get eyes on him?"

He cocks a brow.

He's feeling sorry for me again.

"Is your last name bond?"

He barks a laugh but doesn't answer.

"Head of a drug cartel?"

He blinks before shaking his head. "If that's the case, you're too trusting with your life."

"My life isn't in your hands. What is he going to do?"

He's being dramatic.

He holds my chin. "I don't want to find out."

I sigh, faking disappointment. "You're just a regular businessman, aren't you? I'm not hold up with a mafia boss or anything?"

"Sorry to disappoint you, sweetheart."

He tries to hide it, but I see the worry burning deep. He has his people looking into Rob because he's concerned.

"One week?" he presses.

For once, my head and my heart agree.

My heart knows it might break, but it wants to stay with him, and my head knows it's the sensible thing to do.

And I understand it. It's the same reason I wished my father reached out after he left.

When evil hides in the shadows, it makes you doubt your every move.

My throat burns with bubbling emotion, but I swallow it back down until it dissolves. "One week," I agree.

He kisses me again.

My heart stops.

I'm pretty sure it's the reason I agree with everything. He makes my

255

heart stop so much, my brain is deprived of oxygen.

It's reckless.

"I could always have Nora fire you. I'd pay you to stay here and watch you play the damn piano every day."

I laugh against his mouth. "Have a thing for pianos, do you?"

"I have a thing for a certain sexy brunette playing the piano," he corrects.

He grabs my hip.

"She sounds interesting. I'd love to meet her."

He raises his brows as his hand kneads my breast, running a soothing thumb over my nipple. I fist the sheets to stop my back from arching.

"You'd like her. She's beautiful."

Another kiss.

"Oh? What else?"

His lips leave mine and travel across my cheek.

"She's smart."

"Uh, huh?"

He presses a rough kiss to my lips.

"She has a mouth fit for sinful things."

His hand leaves my breast, and fingers dance over my skin.

Lower.

And lower.

"She's really responsive to touch."

Only yours.

My moan is the only reply.

"She feels amazing."

Painfully slow, he slides two fingers inside me.

My head falls back against the pillow.

My body forgets how sore it is.

I don't care.

I'm already close when his thumb circles my clit.

"Watching her come is more potent than any drug."

"Oh, God," I cry out, eyes fluttering closed.

"Sorry, sweetheart. You won't find him in this room."

In and out.

In and out.

He never changes the rhythm.

It's torturous, and I lose my mind.

"I think my sexy brunette is about to come all over my fingers."

"Uh, huh." I shake my head in agreement, scratching at the headboard as I release a fractured breath.

I do.

He makes me forget.

There's no pain when he touches me like this.

It's always only him.

He works my body into a frenzy, slowing as the world comes back into focus.

I'm flushed and delirious when he positions himself between my legs.

"Shower with me?"

"Mmm." I nod because I haven't found my vocabulary yet.

"I need to leave for an hour, but pack a bag. We're going to the beach house for the night."

Squealing, I kick my legs under him and nod like an enthusiastic puppy.

"Speak?"

"Speechless," I say, out of breath.

He looks around the room like he can't believe what I'm saying.

"Jesus, I've broken her."

THIRTY

Windows down, the wind blows my hair onto my face.

I can smell the ocean.

It's been too long, and I'm desperate to feel the sand under my feet.

The horizon is in the distance, and I try not to burst into tears.

Jake's eyes narrow on me before returning to the road—the open road with the smell of the ocean and the sound of distant waves crashing on the shore.

How is he not freaking out?

I'm in heaven.

"Do you cry over everything?"

"No." I sniffle.

I stopped once, and now I can't stop.

"You give grown men hell. You're the strongest person I've ever met when someone comes to the shelter..."

Okay, heart, calm down.

"But you cry because we're staying by the beach for one night?" I can almost hear the amused smile on his face without looking at him.

"I missed it." Frowning, old bitterness surfaces. "I can't believe you don't remember meeting me here."

He doesn't respond.

I poke his bicep, but he offers nothing beyond a side glance.

I press my feet on the dash. He forces them down just as quickly.

"You won't forget me now, though. You've seen far too much of me." Biting my lips together, I nudge him.

Another side glare.

He's like a tall glass of moody sex.

Yum.

There's silence for a moment until I finally find the courage to ask something that has been gnawing at me since we left.

"Will it be weird that I'm here?"

His head darts back and forth between me and the road.

"Why would it? It's my house."

I sigh, puffing out my cheeks with a long breath. "I know, but your in-laws are here."

The muscles in his jaw twitch.

Sore subject.

"They understand."

My fingers are already tingling to touch him. Going through the night might be difficult.

Lots of wine.

That will do the trick.

"Do you think you'll survive without me for one night?" I tease, trying to lighten the suddenly tense atmosphere in the car.

His knuckles whiten around the steering wheel. "After next week, I'll have to survive without you every night."

That stings more than it should.

At least I know where his head is at.

I can't help but wish I didn't.

I like pretending.

It keeps me whole.

But he doesn't see us existing after I leave our vacuum.

"Fuck," he curses when my face pales. "I didn't mean for it to come out that way."

"It's fine. You're right. It would have been boring in that house if we didn't pass our time with each other, wouldn't it?"

I try to smile, but it's shaky, and my heart is quietly breaking.

You know what this is, Claire.

I do.

But we made rules and broke them, and now I'm dealing with the consequences of hope.

If I could go back in time and change any of it, would I?

No, because my heart is too eager for punishment.

I got myself into this mess. I need to get myself out of it.

He pulls the car to an abrupt stop at the side of the road.

"No," I moan, faking another sob. "We're so close."

"Claire!" he explodes, startling me enough to spin around. Hands on either side of my head, he forces me to look at him.

I can't.

He'll see it.

I'm a horrible liar.

Run, Claire.

"Look. At. Me." I lift my gaze and hate when he sees tears in my eyes.

I want to brush it off. "You said it yourself. I cry over everything."

He ignores me. "You are *not* something to pass time with. Do you hear me?"

The lump in my throat is too big, and I can't speak.

"Do you hear me?" he presses.

I nod, not trusting myself enough to open my mouth.

"That's not what this is."

"Isn't it?" I'm brave enough to ask.

His eyes shut tight. I watch the pulse beat in his neck.

"I'm not supposed to get an after, Claire. It was always only her."

A heavy tear falls from my eye and onto his hand because I know that too.

But some part of me wants him to have more.

The part that lusts after him wants it to be me.

The part that is falling for him just wants him to have everything he deserves. Even if I'm not in the future I've dreamed up for him.

But hearing it is still an agony I haven't experienced before.

I try to retreat—to curl up and disappear—but he holds me tight, and when his eyes open, I'm pinned to my seat.

"I didn't account for you."

My breath escapes me in a wobble, and no matter how hard I try, I can't get enough oxygen into my greedy lungs. The air in the car is too thick, and I'm only aware of him. I focus on his scent, allowing it to invade every part of me.

Anger mars the features on his face.

Who he's angry with, I'm not sure, but when he runs a frustrated hand through his hair and leans back, I know it's with himself.

He turns away, refusing to look at me when he says, "Eight fucking years, Claire. For eight years, I was angry at the world for still turning without her. I got trapped in a memory—too afraid to escape because I thought it meant leaving her behind. But she's right there every day in my son's eyes. And the world kept spinning, even on the days I wished it wouldn't. I was happy to let it pass me by."

My hand is on him before I can think about it. He doesn't scour away from my touch, but he doesn't accept it either. It simply rests on his leg.

"Please don't let the world pass you by," I say quietly.

You're needed on it.

I need you on it.

Jaw tight, he taps his fist against the steering wheel, starts the car, and drives.

With my heart slowly crumbling, I pull my hand away, but his fingers wrap around my wrist to stop it.

"I haven't wished for the world to stop spinning since the day you walked into my office."

But it does.

It stops spinning.

Right here in this car, everything stops.

Gasping, it does little to breathe life into my frozen body.

My skin tingles when he lifts my hand and presses a kiss on my palm.

"I promise I'm trying."

There goes my greedy heart, reaching out and grabbing it. Even when it knows that if he's trying doesn't work, it will shatter.

Without looking, he presses his thumb to the corner of my mouth. "Smile for me, baby."

I try.

I can't.

Because the world stopped spinning.

"Can we just enjoy the beach for tonight?"

I close my eyes and let the final tear fall.

I nod.

I keep nodding.

He grabs my hand again.

The world starts spinning.

THIRTY-ONE

"Well, this isn't the welcome I was expecting."

I stand with my arms crossed, staring at two sleeping bodies on the sofa.

"I know I only saw him yesterday, but Jesus, he obviously didn't miss me as much as I've missed him." Jake frowns, disappointed.

Jay-Jay and Ava are practically comatose, mouths open, flushed cheeks with feet in each other's faces.

"How are they even comfortable?" I ask.

"Ah, young love," Rose whispers, joining us as we gawk at the children. "Alex took them to the playground this morning. They're exhausted."

I look up at Jake. "They won't be this age forever. You know Alex is going to kick your ass, right?"

He blows out a breath. "Yeah, and I'll have to take it."

"And that, honey—" Rose cups Jake's face like he's a child "—will be called karma for all the girl's hearts you broke."

He rolls his eyes, scoffing a laugh as he wraps her in a hug. "If I remember correctly, your daughter was quick to show me my place."

"Oh, Mr. Williams, you were a ladies' man, were you?" I tease, nudging him with my elbow.

I'm not surprised.

"Don't listen to her, Rose. She's trouble and a pain in my ass."

I lean toward her and whisper, "It's my favorite hobby."

Laughing, she pats his chest, her eyes roaming between us. "Hmm," she hums, smiling. "I think I'm getting déjà vu." She cups Jake's face again when he kisses the top of her head.

Their relationship is beautiful.

I know Jake's mother passed away some years ago, but I don't think he was ever short of a mother figure.

"Have they been sleeping long?" Jake asks. "He won't sleep tonight."

"I was about to wake them before you arrived."

I feel my inner child coming out. "Oh, can I do it?"

Jake knows me well enough, so it's no surprise when he casts apprehensive eyes on me.

"Of course, honey." Rose nods.

Poor kids.

Taking a deep breath, I fight the giggle bubbling in my throat when I roar at the top of my lungs, "Jay-Jay. Ava. You're late for school."

Eyes wild with panic, they jump, and scramble to their feet.

Jake shakes his head, but his chest is vibrating with laughter. Rose stands with her hand over her mouth.

"Claire," they whine, blinking away the fog of sleep.

Ava props her hand on her hip like she's twenty. "It's Saturday and summer break."

I watch as it sinks in.

"Auntie Claire," she screams, running to me.

Jay-Jay's glasses are crooked when I look at him in Jake's arms.

After hugging him too, I kneel to Ava, keeping my voice low. "How's project *Make Jay-Jay Your Boyfriend* going?"

She purses her lips and rolls her eyes. "Difficult. He thinks girls are stupid."

Like father, like son then.

"Never mind. Boys are stinky anyway," I add, but a little too loud, and I hear objections from the father and son duo in the corner.

I roll my eyes with her this time.

"I missed your pretty face."

She looks taller, and I've missed it. I've already missed enough of her growing up.

Rubbing my hands together, I stand, loving the sea breeze sweeping through the open doors. "I don't know about all of you, but I'm going to change and get in the water. Will you tell your mom I'm here?"

"Sure," she chirps, grabbing a reluctant Jay-Jay by the hand and taking him with her.

There's a low groan in my ear. "I hope you're wearing a fucking wetsuit because if I have to watch you in a bikini, you're in trouble."

I spin around and wink. "The teeniest one you've ever seen."

"Fucking tease."

"Come on, Grandpa. Show me to my room."

***

"God, I missed this." I stretch out on the sand with Mandy by my side.

"I think you should move in next door."

"That's a great idea, but I don't know how I feel about living on the beach during winter." I close my eyes and enjoy the heat on my skin.

"It's amazing," she replies, her voice heavy as we both relax. "How's life with your Greek god?"

I sigh, reliving the conversation we had in the car. The more I think about it, the more confused I become. "Complicated. How's life with yours?"

She peeks at me through one eye. "He wants to try for a baby after the wedding."

My mouth falls open. "What do you want?"

"To try for a baby after the wedding."

"Sounds like you both want the same thing. Why do you look terrified?"

She swallows, clutching the sand and letting it fall through her fingers. "Because I am."

My heart twists in my chest. She looks beyond scared.

"Sweetie, it's not the same this time. You have your family. Alex isn't going anywhere, and Ava will be the bossiest and best sister ever."

She shrugs, but her lips slowly slip into a smile. "It's exciting. I sometimes still need to pinch myself. It doesn't feel real."

I tip my head toward Ava, making sandcastles with Jake and Jay-Jay.

"She's real, and she's perfect."

Sensing eyes on him, Jake looks up.

He winks.

I liquify.

He changed to black swim trunks, and now I think it should be the law to wear them daily.

Who knew making sandcastles could induce an orgasm?

"You're having sex with your eyes," Mandy says through her teeth, smiling and waving.

"I know." I smile back.

"Have you talked to him?"

I grimace. "We haven't done a lot of talking. But it doesn't matter. I'm leaving in a week."

Her face pales. "Is that a good idea?"

For my heart, no.

For my sanity, yes.

"I can't keep running from it."

The world keeps spinning.

"How's the shelter?"

The smile pulling on my lips is genuine. "It's good. We should have a new baby soon."

"That's exciting."

I love her for not asking more. She knows I can't share it.

"How's Mama Russell?"

There's the same burn in my chest. "She's okay. Amy is good with her. She says she's getting better."

"I called by to see her on the way to the auction. She looked really healthy, Claire."

She's saying it to make me feel better.

"You've seen her more than me then. After my last visit, Amy thought it best if I gave her time."

Mandy kisses the top of my head when I look down. "She really did, you know? She looked good."

I hope so.

I distract myself by drawing shapes in the sand with my finger.

She moves her head to the side. "Are you drawing a penis?"

"Ugh." I wipe my hand over it until it disappears. "Blame the Greek god."

"Anyway, it's more like this." She draws a bigger one, and we both erupt into laughter before it's washed away with a wave.

"Claire?" A shadow looms from behind.

I know that voice.

If I close my eyes and stay still, maybe he'll go away.

"Claire?"

Fuck.

I tip my head back.

"Caleb. Hey."

Mandy attempts to move, but I hold her wrist.

Don't even think about it.

He takes a step around me, and I squint to look up at him.

"It's great to see you." He doesn't try to hide the slow sweep of his eyes down my body.

I cringe.

"You look amazing."

I shift awkwardly. "Thanks."

You don't do it for me anymore.

It's on the tip of my tongue, but I bite it back.

He bends his knees, making it easier for me to see him.

Don't sit.

Please don't sit.

He sits.

I almost groan.

He looks past me to Mandy. "Good to see you."

"Mmm," she hums, not impressed, and I love her for it.

"I didn't know you were back?"

"I'm not. Just visiting."

Please go away.

I thought I'd feel something when I saw him again.

I search for it, but nothing.

No butterflies for those jade eyes, or fingers tingling with the want to run them through his shaggy blond hair.

Zilch.

The Greek god has ruined me.

"You really do look great."

Still nothing.

"She does. She looks incredible."

Here comes the darkest shadow of all, standing over me as the waves come in on his feet.

The circle pissing Adonis.

Mandy clears her throat to stifle her laugh while I die a little inside.

Do I introduce them?

I'm running out of everything else to say.

"Jake, this is Caleb. Caleb, this is Jake."

"Your…" Caleb wonders, like he has any fucking right.

But my tongue still gets tangled around the words.

Because what is he?

My lips simply flap open and shut like a fish.

Jake crouches, knees wide with his elbows on his thighs, somehow looking bigger than he did standing, and doesn't miss a beat when he says, "I'm her sugar daddy."

Karma is a bitch.

Mandy rolls over on the sand, but I feel her body shaking at my side.

I shrug because what else can I do? My head bobs up and down, chewing the inside of my cheek to smother another cackle.

"Well, it was good to see you, Claire." Caleb stands, scratching the back of his neck. "Maybe we can catch up while you're back?"

He's looking for an easy ticket.

I choose to answer before Jake gets a chance. "It was good to see you, Caleb."

He takes the hint.

We will not be catching up.

With a sheepish wave toward the panther crowding me, and a smile for Mandy, he walks away, and I release the breath I don't know I'm holding.

Mandy turns back to me, flushed from laughter…or maybe it's embarrassment. I know I'm feeling both. "I can't believe I was excited for you to marry him."

"That was the asshole you were engaged to?" Jake's jaw is tight.

My breath catches when he feathers his thumb on my ankle.

I don't think he realizes he's doing it.

"Who did you think he was?"

"Some idiot trying to come onto you."

I shake my head. "And that would be a bad thing. How?"

He raises his brow, fingers gripping tighter to my ankle.

"Don't start, Trouble."

I roll my eyes so hard, I'm surprised they don't get stuck.

"I'm going back to build castles with the kids. They're easier to deal with." I stick out my tongue. Tipping his head, he says, "Ladies."

He drives me crazy, but I still love watching him go.

Mandy puts her head on my shoulder. "Oh, Claire, Claire, Claire."

I fall back on the sand with a groan. "I know, I know, I know."

***

I'm not sure if we fall asleep, or if I'm so relaxed, even my mind is empty, but when I hear voices carrying in the wind, I perk up.

"Mine freezes. What about yours?" It's Jake.

Alex barks a laugh. "Mine's a runner."

What the hell?

Propping myself up on my elbows, I throw my hand over my eyes to shield them from the sun.

Mandy stirs when I nudge her. "It looks like the guys are on a mission with the kids."

Four of them stride toward us, determination set in their shoulders.

Screaming, Mandy scrambles to her feet, kicking sand in the air. She grabs my arm, pulling me.

"Claire, run."

"Why?"

"Quick. They're going to throw us in."

Oh, shit.

I'm on my feet and already pointing at him. "Jake," I warn.

He's downright bemused. "I don't know how much power you think that finger holds."

"Get her, Dad," Jay-Jay cheers.

Poor Mandy is already screaming.

"Jay-Jay, I thought you were on my side."

He shrugs. "Sorry, Claire."

"Traitor."

I run.

I'm out of here.

For five seconds.

"Jake," I screech. "Stop it. Right now."

I'm kicking and screaming, but his grip is so tight, I'll never get out of this.

I feel splashes of water on my back before I'm thrown into the air.

Bastard.

I'm submerged.

It's freezing.

Sputtering and gasping for air, I jump up.

"I'll get you back for this." I shiver, teeth chattering.

The words leave my mouth and I'm splashed in the face.

Wiping my eyes, Jay-Jay is laughing his little ass off. Jake is no better.

"You boys are going to be the death of me."

They look at each other and roll their eyes. "Girls."

Boys *are* stinky.

"Well, come on then. I'm in here now. You two better join me."

I'm under the water again when they both dive for me.

***

"Welcome to my world, Claire." Rose hands me a glass of white wine as we sit on the steps leading onto the beach from the house.

The sun is setting.

It's beautiful.

Alex and Jake are busy standing over a barbeque.

"Can I stay in your world?" I cry, breathing in the evening air.

We get lost in comfortable silence for minutes, watching the world go by. The beach is emptying and smoke plumes from the barbeque.

My mouth waters when the smell reaches us.

Jake and Alex are laughing, talking over a beer.

I don't think I've ever seen him so relaxed.

But the same warmth is always in his eyes when his son is near.

His gaze wanders to me. He dips his chin, silently asking if I'm okay. I tip my glass.

I'm good.

Sighing, my shoulders relax as I sip my wine.

"You can hide a touch and an embrace," Rose starts, smiling at me when I look at her. "But you can never hide a look." The lines crinkle around her eyes.

She was watching us.

Fuck.

She strokes the top of my hand. "Don't look so scared, love."

But I am.

I'm petrified.

Stuttering, I swallow my wine before speaking. "It's not what it looks—"

"It's exactly what it looks like."

My heart is pounding. I wipe clammy palms against the thighs of my jeans.

When I look to the sky for help, no one answers my prayer to disappear.

Why isn't this beach covered in quicksand? I'd happily jump in.

Her eyes fix on Jake. "That man loved my baby with his entire heart. I know it because I felt it. It was impossible not to. But they were both too stubborn to admit it."

I don't know if I can do this.

She laughs under her breath. "For years, they masked their love as hate. But when people love so deeply, it eventually explodes." Her next words cause everything in me to crack. "Jess died in his arms where she belonged."

My breath catches in my throat.

I didn't know.

Oh, Jake.

"But sometimes I think he looks down and still sees her there. He sees the long minutes he tried to save her while he waited for the ambulance. He sees his darkest day.

"He tore himself inside out for years. I watched him change. I watched him lose himself. I watched him struggle with decisions she made but loved her anyway. I watched him work himself to the bone just for the distraction. And I watched him come back from the depths of hell. All the while, hiding it and smiling when he looked at his son. I got used to seeing his smiles. The ones for his family, the ones for his son, the ones that were lonely, the ones that were too caught up in the memories, the ones that were so forced and fake, it broke my heart because it would kill her all over again to see it.

"He lost his wedding ring on this beach, and I thought he was going to look under every grain of sand." Her lips curl up. "I think Jess might have just given him a little push because if she was here, she'd say, 'Jesus, take it off and get on with it.'" Her laugh is nostalgic.

My eyes are stinging and I'm holding my breath when she finally looks at me. "Every night, after I pray for the impossible. After I pray to feel my girl in my arms one last time, I pray for his heart. I pray to see a different smile. One that's familiar, but one I haven't seen in a long time." She takes my hand. It's warm and my defenses fail me as tears fall freely. I don't wipe them away. It's no use. "Honey, I've prayed for you." She tips her head toward Jake again. "That's the look I've been waiting for. And it's been so long coming."

My tongue is stuck to the roof of my mouth. My chin quivers, making it impossible to speak any words of sense. But she doesn't need them. She simply squeezes her hand around mine.

"So, when he holds you so tight you can't breathe, there's a reason for it. When he watches your every move, there's a reason for it. Because he knows what it's like to lose.

"He told me you want to leave next week, and where you go from there is up to both of you to decide. I wanted to tell you what I've seen, and what I see now because he'll fight with the past, and the guilt of wanting a future, but don't give up on him."

I'm not supposed to get an after. It was always only her.

I didn't account for you.

He's going to tease me for crying again, but my heart can't take it.

I put my glass down and scrub my hands over my face, sobbing while trying to laugh to ease the tension in my chest.

Her maternal instinct takes over, and she wraps her arms around my shoulders.

"Thank you, Claire. Thank you for making him smile again."

I might not know where we go after next week, but I have him for now.

Today, it's enough.

Jay-Jay comes running up the steps, and I fail miserably to hide what must be blotchy skin around my eyes. Ignoring my emotional state, he sits on the step and rests his head on my shoulder as he yawns.

I hiccup for good measure. "You okay, handsome?"

"Ava isn't talking to me."

"Why?"

He shrugs. "I don't know. Dad said I might never know."

That's terrible advice.

Rose squeezes my shoulder as Jake comes up the steps.

He stops when he sees me. "Jesus, what now? Did you see a dolphin?"

I want to laugh, but looking at him after everything Rose said, I burst into another sob.

I want to throw myself in his arms and never let go.

Pull yourself together, Claire.

I gulp a long drink of wine and sniffle. "I'm fine."

He bends, so he's eye level with me.

Rose pats the side of his face. "I'll leave you to it for a while. You're in good hands, Jake."

His brows draw tight as his eyes zoom between me and Rose.

His shoulders fall with a deep sigh.

He knows.

"It wasn't a dolphin, was it?"

"No," I choke, laughing at myself.

Sitting on my other side, he takes my hand in his and rests it on his thigh. Jay-Jay's breathing evens on my shoulder, and I wrap an arm around him and lie his head on my lap to keep him from falling.

I wish someone would do the same for me.

I catch Jake watching when I look back at him.

He presses a lingering kiss to my forehead. It feels more intimate than all the touches before.

"Smile," he whispers.

When he pulls back, he winks.

He kisses the back of my hand while I run my other hand through Jay-Jay's hair.

The world keeps spinning.

We watch it go by together.

THIRTY-TWO

"Where are we going?" I ask for what feels like the tenth time.

He rolls his eyes. "So impatient."

"That's been your answer for the last hour and a half. I'm not good with surprises."

He rests his hands on my thigh under my sundress and squeezes, slowing my nervous bouncing.

After leaving the beach house, he told me he wanted to show me something on our way home.

We still haven't arrived, and I'm running out of patience.

And I'm on edge because I haven't felt his lips on me for over twenty-four hours.

This is a dangerous addiction.

I blow out a breath and keep my eyes focused on the road. "Sometimes I want to punch you, Williams."

He barks a laugh. "Sometimes I want to gag you, Russell."

I pinch him. "You'd enjoy it."

"Immensely."

I switch up the air conditioning.

He glances at me from the corner of his eye.

"Hot?"

"A little flushed," I admit.

His deep chuckle does little to help.

He motions circles with his thumb around my skin. "We're almost there."

I have no idea where we are. We passed houses, but it's only been trees for minutes.

Back to his tree fetish.

He pulls onto a dirt road, canopied by oak trees in full bloom, blocking the sun. It's chilly in the shade.

Stopping outside a farm gate, he tilts his head and gets out.

What is this place?

I offer a weary smile when he opens the car door for me and grabs a cardboard tube from the back.

He unlocks the bolt on the gate. Confused and still a little heated from his touch, he grabs my hand and walks me into the center of a field.

This is what he wanted to show me?

The land is vast. Tall grass tickles my calves, and the sound of birds is peaceful.

But I'm no less confused than I was when he asked me to come with him.

"Explain yourself."

Stepping closer, he tucks a strand of hair behind my ear and feathers a finger over my bottom lip.

"It's the site for the new shelter."

My jaw goes slack, but nothing comes out of my mouth. Stepping back from his hold, I spin around, utterly dazed and astonished by the sheer size of this place.

"It's huge."

He removes the cap on the cardboard tube and pulls out a large sheet.

Laying it on the grass, he flattens either side with his phone and car keys.

Floor plans.

"That's what you were doing with Alex before the auction," I say, suddenly realizing.

"This one is a joint effort."

I watch in amazement as his excitement pumps through his blood. Passion drips from every word as he walks me around, showing me exactly where everything is going to be.

I don't speak. I'm afraid if I do, I'll ruin it, or the emotions boiling in my throat will sneak past my defenses.

"We'll have private apartments, but we want to build some small houses on the far end of the site," he continues.

I drink in every word, unable to take my eyes off him. He takes my hand and stands right in the center.

"And right here, Ms. Russell, is the music room."

My hand falls to my side again.

My smile fades, the world stands still, and my heart performs the ultimate betrayal.

At least I know in the future, if I'm ever asked if I can pinpoint a moment when I fell in love, I can say yes.

Because right here, in the middle of an open field, I fall in love with Jake Williams.

This place may be vast, but his heart is bigger.

And I get to see it. He's allowing me.

But in doing so, he's caused me to fall harder than I've ever fallen before.

I'm afraid I might keep falling and never get out.

I laugh through my tears. "Don't forget," I tell him, but the lump in my throat chokes my words.

"Don't forget what, Trouble?"

I dab the tears from my chin with the heel of my palm. "Fresh Air Blue."

Hands stuffed into the pockets of his dark slacks, he simply stands and stares at me as we silently relive the memory. He tips his chin with one of those breath-taking smiles. "Fresh Air Blue," he agrees.

Shifting under the heat of his eyes, my mouth opens to ramble. "Please don't ask me to run this place." I laugh, but it sounds like a sob. "It's too big."

There's a comfortable silence for a beat before I walk to him and press my hand over his chest, feeling his heart beat madly beneath my fingers.

"You have a beautiful heart, Jake."

And I've fallen deeply in love with it.

He lowers to press his head against mine and cups my face.

"I never knew so much trouble could teach me what it's like to use it again."

My pulse pounds behind my ears, and I don't hear the birds anymore.

"Jake…"

But I don't say it.

I wouldn't dare.

Not now.

The thread snaps again.

His mouth is on mine before my next breath, and we ravish each other. Starved and possessed, our mouths collide over and over until my head is spinning. He lifts me high around his waist. I don't know where he's bringing me, but I don't care.

A minute later, my skin is on cold metal, but it does little to extinguish the heat.

Hiking up my dress, he unbuckles his belt, pulls my panties to one side, and right here, on the hood of his car, in the middle of an open field, we make love.

THIRTY-THREE

Tummy fluttering, I step out of the bathroom and tiptoe to the bed. I kiss the top of his head, choosing to text him when I leave so he doesn't wake and panic.

He stirs, twisting onto his back. It takes a minute for his eyes to adjust. He's probably wondering why I'm standing over him, fully clothed in the middle of the night.

"Sorry. I didn't want to wake you. Go back to sleep."

Panic washes over him, but I press my hand on his shoulder. "I need to go. Beth just called. The baby is on the way."

He scrubs the heel of his palm over his eyes. "Give me five. I'll drive you."

"No. Go back to sleep. It's fine. We don't want to ruin those nice leather seats of yours."

He pulls my wrist, yanking me on top of him.

I really don't have time for this. I have a woman with a contracting uterus to get to.

"We'll bring towels." He says with a sleepy smile against my mouth.

"Good idea. I'll take yours."

His palm comes down hard on my ass, echoing around the quiet house.

"Ouch." I push off him, secretly wishing I didn't have to. "I really need to go."

Reluctantly, he releases me, and my heart returns to a normal beat.

"Tell Beth I said good luck, or keep pushing, or whatever it is you're supposed to say to a woman giving birth."

I bark a laugh. "It's not keep pushing." I toss my bag over my shoulder. "I'll see you later."

"Claire." He reaches for my hand.

"I know," I whisper. "Stay in contact."

***

"Keep pushing," I cheer.

I'm no better than Jake.

But I've never squeezed a baby through a keyhole.

Grinding her teeth, she glares at me as I dab her sweat-soaked forehead with a wet cloth.

When she squeezes my hand, I try not to flinch. My fingers are turning blue.

But I'm much better on this side of the bed.

Twelve hours.

Twelve hours and thirty-two minutes, to be exact.

"I'm regretting asking you to be my birthing partner," she yells, and I swear, I hear something rip.

I'm going to gag.

When I try to cross my legs, I realize they're already crossed. I think they've been crossed since I arrived.

I don't want anything to go in there again, never mind come out.

I don't reply. I simply wipe her face.

I'm safer staying quiet.

"Can't she have an epidural?" I ask the midwife, but it comes out in more of an off-tune song as Beth is crippled with another contraction, and my blood supply is cut off to my hand.

She peeks under Beth's nightdress. "There's no need. The baby is crowning."

She's what?

This is a fucked up coronation.

The midwife sits between Beth's legs, guiding her on breathing and when to push.

I'm so glad I'm not a midwife…or Beth.

"Would you like to look?"

I glance behind me.

278

There's no one else here.

She's speaking to me.

How can I say no?

So, I don't.

I look.

I come close to passing out.

That isn't a keyhole.

Five pushes later, a broken hand, and a delirious mother later, sounds of tiny cries fill the maternity ward.

"Oh, my God," I cry as the midwife places the baby on Beth's heaving chest. She's covered in blood and other bodily fluids. "She's perfect," I weep because she is. "Beth, you did it."

They should have confetti for these women. Popping champagne bottles. A medal.

Something.

I'm still wiping her forehead. It's muscle memory at this stage, but she doesn't mind.

When I hear a sob crack through the air, I try to comfort her, only to realize it's me.

I'm the blubbering mess.

I'm never having children.

I'd never survive the sheer joy.

Beth rubs the little one's face, soaking in every feature. Ten fingers and ten toes.

"Thanks, Claire."

I run the cloth down her neck.

"You can stop doing that now." She laughs.

How is she laughing? They're doing something that should only be done to ripped trousers between her legs.

I drop the cloth on the chair and go back to staring at the baby.

"Sorry about your hand," she says, noticing how I'm working my wrist back and forth.

I shrug. "I'm sorry about your vagina."

"Yeah," she lets out. "That may take longer to fix."

We stare again.

Biting her lip, she wipes her tears with the sheet. "I hate him, but is it wrong that in times like this, I miss him?"

I stroke her damp hair, but it'll never soothe the heart I'm sure is breaking in her chest. "No. It's not wrong. Nothing you feel is wrong."

Her attention returns to her new daughter. "The shelter is amazing, but I never thought I'd be bringing my new baby there. Although it will be nice to have everyone's support."

I rub her arm. "It's only for a little while longer. You'll be settled in a place of your own before you know it."

Her eyes water again, but she fights it and smiles. "I know you're probably exhausted—"

"Ha! You just gave birth, and you think *I'm* exhausted?"

Her smile is tired, and her eyes are drooping.

"Do you mind bringing Hannah tomorrow? I can't wait for them to meet."

"Of course. I'll bring her after they've come back from their trip to the zoo."

I check my watch. It's three o'clock, but the blinds are closed. I haven't even seen daylight yet. "If you need anything, you only have to call."

She takes my hand and squeezes.

It's gentle, but I wince.

"Sorry," she hisses, dropping her hand like it burns.

Giving birth is painful.

The midwife takes the baby to do some final checks. We simply sit and watch as the cooing bundle of heaven is cleaned up and swaddled.

My womb is all but screaming at me by the time Beth is brought back to her room, and I leave.

I text Jake.

Me: She did it. Baby is perfect, and I have a newfound appreciation for vaginas. See you later.

He doesn't reply.

THIRTY-FOUR

Jake: I'll be home late. Don't wait up. Go to bed.

I stare at the message like he can magically appear through the screen.

I went to work after being with Beth. We all celebrated together at the shelter, but I was exhausted when I got home and didn't even make it to the shower. I passed out the minute my head hit the pillow.

Now I'm staring at a text message that is five hours old, and I don't hear any signs of life in this house.

It's midnight.

Where is he?

And he didn't track me down when I didn't reply.

Something's wrong.

I feel it.

My stomach knots and nausea rocks.

My heart skips a beat when my phone vibrates in my hand, but quickly drops when it's Sam's name flashing at me.

"Sam, what's wrong?"

"Is Jake home yet?"

"No. I mean, I don't think so." I jump out of bed and down the hall. All the lights are off. His bed hasn't been slept in. "No," I confirm.

"Fuck," he grits.

My knees lock.

I hate this.

"Sam, what is going on?"

The front door unlocks. The set of broad shoulders appears, but he doesn't glance my way. Instead, he storms through the house and into the kitchen.

"He's here."

"Claire," Sam says before I end the call. "You need to talk to him, honey."

No shit.

What am I about to walk into?

For now. I promise.

I have a horrible feeling *for now* just ran out.

I don't reply. I simply end the call and take the stairs as fast as my legs can move. A light glows into the hallway from his office, illuminating his memory lane in shadows.

The door creaks when I push it open, uncovering a broken man. Head fallen, heavy rounded shoulders strain against his shirt as he leans on his fists against the table.

Bloody fists.

As if sensing me, his muscles tighten, the veins in his forearms protruding from the strain.

"Jake?" I try to say, but it comes out in a cry.

Just the sight of him makes my throat sting.

Slowly, he turns, and my breath leaves my lungs and forgets to come back.

His white shirt is stained red, knuckles cut, and probably broken. His brows are drawn tight. The heated stare I'm used to is nothing but ice as it dances across my skin.

When my brain finally catches up, I rush to him, frantically searching for the source of the blood.

"Where are you hurt?"

Hand on the back of my head, he forces me to look at him. "It's not mine."

What have you done?

A humorless laugh escapes under his breath. "I got eyes on him."

No.

This can't be happening.

Tears float, threatening to fall. His grip on me tightens. "Don't worry, sweetheart. Unfortunately, he's still breathing. Sam got eyes on him too. I'm sure Beth's face looked worse when we picked her up."

I press my palms to his cheek. He wraps bloodied fingers around mine, trying to ease my tremble.

He's somewhere else entirely when he lifts his head to the photos in the hall.

"Jake," I press.

I don't think he's in shock. He's lucid. He knows what he's doing.

But I've lost the man I'm used to.

I underestimated his anger. His need to protect. To avenge.

The man I see isn't the man I've spent weeks with.

He blows out a tortured breath and kisses the top of my head before pulling away and holding me by my arms. I'm grateful for it because I'm afraid my legs will give out on me.

There's a cut above his brow. He needs ice.

A single tear leaks from the corner of my eye. "You promised me," I whisper, not trusting my voice.

He shrugs and tips his head toward the pictures. "I promised her too, and look where that got everyone. Looks like I'm breaking a lot of promises tonight, Claire."

He offers a small smile when he looks down at me, but it doesn't heat my skin like I'm used to. It leaves nothing but an icy shiver in its wake.

It's that look again. The one where he's in on a secret I'm not aware of, but it's not mischievous or cheeky like I love. It makes my stomach knot with nerves.

"Smile for me, baby," he breathes. I choke on a sob, but I can't let it out. I need to bundle up these emotions and deal with them later. "You're okay. You're still here." I'm not sure if he is saying it to me or reminding himself.

But I echo his words anyway because I think he needs it. "I'm okay. I'm still here."

Careful of his cuts, I take his hand, lead him out of the office and into the kitchen.

"Sit down," I say, nodding toward the chairs. "Let me get those cuts cleaned up."

"I'm fine," he tries to retort, but I slice my palm across the air to stop him. He sighs but doesn't argue before pulling out a chair to sit.

I grab two glasses and the bottle of whiskey because my body is running on pure adrenaline right now, and when that wears off, I'm going to crash, so being slightly tipsy may lessen the blow. Without saying a word, I bring the bottle and glasses to the table, and Jake fills them as I gather some clean cloths, ice, and antiseptic from the first-aid box. He is already pouring his second drink when I bring the damp cloth to his head. It's cut, but not deep, and the ice will help with the swelling.

He hisses once I press the antiseptic against the marked skin.

"Don't be a baby," I mutter tearfully, dabbing the wipe as I take a drink.

My stomach clenches.

"Was he arrested?" I finally find the courage to ask.

He nods.

It does little to ease the tense knot between my shoulder blades.

Once the cut is clean, I take the ice pack and press it against his forehead. "You could have killed him, Jake. He wasn't worth you going to prison and leaving Jay-Jay without a father. Let the police deal with him."

He almost chokes on his drink. "Look what good that was doing." His eyes meet mine as he grabs my hip, pulling me closer. "These animals have been getting away with this for too long."

These?

He doesn't have to say it.

My father.

I set the ice back down and lean my hip against the table. When Jake blows out a long breath and scrubs a frustrated hand across his face, I know it's something he doesn't want to talk about. He closes his eyes so tight I think he's trying to smother the pain seeping from his veins. I can't begin to imagine the memories tonight conjured up, and I have no idea how to comfort him or what to say to make this better.

I just want to make it better.

But somewhere inside, the memories build and creep out of the shadows.

His fist comes down hard on the table, making the glasses vibrate. He stretches his long fingers flat against the surface. I hold back a gasp when his other hand clutches at my hip again, and his palm sprawls out against the skin beneath my sweater. When his head falls against my stomach, and I feel his heavy breaths against my skin, I cup my hand over my mouth to stop the sob wanting to escape.

Oh, Jake.

I don't know what to say.

Why don't I know what to fucking say?

But I don't think anything I say will ease the pain because his agony is so raw, he's practically radiating it. Every day, he hides it, but when it surfaces, it cripples him.

He's sinking. I can sense it. If he is going down, I'm clinging on and going with him. But truth is, the first time I found myself in his arms, I was drowning in him anyway.

"Claire," he rasps, his voice thick with emotion as he clutches me tighter like he'll never want to let go.

Still not finding the right words to soothe the cracks in his interior, I rest my hand against his shoulder and fist my fingers in his hair, repeating the only thing that brought him some comfort earlier. "I'm okay. I'm still here."

"You're safe." He rocks his head against my stomach.

Tonight wasn't entirely about me. There's so much more. But his focus, right now, is on me. I wasn't in harm's way. I don't know if I ever was.

This feels deeper.

There's more.

But I don't press him on it.

My questions can wait until the morning.

Right now, he's safe. He's all that matters.

I take a step back as he stands and wraps his hand around the back of my neck.

"Don't leave tomorrow."

I don't want to have this conversation now. It's not the time.

"We agreed," I remind him.

"Not tomorrow. We'll talk, but don't leave," he pleads, setting my skin on fire with a simple brush of his lips against mine.

Pulling away, his eyes cast to the pictures again.

He's torn.

It's like Rose said: he'll fight the past with wanting a future.

My heart shatters just watching him.

"Go to bed, baby." He feathers his thumb across my cheek. "I promise we'll talk."

I follow his gaze to the hallway.

She'll know what to do.

Look after him, Jess.

After leaving Jake with his memories, I couldn't sleep. I changed for bed, rid myself of the day's makeup, and tried to curl up with a book, but nothing worked. I stared at the ceiling for so long, I have it memorized. When I heard Jake go to bed after his shower, a small part of me was disappointed.

Who am I kidding?

A big part of me was disappointed.

Selfishly, I wanted him to come to me. I wanted to try to soothe the parts that fractured tonight.

But the person most capable of mending him isn't here.

Fighting the urge to leave my room and go to his, I distracted myself with a hot shower, and after more tossing and turning, I knew I wouldn't sleep.

Not when I knew he was down the hall, haunted.

When silence engulfed the house, I tiptoed downstairs, knowing the only thing to rid my mind of the countless thoughts was sitting on the other side of the house.

Not bothering to switch on the light, I pulled out the piano stool and sat. The moon illuminated enough of the keys, but I don't need to see them. My fingers already know.

Playing the first note, I still. I don't want to disturb him, but I already know he won't hear.

Wrapping my hair in a knot on top of my head, my fingers tap over the notes, eventually finding their melody. All my racing thoughts seep through my fingers until I'm left with only music.

I play and play, close my eyes, and lose myself in the sounds lingering in the air around me.

Unsure of how long I've been playing, I feel a familiar tingle along my spine—the same one I always feel when he's nearby.

I keep playing.

He keeps watching.

But I don't break to look up.

He watches me for endless minutes until I feel the heat of his body on my back, and my fingers hesitate over the keys.

"Keep playing," he says and goosebumps dance along my skin. I lean my head back just an inch, but I don't stop playing. Instead, my fingers keep pressing on the keys, switching to a different melody, and I allow the sounds of the music to fill the silence between us.

"I didn't mean to wake you," I whisper, letting my eyes wander over every toned muscle in his bare chest.

"You didn't." He shakes his head.

I meet his gaze before it falls to my lips and my finger slips to the wrong note.

Legs on either side of mine, he sits behind me, pulling me into him, and an uneven breath whooshes from my chest.

I've never been so grateful for muscle memory because I have no idea what I'm playing, and my heart is pounding so loudly behind my ears that I can't hear the music either.

I'm not sure if he does it to comfort me, but when his warm fingers grip firmly to my thigh, we both inhale sharply. I wasn't expecting his touch, and I hate when my body has a response to him, I shouldn't be having. My heart shouldn't be pounding so hard in my chest it's providing a bass to the music, and my hands are trembling. I'm only wearing an oversized t-shirt, so I'm sure his breathing is frantic because he wasn't expecting to feel bare skin. But when he doesn't take his hand away and continues to massage the pads of his fingers into my flesh, I try to concentrate on the notes in my head.

I don't know what to think. I don't know what this is, and I hate it, but I think if he stops touching me, I'll break. Because these brushes of his fingers are holding all the pieces ready to shatter. Those pieces of me will fall apart if I stop pretending for only a second and face reality.

My breath hitches, but before I can turn in his arms, he reaches up and pulls my hair free. It falls over my shoulders. He pulls it over one side, and the clip hits the carpet. I shiver as his lips come to my ear, and his breath sweeps across my neck.

"Jake," I plead, my voice too breathy and wanting. "This isn't what you need tonight."

"You're what I need tonight."

Once again, I try to face him, but his fingers knead my flesh, and his arm around my waist holds me in place.

"I said. Keep. Playing." The demanding rasp of his voice is enough to make me moan. I try to hold it back. I try counting to five to calm my breathing as my fingers go back to dancing over the keys, but nothing is working because I can't concentrate on anything.

And when I feel the soft touch of his lips against my shoulder, my heart stops listening. It hasn't listened to me from the moment my brain whispered that this man wasn't mine.

I'm fighting with it.

Maybe I'm not fighting hard enough.

His fingers roam the flesh of my inner thighs, my body melting into him for support with every inch higher. My defenses are too wounded and tired to fight it.

I shouldn't give in. I should stand and walk away, but I can't.

I won't.

I don't want to.

Slipping the thin material of my underwear aside, he hisses against my neck when his finger pressures against the sensitive bundle of nerves.

My eyes flutter closed, my head falling back on his shoulder, and my fingers slip away from the keys. My body goes slack, but I don't move because he's holding me so tight, I couldn't if I wanted to.

With gentle kisses along my neck, I toss my head back further, fuelled by the groan in his chest.

My nails claw at his thighs as he motions circles around my center, each heavy brush of his fingers making me dizzy, sending me spiraling further into him. Agonizingly slow, he slips two fingers inside me. My body tenses, but only briefly before he begins to move again, the heel of his palm working me into a frenzy.

The delicate strokes of his fingers on my waist are a complete contrast to the onslaught of his fingers in my core.

"Jake," I cry, my every breath erratic.

Another kiss below my ear sends shivers across my body.

"Beautiful.".

It's not the first time he's called me that, but the word leaving his lips always creates heat in my stomach, and there's already too much. The familiar fire unfurls. I grip tighter to his thighs, his arms, anywhere to keep me grounded, to keep me together, because I'm slowly shattering in the most torturous way.

His mouth is against my temple when he orders, "Stop fighting it."

I hate that he can read my body so well.

But this is a war I'm waging against myself and my heart. Not him.

And I am fighting it. For some fucking control because I don't have it anymore.

But my heart wins, my body caves into the feel of his touch, and as if sensing my surrender, he fists my hair around his hand, slowly pulling my head back until our eyes lock, and I'll never fight hard enough when he looks at me like this.

"Come for me, baby." His chest heaves against my back. "Now, Claire," he growls.

Those words are my undoing, and only for he's holding me so tight, I'm sure I'd come apart in his arms. My mouth parts, but he swallows the moan before it escapes. My body goes slack as he begins to slow, and my breathing evens, coming back to him,. Back to reality.

His lips remain on my skin as I turn my head down, and it takes every cell in my body to open my mouth and speak because I can sit here, playing notes that reflect the battle inside me, and I can pretend. I'm good at it. But when I wake, I will have to open my eyes to know that my pretending only cut slices through my own heart. If I pretend, I'll find it harder to breathe when I stop.

I lean closer, allowing just a moment to pass between us where I pretend through his eyes, I'm just me. Because no matter how hard I fight it, there's always a voice echoing, 'This man isn't mine to love. He never was.'

Dropping my head, I whisper, "We can't do this."

It's not what he needs.

Not tonight.

A small groan from his chest causes a lump to form in my throat. I need comfort I can't have. I need his touch that isn't mine. When he inhales, I exhale, and when he sighs in acceptance, my chest cracks wide open.

I give myself permission to press my lips on his cheek. Then my head falls between my shoulders before I stand. "Goodnight, Jake," I whisper, refusing to look at him.

But as I try to walk away—before one foot can follow the other— I feel warm fingers interlock with mine, and I stop. Everything stops. My heart stops. My breathing stops. The pretending stops because his touch brings me back. It brings me out of my head, and I'm here with him. Slowly, I look over my shoulder, and his eyes lock with mine when he stands, towering over me as his chest heaves with harsh breaths.

He clears his throat, not once breaking our gaze.

"I got to her on time, Claire," he says, his voice breaking, but he tries to hide it. His eyes avert to our joined hands, and I'm afraid to move when his thumb motions circles on the flesh of my palm.

Breathe, Claire.

Don't forget to breathe.

I turn fully to face him, and heart be damned because I can't help it when I press my fingers against his bare chest. I need to do something because the pain failing to stay hidden behind his whiskey-colored orbs is killing me. He sighs before taking another deep breath.

The air in the room is thick, and his grip on my hand tightens. When his mouth opens, my legs almost give up on me. He pulls me a little closer. Not much, but enough to feel his skin brush against the material of my t-shirt.

I'm unable to hold back the wobble in my voice when I say, "Jake, I'm not her. I'm not Jess."

I expect him to walk away—to drop his hand and for me to mourn his presence, but he holds me closer until the front of my body is flush with his. His other hand comes up and brushes my hair from my shoulder. The simple touch sends shivers down my spine.

"No, baby, you're you." He pulls my lip away from the hold of my bite, keeping his eyes there as he speaks. "Claire, I'm fucking petrified that I won't get to you."

That's it.

My heart shatters in ways I didn't know it could.

It falls to pieces around me, and his words leave a gaping hole in my chest.

"And what do I do then?" he continues, ripping my heart from its cavity with every word. "If you get hurt?" He composes himself again, but the fire in his eyes never falters. The flicker of his flame dances over my face. "I won't apologize for tonight. I'll do anything to keep my son safe. To keep you safe." He holds either side of my face, pulling me until his head is against mine. "I won't lose you."

His demanding mouth is on me, and I moan into the feel of him.

He steps back with me still in his hold. "I won't lose you, Claire."

Another step.

"Do you hear me?"

Another soul-shattering press of his lips.

"I won't let anyone hurt you."

I know when the thread snaps this time, it will never mend. It's gone forever.

"Because you, baby, are everything."

He pulls my t-shirt over my head.

Another step.

He doesn't take his eyes off me.

Stilling when my back presses against the piano, he whispers against my mouth, "This cold heart has started beating again for you."

Lifting me onto the piano, I wrap my arms around his neck. His kisses trail between my breasts before he sucks each nipple into his mouth. My head falls back, and I think if I don't feel him inside me, I'll go crazy.

With every touch, he erases all the ones before him. They never existed.

It's only him.

It always will be.

"Please, Jake," I cry.

Hand on the small of my back, he fills me as his name rips from my lips and floats in the air around us.

"Don't ever let anyone tell you otherwise." Eyes locked, he thrusts into me, harder and harder. "You're fucking perfect, being you."

Before I can stop it, a single tear leaks from the corner of my eye.

I am hopelessly in love with this man.

Reading me like he always does, he erases the moisture with his lips against my cheek.

I can only hope he feels it too when he says, "I know, baby. Hold on to me. I've got you."

My ankles lock around his waist as he buries himself deeper, and we both fall apart together.

THIRTY-FIVE

Jake wasn't in bed when I woke this morning. Only an empty space took his place on the other side.

Panicking, I grab my phone to call him, only to see a text.

Jake: I've some things I need to do this morning. Come home after work. We need to talk. You're still trouble, but you're my trouble.

A simple text and my stomach turns inside out with butterflies.

I think we might be doing this. Whatever *this* is. I guess I'll find out for sure later. And I need more answers. I need to know what happened last night with Rob. What happened with us.

I dress quickly, deciding to grab a coffee at work. The kids are leaving for a day trip to the zoo, and I don't want to miss them.

When I pull into the parking lot, Sam is the first face to greet me. I like Sam, but I hate him right now.

What is he doing here?

Kids are piling onto the bus in front of the shelter.

"Morning, Claire," they chime, waving at me.

I hold out a hand to Sam. He can wait.

Hannah bounces over to me, the problematic bunny dangling in her arm. "Is Mom coming home today?"

"We're not sure yet, sweetie. Maybe. But when you're done at the zoo, I'll bring you to meet your new baby sister."

Her shoulders bounce up and down before she skips away and onto the bus.

"You sure you don't want to do this instead of me?" Amelia asks.

I shake my head, laughing. "Oh, no. This was your great idea. You're more than welcome to it."

She throws her head back. "Word of warning. Never commit to anything when drunk."

"Do you have enough help with you?"

"Four of the mothers are coming. That's one adult for every three children. We're good."

I pat her arm with my palm, already smelling the freshly brewed coffee from the kitchen. It's calling me. "Enjoy."

She snorts a groan.

Waving them off until they disappear into the long driveway, I finally turn my attention to Sam.

He's already shifting on his feet and running his fingers over his stubble.

I hate when he's nervous.

The last time it happened, I stayed in someone's house for weeks and fell in love.

My heart can't take much more, Sam.

He better say something good.

"Sam," I implore. "This better be a passing visit because you missed my face."

He closes his eyes and sighs.

This isn't a passing visit.

"He was released this morning pending an investigation."

"No," I breathe as my mouth falls open. "No. No. No."

Fuck.

This can't be happening.

"How? You already did an investigation."

His fist comes down on the roof of his cruiser. "I don't fucking know."

"Does Jake know?"

His silence is the only answer I need.

My mouth goes dry, and I can't control the tremble in my hands. "He's going to kill him."

I can't lose him.

Jay-Jay can't lose him.

Now I'm petrified I won't get to *him* on time.

Fuck this.

I need answers now.

"Look, he's friends with the judge. Believe it or not, he's a man known for convictions of domestic abuse cases, but he's too close to this one."

What is he talking about?

"Who?"

He rears back, searching my face as his eyes narrow. "The captain," he drawls.

"I get it, Sam. But is he also going to be responsible for a murder because someday, Beth will have to leave this shelter? Why does she have to be the one living her life in fear? This is about control. Just like the bunny on my doorstep. He doesn't want me or those children. He wants control of his wife and family."

He blinks twice.

Silence ensues.

"Fuck," he curses, pinching the bridge of his nose again. No doubt kneading the headache I'm creating. "Did you speak to Jake?"

"A little."

He shakes his head. "He didn't tell you," he mutters under his breath. I'm unsure if he means for me to hear.

"Sam?"

"Talk to Jake."

"Why?"

"Please, Claire. This will make more sense if you speak to him."

Nothing makes sense.

"I will," I promise, backing away. "After I speak to someone with proper answers."

What other choice do I have?

He calls after me, but I ignore him as I storm out of the parking lot and into my car. My mind is in overdrive.

There are plenty of women that press charges. Some don't succeed, but some do. Most can at least get a restraining order.

But him...I fear he's proving to be as invincible as he believes.

His father is a judge. I get it. But there are people lower on the chain not even trying. As far as I can see, it doesn't pass Sam. Even with the endless evidence, and hours of work, they ignore everything.

Like Beth.

Like Jess.

Like my mother.

The men are invincible while the women they harm are invisible.

And I'm sick of people looking past them.

With a calming breath, I exit my car into the sticky city heat, smoothing the imaginary wrinkles from my blue sundress.

Is it always this stuffy in the city?

I've become accustomed to houses surrounded by forests.

I'm a woman on a mission when I step out in front of the city police station.

This mouth might get me in trouble, but today it's going to open, and it won't shut until I'm heard.

I'm sick of living in the silence.

It's too loud.

But I don't expect to see Jake rushing down the steps toward me.

Just the sight of him tosses me off-kilter.

Maybe he has the same idea I do.

I want to speak to this so-called captain. The one who believes it's okay to leave monsters on the street.

"What are you doing here?"

Hands on my shoulders, he pushes me back onto the car. "Baby, get back in your car."

He's almost shaking.

"No. I want to speak to someone," I demand. "This is bullshit, Jake."

"Claire, please. Just get back in your car. Go home. I'll meet you there. We'll talk."

He's making me uneasy.

"What's going on? What happened?"

But something in my fight-or-flight kicks in and my eyes zone past his shoulder to a man coming down the steps.

I'm glad Jake is holding me because my knees give up.

No.

Our eyes connect.

He freezes.

I think I'm dying.

I can't breathe.

Those eyes.

They're mine.

"Please, get back in your car."

I hardly hear Jake's desperate pleas.

His head falls against mine, defeated. "Claire."

My eyes dart around the station, looking for anything to tell me this is a horrible nightmare, but everything looks real.

Those people walking on the street are real.

The cars passing are real.

The clouds in the sky are real.

I pinch my skin.

It's real.

Nervousness bubbles as he approaches us, and I laugh, but it comes out of my mouth in a choked sob.

It's fear.

I recognize it because I've felt it before.

I look at Jake with tears blurring my vision.

One.

Two.

Three.

Four.

Five.

It's no use. I can't breathe.

It all makes sense.

"You?" I stutter.

Jake holds his hand out toward him. "If you take another step toward her, I'll kill you."

He stops walking, but his eyes don't leave mine.

It's unsettling looking at myself.

Seeing what Mama sees.

"You've been trying to build a case against Rob and looking for backing from him?" My shoulders shake and I'm not sure if I'm crying or laughing anymore.

I don't let him answer me. Instead, I take his face in my hands and focus on his eyes. "We've been so stupid. There's a monster protecting a monster."

"Ms. Marino, that's enough."

Hearing the name I no longer use has me spinning back in time, but I don't scour. I did too much of it.

Head high, I hold his gaze.

My gaze.

"It's Russell now, but you already know that."

He rears back like I've punched him.

He knew where I worked, where I was, who I was, all this time.

Sam said the captain was taking the case more seriously because I was involved.

Now I know why.

How heart-warming.

Every word spilling from my mouth feels like poison when I say, "It's good to see you too, Papa."

He's exactly how I remember. I wish we were somewhere we could sit because he towers over me like he always did. He's bald now. His dark hair is gone, but it makes his ocean blues more prominent, and I hate it.

When my father takes another step, Jake digs a hand into his chest, pushing him back, a silent warning spoken between them.

He swallows when he looks at me again. I wish he'd stop looking at me. "I'm not the same, Claire. I've been sober for years."

I erupt into nothing but uncontrollable laughter. "I'm so happy to hear it. What inspired the change? Almost killing your wife and daughter?"

He shuffles on his feet, looking weaker than he should in the strength his uniform inspires. My eye catches on the gold band on his finger.

Oh, no.

He's hurting other people.

There's not a lot of shock value here, and I have the devastating feeling I'm the last to know.

I turn to Jake, not bothering to wipe the tears. "You knew?" His grip on me tightens. "How long?"

"Yesterday."

He sees it in my eyes when I think, *Yeah, but you fucked me on a piano since then and everything changed.*

At least he didn't hide it all along…or maybe he did. I'm finding it difficult to trust my judgment right now.

"How?" I ask, ignoring the obvious shadow at our side.

Defeated, he pulls a folded paper folder from his inside pocket.

The words *Claire Marino* makes the blood drain from my body.

"What is that?" I gasp.

"Your file," he answers honestly.

"My file? You looked into me?"

He tucks a strand of hair behind my ear. "Only to investigate your father after you told me about him. I wanted to make sure you were safe."

Not just from Rob.

I'm so confused.

My heart doesn't know where to side.

In my hands, the paper feels like a tonne. I open it, but quickly let it fall.

Those pictures are me, but it doesn't feel like it.

Those black and purple bruises on my neck don't feel like mine, yet they're still there.

A photo floats between us before settling on the concrete and pulling all the air with it. A tear falls when I bend over and pluck it between my fingers. I don't look at it, but I make sure my father does. He glances around, desperate for an out, but he's not getting it.

"Look at it," I shout. "You didn't stick around long enough to see. Those bruises are your fingers. Sometimes I still feel them there. Mama was in the intensive care unit for days. They put me into care. And you were nowhere to be found." Ignoring Jake's objection, I walk to him and tip my head back to meet his gaze. "I was your little girl once, remember? You carried me on those shoulders of yours." A heavy tear falls down his face. "But do you remember how I cried for you to stop? You were arrested too, and you were let go like him. Please don't let another little girl fall prey to hands like yours."

He dips his chin but doesn't utter a word.

Something changes in me.

I feel the switch.

The break.

The flower in full bloom about to be sentenced to an endless winter.

I understand my mother more at this moment than I ever have.

But I can't do this now.

Later.

I can break later.

Other people need me.

Blinking, my vision comes back into focus before I hold my head high.

Because Mama taught her girl better.

"I'm going to leave now." I look at my father and try not to crumble. "I have a very excited little girl that needs to see her baby sister. When I'm done, I'm going to come back here and the only air I want that bastard breathing is the air of a prison cell. I don't care who your friends are. If it's not done, every person in this city will know that the police captain of this district choked his baby girl until she almost died, and when she woke, he choked her again to make sure, and was only stopped by the teenage boy living next door."

"Jesus Christ," Jake mutters under his breath, hands balled into fists at his side.

"You remember Nick, right, Papa? For some cruel reason, you're standing in front of me with air in your lungs and he isn't."

My father visibly pales.

Good.

I reach into my purse. Trembling feet carry me until I dig a card into my father's chest.

"That's my phone number at the shelter. Don't ever use it. Please give it to your wife."

Jake reaches for me, but I back away and hold out a shaky hand. "Please don't touch me. Not now."

He flinches, and his hurt is so raw I feel it too.

"Come home to me, baby?"

I nod, unable to focus enough for words.

Shoulders vibrating with nothing but rage, he doesn't object when I get in my car and drive away.

The last thing I see in the rear-view mirror is the sight of Jake's fist connecting with my father's jaw.

THIRTY-SIX

"Hey, baby sis," Amy sing-songs.

I can hardly breathe trying to hold back the sob.

"Hi."

She's quiet for a moment before asking, "Everything okay?"

"Is Mama with you?"

"Yeah. She's here at the shop. Do you want to talk to her?"

My heart is hammering in my chest, and it takes all my power to keep my grip on the steering wheel.

The sounds of pianos and guitars float from the background.

"Please," I agree.

There's silence for what feels like forever, but the second I hear her voice, the break comes. "Hey, Claire Bear."

I sob until the air is leaving my lungs in pants.

She remains calm. "Oh, baby girl, are you okay?"

I bite down on my lip, knowing it will kill her if I tell her. "I'm just having a day, is all. I wanted to hear your voice."

She sounds good.

She sounds healthy.

"I've had my fair share of those. Come visit?"

"I will, Mama. I promise."

I would give the world to have her in my arms right now.

I wanted to hear her voice. I needed to know she was safe.

"Deep breath, baby girl," she instructs when my exhale is shaky.

"You don't have to talk. Just keep me on the phone. I'm not going anywhere."

"Thanks, Mama," I stutter, keeping her on the line as I drive in silence and feel the world fall apart around me.

THIRTY-SEVEN

Hannah stares over the cot at her new sister.

"We should call her Hannah, Mom," she suggests, grimacing when the baby wails.

Beth picks her up and rests her against her shoulder until her cries subside.

"I think one Hannah is more than enough." Beth laughs.

"Here." Hannah holds out her hands and rests her precious bunny on the bed. "She can have this."

My heart swells.

"You don't have to do that, baby. It's your bunny," Beth says, pulling her into a hug. "No, it's hers. I got mine when I was a baby. She needs one too."

Jesus, don't cry, Claire.

Anything could set me off this evening. I'm emotionally drained. I can't think straight. Even the beautiful bundle in Beth's arms isn't enough of a distraction.

Standing, I run my fingers through Hannah's hair. "It'll be dark soon. We should go."

Beth and I share a look.

I want to get her back to the safety of the shelter.

I also want to go home and sleep for days, but I have too much to sort through.

I want Jake most of all.

His arms will fix some of the cracks.

I allow them a moment to say goodbye before Hannah takes my hand.

"See you tomorrow, Mom," she shouts when we're already halfway down the corridor.

I hear Beth's laugh as we leave.

"Do babies always cry so much?" Hannah asks as we exit the hospital. She wasn't overly impressed with how loud her new baby sister was.

"Sometimes, but it's not forever."

We swing our arms as we hold hands on the way to my car.

Instinctively, my eyes scan the parking lot.

I'm being paranoid.

She grimaces and nervously knots her fingers in her hair.

"I bet you're going to be the best big sister."

She shrugs. "I thought Mom was coming home today?"

"The doctors said she should be okay to leave tomorrow. But that means we have to be extra careful around Mommy. She's going to be tired."

Hannah rolls her eyes. "I would be too if I had to listen to *that* cry all day."

I bite my lip to hide the laugh as she climbs into the back seat. "Buckle up."

Another roll of her eyes.

Seriously, what's with the attitude?

"I'm thirsty," she moans.

"You've got juice in your backpack."

She stretches toward the floor. "I can't reach."

She can definitely reach.

Plucking her bag from the floor, I unzip it and hand her the juice.

A white, fluffy head pokes out through the top with the name Hannah stitched to the ear.

Did she not just give this to the baby?

Confused, I look back at her as she swings her legs.

"Hannah, did Sam give you this bunny?"

He would have told me if he gave back the original. I mean, I almost fought him for it.

"The policeman?"

I nod, hating the chill that makes me shiver.

"No. It's my bunny."

"But you gave it to your sister."

I'm so confused.

"No," she giggles. "That one didn't have my name on it. It was hers."

"How did you get it?"

"Daddy gave it to me."

My blood runs cold.

"When sweetie? When did daddy give you the bunny?"

She takes more juice.

"Hannah," I demand, reaching out to touch her leg when I frighten her. "When did daddy give you the bunny?"

Her eyes water, but I can apologize later.

"Today. At the zoo. We have to wait for him, Claire. I told him I was going to see my baby sister tonight. I thought Mom was coming home, and he said he would meet us here. We're going for ice-cream."

Fumbling with the buckle of my belt, I try to dive into the back seat.

Fucking unlock.

"Hannah, get out of your car seat."

The scream gets trapped in my throat when her door opens. "There's daddy's princess."

I try to grab her, but it's no use. I'm clutching at the air.

He has her in his arms in the next breath.

No.

No.

No.

I will my legs to move, getting out and rushing after them.

"Rob, please put her down."

He spins, and the smile curling on his bruised lips makes me shudder.

My eyes dart around the parking lot. There are people in the distance.

Open your mouth, Claire.

Scream.

"Ah," he stops me, waving a finger back and forth. "I wouldn't if I were you. I'll have her in the car and out of here before anyone gets here."

Fuck.

He sets her on her feet. "Get in and buckle up, Princess."

"Hannah," I roar, startling her.

Stay calm, Claire.

"Come over here, sweetie."

She glances at her father, confused. He winks at her and tilts his head toward the car.

She goes.

Why wouldn't she? He's her father. He's supposed to keep her safe.

Every step she takes feels like a mile.

"Please, Rob," I beg. "Don't take her."

"I'm not allowed to see my other daughter. Can you believe that? They're keeping a child from her father."

"I can help," I blurt, desperate and grasping at anything.

His shoulders vibrate with a humorless laugh. "I already asked for your help. You were supposed to be on my side. You weren't meant to be caught up in this. I thought you wanted what was best for Hannah. Do you think keeping her from me is what's best?" He doesn't let me answer. "You're not living in your house anymore. Where have you been?"

Eyes wide, I try to hide the truth from shining through.

He doesn't know.

"With a friend," I lie.

"You're lying," he sing-songs.

There's no heat in the sun around him.

It's cold.

"I bet it was your sister. Was it?" He shrugs. "Doesn't matter now. You didn't do what you were supposed to. You should come with us."

My brain fights to process.

Go with them?

"Or she can come on her own." The words are a threat. And he knows I won't leave her on her own.

Shaking, I bury everything telling me to run.

I can't.

She can't be like me.

I stand here, looking at him, feigning strength I don't have. His blank eyes keep me pinned to the ground. Hands in the pockets of his dark denim jeans, his blond hair is disheveled and greying at the temples. The skin around his eyes is bruised, his lip cut from Jake's fists, but I see no glossiness in his dark orbs. I can't even tell what color they are.

305

He's not drunk.

He's angry.

He snapped.

He's at my back when I walk past him. He's so close I feel the heat of his body, but it makes my blood icy.

"You're a big girl. Up front," he demands when I try to get in the back with Hannah.

My fear is screaming so loud, I can't even cry.

"Buckle up," he prompts, his voice eerily calm.

I do and swallow the bile rising in the back of my throat.

"Put your phone on your lap where I can see it."

I pluck it from the bag hanging over my shoulder and do as he asks.

"Are you okay back there, Hannah?" I wonder, trying to smile for her.

She swings her feet, totally oblivious. If I have my way, she'll stay oblivious.

"She's fine," he answers for her, starting the car, and driving away from any hope of safety.

I run my fingers through my hair, desperate to feel something real.

This is a bad dream.

I'll wake up.

I close my eyes.

When I open them again, I want to be sick.

I'm not dreaming.

I risk glancing at him. His shoulders square, hands rattling on the steering wheel.

"Rob," I start, hoping he will hear me out.

"Jesus, you're a talker, aren't you?"

I shut my mouth.

I stay quiet.

I swallow the scream bubbling.

It's no use.

He's gone too far.

So, I stay calm.

I need to get Hannah out of this.

Think, Claire.

Nothing.

I sit in silence as he chats to Hannah about her summer, like it's the most natural thing in the world.

"When are we getting ice-cream, Daddy?"

"Soon, princess," he promises.

He's lying.

It's twenty minutes before he pulls up outside a beautiful home. There's a bike on the lawn, and flower beds in full bloom. But the curtains are drawn on all the windows, and I know it's not the only cause of darkness inside.

It's dark outside now too.

The street is quiet.

When I attempt to get out before him, he reads my mind and grabs my arm so tight, I'm sure it will bruise.

"Don't be a stupid bitch, Claire."

There he is.

There's the monster.

A heavy tear falls, but I bat it away before Hannah sees.

He waits for me when he has her out of the car. I follow because what else can I do?

Inside, it's cold. It takes a minute for my eyes to adjust when we walk down the long hallway and into the kitchen. He switches on the light and it's blinding. Empty gin bottles are in a neat pile on the counter.

Everything is spotless.

"I wanted to have it ready for when Beth comes home," he explains, reading me. "I thought she was coming home this evening, but I got you instead."

Right here, in this cold, unlived-in-house, a monster is walking the line and is on the verge of toppling.

He sets Hannah on her feet and pulls an ice-cream from the freezer.

"This isn't the right ice-cream," she moans.

"We'll get the good stuff later. Daddy needs to talk to Claire. Why don't you go play in your room?"

"It's boring, Dad," she whines, scooping the ice-cream into her mouth.

She's beautiful.

Innocent.

But depending on how this interaction goes, she may be marred with scars that will never leave her.

"Hannah," he warns, and she stiffens.

He may have never touched her, but she knows.

It's in the tone of his voice, in the way his body straightens.

I kneel, desperate to calm her, to bring her any comfort I can offer. I'm shaking so badly, I'm not sure I have much to give.

"Hannah, can you do something for me?"

She nods and comes to me.

I take the ice-cream from her hands and place it on the floor.

She doesn't notice.

I pull my headphones from my bag and connect them to my phone.

Rob takes a menacing step forward.

"I'm not calling anyone," I assure him. "You can look."

He does. He looms over my shoulder with his breath in my hair.

I'm going to be sick.

Swallowing the fear-soaked lump in my throat, I put the headphones over Hannah's ears.

"You love music, right, sweetie? You play piano with my sister Amy?"

She nods, her smile sparking terror in my belly.

"I need you to go to your room. I'm going to turn this music up really loud. I want you to dance. Dance until you're tired."

"Is this a game?" she asks, breaking my heart.

My chin wobbles, but I refuse to cry.

Not in front of her.

"It's a game. It's so much fun. But you can't come out of that room until somebody comes to get you. Do you hear me?"

She's staring at me like she's seen this fear before.

"Hannah, you need to promise me." I hold out my finger. "Pinky promise." She loops her finger in mine as I press a kiss to her forehead. "Remember, don't come out. Me and your dad are going to talk."

She returns to me with a watery smile before I turn up the volume. "Can you hear me?" I shout.

Her eyes narrow before she slips off the headphones. "What?"

Just checking.

"Nothing, sweetie. Go on. Have some fun." I wink.

She keeps her innocence as she skips away, and I hold my breath until I hear the door close.

Before I look back at the eyes of hell and the fate that surely awaits me there, I roll my shoulders, grasping at courage from thin air.

Smile for me, baby.

With Jake's voice in my head, I force my lips upward. The smile knocks him back for a moment.

I take a step toward the kitchen. "We should have coffee for this talk."

With a bruising arm around my waist, he stops me. "For what? For you to pour boiling water over me?" I look away as he tucks my hair behind my ear. It's the same way Jake does it, but it feels cold. I don't want him to replace all Jake's touches.

"You said you wanted to talk. Let's talk."

He blows out a breath, like this situation is an inconvenience and he's bored. "I want my family back, but either way, that's not going to happen now. That stupid bitch went running to the wrong man, and you didn't help like I thought you would. You didn't do your job, Claire." He pokes my nose. Bile rises in my throat, but I swallow it down. "Such a disappointment."

Pumping steel into my backbone, I stand straight and meet his eyes. "So, what does this achieve?"

"Righting wrongs," he spits, so close his lips almost touch my skin.

"If you wanted to do that, you'd let me take Hannah back to her mother."

Tsking, he releases me to pace. "That still doesn't give me my family back, does it?"

He's rambling, but I hardly hear him as my eyes dart around the room, searching for anything to get myself out of this. I can't leave this house without Hannah.

I need something to knock this bastard out.

"See, Claire," he starts, reaching into the drawer, "She shouldn't get both of them. It's not fair. She doesn't get to take my girls away. She doesn't get to leave me. But if she's sure, then she doesn't deserve both."

Fear traps me. I'm pinned, and I can't move.

He has a fucking gun.

"My wife was always compliant when I pulled this out. Let's see if it works on you."

I don't know why I'm not surprised.

A part of me was expecting it.

He interrupts my scattered thoughts, grabbing my wrist and yanking me to a kitchen chair. I flinch, his fingers digging into the bruise he already caused. "Sorry. Did I do that?"

He pushes me back, and the air whooshes from my lungs.

"You're a flight risk. Let's keep you away from doors and household appliances."

He's crowding me, arms on either side of the table. The chair is painful as it digs into my skin.

And he has a gun.

What am I supposed to do?

He runs a thumb across my lips.

He erases another touch.

"I dated a woman a long time ago." His fingers motion circles on my cheek. "She was beautiful like you. You don't look like her. But she had the brightest blue eyes." He pokes my nose again. "Like you."

This madness isn't even about Jake.

I'm pretty sure that the woman he's referring to is Jess.

He doesn't know about me and Jake.

He's snapped all on his own.

The smell of stale liquor from his breath makes me want to heave. "I'm a man with nothing to lose, Claire, and nothing to gain. I got a call earlier. I thought I had some friends, but apparently, it's not looking good for me. My job is gone. My family is gone. And I won't go to prison."

Oh no.

Did my threat toward my father cause this?

I just need to get Hannah out of here.

"Let Hannah go. She's innocent, Rob. She's your daughter."

He scoffs a humorless laugh, backs away, and grabs the gun from the counter.

I hold my breath for a beat.

And another.

He's still laughing when he pulls canisters from the cupboard.

Gasoline.

"Rob, no."

Fuck. Fuck. Fuck.

I dive for him.

I need to fight, but as if sensing me in some weird hunter versus prey sixth sense, he spins around, and the back of his hand connects with my jaw. "I don't want to hurt you, Claire."

I grip the counter, steadying myself as pain rips through the side of my face. A coppery taste floods my mouth and trickles down my chin.

My vision blurs.

Don't fucking blackout.

The pungent smell invades me, making my head spin.

"You weren't supposed to be here, Claire. Please believe me. You were never supposed to be involved."

But he's too erratic. Not a lot of planning went into this. This was a quick flip. He's giving me too much of a chance to run.

Keeping my upper body still, my feet slide against the tiles at a snail's pace.

He's too occupied with his crazed ramblings when my legs begin to move. I'm running toward the stairs, knowing that if I can just get to Hannah, I can figure something out.

I can't leave this house without her.

A stab of pain explodes at the back of my scalp as he fists my hair, pulling me to the ground with him.

I punch, I kick, I scratch, I fight.

But he's stronger.

He's so much stronger.

"You weren't supposed to be here, Claire."

I see it when all humanity fades from his eyes and his fingers wrap around my throat.

No.

This can't be happening.

"Rob," I scream.

I fight some more. But the more I fight, the more air leaves my lungs.

I need to stop fighting.

Little legs appear at the top of the stairs.

No. No. No.

"Hannah, get back in the room," I shout, but nothing comes out.

"Claire, Jake is on the phone. I told him I'm dancing."

I try to turn to her, but his grip is so tight I can't move.

"Daddy, what are you doing to Claire? Daddy, stop."

He doesn't even flinch.

He can't hear her.

Please, baby girl, go back in the room. Put your headphones on and dance.

"Daddy," she wails.

There's no flicker in his eyes.

He's determined.

No more *almost.*

Hannah screams and screams because that's all she can do.

I'm sorry, Hannah.

My legs jerk, blood from where I tore at his skin staining my blue dress, and I take one last desperate attempt to inhale, but it's choked, breaking through the air in nothing but a wheeze. The blood in my mouth pools in the back of my throat.

The sound only makes him tighten his grip.

Everything burns.

I don't want to die this way.

As my eyes flutter closed and the fight drains from my body, I want to see Jake. I want the comfort his eyes bring.

But I only see myself.

Even in death, my father's eyes haunt me.

Silly, Claire. You can't change history. It's always destined to repeat itself.

It doesn't burn anymore.

Giving up, I let the warmth encompass every nerve because she shouldn't have to witness the struggle.

"You're trouble, aren't you?"

"Smile for me, baby."

"I haven't wished for the world to stop spinning since the day you walked into my office."

"This cold heart has started beating again for you."

"Keep playing. You're beautiful when you play."

With Jake's voice, peace washes over me.

But there's one more voice, and with this one, I know I'm home.

"You're going to change the world someday, Claire Russell."

THIRTY-EIGHT

You need to go back, Claire.
You need to take care of our boys.

***

Everything burns again.

My ears are ringing, and my next breath is the most pain I've ever felt.

This can't be heaven.

It's too painful.

But my eyes are heavy, and the weight of a body is keeping me pinned to the floor.

Fight, Claire.

Fucking fight.

The blackness is coming again, lulling me away.

"Come back."

Go back, Claire.

They need you.

Breathe.

"Come back, baby. We need you. Breathe."

Jake?

He's not supposed to be here.

This isn't heaven.

"Fuck. Wake up, sweetheart. Come on. Keep breathing."

There's a warm hand on my face, in my hair, on my neck.

But it's not squeezing anymore.

He didn't kill me.

I'm alive.

There's warmth on my lips and tears dripping onto my cheeks, but they're not mine.

"The world won't spin without you. Come back to me."

His voice is enough for my lungs to fill. It's tight, and my throat is on fire, but I do it. The taste of blood makes me nauseous and my mouth waters.

"I'm going to get you out of here."

My eyes shoot open, gasping as my body becomes desperate for oxygen, but the air is heavy.

It still burns.

Darkness clouds my vision, stinging with every blink.

Smoke.

He needs to go.

His head is buried in the crook of my neck, and the relief that washes over me is all I need to ease the pain in my chest.

An anguished sob ruptures from his shoulders. I feel every painful cry and my heart breaks in two.

"Jake," I croak, my voice barely a whisper. "I'm okay."

He snaps back. Hot amber eyes dance over me.

But I'm tired.

I've never been so tired.

My head aches, and I think I'm swallowing shards of glass.

His head falls against mine as he holds me up, supporting all my weight. And in the middle of this chaos, he kisses me. It's deep, it's hard, and it breathes every ounce of life I lost back into me.

My life support.

"Keep your head down. I need to get you out of here."

Sparks dance in the air. The orange glow around us triggers another wave of adrenaline.

It's hot.

It's not licking at our skin yet, but it's close.

There's so much smoke.

He went through with it.

Hannah.

Palms digging into the floor, I ignore every pounding in my body and slip out of Jake's arms. But my legs shake, and I collapse against him.

Body don't betray me now.

I need to get her out of here.

It's my fault.

I need to get her.

My lungs fill again, but it's murky.

I just need more air.

Clawing at his shoulders, I manage to stand straight, and I run.

"Claire," he screams.

My knees threaten to buckle, but I'm holding on.

"We need to get her out of here."

He's on my heels as I race upstairs, grabbing me by the waist and yanking me around. I fist his shirt, endless tears streaming from my eyes.

"Hannah."

"Go. I'll get her."

I don't let him drag me back.

It's my fault.

"Fuck," he curses as he reaches out, but I dodge his hold.

Reaching the top of the stairs, I hold my hand out to stop him from coming further.

Rob can't see him.

"Let me try," I whisper.

Something crashes to the floor downstairs, but I hardly hear it.

There's music playing from the bedroom.

Opening the door, my heart falls into my stomach. He stands with Hannah in his arms, a gun swinging from his hand at her back.

He's doing this.

The door opening grabs his attention, and the color drains from his face.

He's seeing a ghost.

I take his moment of shock as my opportunity.

Hannah's tears soak his shoulder as he sings to her.

She's tired too.

His tears fall into her hair.

An utterly broken monster.

"Claire, you were sleeping," Hannah cries, trying to smile.

"Hey, Hannah Banana."

"Don't come in here," Rob warns, turning so Hannah is no longer facing me.

I hold out my hands, keeping my feet in one spot, even when everything in my body is demanding I dive for her. With every breath, I'm aware of eyes on me from the stairs.

"Please don't take her with you. She's scared. She can come with me."

A painful sob rips from his chest.

I step forward, and he doesn't flinch.

Another slow step as I swallow the cough bubbling in my throat.

Resting my hand on his shoulder, my heart pounds painfully as I reach for the gun, but he retreats.

"I want to go with Claire, Daddy," Hannah whispers, so exhausted her eyes are closing.

Dark eyes meet mine, and I hope he can read all the unspoken pleas. *Let me take her.*

Sirens ring out in the distance, and I know I don't have long. There's heat at my feet, and there'll be no way out soon. Jake will come storming in here any second.

"Daddy loves you, sweetheart." He sobs into her hair, collapsing back against the wall with her still in his arms. Eyes soaked with tears, he looks up at me. "I wasn't going to let her burn."

No. He was going to kill both of them first.

"I know," I say softly. "I think I need to take her now."

His head bobs up and down, but his grip tightens.

I do the only thing I can. I rest my hand on his. The contact makes him rear back in shock.

"Show her that her daddy wants to protect her. Be the man she thinks you are."

One by one, his fingers release.

He doesn't object when I reach for her. He doesn't utter a word as he sinks to the floor.

"Come with us, Rob."

He may be a monster, but I'm not.

His justice should be outside this house. Dying this way is too easy.

He shakes his head before holding the gun to his temple and roars, "Get the fuck out."

Nodding, I tell Hannah to nuzzle her face in my neck and not look up.

Jake is still outside when I leave with her in my arms.

He takes a menacing step forward. "Stop," I shout. "Take her. She needs you now."

Face contorted into a rage I've never seen before, he grabs Hannah, places his jacket over her head, and we descend into flames.

Eyes stinging from the smoke, the fire roars everywhere. It's already dancing across the railing on the stairs. But we're close to the door.

We're going to get out.

Choking, Jake pulls the door open.

But he hesitates.

Why is he stopping?

Terror seizes as he turns and places Hannah in my arms.

"No," I sob.

"Get out, baby. Get her out."

He's leaving me with no other choice, and I fucking hate him.

I hate him so much.

Pushing and taking my protest with him, he turns and runs.

I don't see him anymore. The flames swallow him whole.

With fresh air in my lungs, a gunshot is the last thing to ring out in the wind.

THIRTY-NINE

Glass smashes from the windows.
  Fire roars.
  There's heat on my back, but we're out.
  Hannah's in my arms.
  Why is Hannah in my arms?
  "Jake?" someone screams.
  He went back in.
  Sam is here.
  My legs finally buckle, and I fall to my knees on the wet grass.
  It's cold.
  Where's Jake?
  I need him.
  Lights are flashing.
  Hannah is screaming.
  I think I'm trying to soothe her.
  It happened again.
  I couldn't breathe.
  People are rushing toward the flames.
  Others are crowding us.
  Where's Jake?
  I need him.
  People are touching us.
  Every time someone touches Hannah, she screams.

I think it's her.

Maybe it's me.

A woman is snapping her fingers at me.

I do that.

I do that when people are in shock.

"Ma'am?"

Hannah screams again.

"Stop touching her," I whisper, holding her tighter to my body.

Where's Jake?

I need Jake.

Maybe I'm dead because my father's eyes are looking at me again.

But I think he's real.

Hannah screams.

"Please stop touching her."

I rock back and forth on my knees. That should make it better.

I'm tired.

I think we should sleep.

"Ma'am, you need to focus."

Who is this woman? She keeps snapping her fingers at me.

It's so loud here.

The sirens. The fire. The people.

So many people.

They're trying to help.

Where's Jake?

Hannah screams.

She keeps screaming.

"I don't want to go with them, Claire. I want to stay with you."

Something snaps. I feel it. I'm shaking everywhere and they won't stop touching us.

"Stop touching her."

They're not listening. They touch her again. They're trying to take her. They're going to bring her back to the flames. She won't be able to breathe. She'll be like me.

She shouldn't be like me.

She's a baby.

"STOP FUCKING TOUCHING HER."

The woman backs away. "It's okay, Ma'am. You're safe now."

Where's Jake?

My throat hurts.

Papa is here. He kneels. I see my eyes again. He made my throat hurt.

"Claire, you're okay now," he cries.

Why is he crying?

He's reaching for me.

"You're going to hurt Mama," I sob.

His hand is on my shoulder.

He's going to kill me.

I break.

I scream like Hannah.

Where's Mama?

There's another roar in the distance. "Get the fuck away from her."

Papa jumps back, fear in his eyes.

It's like mine.

I can't breathe again.

"Claire?" Jake is here.

He looks dirty, and his skin is red, but he's alive.

He coughs. It sounds painful.

"Are you hurt?" I ask. He shakes his head. He's okay. "Where is he?"

I don't want Hannah to see him again.

He'll take her away.

Jake bends, casting his eyes to the grass for a moment, but he doesn't answer.

What did he do?

"Jake?" I plead.

"It was too late."

Now he can't hurt Hannah anymore.

That's good, right?

Jake reaches out to touch me but stops. "Can I touch you, baby?" He's whispering.

I like that he whispers because everything else is so loud.

I nod.

I'm tired.

Hannah isn't screaming.

"You're safe."

You're safe with me.

He feathers his knuckles along my cheek.

"My throat hurts," I tell him.

He flinches.

I think my throat hurts him too.

"Baby, can I take Hannah? You need to get checked out."

Hannah's grip tightens.

"Please don't touch her," I beg, even when I know he won't hurt her because his arms are the safest place to be.

"Ma'am." The lady snaps her fingers again. Jake doesn't like when she does that. "We need to get you to the hospital. Can you let us help you?"

I don't know.

"She's in a state of shock," I hear her say.

Me?

I'm in shock?

"You should go with them. She's only responding to you. She's not in a good place," Papa tells Jake.

Jake punches him.

Papa doesn't fight back, even when he falls to the ground, and Jake picks him up by the collar.

"Because of us. We put her here. She's like this because of us."

No, Jake. Not you. It was the monsters.

Only the monsters.

Hannah screams.

She's getting heavy.

Jake doesn't roar anymore because his lips are on my face. "I'm so sorry, sweetheart."

I don't know what he's sorry for, but I've already forgiven him.

"I'm tired," I say. "I think I'll sleep now."

"No, baby. Stay with me, okay?"

"Ma'am." The woman snaps again. "Keep your eyes open." She looks at Jake. "She's quite bruised. We need to get her seen."

Jake cups either side of my head, heavy tears floating in his eyes.

I look up because birds are singing in the trees.

It's nighttime.

Birds should be sleeping.

But it's beautiful.

Maybe the fire woke them.

Hannah looks too. She's quiet now.

"Claire?" I look back at him. "We need to get you to the hospital."

"Will you come?" I ask.

"I'll come."

It's painful when he tucks his hands under my arms and lifts me to my feet.

Hannah is so heavy now, but I hold on.

She needs me.

It's bright in the ambulance.

I don't like it.

People are touching me, but Hannah isn't screaming.

Nobody touches her.

I think she's asleep.

Jake is holding my hand.

I'm safe with him.

"I'm tired," I try to tell them, but they don't listen.

Jake listens.

"I know. Put your head here." He presses my head to his shoulder.

It's warm.

He's always warm.

"You got to me on time," I mutter.

My eyes close.

I sleep.

***

"Stop touching her," I roar as I wake.

Someone is trying to take her away.

Lungs burning, I sit up on the bed, gripping Hannah in my arms.

She's still sleeping.

It's Beth.

The sobs come when I see her because I know Hannah is safe with her.

She stops kissing Hannah to cup my face. She presses her head to mine, and everything ruptures.

"You saved my baby," she cries.

She's wrong.

"I put her in danger."

"No." She runs her hands over my hair, my face, my shoulders, until her eyes settle on my neck, and she stills.

What's wrong with my neck?

It happened again.

"I'm sorry." She holds back her cry. "I'm so sorry. I'm sorry it was you."

"But it wasn't her," I whisper because my voice isn't stronger. "It's good that it was me." Something else breaks as I remember. My chest doesn't feel big enough to contain the pain anymore. "She saw things. I'm so sorry."

Beth runs her fingers through my hair like my mother used to. "She's alive. She survived. My baby is here because of you. Everything else we will get through." She keeps rubbing my cheek. "Oh, Claire."

"Do I look that bad?" I try to joke because I can't deal with this. "You should sit," I tell her, trying to come out of the fog in my head. "She's sleeping. Let her sleep."

I will stay here forever if it means she can sleep through most of the pain.

Beth nods and takes a seat in the uncomfortable chair at the bedside.

It looks like the chair I used to sit in when I visited Nick.

It's only then that I feel the warmth of fingers around my hand on the other side.

My chest inflates when I see him.

He looks exhausted, worn out, and in pain.

He tries to smile, but it falters.

His eyes fall to my neck. Guilt riddles the beautiful features I'm used to.

I can't stand it.

I shake my head and run my thumb over his knuckles. "You got to us in time. The blame doesn't lie with you. Jake, he didn't even know about us. He thought I was staying with Amy. This was about him losing control."

Eyes still on our interlocked hands, he stands, only to cup my face and press a kiss to my forehead. "I thought I lost you." His eyes meet mine and knocks the air from my lungs. "The world doesn't spin without you on it."

He tucks the strands of smoky smelling hair behind my ear and nausea rocks in my stomach.

"I'm tired," I whisper. "I think I'll sleep now."

***

"Her sedative should wear off soon. We've prescribed a week of sleeping pills. She needs to sleep. Her state of shock is quite intensive. Exhaustion will creep in, and her past trauma doesn't help. She'll need time off work. A good psychologist will help, but she won't be able to return until she's cleared. Police will want to speak to her soon."

The voices are muffled in the distance.

"Physically, how is she?" someone asks. I think it's Amy.

There's silence for a moment, and I'm not sure if I've drifted off again.

"Physically, she's okay. Her bruises may take some weeks to fully fade. I'm not concerned about her physical state. She arrived to us very traumatized." There's another pause. "But the police will want to speak to her."

My moan scrapes through the air.

I don't feel Hannah's weight anymore.

"Where is she?" I cry, but I hardly hear myself.

"Hush." Amy takes my hand. "She's okay. She's with Beth."

I still smell smoky.

My eyes are too heavy when I ask, "Where's Jake?"

I need him.

"I'm here, sweetheart." His touch brings me round.

I can't be out long. I still feel my dress on my skin.

It stings when I open my eyes to stare at white walls.

"I want to go home," I croak, hating when my sound isn't stronger yet.

Jake turns toward the doctor. "Is she cleared to leave?"

"Well, yes, but the police will want to speak to her."

He plucks a business card from his pocket. "Give them this." Eyes on me, he says, "Head down, baby." He tucks one arm around my back, and the other under my knees as he lifts me. I bury my head in his neck, distracting myself with his scent. Smoke may overpower it, but I can still get a hint of cedarwood and peppermint.

"What are you doing?" the doctor asks.

His answer rolls from his lips like it's the most obvious thing in the world. "Bringing her home. Anyone has any problems, give them my number. They know where to find her."

The bustle of the hospital disappears as he walks away with me.

I was right.

His arms are the safest place to be.

***

"Drink it, sweetheart." Jake holds a glass of water toward me as the tablets settle in my mouth. The smoky clothes are gone.

I drink the water to rid the taste of the medication.

I don't like medication.

It's going to make me sleepy.

I need a shower.

"I want to have a shower."

"You can," he agrees. "Sleep first."

He kisses my forehead as I drift off into the familiar feel of his pillowcase, but I don't think I sleep long before I'm up again, clawing at the pajamas I don't remember changing into and switching on the shower. My hair still reeks.

I stumble against the glass as I pull my clothes off.

I hate feeling like I'm not in my head.

But the shower is warm when I step inside.

So, I stand under the sprays, and I don't move.

I don't think I can.

My arms are heavy.

I simply make the water hotter so I can make sure I'm alive.

I feel it.

I think.

"Claire," my name echoes in the steam. He opens the shower door and I hardly notice how naked I am. "Baby," he whispers, and I hate how desperate it sounds. He brushes a hand through his hair before scrubbing it over his face.

I stand still as I watch him shed his clothes and step inside with me.

He enters the fog.

I'm not alone.

You're safe with me.

I go lax against his body because my legs can't support me anymore. Pulling me into his arms, he sits on the shower ledge. "I've got you, baby."

His fingers massage shampoo into my hair.

It feels amazing.

He washes it out and kneads spasmed muscles until they ease.

When we're done, he dries me off with a towel.

I let him because I don't think I can move.

I'm trapped.

Over his head, I catch sight of myself in the mirror.

I think it's me.

Wet hair dripping, the droplets cascade over black and purple skin. My jaw is swollen. I press a finger to my wrist.

There's a pulse, but my eyes look lifeless.

I touch the tender skin on my neck.

Please, Papa.

When he sees me doing it, he gently removes my hand and replaces it with healing lips.

He kisses away the monster's touch because his touch is the only one.

In the bedroom, he dresses me in clean pajamas.

I hate it.

When I look up at him, the moon casts a glow on his face. It's late. "Where's Jay-Jay?"

His brows narrow for a moment before he strokes my face. "With his grandparents at the beach, remember?"

"You should bring him home now. I'll go home too. He should be here with you."

He nods as I watch him swallow. "He will. He's coming home in a couple of days. He misses you." I smile. It hurts. I miss him too. "But right now, we're going to focus on you."

"Jake?"

Still stroking my hair, he asks, "What is it, Trouble?"

I swing my foot along the carpet. "I think I'm broken." Something has cracked so deep in me, I've fallen through. I'm in a darkness I've never experienced before. I'm sinking. My body is too tired to kick my way out of it.

And I won't drag him with me.

There's silence for a moment, but I need to finish. "I think I've always been broken until I found you. I feel more together around you. All the other pieces come with Jay-Jay. And it's silly because he's not mine. We're not together. Yet, I look at him and I want to dive in front of any danger. I want to be around him." I try to smile. "Because he's more fun than you."

He tries to laugh with me, but we both fail. We're doing a lot of trying. It's not working.

"But something's going on in my head. I need to fix it. You both deserve everything, and I have very little of myself left to give. These bruises are nothing but my own reminders. They'll fade. Nobody will see them. But I'll remember them because these bruises may not scar, but in here…" I dig a finger into my temple, "I'm disfigured. I have been long before today."

He reaches for me, but I walk away.

I'm tired.

I think I'll sleep now.

"I just needed you to know. I always feel the closest thing to whole when I'm in your arms," I mumble, resting my head on the pillow.

His heat is at my back before my eyes close. He pulls me to him, holding me so tight I can hardly breathe, but I don't care.

He's breathing for me.

I don't know how long passes, but his grip never loosens.

I'm sure he thinks I'm sleeping when a guttural sob rips from his chest. "I'm sorry," he whispers over and over. His hands are on my body. Everywhere. It's gentle. Not enough to wake me if I was sleeping.

He's checking I'm still here.

"You're whole, baby. You're everything."

FORTY

The medication makes me feel like I'm outside my body.

I hate it.

But I'm sleeping through most of it. Which is the point, I guess. And the sleeping pills keep the nightmares at bay.

I don't dream at all.

I don't know what time it was when I finally drifted off, but when I wake, I stumble to the window, and peek through the curtain. It's daylight. I go back to bed.

I sleep and sleep and sleep.

I'm grateful for it.

I sometimes feel dips in the bed. It's usually Jake. He's either lying with me or checking I'm still breathing. But he never stays away for long.

When I feel the weight of two bodies on either side of me, I know who it is.

"I missed my musketeers," I whisper, unable to open my eyes yet.

A little while longer.

I'll face it then.

Garry kisses the back of my head. "There's our girl. We missed you."

Mandy takes my hand. "Go back to sleep. We'll be here when you wake."

I'm already drifting off, feeling a crack in my chest fill with just knowing they're here.

***

I'm staring at the stairs.

I can't remember walking here.

I'm showered and I'm dressed. I have no recollection of doing either. I think the police were here earlier. I think that's why I'm dressed.

My mind is blacking out. No matter how hard I fight, I'm always dragged back to the memories.

It's not Rob or that house.

My father's blue eyes are always what haunts me.

It must be the medication.

This can't be how I am now. It needs to get better.

Downstairs, voices float from the kitchen. Voices I recognize. Laughs I love.

My heart pounds and sweat breaks out on the nape of my neck.

Goddammit legs, move.

I put one foot in front of the other. Before I realize I'm moving, I'm standing at the open kitchen door.

Jake is the first to notice. Our stares lock like they always do, but his gaze quickly drops to my neck again.

Stop looking.

I guess I can add another name to the list of who people see when they look at me.

I'm afraid he doesn't see me anymore, just the bruises.

"Claire Bear?" I jump back, startled. "It's okay, baby girl."

"Mama?" I gasp. "What are you doing here? You can't be here." I try to speak louder, but my voice is so hoarse.

"I'm here to take you home. To let you heal."

He'll find her here.

"You're not safe here, Mama. You need to go. He'll find you."

Every feature on her face drops. Everyone's eyes are on me.

"Jesus," she trails off. "Baby girl, what have they done to you?"

"You need to go, Mama. Please." The panic is rising, slowly wrapping dark claws around my lungs and suffocating me.

"She's going to have a panic attack." I don't know who says it, but they're right.

Or the break is coming.

I'm balancing on a tightrope, and every second I'm closer to plummeting into blackness.

"Claire," Mama shouts. "He's not here. You're in Jake's kitchen. You're safe."

Everyone keeps telling me that.

My eyes dart around. Jay-Jay's drawings are still on the fridge. Amy's drinking a cup of coffee. Mandy and Garry look like they want to pick me up and disappear with me. I wouldn't object.

Jake is closer now, ready to wrap me back up in his arms if he needs to. He looks broken.

Like me.

But she's right. I'm not back there.

I blow out a breath and inhale deeply, filling my burning lungs. My hands are seizing up, my knuckles turning white.

"He's here." I shake my head, letting her know I'm okay. "Not here. Not in this house, but he's here."

She rests her hands on my arms, steadying me. "I know. I've always known. I should have told you sooner, but you left. You built a life somewhere else, and I knew you wouldn't settle if you knew he was so close. I didn't realize you would have direct contact with him in your job."

She's safe.

He didn't hurt her.

I run my fingers through her hair, my heart filling as I realize. "You're looking at me, Mama."

I'm broken just like her now—sentenced to an endless winter. Yet, she looks like summer. She's healthy like I remember when I was younger. There's an extra curve in her waist, color in her cheeks, and no glossiness in her eyes. They're clear. She's not drinking. Her hair is longer than mine now.

For the first time, I see a lot of myself when I look at her.

She's getting better.

Maybe I can too.

But with my words, she ruptures. Tears flow like a river. They're endless. They're filled with pain and regret. They're apologies.

"It's okay." I hush her. "I know."

She's looking at me because she sees me. I can't help but wish she didn't.

There's still a hollowness in my chest when we sit. Everyone chatters except Jake. He remains in the silence with me at my side.

I can't focus long enough to know what they're saying or if they're talking to me. But I think they know I don't want to talk.

Jake pushes the plate of uneaten food toward me. I swallow the bile in my throat. "Eat. You need to eat."

I reach out and grab his hand, clinging to it like it's the only thing keeping me planted to the ground.

"I don't want to take the pills anymore. I can't feel anything, and they make me too nauseous."

"No pills," he agrees. "But please eat."

I try, but my mouth waters when I swallow. It hurts, and every bite is a reminder of the tightness in my throat.

I close my eyes and distract myself.

One.

Two.

Three.

Four.

Five.

I keep going until I lose count.

"Claire?"

My head snaps back. "Mmm?"

"You were falling asleep." Garry reaches across the table to take my hand. "You're freezing."

Am I?

I shrug. "Just tired. I'm going to get some air." I excuse myself, not looking back as I step outside and stare up at the birds singing in the tall trees.

They sing and sing.

Ma'am, you need to focus.

She had the bluest eyes. Like yours.

You weren't supposed to be here.

Go back in your room, baby girl. Put your headphones on and dance.

You're going to change the world someday, Claire Russell.

You need to take care of our boys.

Stop screaming, baby girl. Please stop screaming. I love you. I love you. I love you.

I gasp, assaulted by memories.

"Get out of my head."

331

I brush a hand over my cheeks. They're wet.

My body vibrates, and no matter what I do, I can't stop.

Everything burns again.

I can't breathe.

The trees are spinning.

My knees buckle, and I collapse.

I've fallen off the tightrope.

My sobs come out in a wheeze.

I've even lost my fucking voice.

But the birds keep singing.

I need to do something.

If I don't, I fear I'll lose myself, and I won't come back.

When I open my mouth, I fill my lungs, and I scream.

It's swallowed by the trees, so I dig my fingers into the grass and scream again. I'm choking on my sobs, feeling myself shatter with every breath. All the pieces explode. It boils over because the agony is so severe; it needs a way out.

And I need my fucking voice back.

Strong arms are around me with the next strangled roar, muffled against his shoulder. I claw at his chest, throw my fists at it, only to drag him back. He's the only one capable of holding me and making me feel like I can reclaim all those pieces and put myself back together.

I couldn't breathe.

Death must be easier than this.

Roughly, he grabs either side of my head. There's no judgment in those whiskey eyes, only understanding. "Don't stop," he orders. "It's your fucking voice, baby. Don't allow anyone to take it. Use it. Scream."

I might be losing everything else, but I can't lose my voice.

My throat is burning, my eyes are heavy, and I'm on the brink of exhaustion, but I fight through, and I scream.

I scream for my mother, for Hannah, for Beth, for Jake, for Jess. For me.

My voice doesn't give out, but my tired muscles do, and I fall in a heap into Jake's arms. Not moving, he simply holds me until my wails subside and the sobs allow me to have my breath back. The world is a little clearer when I open my eyes.

Building enough energy, I kneel between his legs and sit back on my heels. We're both panting, grasping at anything to hold us together.

My head falls, but he's quick to lift it again. Scrubbing his palms over my face, he dries my sticky cheeks.

Our frantic breaths mingle, and a thousand unspoken words linger between us.

"Keep breathing, sweetheart. One breath at a time."

FORTY-ONE

"Leave? You want me to take leave?"

The word hangs in the air between us like a bomb ready to detonate.

"It's paid leave." She says it like it should make me feel better. It doesn't.

"I don't care if it's paid. I want to go back to work." I'm trying not to shout here, but sweet Jesus. "Nora, this is bullshit, and you know it."

I look to Jake for help, but his head is hanging between his shoulders as he grips the counter. He isn't looking at me. He hasn't done much of it in days.

My blood is boiling and instinctively, I scratch at my neck but drop my hand when she notices.

"You need time. It's only been a week. Your bruises haven't even healed."

"Nora, I can't leave the shelter for too long. I went to see those women yesterday, and I told them I would be back within weeks. I miss them. Besides, I'm leaving today. I'm staying with my mother for a couple of days. My bruises will be healed before I return."

Nora takes my hand from across the table, a sullen smile on her red-painted lips. "You failed the psychological assessment. You need to get better. Those women want you to be better. They'll understand."

I know she's right, but I don't want her to be.

"I'll go to another psychologist."

"Claire, you've suffered a severe trauma," she states matter-of-factly, making my blood run cold. "Honey, I want to see you well. Your job will still be there when you get back. But these stories will carry more weight than they did when you first started. You need to get stronger so you can deal with them. I don't want you to return just to set yourself back."

This can't be happening. I can't be losing everything I worked for.

"There is another option," she says, her eyes glancing toward Jake. He can look at her because she's not the broken one.

I have the unsettling feeling I'm not going to like what she has to say. I hate the knowing look between them.

"What?" I snap, my patience wearing thin.

"An old colleague of mine is conducting a study on the impact of music on domestic abuse survivors. He wants you to help lead it."

That piques my interest and I sit straight on the chair.

It could work. I've assisted in studies before.

If she's insisting I take time off, I can't stay idle. I can't sit at home and look at four walls. I'll go crazier than I already am.

"Okay, that might work. I'm still close enough to the city university. I can help until I go back to the shelter."

She closes her eyes for a moment, containing any emotions on the verge of bubbling over.

With a deep sigh, my shoulders slump against the chair. "It's not the city university, is it?"

She shakes her head. "You'll be overseeing the study in multiple locations around Europe."

I laugh, but this isn't funny. "Europe? Nora, I know I'm half Italian, but the only language I speak is English."

"You won't need to. You're overseeing it," she repeats.

"It could be good for you, Claire," Jake's voice finally breaks through the tense atmosphere.

"Jesus, he speaks."

The flinch is almost unnoticeable, but not to me. There's nothing but pain when he looks at me now.

Fight for me.

I want to beat at his chest and demand it.

"You missed the opportunity to see the world once. You're still young. You shouldn't be stuck here."

Not once has our ten-year age gap been an issue, and he's using this

335

moment to make it one.

I don't respond to him. I'm afraid of what I'll say.

"For how long?" I finally ask, a lump so thick in my throat, I fear I'll choke on it.

"Nine months," she says.

I grip the chair, because if I don't hold on, I'll topple over. "Nine months?" I gasp, feeling like I need to hear everything twice just to get it through my head. Pinching the bridge of my nose, I try to soothe the headache building before running my fingers through my hair. I'm on the verge of tears, but I won't let them fall. I've cried too much.

"It's an amazing opportunity, Claire. Put your PhD to use. It means you still get to do what you love. You still get to work with these women and children, but while taking a step back."

I don't want a fucking step back.

"That means giving up my job at the shelter. It means giving up everything here." I don't look at him, but he knows. And it slowly kills me when he doesn't open his mouth. "You're sending me away."

"We're not sending you away, dear." She takes my hand. I want to back away from her touch, but I don't have the heart to reject her. "I was there. All those years ago when you were a scared fourteen-year-old girl. You fought, and you came through. You just need to fight again. You won't be able to do that here. You give too much of your heart away to others and you'll do so much of that at the shelter. Take the time with your mother to heal physically. The rest you can figure out while you're doing something you love."

It should bring me comfort. It should ease the heavy knot in my stomach. But I feel sick.

I shrug as I stand, the hurt and anger building so much I think my heart is breaking in two. "It doesn't give me much of a choice, does it?" I squeeze Nora's hand, stopping only once as I walk away to look at Jake.

He looks away.

I die a little inside.

"I need to finish packing."

***

It's funny how I can pack up what seems like a lifetime into a suitcase. A suitcase that has been staring at me for weeks. A constant reminder that my time here isn't permanent.

I knew I would have to leave. I never thought it would be under these circumstances.

A part of me is attached to this house, and its pull is so strong, it's a punishment to tear myself away.

I laughed in this house, I cried, I played, I had mind-blowing sex, I fought, and I fell so hopelessly in love with the man occupying it.

My greedy heart doesn't want to leave.

I don't want to go back to a house that was only ever shaded in black clouds. But I need to. I need to face and battle old demons before I ever wage war against the new ones.

And I think my mother needs to see me breathe as much as I need to witness her getting better.

I still have my voice. I made sure of it. Jake made sure I didn't give up on it.

It's a start.

At least I can talk myself out of the dark depths and try to convince myself of brighter days—days when the world is in color.

A hand comes down on my suitcase, slamming it shut. I jump, so lost in my thoughts I didn't hear him come in here.

"Don't leave like this," he demands. His voice coats over me, and the instant tug at my chest makes me want to curl up. He pinches my chin between his fingers. "Look at me."

I meet his gaze, feeling my heart hardening with every second. "I don't have a problem with looking at you, Jake. Can you say the same?"

His grip softens. I can see the fight in him—the want to keep our eye contact but it wavers and drops to my throat.

"I thought as much."

If guilt were a person, it would be Jake.

Pain has made the dent between his brow a constant fixture and there's always tension across his broad chest. His wounds are so raw, I can almost see the peeling flesh and the agony that lies beneath.

But the distance in him makes the air between us cold.

"What is it, Jake? Have I passed the threshold of broken and damaged for you to fuck me?"

Now he looks at me. And I hate it. It's nothing like how it used to be. There's very little warmth in those amber eyes.

I chew my lip between my teeth, feeling him slip away with every second that passes in silence.

"I told you before, you won't break me. I'm not some fragile doll. But if this is how you want to end things with us—whatever *we* are—then have the balls 'big enough to talk to me. Don't do it through Nora." I turn away to close the suitcase. "But I guess you don't have to. You've made sure I'll be out of your life in every way possible."

He grabs my elbow, roughly yanking me around. "Do you think I want to see you walk out that door? Because I'll fucking die inside when you do. I don't want to think of you somewhere else for almost a year. I can't look at you because I still see you lifeless in my arms. I hear you struggling for breath. I see the look in your eyes when you screamed for some fucking control. I still feel your life draining as I held you. I couldn't protect you from him, and it's slowly eating me up." He turns away. Shoulders vibrating, he leans over, presses his hands to his thighs, and roars, "Fuck."

A sob escapes. I hold my hand over my mouth to stifle it.

"I'm sorry," I cry.

His body gives up, and he crouches, head in his hands. He's breaking right here in this room.

"Because I know it's not the first time you held someone in your arms like that." Sitting on the bed so I'm between his legs, I tip his head back. "Look at me, please. I can't deal with you not looking at me."

Eyes swimming when they connect, I'm not sure what he sees in mine, but I see his ghosts. We're both more haunted than we were, and I'm afraid he can't get past seeing someone else. I'm hurting him.

"You can't protect me from the world."

He takes my hand and presses a kiss to my palm. "I'd lock you in this house if I could. I'm too selfish with you, Claire."

Tentatively, he reaches out.

Closer and closer.

He takes my face in his hands, and with his touch, my dams burst.

I know I'm not dead because my heart still beats when he's around.

He makes me feel.

On our first night together, I asked him to help me feel anything but pain. But now, he makes me feel with just the sight of him.

How am I going to get through this without him?

I don't want to lie in a bed and not feel him in it. I don't want to live a day and not hear his voice. I want to see the warmth in his eyes when he looks at his son.

But I don't want to doubt.

And I do—every time he looks at me.

I screamed to get my voice back, and I don't want to leave here not knowing. Worst of all, I don't want to leave without opening my mouth and telling him.

I stand away from his hold. He follows, boring a hole through me with his stare.

"Claire?" Eyes watering, he's blurry when I look up. He exhales. "I know."

I open my mouth, the words tickling the tip of my tongue, but I close it again, hating myself for not just asking.

"Say it," he prompts, reading me like he always does.

I need to see his reaction. I need to know the truth. So, with a shaky breath, I meet his gaze, knowing my words can break us beyond repair.

"Do you see her when you look at me?"

It takes a second, just a flash of confusion before the reality of what I'm asking hits and knocks the air from his lungs. With wide eyes, he takes a step forward but wavers and remains planted on the floor.

"Jesus Christ, Claire." He runs a hand over the stubble on his face.

I need to know.

"Do you?" I persist even when everything in me is gradually falling apart. "Isn't that how we started? I wanted to feel. You wanted to remember. I need to know before I leave. Was any of it how I think? Was it real? Or were we just fucking like we agreed?" Shaking, I bite down on the tender skin of my lip, swallowing the sticky lump in my throat.

The air swirls and thickens between us. Fire rages deep in his amber eyes. It's familiar and foreign all at once as it sizzles over my skin.

I stop breathing, watching as nothing but anger takes hold.

A large stride toward me and he snakes a hand around my waist, holding me until my back is against the wall. "Let me make this clear. I never just fucked you, Claire. I worshipped you."

And I believe it because I felt nothing short of worshipped every time he stripped me bare.

But I've been stripped bare of more than just my clothes.

I hang on to his every word, and despite the pain hammering in my chest, my body becomes desperate for more of his touch. His molten glare is blistering but his touch releases enough for my breathing to slow before his grip tightens and he steals the air from my lungs again.

I give it to him.

He brushes the hair from my shoulders and presses a gentle kiss to the top of my head.

"I broke a rule," I breathe, my voice hardly audible with the admission. But he hears it.

He catches a tear with his finger. "We broke all our rules."

"No. This one I made to myself." I can't swallow it anymore. Closing my eyes because I can't bear to witness the rejection, I finally say it. "I promised myself I wouldn't fall in love with you."

H slips away.

No.

He had to have known.

He drops his hand.

My heart doesn't break.

That would be less painful.

It simply freezes over just like his eyes. It expands, then shatters, all the sharp pieces clawing at me from the inside out.

It was all in my head.

When he tilts his chin, his eyes don't meet mine. They look past me.

You're an idiot, Claire.

The sting of rejection burns too deep, and I can't stand to watch him look at me like this. I attempt to move around him for my suitcase, but his hand grabs the inside of my elbow.

His voice is gruff, tight, and heavy with the weight of his confession when he says, "I broke it, too. It was real for me."

Trembling in his arms, he guides me to the bed. I sit on the edge— exactly how I feel—as he bends and takes my hands in his on my lap.

"I loved her, Claire. For so long, I thought she filled that part of my heart. There wasn't room for anyone else, so I closed it off." He glances at our interlocked hands before returning his attention to me. "Then you walked into my life and taught me you can't put a cap on it. It doesn't work that way. The heart expands and accommodates." I watch as a thousand memories replay in a split second. "I don't see her when I look at you. Sometimes, when I see how you are with Jay-Jay, I get angry for all the times she missed with him. That he doesn't remember her voice, or how she felt. But I never look at you in search of her." Tears coat my skin and trail down his hand as he cups my face. "I never wanted to fall in love with you…Until I did. And I love you so much it scares the shit out of me, because what you see when I look at you is the fear of losing you. Christ, Claire, you make me want to live just to watch you breathe. You brought me back to life."

He's wrong.

He breathed life into my body.

Sometimes, he breathes for me.

He brought *me* back to life.

I don't know how every word breaks and heals me all at once, only to do it all over again.

It's bittersweet because this should be the start of something.

But why does it feel like the end?

We sit.

We stare.

We don't speak because speaking would ruin it.

The familiar electricity bounces between us until it consumes the air.

I pounce.

My mouth collides with his. Tongues dueling, he doesn't stumble when he stands, taking me with him. I lock my ankles around his waist, swallowing his groan and feeling the vibration in his chest.

He's careful with me, placing a gentle hand behind my head as he rests me on the bed. He unbuttons my jeans and I toss my t-shirt over my head. I need to feel him.

Because he makes me feel.

Skin on skin, our eyes lock as he eases himself inside me. A quiet gasp fills my chest. Filled, he stills to look at me.

I don't want to see it in the look we share, but we can't deny it.

There's too much damage done. We need to repair.

One look.

And what we see in each other could be the ultimate break.

We need to repair separately.

We get too lost in each other to mend. Our vacuum isn't the right environment. We'll never be whole together until we fix ourselves because we'll bleed ourselves dry while trying to heal the other.

I want to stay whole. I want to keep all the pieces of myself together. Even if those pieces were few, at least I still recognized the foundation.

But I fear I'm shattered. I've cracked in ways that can't be put back together.

Not quickly.

Too many parts of myself lie with others. They've been smothered in the rubble of my past, and I don't know how to find them.

He deserves a life with someone not looking for pieces of themselves in every step they take.

He deserves whole.

He deserves everything.

I'm not whole.

Not now.

Not yet.

Someday, maybe.

I bite down on my quivering lip.

Fingers gripping the back of my head, he pulls me to him, pressing his head against mine as he begins to move.

Cedarwood and peppermint.

I've never considered anywhere my home, but I think it's Jake's scent. It feels like home.

Our eyes are rimmed red, and our hearts are slowly breaking for the loss of each other.

Because now isn't our time.

He presses forward, lips so close my skin tingles. Even in the darkness, he makes me feel the heat of the sun.

He exhales against my mouth, and I devour it.

My life support.

When he fills me over and over again, working my body until I'm dizzy, my head falls back.

The bruises.

I try to hide them. He shouldn't have to look.

But he doesn't let me. Instead, his fingers tangle in my hair, and with his thumb under my chin, he tilts my head back before pressing his lips to every tender marking. With every kiss, he gives me back every breath that was stolen. With every touch, the words, "I love you," are whispered against my flesh.

Getting lost in him has allowed me to find a part of myself.

But it belongs to him anyway.

Our bodies tense together as I dig my nails into the taut muscles in his back.

The heat builds and builds. A part of me wishes it wouldn't because when this is over, so are we.

A shudder works its way between us as we find our release together.

"Claire," he groans, kissing away the cries of pleasure from my mouth.

Panting, the world settles, and realization blooms.

Brushing my hair off my shoulder, he presses his lips to mine, and I fall into our black hole with a moan. I want to stay here just for a minute. I want to take everything in. I want to remember how he feels, how he touches me, how he tastes. I want to remember this moment, so if our time ever comes, I'll know what it's like when memories don't taint it.

Pulling away, breathless and torn, he holds my face between his fingers, pressing the other hand under the small of my back while I cling to his shoulders.

"I don't want to let you go just yet," I cry.

He rests his head against mine. "When you're ready, we'll do it together."

FORTY-TWO

Amy is sitting on the front step when we arrive. Mama is tending to her flowers.

I don't have my car yet. It's part of evidence. Sam assures us the case will be closed soon. It's pretty open and shut.

I never asked Jake why he ran back in.

I never asked what happened when he did.

I was told Rob shot himself and was already dead when Jake got to him. I won't insult him by questioning it.

I also don't blame him if it's not the truth.

The fire did too much damage to know.

Honestly, I don't want to. Not if he doesn't want to tell me.

My father remains quiet, just like he has for fourteen years. I've heard whispers of retirement, but I don't have it in myself to care.

"Want to dress in Mama's clothes and dance around your room with hairbrushes?" Amy jokes, hugging me as Jake carries my case inside. I still need to get the rest of my things from the house I'm still renting but have hardly lived in.

I kiss her cheek before my mother pulls me into her embrace. I search her eyes.

She's still sober.

I try to laugh. "We never did that, Amy."

"We can always start."

"It's good to have you home, baby girl." My mother squeezes my shoulders and spins me around.

What is she doing?

Maybe she isn't sober.

"We need to feed you."

"Feed me? Why?"

"You've lost weight."

"Last I checked, I'm okay with that." I throw out my hands and nod. "My ass needed it."

"It didn't," she fights back, offended on my behalf. "You're perfect the way you are."

"That, she is." Jake dips his chin when he finds three pairs of eyes staring at him. It's a little adorable.

Smiling, I blow out a breath.

This is it.

The goodbye I always saw coming, but never wanted to happen.

"We'll give you two a minute."

Amy squeezes his arm while Mama takes his face in her hands, needing to press on her tiptoes to reach him properly.

"You're a good man, Jake. Thank you for everything."

My poor heart can't take too much more today, but seeing how he pulls my mother into a tight embrace makes it swell so much, my eyes sting.

She cast me a supportive smile before going inside the house.

It's just us again, and the world fades away.

I sway on my feet.

"Can I get one of those?" I laugh lightly because I'm fighting to keep it together.

He grabs my hand and pulls me to him, wrapping me up so tight I'm almost ready to say I'm okay and I can leave with him again. His heart beats against my ear, and I hold on to the sound for the nights I have without him.

Tipping my head back, I look up while his arms keep me pinned to his chest. He presses a kiss to the top of my head before brushing my hair back from my eyes.

"As much as it's killing me to let you go, I have to." His thumb pulls my lip from the hold of my bite. I can't help but smile because these are memories filled with passion. "You're not a replacement, Claire. You never were. You're everything. If there's ever a day when you're ready, and you trust in this…Come back to me. I'll wait. Always.

345

And if it's not me, then I'll know I was the lucky bastard who found love again in you."

"We found it in each other."

He meets me halfway when I reach up and kiss him. I don't want to believe it's the last time. It can't be.

"You use that voice of yours for everyone else. It's time to scream for you. Find you. Look in the mirror and see you. See what I see because when you do, you'll see that you're perfect. And I can't wait to witness it."

I try to find strength in my worn-out voice to say, "Tell Jay-Jay to keep practicing. I want to hear every song when I get back."

He blows out a shaky breath, and it zings across my skin, making me tingle. "We'll be here."

Building the courage, I finally step away. His grip on me takes a little longer to release.

I follow him, step by step, knowing with each one, I'm staying behind.

"Jake," I call before he gets in the car. "It was real."

A gentle smile curves on the corner of his mouth. "It was real, baby. And don't disappear on me completely. Check in while seeing the world."

Tears cascade over the corners of my smile as I nod. He opens his mouth to say something else but quickly stops.

"What?"

He shakes his head. "Never mind. It's nothing. Tell me something good."

I close my eyes and inhale, feeling a small crack in my chest suddenly become full. My answer is obvious because it's been there since the day they walked into my life. "You and that boy of yours."

Smile dropping, he takes a step forward, but I shake my head and stop him.

I don't want to, but I have to.

They both deserve more of me than what's on offer right now.

"Your turn."

He winks. "Smile for me."

I roll my eyes and force my lips upward.

It hurts.

"A real one," he grumbles, but that smirk hasn't left his lips, and despite the hammering in my chest, the knot in my stomach, and the burning in my eyes, I smile.

I swear, I hear my cheeks creek like old floorboards.

He swallows.

I swallow harder.

I inhale.

He sighs.

"I got to see you smile today. That's my something good. It always is."

Content, he nods before getting in his car and driving away.

I can only watch as he takes my heart with him.

I'll get better.

I have to. For them and for me.

Someday, we might find our way back to each other.

FORTY-THREE

It's always cold in the cemetery.

Always.

It could be the hottest day of the year and there's still a chill when I come here.

Zipping my coat, I ignore the bench at Nick's grave and chose my usual seat on the grass with my back against his stone.

"Hiya, stranger." I fix the potted plants Kate always leaves. "Our girl did it yesterday. You'd be so proud of her. She was stunning."

Mandy made the most beautiful bride. Long blonde curls fell over her shoulders. Barefoot in a white flowing gown, she married Alex on the beach. Thankfully, it wasn't as cold.

Jake didn't go, and I can't help but feel it was for my sake. A part of me is grateful to him for it. I don't think I have the strength just yet.

I like to believe Nick was there in spirit to see for himself, but I'm skeptical, and I don't want him to miss out on a moment, so I tell him things.

I nod a greeting to a couple passing by before going back to my update.

"She's so unbelievably happy. Ava is a firecracker."

I scoot down until I'm on my back, watching the clouds go by for endless minutes. "Mama is sober. She's doing really good. She goes to meetings and sees a therapist. She's back to herself. I don't know what inspired the change, but I'm grateful for it. And she's playing the piano again."

Taking a deep breath, I fight with the burn behind my eyes as I pull at the blades of grass.

"I miss you every day, but I've missed you more than ever lately. I could do with some Nick advice because I've gone and done it. I've fallen in love, and I really wish you were in your room with your window open so I could crawl through and rant until I figured it out." I brush a heavy tear from my cheek. "I'm a little lost, and I don't know if you can hear me, but any help in the right direction would be great right now."

A sob cracks through my chest—raw and painful.

"Truth is, I'm scared because I think I will love him until the day I die. And now I'm leaving for nine months. I'm afraid I might have missed the moment, and I'm scared of all the moments I'm going to miss. But I need to do it." I wipe my eyes with the back of my hand. "So, I've come to say goodbye for now. I'm sure you won't miss my constant nattering, and I'll be back before you know it. I just wanted to sit here for a while. I needed my best friend."

***

"Claire, are you dead?"

I'm hallucinating.

Squinting, I open my eyes only to see a very familiar pair of blue pools looking back at me.

"Jay-Jay," I gasp, and before I can think about it, I leap for him, wrapping him up until he can hardly breathe.

He still gives the best hugs.

He laughs into my shoulder and I'm not looking at him, but I know he's rolling his eyes.

"We missed you too, Claire."

On my knees, I sit back on my heels. I'm touching his face like he's not real. Like this is a wonderful dream. But he feels real. His skin is warm, and that smile is exactly how I remember.

"I missed you so much. But what are you doing here?" I ask.

He stares at me with the same bewilderment I feel.

"We came to visit Mom."

"Oh."

I didn't know she was in this cemetery.

"Where?"

He points. "There."

That could be anyone.

Standing, I brush the grass from my jeans, only to be met with a familiar grey judgment.

"Sharon?"

Scowl a permanent fixture, she blinks at me slowly. "You are the last person I expected to see here. What are you doing?"

She makes me nervous.

I point down. "Visiting my best friend. What are you doing?"

She peeks over the two back-to-back stones before pointing at the ground she's standing on. "Visiting *my* best friend."

We stare for a moment, confusion muffling the truth.

Like mirror images, our mouths fall open.

"No," we gasp in unison.

She's been right there all this time.

Jess and Nick, back-to-back.

My legs are slow to move, but when they do, I'm staring at her picture. Beautiful auburn curls, the kindest smile, and the brightest blue eyes.

They're not mine.

They're Jay-Jay's.

"This is unbelievable." Sharon darts her eyes between me and the picture.

I suddenly feel shy and awkward.

She waves a finger. "Claire, this is Jess. Jess, this is Claire. Bet you've been haunting her, right?"

Horrified, my eyes almost bulge out of my head.

She squeezes my arm, throwing her head back and laughing. "I'm joking, Claire. Truth is, she probably would have liked you more than me."

I highly doubt it.

Jay-Jay tugs at my arm, breaking me out of my shock.

"Dad said you're leaving for a while. When will you be back?"

Looking up to control the threatening tears, I take his hand, choosing to be honest with him. "I don't know, sweetheart. But I know I'm going to miss you so much."

His smile is too sad. I wish there was music here. We could dance our sorrows away.

"Maybe I can ask Ava's mom to call you when we visit the beach, or I could ask Dad if I can video call you?"

"Yeah," I nod, tears betraying me. "I'd love that."

"I've learned lots of new songs."

If he's not careful, I'm going to burst into sobs. "I can't wait to hear them. Keep practicing."

And I mean it.

I want to hear them all a thousand times.

I love when his face breaks into the widest grin. Another part of my heart fills and repairs.

"Can we still do sock races when you get back?"

"It's a date," I tell him, laughing.

"Jay-Jay, can you go wait in the car, honey? I want to speak to Claire for a minute."

I swear, I think all the blood drains from my body and pools at my feet.

"Sure." He shrugs, walking away, but not before I grab him and squeeze him one last time. "I can't breathe, Claire." But he hugs me back, giving me what I've craved for the longest time.

His hugs are better than I remember.

I kiss the top of his head. "I know."

Pulling away long enough for him to escape, I blow him a kiss as he walks again.

He cringes, and scowls when I giggle.

Ah, there's his father.

He's still adorable.

We watch him walk all the way to the car.

Feeling the heat of a stare, I turn around, shifting nervously on my feet.

"He loves you, you know?"

"I do too."

"I can tell." She looks back at Jess's picture, deliberating. "I get what you need to do, Claire. But when you get back, if you choose them, make it work because if you hurt them, I'll have no other choice but to hurt you."

My surprise is short-lived. The familiar nerves bubble until I break into laughter. This time, I'm not alone when Sharon joins me.

She nudges me with her elbow. "Jess is awful quiet these days."

"So is Nick."

Our laughter trails off as she rubs a hand up and down my arm supportively. "I better get going. But Claire, he loves you."

I look back at the car.

"Not just him." She wraps her arms around herself. "She'd want to see him happy. Both of them."

Don't cry.

Do. Not. Cry.

Goddammit, Claire.

With a reassuring dip of her chin, she turns and walks away, leaving me with my tears.

I turn back to stare at the picture.

"Hi," I breathe, wiping the moisture from my cold cheeks. It's going to snow. I can almost smell it, and my chattering teeth are a good indication. "I'm a little lost for words, which is unusual, but I'm pretty sure you've heard my ramblings all these years. Sorry about that." I run my fingers over the engravings on her stone.

Jessica Williams.

"I'm probably not in the best position to ask for favors, but if you could give Nick a hug from me, that would be amazing." My exhale is wobbly, my breath escaping in a cloud as I fight to keep it together. "I'm going to do my best to get back to them, but keep watching over them. They need you. Keep being the brightest star, so they know you're there."

FORTY-FOUR

January

Me: Checking in. Still breathing. It's cold as hell in Berlin. Give Jay-Jay a hug from me.
Something good: I made a snow angel because why not?

Jake: Enjoy every second. Hug received.
Something good: Picturing you making a snow angel.

FORTY-FIVE

February

Me: Checking in. Still breathing. Waiting for my flight to Vienna. Something good: They have a piano at the airport.

Jake: Away on business. Jay-Jay received the music books you sent. Something good: We had some sock races before I left.

FORTY-SIX

March

Jake: Keep breathing. One breath at a time.
Something good: Construction began on the new shelter.

FORTY-SEVEN

April

Jake: The world doesn't spin without you on it.

FORTY-EIGHT

May

Me: Checking in…Sorry, I needed a minute to catch my breath. I'm in Barcelona for two weeks. It's busy.
Something good: Beth tells me they're leaving the shelter and have a place of their own. Hannah is doing well.

Jake: Thanks for telling Jay-Jay what happens if you put Saran wrap on the toilet seat when he called you last week. It made for a great morning.
Something good: He had a recital. He performed a song from the books you sent.

FORTY-NINE

June

Me: Checking in…Currently writing to you from the top of the Eiffel Tower.
Something good: Amy is here. She is trying to rope me into a crazy idea, and I think we're going to do it.

Jake: Whatever Amy is trying to get you to do…do it.
Something good: Some women at the shelter graduated today.

FIFTY

July

Me: Checking in…It's too hot. I think I'm dying. Give Jay-Jay a hug. Something good: Some kids in the study are putting on a concert tonight. Oh, and Gelato in Rome.

Jake: I see you're still as dramatic as ever. Enjoy the concert.

FIFTY-ONE

August

Me: Checking in…I'm high as a kite in Amsterdam. I'm going to get fired.
I didn't get your something good last month. I hope you found one.
Something good: Sweet waffles with ice-cream…and colors. There are so many colors. Who knew?

Jake: I have no words.
Something good: Knowing you're laughing for no reason.

FIFTY-TWO

September

Me: Checking in...Happy Birthday to Jay-Jay.
They're extending the study. I don't know for how long, but I think I'm going to stay and see it out.
Maybe we need to stop checking in now because I still miss you too much and it's not fair to either of us.

Jake: Of course you're going to stay. You're doing amazing.
Keep smiling, Trouble.
Something good: It was still real.

FIFTY-THREE

Four months later

"I can't believe we're doing this." I crane my neck to look at the three-storey building.

"We did it already." Amy nudges me playfully. "Can't you hear?"

I shake my head, still not believing it. But the sounds of instruments floating from the windows and onto the street tell me this is real.

Mama appears from Mandy's family restaurant with three cups of coffee and a donut for me and Amy because sometimes, she still treats us like we're children.

I take the cup and bun. "Thank you."

She joins us, a little awestruck as we gaze up at the sign.

RMA

Russell Music Academy.

When I was away, the building next to Amy's music shop went up for sale. The money was eye-watering, but when she broached the subject of a music school, I knew the moment butterflies swirled in my belly, it was right. I could feel it.

I sold my house in Penrith and cleared my savings. Together, and with some help from the bank, we scraped together enough for this dream.

Amy did most of the heavy lifting because I wasn't here. But when

I came home six weeks ago, we got stuck in. We officially opened four days ago to a full music school and a waiting list longer than my arm.

I even teach.

Who would have thought?

Music was always my life, but my purpose was to help people like Mama, and children like Amy and I used to be.

So…we combined both.

My year away thought me how influential music can be in those circumstances.

I should know.

It saved me more times than I can count.

Taking the idea I had with the music room in the shelter, we ran with it. Along with regular lessons, we started a music program for people just like us.

We see the impact it has in the shelter, but the kids didn't have many options to continue when they left. Now, they'll come to us to continue studying.

"I'm so proud of my girls." Mama wipes a tear from her eye, and we instantly crowd her for a hug.

"Don't cry, Mama."

Standing back, I sip from the cup and try to hide my grimace.

"I thought you loved that coffee, Claire."

I open my mouth to defend myself, but Amy buts in. "Ah, she's cultured now, Mama. She experienced French and Italian coffee. This is muck to our world traveller."

I roll my eyes.

"Our *award-winning* world traveller," my mother adds, pride gleaming in her smile.

"You know I didn't win the award by myself, right? I was part of the team conducting the study."

She shrugs.

I've told her this many times since I came home last month, but she still tells everyone it was just me. She's added *award-winning* to the end of my name.

It makes me cringe, but I love her for it.

Amy checks her watch. "Shit. I need to go. I have lessons at the shelter at six."

"Yeah," I agree. "I have a lesson at six, too."

She wiggles her eyebrows in a way that always freaks me out.

"What?"

"It's good you look hot today."

I look down at my red shirtdress. I don't think it's anything special. "Why?"

"Your six o'clock? The dad is more delicious than your donut." She winks, taking backward steps to her car.

I bite into the sugary glaze and moan. "That's impossible. This donut is heaven."

I don't know if it's the donuts or speaking of hot dads but an ache ruptures in my chest.

My heart has healed...mostly.

I still have days when the memories consume me, my throat closes, and I need to remind myself I can breathe. But I look in the mirror now and I see myself. I don't see another person looking back at me, and I can sit through a thunderstorm without a panic attack. I attended therapy while I was away. I still do.

Over the year, I've learned that forgiving other people isn't my issue. It's not the key to moving on.

Not for me.

I needed to forgive myself.

And I did.

I forgave myself for the years I carried my father's burden. For the guilt that ate me up until it left me wounded and raw. For the weight of knowing if maybe I had done things differently, Hannah would have never witnessed what she did. For the years I missed with my mother because of the memories we saw in each other.

We always make new memories.

I'm not what happened to me. No one is.

There's good in our days.

I still see Jake and Jay-Jay when I think of my good, even if it causes the deepest ache in my chest. It's worth it. It gets me through.

It helps me breathe.

And I can do it on my own now. The air in my lungs is mine. I don't need life support.

I know why we let each other go. We needed to fix ourselves, and I'm so grateful for it. I'm stronger for it.

But I still miss him.

It's been over a year since I left his house. Nine of those months were nothing but a single text once a month to check in. I found myself waiting for the day I allowed myself to contact him. I became dependent on it. I needed to let that go too. I needed to know I could do it on my own.

He never objected. Never put any pressure on me. He just let me be.

He let me go for me.

I'm sure if one of those texts asked for him to come to me, he would have been on a jet in the next breath.

But just because my contact with Jake ceased, I kept the connection with Jay-Jay. We video call once a week. We have for over a year. I still give him advice on the best ways to prank his father.

I'm excited to see him. To see how much he has grown.

I've been home six weeks, and I'm too nervous to face the man who probably knows the deepest parts of my soul.

I know it was real.

But a year is a long time.

Has he moved on?

Is he happier without me?

Will my coming back also bring him back in time?

I haven't reached out because I fear the answers.

"See you later, baby girl." My mother kisses my cheek.

"Bye, Mama."

Music spills from every room when I go inside. The smell of fresh paint still lingers in the air. My smile is so wide it's painful as I stroll down the halls, peeking through the windows to see happy children.

My room is on the ground floor, with a brand new piano in the center, and Fresh Air Blue on the walls.

Running my fingers through my hair—it's still shoulder length because I don't need it to hide behind anymore—I sit at the piano and play while I wait.

The bell rings, indicating the end of a lesson and the start of a new one, but I keep playing.

I try to convince myself I'm imagining the tingle along my spine, the familiar awareness that prickles on my skin. But it's so powerful, I can't ignore it. Turning, I slowly lift my head, and my fingers slip from the keys.

Home.

Dressed head to toe in a dark tailored suit, white dress shirt, black tie, and the most breath-taking smirk. He still doesn't have a hair out of place.

All the best memories come flooding back.

It knocks the breath out of me in a whoosh. And with the sight of him—hands in his pockets and muscular shoulders almost filling my doorway—my eyes water whether I want them to or not.

"Hi," I say, but my voice is trembling, and it sounds more like a choked whisper.

His eyes stay on mine and in a second, every memory washes over me.

Every time he touched me.

Every whisper.

Every kiss.

Every time I screamed his name.

Every time he held me just to keep me together.

He's only a couple of feet away, but it feels like miles.

A slow curl on the corner of his mouth and I melt all the way to my feet.

I thought the time away would lessen the zing that echoes in my chest from just the sight of him. I thought leaving our vacuum would put things into perspective.

It does, but not in the way I expected.

The pull is still there—the unexplainable need to put one foot in front of the other just to be near him. I stand from the stool to feel closer.

It wasn't all in my head.

He's the same man.

Same look.

The same need to feel his touch.

The same longing in our eyes.

I don't see his ghosts anymore.

He smirks how I remember and dips his chin, making no apology when he takes a long sweep of my body and blows out a breath. It swirls around in my blood like a warm drink.

"Hi, Trouble," he breathes.

I want to burst into tears and instantly blush.

Filling the silence, I laugh. "Are you my student?"

He chuckles, deep in his throat, and it still makes my knees lock. He shakes his head. "No. He's coming." Another sweep of his eyes. "You look beautiful, Claire. Happy."

I swoon on the spot.

My chest swells. "You too, Jake."

"Claire." My name echoes around the room as the sight of a very familiar pair of baby blues catch mine.

"Oh, my God," I gasp. "What have you been feeding him? Jay-Jay, you're practically a man."

He rolls his eyes.

Some things never change.

I hold out my arms. "Will I have to stand here all day, or are you going to give me a hug?"

A big smile and my throat stings with emotion. When his arms come around my waist, I hold him tight, ignoring his pleas to let him breathe. His hugs are still the best.

Backing away, he fixes his glasses. "You're my music teacher?"

"It looks that way." I glance between him and Jake. "Did you not know?"

I certainly didn't.

"Amy." It's all Jake says, and we instantly know.

She's so sneaky.

He taps his knuckles against the door. "I'll let you two to your lesson. I'll see you in thirty minutes, buddy."

After a wink in my direction, he leaves, and it takes all my power to stop my feet from running after him.

With a shaky breath, I keep my attention on Jay-Jay. "Okay, I want to hear every song you learned while I was gone."

***

"You look a little flush, sis," Amy teases as I open the gate to my mother's house. I move into my new place next week, but until then, I'm here.

It's freezing.

Why are they sitting outside?

But I already know. They've been waiting to see how my day went. How my six o'clock lesson went, to be specific.

I try to glare at her, but I smile despite myself. "Why didn't you say something? I stood there like a gob smacked fish."

367

She shrugs. It's smug and proud.

Mama stands, taking my hands and warming them in hers. "You're shaking. Did it bring back too many memories?"

Only the good ones.

I blow out a breath. "That's just the effect he has."

"It's still there then?"

My eyes water, picturing him standing in the doorway. I've thought about him for over a year. The image in my mind didn't do him justice.

"Yeah, Mama. It's still there."

Amy clicks her tongue against the roof of her mouth, whistling as she looks up at the darkening sky. "You need to tell her, Mama," she sing-songs.

"Tell me what?"

My mother puffs out her cheeks, taking my hand and guiding me to the step. "Sit down, Claire."

I do because the ground feels unstable under my feet.

A long moment before I explode. "Someone spit it out. You're killing me."

One last hard swallow before Mama begins. "Amy told me about the night you were here with Jake." Shame flashes across her face. She doesn't remember. I didn't think she would.

"It's okay. I understand."

"Jake came back," she blurts.

I'm glad I'm sitting down.

"He did what?"

"The next day, he came back. I was embarrassed because I couldn't remember him. Amy was here to explain. We talked for hours. He told me about his past. About his darkest days. I told him about mine. But I didn't want to help myself. So, when he left, he gave me a letter. I still remember what he said because of the look in his eyes when he said it. *'I know what it's like not wanting to get better for yourself, but I promise she's worth it.'* I agreed to his help because a man that loves my daughter that much only has good intentions."

"He set her up with the best of every doctor, Claire," Amy adds, like my world isn't spinning at lightning speed.

He came back.

"Why didn't anyone tell me?" I choke, my voice breaking with every word.

"Because I asked him not to say it. I wanted to be sure I could do it. And he didn't want you to know. After everything that happened, if you read the letter, you would have stayed when you needed to go."

I'm too shocked to cry. "What was in the letter?"

Her mouth curls into a grin. "I'll give it to you. I wanted to be sure it was still there between you two before I did."

With a sigh, she stands and walks away.

Amy shrugs, looking like her mystified self.

"Why didn't you tell me?" I whisper-yell.

"Because you didn't need to know. You fell in love with him all on your own."

He's the reason I have my mother back.

And he didn't want me to know. He just did it.

A part of me isn't surprised because he cares that much, but my heart swells anyway.

Mama arrives back and places a white envelope in my lap. It's as light as a feather, but I know whatever he wrote in there will carry the weight of my heart.

"Read it," she says, nodding at Amy to give me time.

With shaking hands, I remove the page from the envelope, my tears already soaking the sheet.

I read.

I cry

I fall in love again.

FIFTY-FOUR

The letter

This might not be my place. If so, tear up this letter, and throw it away. If you never open it, I have nothing to lose.

I understand I'm nothing but a stranger, and you don't have to accept anything from me. But I'm asking anyway.

Pain has a funny way of showing itself. It keeps us frozen in time, too trapped to move forward or see past it. I know it when I see it because I recognize it. The endless cycle of wanting to go back in time, wondering what if we had done things differently? If we spoke a minute sooner or said nothing at all, would life be different?

For such a long time, I was stuck back there too.

Until Claire walked into my life.

Though I don't think Claire walks into anyone's life. She blazes.

I promise she can heal the deepest cuts, and the wounds that won't stop bleeding with just her laugh. It's loud but contagious.

I know she can help your healing because she has a heart so big she's unable to contain it. It overflows.

She's one of the strongest people I've ever met, and I promise she's worth getting to know.

On the days when life is hard, and she wants to hide it from the world, she puts two sugars in her coffee like it can cure all her problems. She dances barefoot in her office, and she doesn't care who sees. She talks to herself when she's stressed. And she plays the piano as a tribute to you. I see it every time she plays and gets lost. She's right there with you.

I promise she's worth it. She's worth getting better for.

She's better than any high or the numbness you get from the bottom of a bottle.

Claire even heals the wounds you don't know you have, all without showing she has so many of her own.

I should know. She healed me.

I promise, she's worth every single second.

Now it's my turn to heal her.

She would never ask, and I'm sure she would kick me in some painful places if she knew I was doing this. But I'm asking for Claire and her memories.

I'm asking for the little girl whose mother once told her that if she never jumped in the cold water, she would miss out on a great adventure.

If it's judgment you're worried about, then don't. She's never judged you. It's not in her nature. It's not who she is.

If you're ever ready, all you have to do is call.

Best wishes,

Jake Williams.

This won't make sense, but when you're through this, and you get to hold your daughter again, you can ask her about it. But I think I started falling in love with Claire from the moment she smiled at me with sugar on her lips.

FIFTY-FIVE

The smell of the surrounding oak trees washes over me with familiar heat.

After reading his letter, I had to see him. I need him to know. I need to see it in his eyes.

It's Friday night, so Jay-Jay is probably with his grandparents. His car is here, but there's no answer on this goddamn door.

Oh, shit.

What if he has a woman in there?

Bile rises in my throat.

Walk away, Claire.

Walk. Away.

Jittery and resigned, I turn back to go to my car but stop dead in my tracks when I hear the door swing open.

"Can I help you?"

That's not Jake's voice.

I spin around.

"Logan," I breathe.

His eyes go wide as he steps back. "Claire?"

Poker night.

Great.

Embarrassed, I wave my hand at him and try my best to smile. My cheeks are wet with tears, and I'm standing in the freezing cold with no coat.

He's going to think I'm losing it again.

"I can come back another time. I didn't mean to interrupt."

Run.

He takes a step forward. "Claire, please. He'll kill me if he knows you were here, and I let you leave. Come in."

Laughing nervously, I waver in my steps, not sure if I'm ready for the tsunami of memories that awaits me inside.

A furious blush rushes over my skin. "It's okay. I think I'll just wait out here."

He's about to object, but I wrap my arms around myself and keep my feet planted on the ground.

Defeated, he blows out a breath before disappearing.

It's only seconds, but it feels like forever before Jake storms to the door, panic wild in those whiskey eyes. "Claire? Jesus, woman, it's freezing. Get in here." He reaches for me, but I back away.

"It was you," I say, voice shaky and thick from crying.

"What was?"

A heavy tear escapes before I can catch it.

"Fuck. Come in, Claire. Please. Just give me a minute."

Teeth chattering, I nod as he steps aside to let me through. I'll never get my words out when I'm shivering so much.

My arm brushes against his shirt and the heat from his skin sends a jolt down my spine. "Should I wait in the living room?"

"Sure."

It's like second nature when he reaches up and wipes the tear away with his thumb.

The brief contact makes my heart seize.

I remind myself to breathe.

It doesn't work.

I can't think straight when he stands this close.

I manage a small smile before going to the living room.

Everything's the same, yet so different.

Fresh eyes.

Eyes that see in color.

I comforted Jay-Jay in this room.

We danced on the floor under my feet.

I look at the couch and remember how Jake took me there and made me his. Branding me and ruining me for all others.

A few minutes later, I hear chatter from the hall.

He's making them leave.

"Your friends must really hate me. I've ruined poker night twice," I say as he steps inside, making the room smaller with just his presence. "You shouldn't have done that. I could have come back."

"This is more important."

A step closer.

"You don't even know why I'm here."

Another step.

My gaze lifts the closer he gets, my heart hammering in my chest when he crowds me.

"It's still more important."

"Why didn't you tell me you helped my mother to get better?"

He takes a breath, holds it, and lets it out again. "She got better all on her own."

I know he won't take any compliment I give, so I simply say, "Thank you, Jake." I bite my lips together before building enough courage to speak again. I can hardly hear anything over my pulse beating frantically behind my ears. "I read the letter."

With a smile edging on his full lips, he drops his head before meeting my gaze again. "You honestly didn't think I'd be able to forget you, Trouble, did you?"

I shake my head, not knowing whether to laugh or cry. I do both. "Why didn't you say something?"

One large stride forward, and his breath is in my hair, hands cupping my face, and like all the times before, his touch reminds me of who my heart truly belongs to.

"Because you scared the hell out of me. That day when we met, I told you to see the good in your days when, apart from Jay-Jay, I was struggling to see any. That night, when I tried to think of something, I closed my eyes, and I saw the smile of a stranger." He brushes my hair behind my ear before feathering his knuckles across my cheek. "So, when you walked into my office, I did the only thing I could think of. Anything to close you off. Anything to not—"

"Fall in love with me," I finish.

He nods, pressing his forehead against mine. I smooth my palms against his chest, fingers tingling as I fist at his shirt.

"But you did," I add.

Another nod. "So fucking much."

"Do you still? I understand. It's been over a year."

374

"Christ, yes." He kisses the top of my head before curling his fingers under my chin. "I lived with a fear that you wouldn't come back, and I was happy loving you from a distance if it meant that you were happy. But seeing you today. Seeing how you're the same yet so different. I knew—even if you decided it's not where you belong—I knew you'd always be mine."

I was never meant for anyone else.

Two halves of a soul would never fit together as perfectly as ours.

My hands are trembling when I whisper under my breath, "Yours." Stifling a sob, my heart swells so much that I can hardly breathe. "I am. I belong with you because I'm yours, Jake. I've always been yours."

"Oh, thank fuck," he sighs, laughing against my mouth. His fingers tangle in my hair, gently gripping it until my head falls back. Throat exposed, I'm sure he can see me swallow my nerves. "Can I kiss you?"

"If you don't, I'm going to teach Jay-Jay the worst pranks, and—"

He doesn't let me finish.

Lips on mine, the words melt away, and I moan into his dizzying kiss.

It reaches so deep, we become part of each other.

My mouth parts in a gasp. Our tongues devour. We claim each other as our lips collide over and over.

With a vibration of pleasure from his throat, we're everywhere. My skin burns from his touch as he snakes a hand around my waist and presses me flush against him.

I don't need him as life support anymore, but I want it.

"Fuck," he growls, holding my head and pulling away.

Why is he pulling away?

He rests his head against mine, frantic breaths making our chests heave.

Breathless, we look at each other and laugh.

"Why are you stopping?"

"Believe me. It's taking every ounce of strength I have not to have you. But you deserve more than what I gave you before. If we're doing this, I want to do it right."

I chew my lip between my teeth. "But it's so much fun doing it wrong."

His jaw tenses as he grinds down before pulling my lip away from the hold of my bite.

"Trouble," he warns.

He takes a step back, cold air taking his place.

I shift on my feet to ease the ache between my legs.

It's been over a year.

Give a girl a break.

There was never another when I was away. How could there be when this is how he makes me feel?

"Eight o'clock tomorrow night," he says, shoulders still rising and falling erratically.

Confused, I ask. "What's going on tomorrow night?"

"Come to dinner with me?"

The air leaves my lungs in a fractured exhale, and I try to smile. "Are you asking me out on a date, Mr. Williams?"

"Yes, Ms. Russell, I am."

Teasing, I rock back and forth. "I thought you didn't date?"

He reaches out and grabs my hand, pulling me to him. His thumb traces the blush on my cheeks.

"I want this one. I want all the dates after. I wanted you yesterday. I want you today. I want your every tomorrow. Because you're mine. You'll always be mine. And since I saw you this evening, I've been wondering how long is appropriate before I ask my son's music teacher on a date."

Farewell heart.

"I think almost two years is reasonable."

Lips tingling to taste him, I stretch on my tiptoes, but he rears back with that smug smirk I love so much.

"If we're doing this, I have rules."

My heart sinks.

"Jake—"

"I don't want one night. I want every night. I want to kiss you every damn time I like. And I'm going to fall in love with you every day."

"I like these rules."

Finally, his lips are on mine, so deliriously happy—I'm dizzy.

Taking my hand, he spins me around, and in his arms, we dance.

We don't have any music, but we don't need it.

The world keeps spinning.

And it never stops.

EPILOGUE

Three years later.

"Keep pushing, baby."

Even through the agonizing pain of a contraction, I find it in myself to glare at him.

"You're getting a vasectomy," I scream.

Apparently, this is what they call a natural birth.

There's nothing natural about this pain.

My organs are being ripped out.

"Just another few pushes, Mrs. Williams." I can't even see the midwife. My vision is too blurry.

"Please, call me Claire," I cry. She's between my legs. I think we're on a first-name basis.

Sweat soaking every inch of my body, I push and push until my lungs are burning.

And oh, sweet fuck.

Everything burns.

And I mean *everything*.

Holy shit.

The midwife turns to Jake, smiling.

Why is she smiling?

"Dad, would you like to look?"

He turns a shade of green.

"Oh, he wants to look," I grit through clenched teeth, squeezing his hand. The bastard doesn't flinch.

He looks.

He visibly pales.

Good.

He's not allowed near me with that thing ever again.

He kisses my forehead.

I want to punch him in the throat.

Chin to my chest, it takes one last final push, and the rest of the world disappears.

There's a weight on my chest.

Oh, God.

There's a baby on my chest.

My baby.

Our baby.

Shaking, I brush my fingers over tiny cheeks, eyes, nose, and ears.

"Congratulations, you have a daughter." The midwife smiles again.

I like her smile now.

"Hi, baby girl," I whisper as her eyes begin to open.

The bluest, most perfect eyes I've ever seen.

I look at my husband.

My blubbering husband.

"I thought I was going to be the mess here." I laugh as he takes my hand and kisses me.

"Hey, Princess." His eyes gloss over, and he runs a finger over her arm. "You're perfect, just like your mama."

One look.

That's all it takes.

And I've lost him forever.

I don't care.

It's stiff competition around here.

I wipe the stray tear from his cheek.

I kiss the top of her head, her little fingers, her chubby arms. "You have a big brother that's going to be very excited to meet you."

Jake brushes my hair back from my face. "You're amazing, baby."

"I am, aren't I?" I joke.

I throw my head back on the pillow, exhausted, but there's too much adrenaline rushing through my blood.

"I'm sorry. I don't want you to get a vasectomy. But doing this once is enough. Two kids are plenty for anyone."

He chuckles as the midwife takes our daughter for her measurements.

He kisses me again and again and again.

"I love you so much."

"Always," I agree.

***

My eyes flutter open, heavy with sleep. I stretch out on the bed, my muscles lax and well rested.

Too well rested.

I glance beside me. Jake is stirring now too, and I watch as realization flashes across his face.

"Did you get up with Ella this morning?"

He shakes his head and panic washes over us.

The clock says it's seven.

We both leap, scrambling to her nursery next to our room. I reach it first but halt at the door. Holding my finger over my mouth, I wave Jake forward.

My heart expands so much, I feel it in my throat.

Jay-Jay sways back and forth, staring at his little sister as he hushes her.

"He's the best big brother," I whisper.

Jake wraps his arms around my waist and rests his chin on my head as we soak up the scene.

"That's my boy," he breathes.

We give it another long minute before Jake leaves my side and creeps in, careful not to wake the sleeping baby.

It's the first full night's sleep we've had in three months.

"Thanks, buddy." He takes Ella from Jay-Jay's arms.

"It's no problem. I knew you two were tired, and I was up anyway."

I know he wasn't. He's just a great kid.

When he steps outside, I wrap my arms around his waist and squeeze him tight. He's thirteen, and he's taller than me.

Handsome, like his father, with a heart as big as his, too.

"Thanks, sweetie. Want some breakfast?"

He throws a hand over my shoulders for a one-arm hug because he's too cool for two arms now. "Sure."

"I'll be down in a sec."

I have another scene to soak up.

Crossing my arms over my chest, I lean against the door frame and watch as Jake maneuvers a three-month-old and takes his t-shirt off with expertise.

Placing her on the heat of his chest, he paces back and forth. She's already asleep, but he doesn't care.

He's the pro here. He's done it before—all on his own, and I'm thankful every day that we have each other.

He whispers hushed lullabies against the top of Ella's head.

The sight makes me drool.

"Careful, Mr. Williams, you'll make me want another one."

He winks. "Careful, Mrs. Williams, I'll enjoy giving you one."

Smiling, I turn to walk away.

"Claire," he calls in a whisper.

"Hmm?"

"Happy anniversary, baby."

One year since we said, *I do.*

I'm pretty sure he knocked me up that night.

Tiptoeing into the room, my fingers tingle when I smooth my palm over his bare chest. His skin is hot, but my blood gushes hotter.

It has since the day I set eyes on him.

I still get a little dizzy when I kiss him. "Happy anniversary. I love you."

"More and more every day."

BONUS EPILOGUE

Jake

"Hey, beautiful." I place the fresh lilies on the grass and crouch while running my fingers over every feature in the photo. "I can't believe it's almost sixteen years, Jess."

The wind picks up, and I swear, I smell the hint of vanilla.

"Jay-Jay is doing good. He's keeping his grades up. He's still playing the piano, but he's traded it in for a very loud electric guitar…and girls. I guess I'm getting a taste of my own medicine. But we're going to the beach house today, so I think those girls will fall to the wayside for one in particular."

I know she's laughing wherever she is.

For an hour, I sit, I talk, I relive memories.

When I stand, I press a kiss to my fingers and place it on the picture. "I love you. I'll be back soon."

I feared after Jess died that if the impossible happened, and I found love again, I couldn't love them as much.

But that's not how it works.

I never loved one more than the other because when you love like that, it's everything, it's all-consuming, it fills every gap, and every injured crack in our interior.

It just is.

And I was lucky enough to find it twice.

***

"Daddy!" Little legs come running toward me from the piano room and my goddamn heart constricts in my chest.

"There's daddy's princess." I scoop her up. Long eyelashes flutter over bright blue eyes.

I'm screwed.

She's her mother all over again. Three years old and she has me wrapped around her little finger.

The sounds of the piano float through the air.

"Is Mama playing?"

She nods, holding a tiny finger over my lips. "I wanted her to play for me, so we have to be really, really quiet, Daddy."

She squeals when I lift her onto my shoulders.

I never thought I could find a piano sexy until I watched my wife play one.

She sits there every chance she gets, eyes closed, that beautiful full mouth slightly parted, and she sways as her fingers work their magic, moving at an unnatural pace. Always barefoot, her pink-painted toes press up and down on the pedals, her long legs bare in only sleep shorts, and it takes everything in me to stay in one spot.

Once upon a time, I thought I could have her only once, kiss her only once, and simply get her out of my system.

I was such a fool.

Only hours since I last had her, when she woke me in the middle of the night, her sleepy eyes making me hard the minute they locked with mine, and I'm getting withdrawals.

It's been almost eight years since she walked into my office for the first time, and I'm still addicted to her.

My thirsty eyes drink in every curve as she moves on the seat, lost in her own creation.

Sometimes she plays music I recognize, but mostly I think she's making it up because she's that brilliant.

Pieces of her hair fall from the knot she's tied it in.

I could watch her forever and never get bored.

Her fingers slow, and a smile curls on the corner of her mouth, but I can only see half of it, and I feel cheated.

The world should see her smile.

"You're creeping again," she teases.

"I'm the biggest pervert."

She laughs, and I think it sounds better than the music she was just playing.

Turning, she presses her palms flat against her thighs, stands, and takes a bow when me and Ella clap.

"Great audience." She smiles and my chest tightens like it always does when she flashes that smile.

I made a vow to her—to love and to cherish. But I also made a vow to myself—to make sure I see that smile every day.

Ella ducks close to my ear, still holding onto my head. "Give Mama a kiss, Daddy."

I dip my chin. "My wish is your command, Princess Ella."

Claire puts her hands behind her back and sways. I tilt her face back with my fingers under her chin, needing to look at her properly. Her breath sweeps across my wrist. I pull at her mouth, parting her lips, needing my next fix.

The kiss is deep but too quick.

Not enough.

"Okay, little lady." I scoop Ella from my shoulders. "I think it's your nap time."

Claire rolls her eyes, giggling.

Bending, she takes Ella's hands and kisses each of her fingers like she always does. "Sweet dreams, baby girl."

She eyes me when she stands, a mischievous curl to her lips before she stretches to reach my ear.

This woman will be the death of me.

"If you can get her to sleep quick enough, I'll be in the shower."

I've never tucked my daughter in so fast.

***

"Get 'em, Ella," Claire roars as the waves wash in on our feet.

My breath escapes in a whoosh as a bucket of cold water is poured over my back. Jay-Jay is the next victim.

Scooping Ella in her arms, Claire runs, both of them laughing hysterically.

When we stand, she nods smugly with Ella on her hip, clapping her delight at our reactions.

"I have backup this time. Bet you didn't think of that every time you ganged up on me."

I run my finger over my jaw, trying to hide the smirk.

Her face drops.

"No, Jake. I have the baby."

"You can't use our daughter as your shield."

When she doesn't like my response, she turns to Jay-Jay. "Come on, buddy. Have pity on me."

He lifts his shoulder. "Can't do it, Claire. Sorry. I do love you, though, just so you know."

I watch her melt a little.

Their relationship is one thing I'm most proud of in my life. They connected from the beginning, but Claire nourished it until it bloomed. Throughout the years, she gave him space when he needed it, and had the maternal instinct strong enough to know when he didn't. She never wanted to replace Jess in his life, but she's the most amazing mother figure and friend.

He trusts and loves her, and I see how much she adores him every time she looks at him.

I'm the luckiest man alive.

Claire is ready to burst into laughter. I can almost see the nerves in her eyes and the twitch of her lips.

Me and Jay-Jay share a look.

He tips his chin. "I've got your back, Dad."

And I'll always have yours, son.

Sometimes, I still look down when he speaks to me, expecting to see the boy with glasses and shaggy hair.

But at sixteen, he's almost my height, and football has broadened his shoulders.

I don't want to go back in time, but sometimes I wish I could slow it.

He's my right-hand man...In everything. Including getting his stepmother into the water, whether she likes it or not.

High-fiving, we take off in a sprint.

She's predictable and freezes on the spot.

When we reach her, we're too quick. Jay-Jay grabs his little sister as I bend and wrap my arms around Claire's knees.

"You two are the worst," she shouts, pounding her fists against my back.

I slap my palm down on her ass. "Baby, you should know better by now."

She's about to reply, but we're both under water before she opens her mouth.

Sputtering, she jumps up, panting and feigning rage.

"Asshole," she chokes. "You're too old to be carrying me around like that."

I grab her waist, and her chest heaves against mine. "You didn't say that this morning."

Rolling her eyes, she slaps my chest, her laugh vibrating against my mouth.

Just as dramatic as her mother, Ella squeals on Jay-Jay's shoulders as he runs into the water, cold droplets splashing on her feet.

I take the moment and soak it up because right here, in our own little circle, is my entire world.

***

"She's snoring," Claire says, wrapping her sweater around herself and climbing onto my lap.

I hold her tight as she rests her head on my shoulder and we watch the ocean in the darkness.

I always cherish when she's in my arms, always grab on and never want to let go because the fear will always remain that there'll be a day she won't be there.

She sighs, moaning her comfort.

"What are they doing?" she asks, staring down at Jay-Jay and Ava, lying on the sand and staring up at the night sky.

"Looking at the stars."

Her eyes water when she looks at me. "Jesus, woman, you don't need to cry over it."

"It's sweet, and some of these tears are for you."

My brows almost reach my hairline. "Me? Why?"

"Because Alex is going to kill you."

She's not wrong. I see the look in my son's eyes—all googly and stupid when Ava is around.

They're best friends. They have been since they were eight years old, and now he stutters when she stands too close.

"They're kids," I defend.

She eyes me, tilting her head. "What were you doing when you were sixteen?"

Nothing good.

I blow out a breath. "Fuck."

Risking a glance at Mandy and Alex sitting on their steps, I immediately regret it.

If he wasn't holding their six-year-old son, I'm pretty sure Alex would drown my kid.

Mandy waves. Alex shakes his head.

"And we both know what Mandy was doing at that age," Claire adds, laughing. "Because it led to…well…Ava."

"Okay," I drawl, tapping my fingers against her thigh. I can deal with this tomorrow. "I think it's time for a drink. Something strong. Wine for you?"

She chews her lips between her teeth and plucks the material of my shirt between her fingers, fidgeting.

Silence.

And more silence.

She swallows hard. I can tell whatever it is, is bubbling on the tip of her tongue. "Spit it out, Trouble."

"I can't."

"Why? Cat got your tongue?"

She puffs out her cheeks, eyes anywhere but on me. "I can't drink wine. I can't drink any alcohol for a while."

"Why?"

She casts imploring eyes on me as she waits.

"Oh."

Oh.

"Claire…" I leap to my feet, taking her with me. The realization hits me like a punch to the gut.

"No more babies, Jake. This is the last time. You're not allowed to touch me ever again." She's laughing and crying all at once.

It would be an easy promise to make if I could keep my hands off her for more than ten minutes.

Curling my fingers under her chin, I tilt her head back, wiping away the fresh tears.

I don't know how it's possible, but I think she's more breath-taking in this moment than she was the first day I met her.

My stomach is tying in knots with all the best nerves. "How long have you known?"

"About ten minutes."

I don't answer. I kiss her until we're both breathless and stealing the air from each other.

A sob makes her voice thick when she asks, "You're happy?"

"So fucking happy, baby." I press my thumb to the corner of her mouth. "Now smile for me."

She does. Despite her tears, her mouth curls up into the most beautiful smile.

Her arms drape around my neck as I press my hands to the small of her back and feel the curve of her waist.

My world is about to get a little bigger.

It spins a little faster too.

Hand on her waist, I lace my fingers in hers. "Dance with me?"

After one more kiss, she rests her head on my chest and whispers, "Forever."

The End

We love hearing your thoughts.
If you enjoyed If By Chance, please consider leaving a review on
Amazon or Goodreads.

What Will Be Book Series

GET IN TOUCH

You can reach me on my website. I would love to see you there.
www.lauraashleygallagher.com

You will also find me on Facebook, Instagram, and TikTok.

ACKNOWLEDGMENTS

Where do I begin with this one?

Wow!

What a rollercoaster.

Twelve years ago, when I sat down to write Watch Over My Life, Jake Williams was the first hero I ever wrote about.

Twelve years!

He's been with me as long as my husband.

When I finished Jake and Jess's story, I was adamant that I wouldn't go back. After all, they had a triadically epic love story. He wasn't going to find it again, was he? So, I didn't want to touch it...Until I wrote Losing Love.

I knew I wanted to combine these two worlds somehow, and believe it or not, this book originally began as Ava and Jay-Jay's story. But there was something about Claire in Losing Love that stuck with me. No matter what I did, I kept thinking, "She would be a great match for Jake." And subconsciously, I created too many coincidences between the two books. I always imagined Jake would go on to help women like Jess...and so did Claire. It was only a matter of time before their worlds collided.

And I finally admitted his story wasn't over.

I was diving back in. It was like catching up with old friends.

But if only I knew what I was getting myself into.

Their individual stories carried weight, but together, their story was a dark and heavy one for me to write.

Writing this book tore me to shreds. I didn't sleep. I cried more than I care to admit, but it healed more than it broke.

I hope I brought all the sensitivity, care, and love to Claire and Jake's story that it deserved, and all the respect to Jess's character.

I might be crying—just a little—as I write this, but after twelve years, I'm saying goodbye to the characters in this series...For now, at least.

It has been the craziest and best year. Here's to hoping for many more.

Shane…you're still the most amazing husband. In previous acknowledgments, I apologized for all my future freak-outs, but I think this one requires a special apology. Thank you for not making me feel like a crazy person while I cried every night writing this. I swear, I'll switch to comedy (That's a lie). I love you.

To my little man, Liam…Mommy still loves you more. (It's printed now. It's forever.)

To my parents…I love you both so much. And I'm sorry. Please only read the acknowledgements. Don't read the rest. You can't unsee it.

Liz…we're another day closer to building our cellar or eating caviar on a boat—it might be a yacht or a rowboat, but we'll get there. Always remember, cedarwood and peppermint. Strap yourself in because the books only get spicier from here. Tell your husband to practice his impressions. I love you.

Thank you to the amazing Booktok, Bookstagram, and Facebook communities. Your support means the entire world.

To my incredible ARC team, thank you for giving this book a chance. You are all amazing. I hope you enjoyed If By Chance.

And to my wonderful readers…there's not enough words to describe how grateful I am. I hope you fall in love with these characters as I have. None of this would be possible without you. It means everything.